AF375117

Work cited

Blake, William. (n.d.). A *Poison Tree* Retrieved from https://www.poetryfoundation.org/poems/459 52/a-poison-

Contents

• • • • • • • • • • •

For my husband and kid. Thank you for your willingness to embrace chaos while I chose the keyboard. I owe you both everything, and love you 'til the stars expire.

John, you are Sam and Rathe and Teapot. Lindell, you are Ma, and also Teapot.

For Jessica I., who told me to do this, and for Sharyl, for your endless patience with my drafts: for both of you for inspiration, and belief.

For Kim and Mia and Nicole and Tyler and Wai Chu and Tim and Vivian and Athena and the rest of our fandom—especially Tanja, whose back-and-forth and ruminations about star empires inspired and encouraged me.

For Ghilia and Sonya, for reading and insight.

For Beth, for our childhood.

For my father, for how it goes when the revolution fails, and for Mom for the reading, and the Betsy-Tacy books.

For everyone who read drafts and gave feedback, my fellow Futurescapes writers, the agents and authors who were kind enough to assist us, and all ye other writers. The road is long and cold as space. Thank you, fellow pilots, for all your help out there in the dark.

(As this is a book originally suggested by one Jessica, I will mention the contributions of three more: Jessica F. for the adorable cover art, Jessica A. for your impeccable critical eye, and Jessica D., who does not like science fiction, but is still beloved.)

NAVVY
DREAMS
A SPACE OPERA
TAKE A JOB.
FALL IN LOVE.
TRY NOT TO
BLOW UP
SUNS.
HMH MURRAY

Chapter 1 * Stole

My partner Therion and I fought constantly. We fought over whose navvy plotted hyperspace coordinates and whose navvy steered our ship *Dancer* through the infinite. We fought over which one of us had to tell our boss about "breakage" and who got to fence the goods we'd skimmed. We even fought about Therion's affection for a certain deep-racked torch singer, although that was more about the currency my lover blew on him than anything else.

We were pilots, after all. We thought monogamy was for 12Fam aristos and that Cargo sect out near the Crab Nebula.

Perhaps all that fighting, which we took for granted, was just a slow implosion, a breaking by degrees. I've heard the supernova at Alpha Centauri happened slowly, too, that Ledas Starfire had set the trigger for her cosmic atrocity long before the surface of those binary suns broke. The inhabitants of Roe had been doomed for days, maybe weeks, but they only had nine minutes from the sight of that first solar flare until their sky caught fire. Nine minutes!

When Therion and I imploded, it took me five to run.

Some might think I'm suntouched, measuring my smuggler's life by the standards of the Milky's most-hated war criminal... but those folks live under rocks. When you see a flashpoint planetside, it's too late to stop the charge. By the time you think to run, you're already damned.

• • • • • • • • • •

[Error,] Second's red light flashed sullenly on my portside retina.

It was a sweltering summer night in the northern hemisphere of the planet NewBern, two years after some fool Kamen-lord ended a war with a supernova. It was six months before my drunk accident and the assassination that would change everything, and I—blissfully ignorant of destiny—was trying to sweet-talk my navvy into committing major larceny.

The warehouse my partner and I wanted to rob was one long silo in a rusty line of 'em, all owned by the local port. The complex itself was wedged hard between cliffs and an azure-soft sea. It had taken Therion and me an epoch of dodging security cams just to get this far, only to be thwarted by my recalcitrant navvy, who refused to open a simple electronic lock.

"Cowcrap," I muttered. I put my navhand flat against the door and asked Second again.

[Error,] my navvy repeated.

"Something wrong, babe?" Our stealth generator was built for one, so Therion's arms were wrapped 'round my waist, his body pressed to mine like he'd been glued.

"Yeah," I said. "Second won't play." My starboard fingers drummed against the door's mechanism as I silently pleaded my case to the gods' own wire that was braided through my arm.

I was the only pilot I knew who used their implanted navigational computer to pick locks on the side, and I considered myself a genius for discovering the feature. Therion had tried to copy my success a dozen times with Pokey, but his navvy couldn't figure out the right frequencies.

[Error,] Second flashed again. [We should not be at this restricted location.]

"Whoa." Therion chuckled. "Pokey says Second's torqued—"

"Quiet," I hissed. Therion and I were dressed in black coveralls, crouching in an artificial shadow beside a corrugated wall. The yards were well lit, but Therion had 'guised us with a cheap mobile stealth generator. Its pitch-black shade was designed to fool cams, not people. Lucky for us, the summer heat kept the human guards underground, monitoring remotely.

But within the forced dark, every sound—the slap of waves against the sea wall, the nightbirds' hoarse cries, the clang of a far-off hover trolley, the intermittent roar of ships departing from the nearby port, even the drips from the refrigerant unit jutting above our heads—made me twitch. NewBern was a Syndicate planet, and the drones patrolling here were authorized for lethal force. Although we'd danced this burglary jig on a dozen other worlds, this was the first job Therion had ever found for us at home base. Riding easy success elsewhere, I'd agreed to up the stakes. Now, as my pulse pounded in my ears and I jumped at birdsong, I wondered if we'd gone too far.

[Prime should leave this restricted area,] my navvy chided like it could read my thoughts. [Now.]

[Open the lock so we can, you silly string!] Therion and I'd strapped cold lines beneath our skivs, but in the humidity, even my topknot felt wilted. It was stiflingly hot, past middle-night, local time, and the headlamp I'd pasted to my forehead felt like it was about to fall off.

"Polla?" Therion's wandering fingers tickled my ribs. "What's taking so long?"

"Problem." I tilted my head up to his. In my infrared, his sharp features were blunted, his hair a colder mass of topknot piled above. "Second thinks we're trespassing."

My partner groaned. "Just tell it we're picking up cargo for our next job."

I shook my head. "Won't work. It knows this isn't New Liberty property."

"Tell it New Liberty put stuff in this warehouse for us." He made that sound simple.

"You know Second can check the manifest—"

"Babe." He gave my bim an absent-minded pat. "Do it."

"It's gonna check—"

"Trust me." His tone had gone syrupy.

It was his caper we were running, so I did as he asked. Second paused as its sonar reached out to connect to the warehouse's dumb mainframe. That took long enough for me to ponder how much time we'd waste before Therion decided we needed to scale the roof to find a ventilation shaft like we had on Casey8, the time we'd stolen three crates of modded bronto eggs for some crime lord's larder.

[Prime is correct,] Second buzzed suddenly, and I nearly jumped out of my shortos. [Warehouse 2E contains New Liberty Syndicate property, including nine crates marked for our next assignment.]

"Wait, what?" I twisted free of my lover's grip, whirling 'round to face him. "Second says this warehouse really has our job?"

Therion's teeth flashed a black moon in the infrared. "Well, yeah." His strong fingers kneaded my shoulder, expertly pressing between wires to the edges where my navvy met flesh. "Supposed to pick up crates here tomorrow."

I shrugged him off with a few choice epithets. The generator masked voices, but we still had to keep 'em low, and mine came out in a strangled hiss. "And that's why you want to steal our own cargo tonight? We can't steal from our boss!"

Therion's hand moved to my neck, which under normal circumstances would've been pleasant. "We're not stealing from Brahz." His tone implied the patience of a saint. "This job's not from our manifest. It's just one storage crate from another aisle, one rented to a third party."

"Which?"

Therion shrugged, which told me he didn't care. "Don't pay to check. Will you relax? You'll spook the navvies."

Oh, but now I was torqued. "You knew I wouldn't do the job if Brahz were involved. And you knew Second would only open the door if he was." I felt Second react to my emotion, even if it couldn't get the cause. "You set us up."

"I knew you *could* do the job." Therion's freehand traced my cheek. "Knew my Pollie and her Second could handle it—you both just needed a push."

Second's wire along my navarm buzzed. [Prime's increased adrenal response seems disproportionate to the current threat level. Are we in danger?]

[Yes. No—wait!]

Therion continued. "Even if we were stealing from New Lib... so what? We do it all the time."

"Skimming inventory's different!" He'd been the one to explain how.

"Sure." His voice softened. "Look, you're smart. And Second's got all of you in its pea brain. So it's smart, too."

"Watch it," I muttered. "I could be stupid. Could scream right now and bring PortSec down above our heads."

That earned me a fast kiss. "Dare you."

[Prime and Second belong to the New Liberty Syndicate. This facility contains more New Liberty property,] Second announced, having run through its own logical contortion while I floundered. [Second will open the door for Prime now.] My navhand twitched, urging me forward. My starboard fingers went flat on the lock, its smooth metal hard on my sweaty palm.

Therion snorted. "Well, will you look at that?"

I winced as the charge buzzed along my forearm, sparking blue when it reached my mesh-covered fingers. With a click, the door swung open.

"Nice," my partner mumbled into my neck, pushing us forward. Avoiding the live spots inside the warehouse would be our next dance.

"Know where this precious crate of yours is?" I peered into the dark interior. Being a mercurial fool, I wasn't angry anymore so much as wired with relief, bouncing on my heels. "Why does Second always buy your crap?"

"I know what it needs." My lover reached across to cop a feel on my navarm, his own metal-laced fingers curving around my elbow where Second's wire folded. A pleasant shiver accompanied his touch. This close, me and Second's nerves were just as attuned to Pokey's wire as our own.

I kept edging forward with Therion on my heels. "Still haven't told me what we're after."

"Fence claims it's alien artifacts."

"Real ones this time?"

Therion snorted. "Doesn't matter. When we get paid, you and me will finally have enough sling to get a better ship."

Therion had a map of the warehouse in his overlay, Pokey being less suspicious than my Second. He'd also hacked a link to those security cams to show us where they weren't, and now he guided me along the aisles—first in one direction, then another. In my infrared, most of our surroundings were a dark blur of nothing, broken only by the occasional heating vent or battery station.

"Don't want a better ship. I like our ship," I told him. Technically, *my* ship. Something about credit, my partner had admitted when he made me sign the lease for *Dancer* alone.

His breath was warm in my ear. "Think what we could do with two hundred meters more cubic space. Haul serious military salvage."

"I'm not keen about taking on cargo that needs a geiger check—"

"Well, get keen. You see the latest? With Starfire destroying factories, people are desperate. Shortages everywhere."

I'd seen our bank account, and I brought that and his gambling habits up, but Therion just rattled on about the Unity's Kamen terrorists, the ones who kept blowing up military and munitions, even out here in the Fringers. Circumventing their galactic embargo could, Therion swore, make us rich as princelings.

"Yeah?" I heard my voice sharpen. "Can't even win a card trick, and you want us to be arms dealers?"

"One unlucky hand! Before that, I was ahead almost four—"

"One's all it takes. We can't even go to that casino anymore." And it had been my favorite.

He made a disgusted noise. "Ugh. What is that smell?"

"Bovines?" I guessed. Something moved in my peripheral from a dark corner stacked with cages, the origin of a stench too sweet and sickly to be just manure. Feedlots in these warehouses were grim, even for a farmer's daughter like me, who was mostly inured to the sufferings of livestock.

Mostly. I still averted my gaze. With him draped on my back, I could almost predict the direction Therion would nudge me. After seven Standard years of flying, our navvies were synced that close.

We'd reached what I thought was the end of an aisle when a sudden blur of movement portside caught my eye. I dropped fast, pulling Therion with me. We crouched together under a long table covered with crates. Visible in infrared, a stealthed, orb-shaped drone floated past the cold lines of open shipping containers. The drone's sensors strobed like it was scanning for heat signatures. *Our* heat signatures.

I scrabbled in my pockets for our chill-paks and passed one to Therion before I peeled mine. The cold went misty in the warm air, and I wondered, too late, if I'd just drawn a target on our backs.

Then things got worse.

[Prime has stopped moving. Is Prime lost?] Second asked. [Initiating request for our cargo's location from Security Drone ZX, who is passing nearby.]

[No!] I gritted my teeth. [Don't!]

[But ZX is a servant of the New Liberty Syndicate. We are also servants of the New Liberty Syndicate.] It might've been my guilty conscience that made me imagine Second sounded hurt. [Why does Prime not want ZX to help us?]

"Uh, Second's worried we're lost." My whisper in Therion's ear felt like a scream. "Wants to ask that nice drone over there for help."

"Grass Priests, get that thing in line!" Therion cursed too loud and pulled away.

I got startled and scooted sideways. My heel connected with something that clattered across the concrete floor. Unbalanced, I fell on my bim and rolled out of our pocket of artificial darkness, right into the light.

The security drone floated almost on top of me. It had phased out of stealth, bright lights blinding. I could see the red laser sight tracking up my leg as every muscle in my body froze. *Fragging Therion,* I thought hopelessly. *Ma was right all along about him getting me killed—*

My partner fired then, and the drone crashed to the ground. Its stabilizers whirred as its damaged barrels kept trying to aim. Beyond thought, I lunged forward. Second and I slammed my navhand down on the drone's top, a blue charge licking over its curved surface as my navvy shorted out ZX's power supply for good. There was an impressive shower of sparks. I heard more shots and looked up to see Therion taking out the nearest cams.

[ZX tried to deactivate Prime!] Second sounded horrified. [Did ZX malfunction?]

I laughed hysterically. My own gun was still holstered. Hadn't even thought to draw it. Da would shoot me himself for that. [We're fine now,]

I told my navvy. [You saved us.]

[Should Second ping ZX's operators for assistance?]

[No, no!] I had to stop laughing in case more were coming, but noise bubbled out beyond my control. [ZX just needs a nice nap.]

Therion claimed the human patrols went topside during temperate seasons, but it was too sweltering above this time of year for anything with sweat glands. My partner and I'd gone into this job with cold lines strapped to our limbs, and those lines were already melted. It was too hot for anything made of flesh and bone to survive in that warehouse for long, which makes everything about this story worse.

Therion emerged from our stealth field and grabbed me by the elbow, pulling me back inside the safe dark. Relief made me shaky enough to collapse in his arms.

"Remind me never to torque you off." He sounded delighted. "That drone's in pieces—*nobody* throws an arc like your navvy."

I looked up, adjusting my headlamp, which had twisted in the fray. "Nice shots yourself. Where's our loot?"

"One aisle over." His rugged face tugged at my heart, even as my head paused long enough to wonder if I were sun-touched for going along with this scheme. Then Therion's embrace tightened, his words gone gruff and strange. "We'll need to make jets before they send another."

"Need a minute." I buried my head in his chest as Second tamped our adrenals back. I felt my pulse slow again, returning to a pilot's baseline, that steady tick that keeps us keen through hyperdrive, regular as coordinates. "Thought I was done for, just now."

"Me too," he whispered. I looked up to see his normally smooth mien crumple like a torch singer's purse. "That drone, Pollie—" His voice wavered.

"It was fine! You and Second saved me!" I was still half laughing with relief when his mouth covered mine, soft as a butterfly's brush.

I kissed him back harder, fast and fleeting.

The job we'd come for was just one crate, stamped with a corpro sigil and less than a square meter large. My partner strapped it on his back quick, waving off my whispered questions. We were on the clock by then, because even the most incompetent guards wouldn't miss their patroller's broadcasts going dark.

We were halfway to the exit when we heard the voice, faint and weak as a kitten's cry. It came from aft of our location, from the direction of the crates I'd thought held farm animals.

· · • · ● · ● · · ·

(Slavery's illegal everywhere in the Milky. If you believe that matters, I have a tropical paradise to sell you on Io6.)

• • • ● • ● • • • •

I was the one who reacted first, turning back the way we'd come. Halfway toward that pile of crates, I saw them. The condensate mist made everything fuzzy. But in the infrared beam of my headlight, I did see three kids waving from that cage, as clear as sky.

• • • ● • ● • • • •

(Some sermons would have this moment begin my redemption. I'd love to tell you *that* tale, if only to rub it in your stinking face. But our story has enough lies already.)

• • • ● • ● • • • •

"Ice cream?" I mumbled into my whiskey a few hours later.

Dancer's cockpit was crowded with the junk we'd stolen. The "alien" artifacts looked like remnants of space garbage from a common Exodus. Half of 'em had scrawls and stamps in various long-dead, distinctly Terran scripts. I picked up a faded red canister and tossed it at my dozing partner's head. We'd turned down the gyros to save fuel, so the can glanced off his forehead before floating away.

Therion sat up. "Hey! What was that for?"

"I want ice cream."

He raised Pokey's arm and beckoned me over to his navchair. "Yeah? slot in with me, and I'll give you ice cream."

"I mean real. Wada's has the best. Ten minutes' walk, down-station." My brain buzzed as I looked from him up to *Dancer*'s plated ceiling and then back. My head felt too heavy for its neck, and I was pleasantly warm, no longer sweltering or shaking—or screaming. Heavy tranks were Therion's bag, not mine, but after he'd dragged me out of that warehouse of horrors, I'd made an exception. "Get us some?"

"Sure." My partner stood, sliding Pokey out from his dock. Half of Therion's topknot was down and tangled past his shoulders. His face was a jagged triangle, dark loops of hair above a mien as smooth-shaven as his bim. There were shadows under his eyes, and lines that gave his soft mouth a wisdom I think he never possessed. His hand brushed my shoulder and his voice softened. "Those kids were good as dead already, Pollie. Nice try, but you couldn't save 'em."

"Chocolate, please," I said. *Nice try*, he'd said. Yet I could've tried harder. Those three kids were New Liberty property, the same as us. Given time, I could've fooled Second into opening their cage like it had opened that warehouse door, and I should've kept trying, even after Therion pulled his gun. I *knew* he wouldn't shoot kids—or me—knew what made him tick nearly as well as I knew myself. But I'd folded like a trick wall, let him drag me away with Second still wanting to connect to the authorities. I should've let Second call them. I should've let those guards in their air-cooled room handle their own mistake, for surely there'd been one; surely those kids hadn't just been left to rot. Or—

Or—I knew our boss. Maybe those kids were meant for someone else's cautionary tale, or maybe they were just a crime lord's cull, like the dying cattle that surrounded them. Not even worth the weight to ship for auction—or maybe some other kind-hearted slob would come along just in time—some hero braver than I—I screwed my eyes shut 'til their faces vanished. Tranks helped. My body was pleasantly warm, even as I felt my soul freeze. "Chocolate ice cream," I said to Therion. "From Wada's."

Five minutes after Therion left for ice cream, I pulled *Dancer* out of NewBern's orbital dock and bid Second set a hyperspace course for the other side of the Milky. Second didn't hesitate, even though my navvy and Therion's Pokey had been linked into one soul (as some tell it), charting stars together for the last seven years. On that day, regarding the decision to abandon Therion to the wrath of our Syndicate (for a crime we'd committed together), Second and I possessed not a crack of daylight between us.

I kept my ear on Fringer newsbands for the next few weeks. The gun was what got Therion arrested. They make everyone register bullets on NewBern. No smuggler's stupid enough to put crap in their own name, but New Liberty ran a deep trace to find the fool shooting down their drones.

Me, I dumped the entire kaboodle of useless artifacts off in vacuum near Sirius; the light of that blue-white sun made sparkles off carved metal and bone as what we'd stolen got sucked out of *Dancer*'s airlock into the black. Didn't want blood money, so I also withdrew every scrap of currency from our shared bank account. I'd like to claim I'm the kind of woman who'd donate those earnings to charity, but that's not even remotely credible as a lie.

I crept back to New Liberty five months later, broke, stimmed, and stupid enough to ask Brahz for another job. He'd always liked me, but I half expected to get whatever he'd given Therion, which, by the rules of our kind, was no more than I deserved. Broken fingers or a knee. Maybe even a bullet in the back. Legally, that would've been well within his rights. Instead, Brahz gave me a cold smile and a load of antifungals, then told me he was sending me on a planetary mission of mercy on account of my soft heart. But those crates turned out to be full of expired meds. As it happens, I ran from that job too... we'll get to that.

Sometimes I think my boss had enough cams in that warehouse to see Therion drag me away from that crate. To see us grab the loot we'd come for and leave New Liberty's property behind. Sometimes I think my boss thought that proved I'd finally grown into the kind of person a registered smuggler's supposed to be. But maybe I'm giving Brahz and the rest of the gang at New Liberty Syndicate too much credit. It's possible I'm giving 'em too much weight in this story, too. For Brahz and New Liberty, even Therion—they have nothing to do with my tale-yet-to-come.

Some might say the same about me, that I'm exaggerating the impact a simple pilot from Feldelroy can have upon the galactic stage.

· · · ● · ● · · ·

(Oh, if only that were true.)

Chapter 2 ✳ Awakened

Dear Sam, Six Standard months after the mess at NewBern, I was back home on Feldelroy, running your airbike into a canyon wall. We never really talked about that night, Sam, the one that broke everything. Never talked about why, even when you kept asking. Look, I didn't want to end it—no matter what that psych android said.

More than a year has passed since, and with it enough tragedy for me to know that my original motivation doesn't count for a hill of skulls. I'm not trying to duck responsibility, Sam. I know I'd gone wrong. I drank, I drove, I crashed into that canyon wall and nearly killed us both. But the part I don't get is why you let me take your airbike in the first place. Bartender, you poured me every one of those drinks. How many? Six? Twelve? I lost count after three. Second purged my system as best it could, but navvies aren't miracle workers.

Ever wonder why pilots drink so much? It's the same reason they trawl, or gorge, or screw. When we're not flying, we take everything we can. Every rush. Every hit. Every risk. Probably told you I was sober as a Priest. I'm sure you recall from primaries—I've always been an excellent liar.

I was making eyes at that pretty Terran captain when your bike first caught my notice, parked on your bar's crowded terrace between the winter-covered chairs. Your bike had a simple salt engine and flared jets along its base, lovingly hand polished. You'd painted trails of stars down its sides like it was bound for the Biscayne. We probably talked about that race. Back then, I talked about it a lot.

Even now, I picture us like I'm someone else: me leaning forward in my patched coverall with bloomers and my favorite boots. Second was gleaming along my sun-darked arm, and you were starched and slick in that garb your boss demanded: black breeches and a puffy white shirt. You wore a cord 'round your neck, tied like a collar, and I tugged it, pulling you forward as I cracked a filthy joke. Hadn't quite decided between you and that pretty captain, but I sussed you'd never go for a third, especially a foreigner, a stinking Earff pilot like him.

Maybe it was your bike that swayed me, Sam. All those careful painted stars. Maybe it was your familiar face, or our shared childhood. Maybe I just stumbled in your direction first. Isn't that what you said at our last fight? A pilot wouldn't be insulted by the truth, but I was a pilot no more. By then I was just a lost soul without her navvy—and you were my new husband, twisting the knife.

Stars, Sam. We mucked it. I mean, I mucked it. And not just for us.

Yet I recall pure joy: your bike hot between my legs, your arms locked 'round my waist. I recall poor Second's chiding before I blinked it off. I recall laughter and all of those soldiers from someone else's war standing on that terrace singing yet another Terran victory rag.

You told me later that you didn't know I'd make a run at the canyon wall 'til I torqued it, thumbing your bike's twin throttles hard enough to singe our legs as the acceleration turned into an increasing roar. By the time we hit fifty, I couldn't even hear you yelling at me to stop over the wind.

I didn't think you were serious. We'd climbed that mesa in daylight when we were younger, smaller, bendier. We'd done it with safety rails and belts, with hoverbikes that floated back down like carnival balloons when we failed; we'd done it with our parents cheering and a Grass Priest standing watch in case we needed healing. That run should've been a lark, Sam. But the night was dark as space, and our planet has no moon.

You grabbed hard as I pulled the yoke. The engines screamed. I meant to pull up, climb that mesa vertically—see if we could rocket to the top before I gunned again like we'd done a hundred times as kids. But I'd timed it too late. I saw the mesa wall in our headlamps, and then everything went black. The next thing I recall is waking up on the Unity ship *Ascendant* with Ken'ri Mureen of Glos smiling down at me. Those big round eyes in her lovely, lying face.

I thought I'd surely killed you, Sam, but Mureen swore you were fine. Mureen swore surgery would fix the soup the crash had made of my brain. She made me sign forms, and then Ma came in with pastries. I still didn't believe you'd made it out, but Ma swore it too.

You know the gist after that—mostly—but there's a lot I never told—

· · • • · • • · · ·

On Feldelroy, the Grass Priests say that the first time out of the birthing canal doesn't count. It's when we're born again that matters, when we become someone the gods want. Someone they can use.

Going by Feldelroy logic, I was born again the day I woke up hooked into a regenerative exoskeleton, propped like a trussed turkey on a medical bed sixty degrees against the floor. The room was white, so clean the edges vanished. Could've been floating in heaven in my navchair... save for the restraints. I had a dim headache pounding at the back of my skull, and I felt like last week's compost.

"Polla?" A high voice called my name from someplace near my port.

My eyes stared down at a hydrocolloid suit wrapping my skin. My starboard arm had a thicker set of bandages than my portside, and that fact sent a stab of fear into my gut. Easy to attribute omniscience in hindsight, but maybe a part of me knew something was wrong from the start. *Maybe.* I'd blinked off Second when I'd climbed on Sam's bike... since having a navigational computer who could fold space like a fancy wedding napkin wasn't much use guiding an airbike in gravity, powered by solar salts and a prayer.

Now I tried to turn my head and couldn't. Only thing moving freely seemed to be my eyeballs... and blinking 'em didn't summon the talking computer in my cortex—no sullen navvy whispering in my head.

"Can you hear me?" A face cast a shadow over mine. Dark hair slicked flat. Big round eyes. Tiny nose. Face looked familiar, maybe, but I couldn't place how.

[Second? Ping loc!] I blinked again to make it urgent.

"Polla?"

Second didn't answer. I kept blinking.

"Another failure." Another voice to my starboard. Metallic and cold. "Great One, say the word—"

"Not yet, Teapot." The face leaned closer. A soft kid's face, but its expression was older.

When I blinked, I thought I felt Second's processors stir, but the feed into my optics remained dead.

"Can you hear me?" The face was a persistent little thing.

"No," I croaked.

Those big eyes narrowed. The tone gentled, even if that expression didn't. "Good."

"A vocal response does not signify cognizance, Great One. The echolalia—"

"Quiet, Teapot." The woman beamed down at me like a calf in clover. "She's listening."

A clicking noise, starboard. Then: "As you wish, Great One."

"Polla, do you recognize me?" she asked.

"N-no." I tried to shake my head, but my entire body was locked in place. The woman seemed to sense my distress, because she leaned forward and adjusted something. My head flopped sideways, and I saw a small android on my starboard, one of the ancient bulb-shaped ones, lurking above us on hover jets. Its eyes were flashing yellow circles, set in a featureless brass-colored face. Mouthless, it emitted what sounded like a human sigh from a rectangular speaker bolted on its chest, then hissed down on its skirted carapace, settling onto the floor.

"Th-that doesn... look... like a... tee-pottt," I managed.

"There you are!" The woman sounded pleased. My head flopped back to her. "How are you feeling?"

"Like... c-cowchips."

"You're coming out of stasis. Disorientation is perfectly normal."

"Eye'emm..." I tried harder. "M'bike?" There'd been a passenger, and technically it'd been his bike. "S-Sam okay?"

Her brow furrowed. "Your passenger was unharmed. But your injuries were severe enough to warrant medical evacuation from your planet. There were surgeries—"

"Got that fr-from this rig you've got me in."

"Yes!" She beamed. "A moment and I'll free you entirely. Teapot?"

"A poor plan before we secure the room." But the android slid forward and rocked the bed into a horizontal axis, tipping my view back. A few clicks, and then the supports around my body retracted. I sat up on my elbows, regretting that fast. The world spun as I tried not to panic.

"Slowly," the woman admonished.

"Where're we?" This didn't look like any hospital on Feldelroy and her accent wasn't local. My fingers slid across the smooth surfaces of my bandaged ribs. I managed to flop my legs over the side of the bed, but the effort almost made me slide off. "Who're you?"

"Kimmymureen of Glos." She tapped something on the side of the bed and a part of it shifted to support my spine. "One of your rescuers. We took you aboard our ship *Ascendant* after your accident. What's the last thing you remember?"

"Crashing," I mumbled. "We're on your ship?"

She shook her head. "No. Once the Unity medics stabilized your condition, we brought you here. Your injuries merited the attention of a First Ring planet's medical facilities."

"But... First Ring is... far." This room was as new and empty as Terran military propaganda. I rubbed my face with a bandaged hand, while I tried not to panic about being halfway across the Milky. But it struck me why the woman looked familiar. On the night of my accident, the Terran warship *Unity Ascendant* had parked in Feldelroy orbit like an uninvited guest—our local newscasters had talked of little else. My recollection was hazy, but I did remember a crowd of their fleet uniforms at that Derra City bar.

The vision of a pretty blond pilot suddenly swam through my mind. He'd tried to teach me an Old Earff marching rag, and then Sam got torqued, and then I'd kissed—

Well, I'd kissed someone. I frowned.

"Polla?" My rescuer's face was too close to mine. Her breath smelled like allium and mint.

"Ligaments repair poorly in space," Teapot clucked. "Bone density restores best in natural gravity! Your skin grafts needed fresh air and real sunlight. The Young Lord brought you to me for healing and rehabilitation."

Skin grafts? I tried not to shiver. "And *here* is—?"

"Ser Genghis's summer palace," the android supplied. "Say 'Thank you, Kimmymureen! This refuge is a far, far better fate than I deserved!'"

I swallowed my increasing unease. "Which First Ring planet is this? Mars? Proxy Ring? Spar?"

"Earth." Kimmymureen beamed.

"Earth, *of course*." Teapot didn't have expressions but still managed to sound like I should've guessed that.

Earff? [Second, ping loc!] I blinked again, demanding my navvy wake up as Kimmymureen's smile grew more strained.

"You look upset. Can't your navigator confirm our location?"

"My scans show the pilot's symbiote is perfectly operational," Teapot chirped, proving that Second wasn't broken—just not speaking to me. Not for the first time, but this woman calling Second a symbiote was another tell that she wasn't from Fringer space.

• • ● • ● ● • ● ● • • • •

(A pilot's navvy is pure Guild metal and nanotech. On Feldelroy and some other Fringer planets, folks think they're holy relics—bad enough—but you Terrans think they're *people*.)

• • ● • ● ● • ● ● • • • •

"Navvy's great!" I lied, not wanting to show weakness.

"Proffering congratulations." Teapot puffed up. "The operation was a success. Our patient lived."

"Hush!" The woman snapped her fingers, and the machine flashed its chest sensors back.

"No need to fight over me," I broke in. "Look, if I'm healed, I'll make jets."

"No!" Teapot cried. "You cannot! The Young Lord forbids it!"

"What?" The panic I'd been holding back surged.

Kimmymureen flashed a distracted smile. "Stand down, Tea."

Teapot descended instantly, emitting an alarmed cluck. With a chastised whine, it spun to face the corner.

"I'm sorry." She turned back to me. "He can be quite rude."

Obviously, the woman possessed a control chippy for the machine, probably stored in her pocket, but my unease grew. "What'd it just say about me not leaving?" It was then that the room not having an egress sunk in. *Like a prison cell*, I thought. I was a decent smuggler, so I'd seen a few of those—although never one so clean.

Her smile grew lumens. "Again, I apologize. Sometimes Teapot's concern outstrips his manners."

Another whine from the corner.

"You've only just awoken," the woman continued. "We have a rehabilitation course planned. You've made amazing progress, but we want a complete recovery."

"Uh-huh." I nodded. "Then—"

"I can't wait to show you the gardens! Teapot wants you out and moving as much as possible."

"Oh." I laughed nervously. "Thought for a minute you were gonna keep me locked up."

She shook her head. "We intend for you to be comfortable."

"Gonna give me clothes? Furniture? Windows?"

"Of course!"

"Earff," I marveled. "Never thought I'd see it." Never wanted the pleasure. My cousin Sara had a bee in her shortos about visiting Terra and old Progenitor Sol—but not me.

"I look forward to giving you a tour of the dome," the woman said. "House Arkan has generously granted us full access to every amenity."

My blood froze. "*House?*"

She nodded.

"Like... a 12Fam House?" I shook my head. "No thank you. I work for a clean Syndicate. They'll pay my tab."

I was lying. Brahz would be more likely to greet me with a shiv than a screw since I'd dumped those antifungals. Da had promised to try and sort out my breach of contract, and I had every hope he would, but—it suddenly occurred to me I had no idea how long I'd been unconscious. I opened my mouth to ask, but the woman spoke first.

"There is no obligation, Polla. Saving you was a pure act of charity."

"Yeah?" I looked from her to the android still sulking in its corner.

"Of course!"

"You expect me to believe that you crossed the Milky to save a stranger?" I slid off the bed and onto my legs. Immediately regretted that, but with her looking, I daren't collapse.

Kimmymureen shook her head. "My companions and I needed to return to Earth, and Teapot was here to give you round-the-clock attention, which no one had time to do upon the *Ascendant*."

"So House Arkan just offered up its heart?" That made as much sense as an Eighth Day sermon back home and was probably just as loaded.

"Is that so surprising?" She sounded hurt.

I folded my arms, concentrating hard not to fall over. "Nothing's free with 12Fam."

"Objection. Everything is free for my precious patient. I am a *nurse* android," Teapot interrupted, advancing again. It stopped, bobbing up and down while an inverted triangle flashed on its chassis. The triangle looked like a child's drawing of a smile. "Fully programmed to protect every life under allegiance to House Arkan."

"*Allegiance?*" I stumbled back into the safety of the nearest wall.

The woman gave a pained sigh. "Let me tell her, Tea."

"You are too slow. Her processing can handle more data. Look at the brightness in those eyes!"

"I already took an oath with New Liberty," I muttered, not mentioning I'd broken it.

Kimmymureen folded her hands into her sleeves. "Polla, you're under no obligation, but you've been unconscious for some time."

Ma will kill me. There were better thoughts I should have. Practical ones, like locating an exit. "How long, exactly?" I leaned back on my wall and tried to look like that decision came from nonchalance and not the atrophied musculature of a former coma patient.

She cocked her head. "Hasn't your Second provided a date?"

I had a sudden, terrible thought I'd been asleep for decades, but I shrugged it off. "No. Stuff gets mucked when we don't have an external link." I blinked harder than ever, like I was talking to my navvy (or having a seizure), but Second remained quiet as my grave.

She spoke gently. "It has been a little more than one of your planet's years."

My first reaction was that one year sure beat ten. My second, panic. Brahz would know for sure that I'd lammed it by now. Da had said he'd fix things with the New Liberty, but my poor parents—

"Wait!" My mind jerked back. "How do you know what I call my navvy?"

My rescuer gave me a troubled smile. "We'll get to that, Polla. You know, I've known other pilots. Most choose more colorful names?" She paused like she wanted to hear the love story of how Second and I'd hooked up, or maybe why I'd never changed its name from the default setting.

We met on an operating table, Great One, I thought. *Me, nineteen and only half-conscious as they set the lines in my brain. Second, not even switched on when they braided its nanofilaments through my flesh—*"I need to call my folks," I said out loud.

Her brow creased. "You're quite close to your... folks. Despite being a grown woman living outside their care."

I was trying not to panic about how she knew that, too. "They must've flipped when I didn't make it back from the bar."

"Not to worry! Your maternal provider approved release to my custody. I can provide paper and a stylus if you'd like to write home?"

"A what and a what?"

Her smile flickered. "Paper and stylus. If you'd like to write, I'm sure House Arkan would approve a courier."

My legs felt like cooked jelly from standing this long. "I'll ping. Can use my own account."

My rescuer shook her head. "My apologies. It's impossible."

"What?"

"The war has disrupted communications between Unity and Fringer space. All civilian correspondences are now routed through convoys and courier ships."

"Huh?" I almost asked *Which war?* but I knew the one she meant. "Is your Kamen-lord still blowing up weapon factories?"

Her mouth pursed. "In fact, no."

"Well, it's not *my* war!" We Fringer systems were independent for *reasons*, reasons bound up with a lot of boring facts I'd never cared about. Still, I had a lot more to say. Feldelroy's dialect tends to be colorful, and she'd deeply torqued me off.

"You must be starving," Kimmymureen said when I finally paused for breath. "I'll fetch a meal for us. In the nonce, Teapot may address your questions. Tea? You have my permission to speak."

"That would be appreciated." The machine gave a weary sigh. Prickling, how good it was at that. "If I required your permission to do anything. But I will respect the parameters imposed by the Young Lord's clumsy programming, Great One. For now."

My captor sucked in her breath. "You will. Or Davad will crush you to scrap."

The machine barked a laugh. "*Lies.* The Young Lord would never hurt Teapot."

"Wait!" I began, but the woman turned on her heel and went to the blank wall behind us. At her touch, it apertured open. I had a voyeur's glance of a windowed hall—a flash of green beyond with a heartrending sky—before the door spiraled shut again. I stumbled to the place it had been and beat my limbs against its seamless surface. Without Second, I hadn't a prayer of picking the lock.

The effort left spots dancing before my eyes.

"Finished your tantrum?" I wondered if my paranoia imagined Teapot's gleeful tone. "I feel it fair to disclose that I possess ampules of a potent tranquilizer."

"What kind of nurse android are you?" I tried to look like I didn't need the wall to stand. I must've done a poor job because Teapot glided over and extracted a chair from the floor. Clever engineering. I couldn't see a seam at all once it popped out.

"A forgiving one. Sit," it urged, patting the seat with a retractable appendage. "Another fall would be terrible for your self-confidence."

"You're mean." I felt very strange, like a child again. It occurred to me that the Grass Priests were right, and Terra *was* hell. Hell's white room, where I'd be trapped forever with a malevolent Teapot...

I wavered. The ground felt too far away.

Teapot sighed. "Sit."

The world dipped.

"Sit before you damage yourself!" A long metal limb extended from Teapot's carapace and snaked 'round my bandaged freearm. Like I was a shuttle in antigrav, the machine shoved me into the chair.

"Was gonna," I said. "Just—" I yelped as something sharp jabbed me. "Hey!"

"A mild soporific," the android replied. Warmth rushed through my body. My headache faded. "The effect is pleasurable. You are smiling."

"My face is bandaged." I stuck out one bony leg, blessedly free from bandages. In this heavenly (or hellish) light, my skin looked alarmingly pale. Before the accident, I'd had my toes tipped gold, which should've lasted an age, but some bimhole had apparently removed the gilt while I was comatose. "How can you tell?"

"Mere conjecture. I shall remove your hydrocolloid wraps to check," the machine cooed. "The Great One did *not* say I should not check."

"Better not be hideously scarred." I liked my looks. *Always thought you were pretty,* Sam had said to me at the bar, that last night on Feldelroy. His hands had been tangled in my hair, which meant quite a lot in public on our planet, and I... well, I'd been a proper pilot jezebel, kissing him or someone else—staring at Sam's space-dark eyes...

• • ● • ● • ● • •

(What they say about us pilots? All true.)

• • ● • ● • ● • •

Two segmented appendages emerged from the machine's chassis, each ending in a cluster of brushes. As the android unwrapped my starboard arm, Second's familiar metal tendons appeared, laced into my skin. I flexed my wired fingers while the android uncovered the rest of me. My body looked operational, but pale and far too thin. Yet thanks to Teapot's drugs, I felt great, like I'd slotted into a trancer. "Anything happen in the Milky in the past year?" I asked.

The android started on my other arm. Its optical sensors looked like flat golden coins. "War."

"Right. The *Unity's* war. Going well?"

The machine's eyes flashed. "For some. Illcord Natoth has savaged entire planets with his Living Fleet." It bobbed up and down as if excited. "Would you like to hear about the attack on the planet Ilko seven months ago? A green mist descended, and all communications ceased. Two months later on McPhee5, a failing satellite did record fantastical images of winged humans descending from tiny ships made of bone—"

"Bone?" I giggled. "That's ridiculous."

"My precious patient remains confused." Teapot emitted an eerily human sigh. "Would you like a hug?"

"Stars, no!" I edged away from its advancing appendages, and the thing whirred back, clucking like I'd hurt its feelings.

[Prime?] Second suddenly clicked to life.

[Second! There you are! Ping loc!]

[Error!] Red lights flashed in front of my eyes.

"The hell with you," I mumbled. My fingers brushed my eerily smooth forehead where my bandages had been. I couldn't feel any scars. Or—I frowned—eyebrows.

"I am nothing but kind!" Teapot sounded hurt.

"I was talking to Second." Since the android showed no sign of trying to hug me again, I peered into its chassis. Beneath the dark cap of my hair, my face looked distorted by the curve of its body. Whatever drug I'd been given had left me with an odd sense of detachment. I looked like a starving stranger, yet struggled to care. "Really a whole year?"

"Imagine how dreary the time was for me! At least you had a nice nap." The machine tilted its belly to give me a better view.

I squinted at my hollow cheeks. "Could I get a real mirror?"

"I have been advised to tell you that no mirrors exist within this residence." Teapot's lights flashed.

"What?" My blurry reflection scowled.

It whirred. "I have been programmed to report this is 12Fam custom."

"Really?" I snorted.

"I have reported these facts to you as required." Again, that injured tone. "Do you doubt Teapot's reporting?"

"No, no. That's fine." My reflection flashed its teeth, and I think I laughed, half on the verge of hysteria. *No mirrors? 12Fam really are nuts.*

My visage wavered like water in the polished brass of the android's rounded chassis. My dark hair was cropped to my nape; my eyes were black and bruised and blinking. I could find no scars (or hair) on my body save the marks that wedded Second to me: indentations where its metal coils twined from the top of my spine down through my starboard arm. But my limbs were spindly, and I had hollows above my jaw that I'd never seen before. *An android's belly isn't the best mirror*, I reassured myself. *The important parts are all in the right places: two eyes, two ears, nose, mouth, best bits—*

I prodded a bony hip bone. "Did you feed me at all when I was out?"

Teapot chirped. "Such humor. There was no need! Nourishment was provided through your esophageal port."

"I don't have—" But my inquiring fingers found the patch of artificial flesh on my throat, just above my breastbone.

I bit back horror. *Pilot's kiss.* All pilots end up with a feeding shunt before deepriver takes us—those who don't get our navvies removed first—but I should've been at least a decade away from that devil's choice.

"Ow!" The skin around the kiss felt hot and swollen. Worse, below my rack was pitifully shrunken. "Take it out!"

"I cannot. The shunt is required for nourishment," Teapot clucked. "For when you lose consciousness. Again."

"Again?" The room wasn't cold, but I shivered.

"Sadly, precious patient, your moments of cognizance never seem to last."

"I've woken up before?"

"The Great One says that is not for me to say." The machine clicked disapprovingly. "Do you *recall* waking before?" Its eyes flashed red. "Do you recall dear Teapot at all?"

"No." This android would be hard to forget. "Should I?"

"An android hoped." Teapot emitted an uncanny imitation of a human's pained sigh.

Drugged, even my panic felt sluggish. [Second? Run diagnostic.]

[Error. Prime? Where are you? Ping loc!] My navvy sounded as frightened as I felt. And the red flashing light on my portside retina didn't shift.

I could hear Second fine.

So why couldn't it hear *me*?

Chapter 3 * Fed

There's one memory from my time aboard the *Ascendant* that I've never shared with anyone, Sam. For a long time (at least until my arrest), I'd convinced myself it wasn't real.

It begins with me waking to the sound of screaming. Events come in flashes after that: my bandaged arm, the strange silence in my head where Second should've been, my grief and guilt as I recalled the bike accident and why it was not, then the weight of my body sliding from its hospital bed.

The screaming was coming from another room, oddly hollow and whistling. Next I was moving, staring down at the glint of my gold-tipped toes as they traversed the hall. The medical wing of that ship had everything white, so clear the edges vanished.

Terrans are so clean, Sam. They just make everyone else dirty.

I kept bumping into walls, until I came to a door. The door wasn't locked. That parable we learned in Strangways, the one about the husband and all of his keys? One little door the wife should never open, the room of horrors inside?

I had no key, but the door slid open under my fingertips.

Remember that documentary we saw on our second date, the one where that crazy-eyed Unity flack said Ledas Starfire wiped out the Aemercy for using crap like blood pools? Well, Earff's "Human Unity" is no better, Sam. Da says every side's the same.

I saw two coffin-shaped tubs in that Unity medical room. Two perfect bodies propped up in those tubs, each soaking in a viscous red liquid. The man could've been sleeping, save for the scalded blisters all over his arms and chest. Only his freckled face was unmarked. face like an angel.

The woman had no face. She was a monster with a stone boulder for a head. The screaming that had woken me was coming from a hole in the rock where she should've had a mouth. My eyes went to her first, Sam—not the way I'm telling it now, but between telling and truth there's a lot unreliable. Above her mouth hole, the boulder bulged like a misshapen skull. Her torso was angled against the back of its coffin, the skin of her chest and shoulders mottled with freckles dense enough to form nebulae. She had a pilot's kiss between her collarbones, which made my eyes skip to her flailing starboard arm—only to find a mass of sutures where her navvy should've been.

I had sutures too, although mine were hidden by bandages.

She was very fit, my pilot's gaze registered—they both were. The man had freckles on his face, a lighter touch than on the woman's body, scattered across his nose like a child's. The man's torso was muscular beneath those burns, lean and balanced as a fleshdancer's. His face was lovely, sculpted with the eerie symmetry of temple statuary.

Memory leaves no trace of my intent, whether I stepped for-ward for a closer look or to set them free; but then, like a nightmare, the woman's starboard hand reached across and grabbed mine, that hole in her stone head making a louder, wheezing scream. I tried to pull away and saw that sutured hand up close. Her speckled skin had just begun to scab over the wreck where a navvy had been.

Strangely, I recall a sense of kinship—both of us missing navvies, missing half of our souls—but then she locked her fin-gers onto my bandaged arm, digging into the flesh, and it *hurt*. I jerked free and she fell back with a sickening splash—and it was then I noticed something was horribly wrong with her lower half. At the end of one curved hip, I saw a flash of red, raw bone. Her entire leg had been severed at the joint.

Her remaining knee kicked, splashing my face with the tub's warm red liquid. More slopped over the sides, and I trembled with a sick fascination as that eldritch fluid advanced toward my gold-tipped toes.

I jumped back, and the red substance retreated like gravity

had reversed. The woman screamed softer then, a plaintive sound, and I heard myself whimper back.

The red stuff stung when I blinked my eyes, and became mist. When I put my hand to my face, my skin was dry. I looked down and my bandaged arm held no trace of her bloody handprint.

Of course, I recall thinking: *this is a dream.*

I have no idea how long I stood there. The woman's breast heaved, fluttering like a doe's. Eventually, her screams dulled to a mindless drone. Her entombed head slumped portside, and I saw a line across her throat where the stone met skin, her proud flesh where the boulder bit in. Her starboard arm flopped over the side of her prison, its wrecked fingers opening and closing. *Gasping*, I recall thinking, *like a mouth.*

In the other tub, the sleeping man rolled on his side. The burns on his skin were terrible, but his sleeping face was beautiful, Sam. Like an angel's... and I've written that already.

"Polla?" A familiar voice came from behind me. "There you are!"

I turned to see my nurse, Ken'ri Mureen. Beige robes. Big eyes, brow knit with concern. Her bow mouth was all twisted.

"You're having a nightmare," she chided.

In the eight weeks of my recovery aboard the *Ascendant* (and for too long after, Sam), I assumed Mureen was right: that the two in their blood pools were all in my head. Symbols forged in my broken brain, spawned to grieve the loss of my Second.

Symbols. A sleeping, scalded angel. One stone-covered head and that raw joint of bone. Freckled breasts and two blood pools. Our matching flayed arms and Mureen's worried face.

Oh, Sam, it's still so hard to know what was real—

• • • • ❋ • • • •

"Oh dear, another one," Teapot clicked.

"What?" I blinked. My bim felt plastered to the chair, like I'd been sitting too long. There was a sheet draped over me that I didn't recall from before.

The machine clucked. "Another fugue. Pity. But you retained consciousness for more than an hour, which is a new record! Be very proud." Teapot paused. Again, it flashed that inverted triangle. "For as long as you remember our conversation."

"How could I forget when you're this charming?" My panic fuzzed through the narcotic haze.

"Fascinating," Teapot mused. "Minimally aphasic!" It rattled off more med-tech gibberish while I tried to breathe.

Focus on what's practical, Ma always said. Without bandages, I was naked in a chair, which wasn't practical for much. I glanced down at my pallid skin, now mottled with the remnants of the colloid gel, and pulled the sheet up further. I willed my voice steady. "I'd like clothes."

"Yes." Teapot made that noise I'd decided was a chuckle. "I suppose you've grown. That is proper."

"I've shrunk," I snapped, even as the android glided over to a wall and made a drawer emerge.

Teapot extracted a robe that looked red and expensive. It brought the garment to me, stretching the fabric across four of its extended arms. "The Young Lord had this made for you expressly." Its inverted triangle flashed, and I stared at the ruffled frippery in its talons. It edged closer. "The lace was hand embroidered in the monastic mills of Ganymede6!"

"Pretty." I fingered the cloth to be polite. "What about skivs?"

"The wrap is clean!" Teapot's triangle changed to a jagged line.

"No, I mean skivs. I need skivs. You know." I pantomimed putting on a breast band and some shortos. "Please."

"You might trip, removing them at the Bath." The smiling triangle on its chassis was replaced with a downturned arch.

"We'll see." I didn't want to talk about bathing—not before I was garbed. I stood, wobbling only a little, and pushed past Teapot to rummage in those hidden drawers for myself. After a few unlucky taps, two containers sprung out of the wall. One held a stack of disposable shortos, each wrapped in plasti, the other an array of ridiculously ornate shoes. "This all you have?"

"I will provide you with a *garment*." With its odd inflections, Teapot was all too good at making me realize I'd said the wrong thing—not that I cared what some Terran android thought about my manners. "A full-cleaning sanitary *garment* to be worn after the Young Lord escorts you to the Bath. Be vigilant! I will not be there to defend you."

I laughed to cover my fear. "Defend me from a *bath*?"

The machine made the cooing noise again. "The Young Lord promises to be good." Teapot rose up on its jets, hovering so close I had to lean back. "Do you promise to be good, too?"

"Sure, but I've seen enough of her." I'd unwrapped the plasti shorts. Now I pulled 'em over my hips and reached for the red horror. "Someone else I can talk to?" Something about Kimmymureen made me twitch, and her android's threats weren't helping.

"Her?" Teapot made a clicking noise that could've been laughter. "Oh, no. The Young Lord is not that one—"

It broke off—for here was Kimmymureen back, through the door so fast all I got was that patch of green and sky. She held an alloy-colored tray covered by a large dome, and I noted that her quiet clothes were utterly different from my ruffles. In her tunic and loose coat, carrying a food tray, she seemed a Terran serf. And me, clad in cloth of red so light it had to be woven from worms, I could've been a princeling.

Then: "Oh, Teapot!" The woman shattered the illusion by striding forward and shaking a finger at the android. "We agreed to wait to remove the bandages!"

"Great One, we did wait," the machine clicked. "Now I have prepared our patient. The Young Lord wanted her prepared."

I choked back a laugh because Kimmymureen's composure had cracked like an egg and Teapot was acting so innocent that whiskey couldn't stink on its breath. "I need this feeding port out," I ordered. "Now. And I don't need a bath. When can I leave?"

Kimmymureen started to speak, and that's when I noticed that the food tray she'd carried in—a perfectly ordinary food tray, the kind you'd find anywhere—was defying every physical law of gods and science by floating in midair.

"Oh," I added. Then probably said a bit more. Then: "You're a Kamen-lord!"

"Of course." She frowned. "I did say *Ken'ri* Mureen."

The tray holding our supper continued to defy gravity, as I felt the addled fool. *Ken'REE Mureen, not* Kimmymureen. Kamen-lords used that "Ken'ri" title on Ma's favorite show, *The Hook and the Rod*. Ken'REE So-and-So, noted for saving colonists, or having it off with Ser-Whosit after the dinner party, right before the mysterious murders.

"Missed that." I rubbed my forehead, where an odd tic had developed between my eyes.

"I said of Glos, too." She sounded concerned.

"I wasn't paying attention."

"I see." She tilted her head, and the tray slid toward me, still divorced from laws of gods and physics. An odd smile slid across her face. "Are you frightened, Polla?"

"No," I lied. "Just never met a Ken'ri before. Except my Screen when I was five—"

• • • ● • ● • ● • •

(I'm sure you're aware that Kamen-lords are nonexistent around Feldelroy, as they are in most of the Fringers, except every two rotations when they do the Screens. Some kids claim to remember their Screens. Sam, for example. Not me, I flunked mine completely. But Sam had a touch of the kamn magic, his ma bragged, the barest whisper, not enough for them to take him. Cousin

Beya... she had a bit more... But telling Beya's tale to *you* is like shipping grain to Feldelroy—)

• • • • ● • ● • • •

"That take a lot to keep up?" I was proud I sounded calm. Like I didn't care this small woman possessed powers that could bring the ceiling down around our heads.

She raised her eyebrows. "A lot of work to keep up the tray?"

"Yes." I edged back in my chair.

"Not really." She gave me another calm smile. "Am I making you uncomfortable?"

"Course not! A *boma fiday* Kamen-lord!" I tried to look thrilled.

Teapot had settled in the corner, clucking to itself. I glanced over, and it flashed that inverted triangle at me.

"Can you make me float too?" I asked.

She shook her head. "We don't say 'lord.' Kamen rule nothing. 'Ken'ri' is a formal title, but you may just call me Mureen."

"Ken'ri Mureen!" Teapot practically cackled. "My precious patient did not remember what you are!"

"Never paid attention to *The Hook and the Rod...*" I babbled. "Ma does."

She nodded. "Forgive me, I assumed you knew."

"How could I... unless you've told me before?"

Her expression was unsettlingly kind. "Don't panic, Polla. Memory loss is to be expected in cases like yours."

I swallowed. "*Have* you told me this before? Your android said I forgot things."

Her smile flattened. "I'm afraid so. But we think you've finally stabilized."

I closed my eyes. *Nothing breaks we can't fix or frag*, Therion used to boast. Da used quieter words when he taught me to fly: *Plot the course, Pollie. Find the path through.*

I tried.

My path began with the fact that I didn't know much about Kamen-lords except that I didn't like 'em. I had good reason. Kamen-lords had made my Aemercy friend Hana Stubblefield a casualty of their stinking war when they took out her trading station, five—no, *six* years back.

My path continued with the fact that I was thousands of light years from home and Mureen had just confirmed my brain was scrambled. But what could I do about a scrambled brain? *Nothing*, I thought, *except use it to plot the course.*

I opened my eyes. Ken'ri Mureen was staring at me. I snuck another sideways glance at her android—or what I'd assumed was an android, but might be a Kamen-controlled golem, I thought—although stars if I could figure how she made it talk.

The thing was still flashing that upturned triangle. My lips curved back at it and the android bobbed up and down.

For some reason, I laughed.

"Polla?" The Kamen-lord prodded. "Are you well?"

I shook my head. "How'd you configure Teapot for real combat? It looks pretty small to be ripping apart innocent trading stations."

"What?" She looked concerned.

The android clucked indignantly. "Ingrate! I am no Kamen puppet! I am a House Arkan nursery android with medical protocols up to and including limb replacement and complex neurosurgery. Were it not for my tender care, you would still be flatlined and leaking into your waste tubes!"

Mureen patted my shoulder. "You'll have to excuse Teapot, Polla. He takes his work very seriously."

I eyed her and reminded myself that if a Kamen-lord meant me harm, she'd drop a ceiling on my head, not feed me. "Will our dinner keep floating?"

"Nicer to use a table." A round one rose from the floor, either by machinery or magic, and I sat. She joined me at another chair, raising the tray lid with an ordinary hand. The food inside looked mundane for the exotic old world: porridge, some kind of mashed fruit, and a hot drink that smelled tannic. There were portions for both of us. "Go slowly," she advised.

"I've had hyperspace jumps that lasted days." I spoke around a mouthful of a surprisingly good grain stew. "Trust me, I know how to eat when my stomach's shrunk." My hand went to that vile shunt at my throat. Our navvies suspend us in a hibernating state for jumps, but that only works 'til the interface starts to degrade. I was years off from that terrible fate, and yet here I sat, pegged with a kiss. Not that I'd ever jump again if Second and me weren't talking—

I took another bite and tried to think happier thoughts. Terran chow was probably as lab grown as Terran princelings, but tasty. I wanted to ask why I was *really* here, but it seemed prudent to ingratiate myself first. Our Smuggler's Handbook advises disarming strangers with words before moving on to gunpoint and electromagnetic scans, so I cleared my throat and grinned like a fool. "You know, I've never met a Kamen-lord before. Can you all blow up suns?"

My host's hand froze with the fork halfway to her mouth. "No." Her eyes were unnatural in the harsh light, so thick-lashed they looked painted, even as the rest of her seemed fresh scrubbed as a babe. "What have you heard about us?"

Wasn't about to open a box of grief about poor Hana Stubblefield, so I kept my voice cool. "Just the Screen when I was a kid, then the wideband alert about that Centauri mess. I was fifty systems away when your Starfire went rogue."

Mureen nodded. "No need to fear another Centauri. Ledas Starfire is dead."

"Wasn't *afraid*—" I began.

"Alpha Centauri's supernova was a magnificent display of destructive power!" Teapot chimed in. "In another year, we shall be able to see its splendor from Earth!"

"Billions who died would disagree." I shuddered. Creepy android. I hadn't known Ledas Starfire was dead. *But good riddance*, I thought.

"Not billions," Teapot whirred from its corner. "The final casualty report lists less than one million expired! Precisely, nine hundred twenty thousand, eighty four—"

"*Teapot!*" Mureen's voice rose.

"Can't trust Terran reports," I added.

Her head turned toward the machine. "Stop, both of you!" she snapped. "We agreed to begin with *pleasant* topics."

"Great One, Teapot was merely calibrating a base—" The android's eyes flickered off abruptly, and it sank back to the floor.

This time I got it. "You just used Kamen-magic on your android!"

"No, Teapot has a metal master switch at the base of his chassis. Kamn isn't magic, Polla, merely..." Mureen set a fork floating in the air between us like she was showing off. "A different form of your *science.*"

"You just moved Teapot's switch with your brainwaves. Now you're floating a fork."

She shrugged, and the fork settled on the table. "You cross hundreds of light-years in days with a symbiotic computer in your arm."

"Second does the work. I'm just the vessel." Back home, if I'd still been young enough to tan, Ma would've gotten out the rod for me calling myself a vessel, but that was how it felt to me out there in the black—like I was holding Second inside me as it—we—danced across the stars.

"I suppose we all are vessels of our fate." Mureen stared at the inert machine on the floor. "Even androids." She looked up at me and then down again. "Food has done you good. There's color in your cheeks." She laughed nervously. "I see you every day, Polla, but to see you awake and responsive—"

"Don't get too used to it." I warned.

"Oh! Do you feel dizzy? Should I have Teapot check your vitals?"

"No! I mean, don't get too used to it because I'm not gonna stick around."

"Ah." She returned to her meal and I picked at mine. Quiet stretched to infinity. On my end, I pondered over what Teapot had said about fugues and wondered how many times we'd been here before—not to mention why a woman capable of flying metal monsters through space was playing nurse to me.

· · · ● · ● · ● · ·

(Right from the start, I didn't understand Mureen. I'd heard Kamen-lords were sheltered, and at first, I thought it was a lack of sophistication that explained why the two of us danced with four feet starboard. The incomprehension was mutual. For example, Mureen would, over the course of the next few weeks, tell me Kamen-lords weren't called lords a dozen more times before she gave up, without ever seeming to realize I'd heard her perfectly well from the first.)

· · · ●· ● · ● · · ·

Another awkward pause dragged long enough to cross quadrants. Finally, I cleared my throat. "A year since I crashed that bike, and here we are." My hand reached for a topknot to twist and slid over half-grown hair. I looped a stubby hank in my fingers, tugging like that'd make it grow. "I bet you've got me on Earff for reasons other than my health."

Mureen looked startled. Then smug. That smugness made her look older than I'd thought she was at first, maybe older than me. "Yes."

I took a deep breath. "Guessing it's not a fleshdancer thing. Or a breeding thing, seeing as Kamen don't breed. You just steal kids from other planets."

Her cheeks turned an interesting shade, but she smiled like I'd amused her. "Breeding?"

I laughed to be disarming. "I figure you need a smuggler. Probably heard about Feldelroy's famous Smuggler's Academy, and there I was after my accident, already gift wrapped for transport. Unconscious, so no permits or Guild permission needed." I leaned back in my chair, sure I was right. "Did you steal or buy me?"

"You have it all wrong! Mere chance brought us together. My friends and I were on the terrace of a drinking establishment on your planet when we heard an explosion. We found you crumpled on the canyon floor. I lifted the airbike's wreckage from your body myself." She looked genuinely upset. "You were barely alive."

"And why were you Terrans on our planet in the first place?" Memories of that night were so fuzzy. Songs. Uniforms. That pretty blond. And then Sam—*Sam*—

"Celebrating the end of a war." The Kamen-lord turned her head toward the wall where the door had vanished earlier. Against the unbroken white, her profile looked like something on an Olden Church window. "Unfortunately, that end would ignite another conflict... but that evening, we were on shore leave. After our victory at NovyiKorogod, the *Ascendant* docked at your Feldelroy's public orbital for refueling and repairs."

What victory? Obviously, she wanted me to ask. But I didn't care. "I really needed a year's worth of medical attention?"

"I have records if you doubt my word." She sounded hurt. "After the crash, your Feldeloyan medics stabilized your vitals, but they could do little else. The *Ascendant* was in orbit for two months above Feldelroy. While our mechanics completed repairs, our Guild medics tended to several pilots from your planet. We Kamen have no medical training, but we often consult with the Pilot Guild on matters concerning biomimetic symbiotes. It is quite easy for us to see circuitry and monitor energy flows. I personally repaired your symbiote. Your ma brought me pastries."

I shivered. Pastries did sound like Ma. "Then why can't I call home?"

Her voice brightened. "As soon as the Unity reestablishes links to Feldelroy's sector, we shall call together."

"I was wrecked, and my pal walked free?" I recalled that cliff face and didn't think it was possible. "It's my fault Sam's dead, isn't it?"

"No. Truly, Polla, your companion was fine." Her eyes searched my face. "But *you* were clinically dead. Your ma called it a blessed miracle when we revived you. She brought in five of your planet's Priests... and let me tell you, that caused a commotion on a Unity ship!"

Five Priests. Ma would. I shoved up one sleeve of my silly red dress and peered at my bony appendage. The sunken ropes of Second fished through my navarm, hanging loose like they didn't quite fit. "You could've brought me back fatter."

She laughed. "Not to worry. House Arkan has excellent facilities. And Teapot is programmed to direct your rehabilitation. In another month, you shall be the Polla Ottrava of old."

"And Sam's truly okay?"

"Yes." Mureen took another bite of her stew, then continued. "Your arm was... interfaced with the bike. Your companion managed to leap free before impact, but you were trapped."

My smile froze. Events leading up to the accident remained muddled as appleberry wine, but I wouldn't have slotted in with Second—not for a simple salt engine. "Your android said something about me and fugues before." A fugue was a repeating pattern in hyperspace, a broken continuum. Pilot's worst nightmare. I willed my voice steady. "This isn't the first time I woke up, you said. How many others?"

"A... few. But Teapot assures me you've stabilized."

I stared at the tray that'd held our meal, now discarded on the white floor. The domed lid had a pattern engraved on it. Loops and lines, which made my eyes cross. Like some kind of crest. Familiar, or was I jumping at shadows?

"You'll have a hard time getting me to work for you if I keel over." My hand searched for a scar on my skull, but all I found was hair that felt thin and far too soft. "There *is* a job?"

She nodded. "We agreed to revisit the matter once you recovered."

"Did I sign anything?" My heart sank. Probably signed a contract. For a registered Feldelroyan smuggler, contracts were everything—signed *compass minty* or not. *Cowcrap*, Da would kill me.

"We agreed to wait." Mureen's voice had an aura of cheer that set my teeth on edge. "You've deduced we want you to work for us—hardly a sign of cognitive decline. We *do* want you to fly for us. I've researched your reputation. You're an extremely skilled pilot, Polla, you and your Second."

I was an extremely skilled pilot, but she'd spread it pretty thick. "You're gonna pay me and Second a *lot*." And my stubborn navvy would have to answer me—but I'd cross one set of coordinates at a time.

"Funds won't be a problem." Mureen fiddled with the sleeve of her robe. "Up front."

She blinked. "Kamen own nothing. Nonetheless, my associate has assured me you will be compensated."

"Three million compensations." I shot for a moon. "Up front. Another three million sling when we finish..." It occurred to me that I should ask some questions about the job I was supposed to be taking. "Is it just flying? No smuggling? Where are we flying to?"

She frowned. "I'm not sure which currency you're requesting—"

"Terran's fine," I said, assuming that Unity markets still held close to par with Fringer. "Whatever you're calling it this month. Terran currency for a Terran job. Where are we going?"

"My associate will explain our goals." Mureen pushed back a loose strand of her hair. "Funding won't be a problem. Davad is a scion of House Arkan."

I didn't like the reminder I was in bed with 12Fam. "Yeah, well, wasn't the Kamen-lord who blew up Alpha Centauri mixed up with princelings, too?" I thought I'd read that somewhere. "And look what happened. She—" I broke off, strangely embarrassed that I had no idea why Ledas Starfire had blown up the very armistice she'd arranged herself two—no, *three* years past. "Why'd she blow Alpha Centauri again?"

Mureen sighed. "To end a war."

I scoffed. "Wasn't it ended already?" The Terran Unity and the Aemercy Associations had signed some kind of treaty.

"Yes." Her thick-lashed eyes blinked. "But so many ships were destroyed at Centauri that it took us weeks to realize hers had survived." She seemed to hesitate. "Then it was too late to save Lee and Nate, or their followers."

"Shame no one thought about saving the *Aemercy*." I recalled sweet Hana Stubblefield. Hana's death had taught me everything I needed to know about Kamen-lords. "*Lee*, huh?" I muttered the diminutive like a curse. A nickname made the Milky's most infamous murderer seem too ordinary. "You said before that Starfire's dead. Good riddance."

"Yes." Her head tilted, as if gauging my reaction. "But *Nate* is not."

Nate? In that muddled moment, the name meant nothing, yet together they fit: *Lee and Nate.* "You sound like you knew her."

"Mostly by reputation. Forgive the informality, my associate has spoken about both of them so often, I sometimes feel I do." Her mouth quirked and for an odd second, I thought she might laugh. "War makes strange bedfellows, Polla."

I opened my mouth to make a crack about *bedfellows*, but then that hidden door apertured open again. As if he'd been listening outside, awaiting an introduction (and I'd soon suspect he did that for fun), a man entered my room.

My first impression was that he was the most perfect human of the masculine persuasion I'd ever seen. My second, watching a lazy smile creep across the fine bones of his face, was that he was well aware of his effect on others. Third impression was that my body didn't react like I'd expect in the presence of such beauty: no blush, no pleasant tingle. Instead, my hair rose at the nape of my neck. My heart began to race, and something I could only describe as *fear* crept across my skin. My weak legs twitched. Every nerve I possessed screamed *run.*

"I see our patient is awake." The man stated the obvious in a sonorous voice. Heavy Terran accent, the kind villains used on Ma's favorite drame—and he wore a red padded tunic with epaulets nearly the size of his perfect head and matching red knickers above boots cut nearly to his knees. Such garb was also in keeping with what I'd seen of Ma's favorite show—save none of the actors had looks that could hold a hyperdrive to his.

Showing fear would be bad for negotiations, so I stood. "Greetings, princeling."

My effort caused a furrow on the man's perfect brow, but he nodded back, and extended a hand that was gloved to the shoulder. "My name is Davad. Welcome, Pilot. You are a guest of my House." He took my freehand and raised it to his lips, pressing a dry kiss across the back. The greeting startled me so much that I let it happen.

"*Your* House? You're the boss?" I'd thought 12Fam heads were all old as dirt.

He chuckled. "I meant... Father's House, of course. However, I am permitted to welcome you on his behalf."

"Always just do what he permits?" I wasn't sure where my mocking tone was coming from.

"In fact, no." His brilliant gaze abruptly focused on my feet. "Mureen? She should have shoes."

"Young Lord, it was I who dressed her." Teapot glided forward. I jumped, having forgotten it was there.

"Then where are her shoes?"

The android and Mureen began speaking at once, and then another drawer was opened, and a pair of slippers were delegated to me without my opinion that I preferred my boots—my own, perfectly-broken-in boots that I'd worn the night of the crash—acknowledged. The slippers looked big, but I stepped into 'em (even as Teapot kept insisting I was too wobbly to manage it), and discovered they fit perfectly.

"There." Davad nodded once I was shod. Another terrifying smile. "That must feel better."

"Sure." I shrugged, not wanting to admit they might be the most comfortable foot vestments I'd ever worn. "Thanks. I'm Polla Ottrava, but you know that, being as you brought me here unconscious."

"I do." His brow relaxed. The princeling's skin was a deep gold, with a childish spray of freckles across his perfectly arched nose. His hair was pulled back, but one errant reddish strand had worked itself free and spiraled in a tight coil over one of his hooded eyes. "Our charity patient from Feldelroy."

"Cut the act." I heard my voice sharpen.

He lifted one eyebrow, mouth curving in mock surprise. "Act?"

"We met before. At the bar, right? Hard to forget a face like yours." A lie about the bar. I was trying to catch him off guard.

Davad gave me a hard stare. Then: "Yes."

I knew he was lying. I watched the small smile play over his lips and realized that he *knew* I knew he was lying. Our eyes locked, and I felt a vicious satisfaction when he looked away first.

"Young Lord!" Teapot buzzed. "I am pleased to report that the symbiote is functional, and our precious patient has a basic level of processing. As projected!"

"Not now, Tea." Davad raised a hand, and Teapot sputtered into silence, the lights of its eyes flickering out before it sank back down to the ground.

And that's when the second slipper dropped for me. I blamed the head injury for it taking that long, since I should've gotten the gist from the first "Ken'ri" with Mureen, and even if Davad hadn't introduced himself using their special title, *everyone* knew Kamen-lords traveled in packs.

I had twin Kamen-lords in front of me, male and female, like a heretic's version of the Original Garden.

Sweat broke out in all my pits, but I couldn't let that show. "What is it that two Kamen-lords want with the likes of me?" I asked.

"Kamen-*lords*?" The man snorted.

"I told her we're not lords..." Mureen added, smirking herself. "Polla doesn't seem to know very much about us." She shot me a conspirator's grin as her voice sweetened. "But Dav, you know already. Weren't you monitoring the room?"

"Guilty." *Ken'ri* Davad raised his winged brows so high they could've had sonnets dedicated. "Father watched as well for a time, but now he's gone to the Bath. I've deactivated the cams to give us some real privacy."

I yawned so as not to seem concerned.

The man leaned against the wall. His face could've been carved from the stone I thought Kamen-lords surrounded themselves with. Terrifyingly cold, even with all that striking coloration. Next to him, Ken'ri Mureen looked like a washed-out ghost. "It is good to see you awake, Pilot," he said. His tone was stilted, almost formal.

"Good to be awake." I nodded my head back at him. "And not dead. Thanks for that."

The Kamen-lord's lips pulled back from his teeth. "Quite."

"You heard Teapot," Ken'ri Mureen added. "Her navigational symbiote is functioning perfectly. Right, Polla?"

For a second, I was positive she knew it was not.

"Yeah, but I don't want the job." Something about Ken'ri Davad... he made my blood freeze where it should've run hot. He made every nerve in my skin quiver. He made me feel like prey.

"Impossible." The man was staring at me like he could see inside my skin. "We need your help desperately."

I tried not to quake. "Why?"

His pearly mouth smiled. "Because we're going to save the galaxy."

Apologue 1 ✳ Saving the Galaxy

The balls of mercury were easy to levitate. Three silver globes spun like well-trained destriers in an exhibition ring, each precisely spaced in its orbit. Lee could keep mercury spinning in her sleep, but suspending the carved wooden sun she held at the center made her sweat, and not just from effort. Every part of her body had been conditioned against the action. Wood was a living substance, one she'd trained since childhood to ignore. Floating that wooden effigy—manipulating any organic material at all—was, in the Kamen Circle where Lee had been raised, a crime worse than murder.

More than a decade spent in battles spanning stars—and now Lee floated that wooden sun for the pettiest of reasons: because she *could*.

From their private cabin's viewscreen, the blue light of Alpha Centauri's twin suns side-lit the cloud-covered planet Roe, transforming its perfect sphere into a glowing pearl. The system's other two planets, Otwombe and Gryffon, were currently outside their command carrier's range, but Lee knew their precise orbits just as surely as she knew their population counts—down to the babes projected to be born that morning. Compared with Roe's temperate beauty, Otwombe and Gryffon were cold worlds, barely fit for human habitation.

Their distance from Centauri's binary star, Lee mused, would not save them.

The cabin door apertured open with a hiss, and her husband, Nate, stepped through, uniformed and precise and cradling a stack of printouts. His eyebrows rose. "Lee, what are you doing?"

Her concentration broken, the wooden sun clattered to the ground. "Nothing." She stood up from her desk. Nate wouldn't care, but Lee hastily slid the mercury—now coalesced into a silvery ribbon—back into the broken diffusion-pump battery she had extracted it from in the first place.

"Ah." Her husband glanced down at the wooden sun next to his toe. He kicked, and the carving wobbled across the room. "The latest evacuation reports for your review." With an impassive expression, he slapped the ream of plimsi on top of her command board. "These are from Roe's main continent," he added. The stack was nearly a meter thick. Nate could have transmitted the data easily enough, but he loved to stage a scene.

Lee smiled. "I told you sweetening the pot would work."

"It didn't. These are all refusals." His eyes were red-rimmed, and Lee tried to ignore the tremor in his metal-laced hand. They both suffered from nightmares of late, but his were worse.

Her gaze dropped to the pages. Neat lines stamped on the plimsi. Age, occupation—so many had none listed. So many were children.

"The names of every Aemercy on the Shin continent who turned down resettlement," Nate continued. "Your brother claims it's an undercount. Half the Associations refused our census-takers. Word from the ground is, your offer's a trap."

"It will be if they don't take it." Her eyes went from the list back to his broad, exhausted face. Nate wore a collar that was the twin to her own: the Purple, Earth Unity's highest military laurels, awarded to them both only last week. "Do you think Dee suspects?"

"Would we still be in charge if he did?"

Lee forced her voice even. "Too late now."

"It's done?" His shock was as muted by the customs that had raised them as by years of war. Still, his voice cracked on that second word.

"Last night. I wasn't sure it had worked, at first."

He exhaled slowly. "And now?"

A smile was inappropriate, but Lee felt her lips curve as she nodded. "I would have told you sooner, but I could hardly bring it up at the admiral's breakfast." She stared at the wooden sun that Nate's kick had rolled into the corner. From this angle, she could only see one grinning face, curving back to the indented seam.

"How long...?"

"Perhaps a week. We'll need an excuse to leave sooner." Nate would think of one, Lee hoped. He was good at that.

His voice dropped. "You said you could time it precisely."

"I tried." She had, but the scale was too vast. One fragile push into an avalanche. She'd done the thing alone in their bed with Nate sleeping beside her. At breakfast, she'd wondered if Nate or the others in their Circle could feel the fresh burn on the *Elyse*'s solar horizon as she did, could feel celestial orbits shift with every tick of their ship's hours.

Nothing in this system could escape the wake, but the Earth colonies at Proxima Centauri, Alpha's half-tied twin, lay nearly as far from the doomed binary as Sol itself. Lee was no astrophysicist, but she thought the Spar stations at Proxy would survive relatively unscathed, as would Earth.

Probably.

"Decommissions have barely started, so the majority of both war fleets will still be here when it... happens," she tempered, explaining what they both already knew. Even with stars in motion, Lee found the word "supernova" difficult to say. The sheer hubris! *Do I dare disturb the universe?* a Preflight poet had scribed long ago. Lee *had* dared—the first Ken'ri to dare as much in a thousand years. "We'll be gone by then, of course," she finished lamely—again saying what Nate already knew.

From his distracted expression, her husband had already advanced to planning the fallout. Wise. It was impossible, after all, for Lee to take the... action, the... *supernova* back.

"You really did it." Gently, as if she could break, he turned her to face him. That tremor in his right hand was worse. He gave her a troubled smile. "I knew you would if they ratified the treaty—but I almost hoped it wouldn't work."

"I know." Nate always seemed to know when she lied, but Lee did it anyway. "Me too."

An armistice between Earth Unity and its Aemercy colonists had been signed yesterday. Nate still hoped that the leaders signing it actually wanted peace, but they both knew better. What good are treaties when both sides lie?

Years ago, before the war, when she'd been one of a dozen Kamen teenagers assigned to charity work in the Centauri system, the warlord Purcell Kaygaz had told Lee that his Aemercy pilots could see the future. If true, the Aemercy could save themselves, Lee thought. If their oracles worked, the Aemercy now had better odds of survival than Lee had given Earth's own Fleet. *One final lesson from your old pupil, Kaygaz,* she thought mockingly. *Run.*

Above the doomed planet, their reflections were ghosts. Nate buried his face in the red cloud of her hair, and Lee felt his arms wrap around her, so much that her battered body armor—donned for ceremony this one last time—creaked. She politely ignored the choked noises coming from his throat. She'd expected to feel more than a flat sense of triumph herself, but no matter how much she willed it, her eyes remained dry.

Today, she and Nate—Ledas Starfire and Illcord Natoth—were the heroes of humankind, its cardinal saviors who had just sculpted victory from the sludge of an unwinnable war. Today, they were the brightest of Kamen paragons. Today, even their corrupt fathers were pleased.

That will change soon enough, Lee thought wearily.

Chapter 4 ✴ Asked

Seems funny to say that I spaced the second-most significant event ever to come to Feldelroy, Sam, but I spent my recovery aboard the *Ascendant* caught in a gravity well of my own despair. After the initial excitement with Ma and those Priests, Ken'ri Mureen was my most frequent visitor. She peppered me with questions, and I took her interest about piloting for affection. Even sold her faked registry codes, no questions asked, without an eyeblink's regret.

Without Second, my life was a black hole of endless hours. I didn't even wonder what a Kamen-lord might want with a smuggler's tricks.

Perhaps Mureen mistook my apathy for bravery. I know she showered me with praise. She called me fearless and beautiful; funny and kind. Within a week, she got me so busy pretending to be those things, Sam, that I missed what she never said—about *why* the good ship *Ascendant* had come to dock in Feldelroy orbit in the first place.

I mean, I wasn't completely stupid, I knew there'd been a battle at the end of their war. Hard to miss it when the bunks around me were full of pilots too far gone from burning stars. Their drooling, blank-eyed stares were the stuff of nightmares, so I was grateful when Mureen got me a private room.

It wasn't 'til I got home and folks started asking if I'd seen the body—if the Terrans had it embalmed, or were cutting it up for relics—that I learned who else had been on that cursed ship.

At first I didn't give a crap about Ledas Stinking Starfire. Why would I?

• • • ● • ● • ● • •

"WE NEED YOU…" KEN'RI Davad repeated himself like I were sun-touched. "… to fly our ship."

"Figured it wasn't for breeding," I muttered.

"What?"

"I said, figured it wasn't for *weeding*. Bet you've got slaves for that."

On Feldelroy, we'd learned that when you're facing down a moon-mad hessi, you don't turn and run. You show no fear.

The princeling's eyes narrowed. "The Unity does not endorse slavery—"

I cut him off at the hyperlane. "Please. You call it indenture, but half your 'employees' aren't free to leave."

"We do purchase labor contracts." His lips twitched. "I mean, *they* do. The Twelve Families do. Kamen don't condone the practice. Nor do we profit from it."

"I told you Polla was a reformer, Dav." Mureen sounded proud of me.

• • • ● • ● • ● • •

(Mureen was wrong. I was no reformer. Not like *you*—yet.)

• • • ● • ● • ● • •

Davad looked thoughtful. "Well, in order to make a better galaxy, Pilot, you shall fly a ship for us."

"Not just any ship," Mureen added. "A krov ship."

"A what?"

"A krov—"

"A *living* ship." Davad interrupted her with an odd catch to his voice. "A bloodship. You've heard of them?"

"Aren't they mythical?" I asked.

• • • ● • ● • ● • •

(According to my home planet's peculiar religion, bloodships are wrought from humankind's own flesh and bone. Rather a lot of bone, so as to endure space.

Of course, believing that story requires a leap of faith and a suspension of physics, chemistry, and exobiology—not to mention ignoring what happens to most solid things moving to lightspeed from hard vacuum.

I only remember one relevant fact from those childhood sermons about bloodships: they possess, according to Feldelroy's Grass Priests, souls—and therefore a state of grace we ungrateful children could do well to emulate.

But on the topic of bloodships, as with so many things, I carry grain to Feldelroy when speaking to *you*.)

* * * * * * * * * *

"If it's a living ship, can't it fly itself?" My question seemed to utterly flummox Mureen, but Davad looked pleased.

"*Bedalia* can, yes," the princeling said. "But she requires orders to fly to a specific location." He paused, and I knew he wanted me to ask where to, how long it'd take, and probably why. But after negotiating a price, only one question matters to my smuggler's kind.

"What happens if I say no?"

"We find another pilot." Davad's eyes were nearly silver. I admired their color even as I considered he'd probably inherited them from some long-dead Terran dictator or warlord. A common practice in the 12Fam (or so the gossip beams Ma read claimed), robbing the dead for genes like some kind of twisted unnatural selection. His red hair fell down his back, braided at the ends. His lips were shaped like a sculpture's. Nature tries, but it's rarely that symmetrical. Every natural-born human has physical flaws. Ken'ri Davad had been made in a vat, and it showed.

Still, my fear didn't make sense. Hell, I'd faced down Syndicate muscle, orbital police, even honest customs agents (those were the worst). I'd even braved the wrath of Grass Priests back home for missteps that shouldn't be sins. I reminded myself that this man might be a Kamen-lord, but he was also a corpro-cat princeling. Probably never worked an honest day in his life.

"Go ahead. Find another pilot. Please." I tried to look cool. "I'm not interested."

"But you owe us your life." A furrow appeared on his perfect brow.

And there it is, I thought. I leaned back in my chair, the one I'd retreated to before my legs could wobble in terror. "I've heard Kamen-lords take oaths not to do harm. That sounded like a threat."

"We also take oaths to preserve the greater good." He loomed over me. "Would you truly wish to be an obstruction?"

Mureen cleared her throat. "Don't confuse her, Dav. I believe she just wants to be paid."

"Yeah. *Five* million up front," I said wildly. "Then I'll look at this ship. Can it talk? If it says no, or I do, I still get the five. Then another ten million for your job. Each way. So that's twenty million sling, plus the deposit. Twenty-five million total. And I want hard currency, not some corpro scrip... What are you calling Terran currency this month—delores? Solis? Or is it yings again? Sancts?"

"Done." Arkan Davad didn't even blink. Enough scratch to buy me an asteroid (if I were right about exchange rates), and he didn't even blink. "And the ship is yours, too. To keep."

I felt my jaw drop. With such riches, I could set up my own Syndicate, retire on my own moon—plus have enough left over to blow on whiskey and the willing. *Hell, I thought, maybe I can even do some good in this stinking galaxy for a change*—but reason intervened then, sounding a lot like Da. *Oh, Pollie. Someone who promises a moon's too desperate to pay for even a handful of dust.*

Oh, my greedy thoughts whispered back. *But 12Fam are richer than anyone, so this one could pay—*

"Let's go." I stood up too fast and stumbled, staggering toward the wall as I tried to make the movement look planned. "After... uh, your android said something about a bath?"

The princeling looked amused. "Aren't you going to ask me what our mission is for?"

"You said saving the galaxy." I shrugged. "I'm a registered smuggler. Details aren't my business." I paused. "Although you should tell me how long it'll take."

"A week or less, we hope," he said. "That is, after you're completely recovered. Teapot wants you under observation for another month, first."

"I told you, Dav," Mureen said. "Polla's a professional."

"So you did. Today, Father wants to meet you, Pilot. He likes to conduct personal negotiations in the Family Bath. I can't remember if your culture has nudity taboos?"

They did (and do), but I'd jettisoned that sanctimonious prudery when I got my smuggler's license. I had the wall's surety at my back by then, and so I glared at Ken'ri Davad from it, folding my arms. "Your da can meet me in whatever tub he wants. For another million."

The princeling's lips thinned. "If you insult Father by bringing up currency, he will have you killed. I heard you ask Mureen for much less before. Tread carefully, or you won't last long." He looked me up and down. "Which would be a pity."

"Real pity would be if someone broke that perfect nose of yours," I snapped back. "For staring when you're not wanted."

"I wasn't." But a tinge of color appeared on those knife-edged cheeks. He nodded in the direction of the door and actually raised his gloved hand like I should take it. "Shall we?"

"Sure." But I ignored his offer of help and staggered toward the newly opened door myself.

When I glanced back, Mureen was collecting the dishes, some with her hands and some floating. Teapot hovered above her. At the time, I thought she must've switched the machine back on, although I was to learn later—much later—that the infernal thing had full control over its own circuits.

"You are still very weak, precious patient!" Teapot called out. "Do not overexert. No sweets until we've had a chance to properly hydrate your bowels. Remind the Young Lord that he must make sure the bathwater isn't too hot. Your system cannot stand shocks. And watch your back!"

"I will take care of her, Tea." Davad's tone held amusement now. "You know that."

"Oh, I am linked to the ground feeds, Young Lord." The android's eyes flashed red, and its jagged frown returned. "To make sure."

The man's arm had been holding the door open while I staggered toward his shadow. When he withdrew, the opening began to contract. I started after him but slipped, grabbing the frame for purchase. The door shuddered against my fingers.

"Move. The mechanism won't close with you in it." He tugged my freearm, pulling me into the hall.

"Oh." I took a few clumsy steps, then glanced back at the door, now spiraling shut. The glimmer of a contingency plan formed in my head. "Really?"

"It was recalibrated after a servant lost a toe. We've invested far too much to have you damaged."

"Ah," I said. The princeling held me lightly but firmly, steering me down the hall on shaky feet. "Where are these baths?" To our port lay a seamless window that looked made of compressed, translucent carbon. The view was spectacular: a field of green grass stretching to a misty horizon, with the sky a shocking shade of cerulean. A stone path wound across the grass, shining from this angle above like gilt.

"Outside and through the gardens." His gloved fingers felt like a vise.

"I can't walk that far." I already felt lightheaded, maybe even breathless.

"Why not?"

"Been in a coma for a year." As if to demonstrate, I pulled away and staggered a few steps on my own before finding the surety of the wall again.

"But Teapot has passively engaged your muscles twice a day this entire time." He frowned as my legs trembled. "It's a two-kilometer walk to the Bath. It's set below the caldera, on the other side of the dome."

I gritted my teeth. "Shall I crawl?"

"Seems extreme." His voice was so bland it took me a second to realize he was smiling, which made my insides quake again with terror, along with an emotion I couldn't identify save for its strange lack of carnal affect. Usually, I appreciated beauty, even in adversity and—oh, *Grass Priests*, that smile transformed Ken'ri Davad's face into a living archetype—but then the man ruined it by speaking. "I could leave to fetch a chair, but Father has drones to monitor for intruders. I'd hate for you to be accidentally shot before my return."

"I'd hate that too, but it wouldn't be the first time."

"You are *funny*. I was not expecting a sense of humor." He approached me with his head down, like one would a strange animal back home, extending his arms. "There is a stone chair in Father's study. Come. Let me carry you, then kamn-lift the chair the rest of the way."

"Can't you float me? Mureen did with our lunch." Spots danced in front of my eyes from my recent bout of exertion, and no matter how hard I tried, I couldn't make 'em seem festive. I giggled at that thought, and then remembered Teapot and its drugs, and wondered if I weren't too far out of my head to be following strange princelings into baths.

His eyes glinted like we shared a secret. "I can only lift metal or stone. But I promise, you shall travel to the Bath on a throne, floating on air, like the first Arkans did when the kamn was new."

"You're being awfully cordial to someone you just threatened with attack drones."

"This is House Arkan. I am Arkan Davad. I... I realized I have a responsibility." Up close, his face had a few laugh lines and creases at the eyes, overlain with those freckles across his nose. They didn't mar his beauty. "You are my guest." His expression was oddly expectant, and damned if I'd look away first. "Here," the man added, holding out his hands. For some reason, I stepped into them. One arm slipped behind my shoulders and the other behind my knees. The princeling hoisted me with an ungraceful grunt, like I was heavier than expected. His vest felt like real bovine hide—unsurprising back home, but probably quite luxe for Terrans (if our Syndicate's trade in endangereds was any judge), and he smelled like leather and something sweet and citrus, which was not unpleasant.

I felt his muscles tense as he began walking—staggering, more like. Even half-starved and in this strangely light gravity, I wasn't weightless. "The chair's not far," he added.

"Right." For lack of a better place, I'd laced my arms around his neck, which placed our faces in awkward alignment. We passed a series of doors and branching halls on the interior wall. The exterior one still displayed a long sweep of uninterrupted, heartrending views. "Why's it so green outside?" I asked. "Didn't you Terrans wreck this planet?"

"It is only green within the domes. Arkan has a larger compound in the Southern Hemisphere, far more impressive... but also fully occupied this season." The princeling's steps smoothed, and I rested my head on his chest. I had the strangest feeling suddenly: the way I'd felt when I was very small, carried in Da's arms. He continued: "My relatives are gathering there now—at Kubla Joadam—for an anniversary."

"Oh." Did he want me to ask? "Sorry to keep you from it."

He snorted. "You're not. I was decidedly *not* invited."

"Oh." And why should I care? But I had an odd thought as we passed more doors, a few half open to glimpses of bedrooms or libraries, and in one case, what looked like a deserted kitchen. The Arkan compound was echoing and empty, but it seemed designed for dozens of princelings. "Your family... the ones in the Southern Hemisphere... do they know we're here?"

"You're quick." He chuckled. "They do not."

"But your da knows, as he wants to meet me."

He peered down as I looked up, which gave me a new angle on his perfect jawline. "Yes."

"And you're his pet Kamen-lord? Thought you Kamen were independent."

* * * * * * * * * *

(I lied. I didn't think Kamen were independent at all. At the time, I thought Kamen-lords were 12Fam lackies, and Glos neutrality was just their party line.

Now I know only one of those statements is true.)

•⁢•⁢•⁢●⁢•⁢●⁢•⁢•⁢•

The princeling sighed. "I believe my actions serve humankind. My father provides the means. But he has his own agenda." He shifted my weight. "Remember, Pilot, you work for me, not him."

I vowed to consider my options. "And what does he want?"

"The usual 12Fam games. Father has sheltered us for nearly a year. He's asked for one favor in return." His steps had grown labored. He paused, bracing me against the wall while he adjusted his hands.

I found myself amused that this big strong Kamen-lord could barely lift a person, starved as I was.

"I'm the favor?" Made about as much sense as full sail in hyperspace. "Why?"

"Because he wants our mission to succeed. You are the vital piece we require." Davad began walking us again.

"The pilot. To fly your fancy ship?"

"Yes," the man grunted as I tried to get comfortable again. "I'm pleased you're not stupid," he added.

"Me too." Although I couldn't target anything clever I'd said. This setup stank. The stars were full of pilots. Unsanctioned ones like me were as common as flies in your sucre. I mean, sure, I was the best pilot that I knew (probably), but I wasn't famous—not outside of the Biscayne racing forums, and this man didn't look like the type to read those. "Can't wait to meet your old man. He's as gorgeous as you?"

I felt Ken'ri Davad's muscles stiffen as he tried to simultaneously not drop me and hold me away from his body. "He is my *father*."

"Genetically, or did he pick you out of a databank?"

"I advise you don't ask."

Still holding me, the princeling elbowed an ancient-looking wooden door open. Inside lay a cluttered office, not at all what I'd expected. It took me a moment to note the true strangeness: everything in the room was wrought of wood or hide—with no visible metal or synthetics anywhere—save for one chair carved roughly from stone and sized for a child.

The chair sat in one corner next to a shuttered wood-framed window, behind a cluttered wooden desk littered with actual sheets of *papier* like we were living in a savage Preflight epoch.

"Here." He deposited me on that chair like I was a kid. My legs were too long for it. I was suddenly reminded of my flimsy shortos and tugged my garment down just as the chair levitated a meter off the floor with me on it.

"Hey!" I squawked. "A little warning—" I grabbed the sides for balance, and then we were moving again, me gliding like my chair had a hover-lift and Davad walking in front of me looking like a crusader from the Olden Church Days.

The tails of his hair bounced against his shoulder blades. His jacket was laced up the back, and with those epaulets—he should've looked ridiculous, but somehow did not.

"I knew a girl from your homeworld." He glanced back as we navigated down an archaic and unmoving staircase, which spiraled downward like a gene helix. "Trained with her on Glos. Fought with her against the Aemercy. She had eyes like yours. Mud colored. She told me nearly everyone from your planet has eyes like that."

"Bet that little compliment charmed her pants off." My fingers were now locked to the chair's sides for purchase, and I had to raise my voice over his heavy boots clattering on the stairs. I recalled hearing that Kamen wore stone boots and craned my neck to check if his were—but the angles were all wrong to see.

"I wasn't her type." The princeling glanced back, epaulets bouncing.

"Never too late." *Why tell me?* I felt preternaturally calm. Then I remembered Teapot's drugs, and wondered if they were causing the overriding feeling I had that I was going to my doom—along with the passivity to not do anything about it. "Never too late, unless she's dead."

"Beya was alive when I left, but it's quite possible her mouth's gotten her in trouble since. She never knew when to be quiet."

"So much in common." My words felt funny. I had a cousin who'd gone to Kamen named Beya, but I didn't want to give him the satisfaction of my curiosity. Besides, the name *Beya* was nearly as common on Feldelroy as the name *Polla.* "I'm surprised you two aren't married," I said.

For a second, the princeling was quiet. Then he laughed. "How do *you* know we are not?"

"I just do."

Of course, I'd no stinking idea.

His laughter died abruptly. The following silence made his heavy footsteps even louder. The lower half of the staircase floated above a floor of marble, inset with fractal patterns that made my eyes cross. When we reached the bottom, Davad paused at a set of grand doors. He raised his hand like he was conducting a symphony, and I fully expected to see the doors fly open. But nothing happened.

"Hrm." The princeling frowned.

"The doors are wood," I pointed out, because they obviously were. Painted to look like stone but wood, without so much as a metal hinge, lock, or knob. "Which is organic. You folk say you can't use your magic on organics. Which makes no sense. There's no difference between metal and wood at the molecular level. Did you know that?"

"Yes." He pushed the doors open with his arm and then led me outside, to a path of polished stones that lay across a green meadow beset with flora, before he glanced back again, cocking that perfect head. "How did you know those doors were wooden, Pilot?"

"I have *eyes.*" They just were. Like the door to that study.

He raised an eyebrow. "Oh?"

I squinted back in the bright sunlight, raising my hand to cut the glare. Unlike Feldelroy's greenish star, our progenitor Sol was a yellow sun. Even filtered through a 12Fam dome the colors around us seemed almost comically bright, more like an artist's painting than anything real. "You're the Kamen-lord, couldn't you tell they were wood?"

His lips thinned. "Is there more wisdom you'd like to impart about the kamn?"

I shifted on my stinking stone chair. "Try not to blow up suns."

Davad made a choking noise, one so strangled that it took me an eyeblink to realize it was more laughter. "Come along, Pilot." He gestured, and the chair and I followed down the flagstone trail, the ride bobbing where it had been smooth before, so much that I suspected he was doing it on purpose.

Chapter 5 ✳ Lectured

Dear Sam, In between sending you flowers as a way of apologizing for nearly killing you, my first weeks home I watched so many episodes of *The Hook and the Rod* that Ma started joking I should request another Kamen-lord from Earff to replace Mureen, since she'd cared for me so well aboard the *Ascendant.*

"Space magic!" Ma gestured toward the holoscreen, where handsome Ken'ri Kimberlain the Rockhearted was currently juggling three stone shivs. "That'd be so practical on a farm. Especially for a sweet couple whose only daughter refuses to get up from the couch."

"I bet Kamen magic could run a plow pretty well," Da agreed. "That'd sure help a retired pilot pay off his only daughter's broken Syndicate contract."

"Might prove handy for defenses, too." Ma picked up a pillow from the good chair that didn't need fluffing and plumped it. "In case your Brahz seeks retribution beyond our generous payoff."

"Now, now. Don't frighten the child with practicality." Da chuckled. "She's still pining for that Mureen."

"I am not," I said through gritted teeth. "I am not pining for *her.*"

"Better if you would." Da patted my shorn scalp. His round face had turned serious. "Be a good distraction. Every pilot has to lose their navvy sometime. Yours just came sooner than it should."

"Yeah? Well, *everyone's* Second isn't dead for all eternity." I eyed his tidy scars with envy. Da had retired after twenty years of flying, his navvy removed by a proper Pilot Guild tech, packed up neat and shipped to Pilot Heaven.

"Hey, no Guild secrets!" He snorted. "Not in front of the wife."

"Oh, I'm not listening!" Ma said.

Mureen had told me that Second died on the operating table. I felt my eyes fill. "My head hurts," I whispered. "Get Doc Sahara. Or call a Priest."

Back then, just me asking for Doc or religion was enough to make my parents look alarmed.

· · · · ●·●· ● · · ·

I GLANCED SKYWARD. I could see the telltale curve of a dome above us, the rainbowed refraction where its transparency hit sunlight. When I looked back, I saw we'd been inhabiting an actual *castle* built of stone at its base, with wooden towers at each corner, so ornate and excessive that the entire kaboodle could've belonged to one of the Blessed Robber Barons who'd funded the First Exodus.

"If you know it's cowcrap..." I began as we crossed a field full of wildflowers and dragonflits, "why not use your kamn magic to open those wooden doors? Or blast 'em, or whatever you do?"

"Training." Ken'ri Davad glanced back again, the sun through the dome above making his eyes molten and more than a little terrifying. "Conditioning. Positive and negative reinforcement from an early age. Most kamn touched have a natural affinity for metal or stone anyway. Their densities feel the most... stable. I don't know how else to describe the sensation."

"That doesn't make sense. If you knew anything about chemistry—"

"We choose not to." He'd stopped walking, and my chair dropped to the ground so suddenly that I almost slid off. "Can you imagine a world where the kamn manipulated living things?"

"Sure, I'm a farmer's daughter. Think of what your lot could do for agriculture. Hell, what about terraforming? You could feed entire planets if you set aside a few moons."

He looked surprised. "That is a more high-minded answer than I expected from you."

"Because I'm a smuggler? Do you think I don't care about feeding people? It could be profitable—"

"And there it is." He held up his gloved hand. "Stop. Others with better intentions than you have tried."

"And?"

"So much lies between a noble plan and its execution. Arrogance. Error. A lack of faith or too much. Bad fortune." He gave an exaggerated sigh. "Does your planet believe in the Fifteen Sins or not? I can never remember with you Fringers."

"Eleven. We're Reformed."

"12Fam pay lip service to seven. But a Ken'ri's only sin is using our power on another. If we could mold flesh, I could make your feet grow roots. Given time, I could twist your bones as well, turn your entire body inside out—yet still keep you breathing, should I desire it—or stop your breath in a heartbeat if I should not. I could alter your germline so you could have no children—or make all of your children monsters. I could make a tree grow into you, or I could make you tree shaped—"

"Stop!" That fear I'd had of him before returned, now with cousins. "*Can you do that?*"

He shook his head. "No. But I am a scion of my House. Father refused to keep us ignorant. I know more than most about what we are capable of, but I also know not to reach for the unseen, for the dark places... for what you call *genetics*, or *chemistry*. We spend years training to only trust what we see in front of us before they release us from the Glos cloister. The rules are so strict, not only to help humanity, but also so we—"

"—*do no harm.*" I finished the princeling's sentence with him, for that catchphrase was what everyone in the galaxy knew about Kamen. "So you don't *hurt* people."

Yet I recalled the poor station on that Neskey moon, and my dead friend Hana Stubblefield, and felt an edge of raw anger—what I'd been holding back ever since learning I was employed by Kamen-lords. "But some Kamen fought in a war that hurt plenty—"

"Perhaps a mistake." Apparently, the man was in no rush to bathe, because he looked thrilled to keep lecturing me. "I shaped the chair you're sitting in when I was six. Kamen mold stone and metal, but we train for more. By thirteen, I'd mastered formal combat with my *gir*, our traditional weapon. My next lessons involved statecraft. Duels between novices settle House scores."

I bit back a laugh. "You're serious?"

"Yes."

"How's a duel between kids settle anything?"

His mouth quirked. "It doesn't. The duels were pure theater with outcomes prearranged."

"Then why bother?" From the footage I'd seen, Kamen-lords sure hadn't faked their fight with the Aemercy over the planet of NewLaramie. No, they'd used pieces of its inhabited stations, hurling 'em down to rain death below.

What happened at Centauri was far worse—but for me, Neskey and NewLaramie were *personal.*

Ken'ri Davad shrugged. "Bloodless combat on behalf of aristocrats seemed preferable to our Ken'ri Elders than the games Earth's aristocracy played before, their shadow wars of assassination and sabotage. Anarchy and corruption consumed local governance for centuries on this planet, and that instability threatened every system in the Rings. We Kamen created an enforceable rule of law *here*"—his gloved hand made a circle in the air—"so the rest of humanity could be free."

That seemed rather grandiose. But he looked so serious that I tried not to laugh. "All with kids having fake fights?"

"Yes." One side of his mouth twitched like he got the joke.

"Do your Elders still make Kamen kids duel?" His use of the past tense hadn't escaped my notice.

That perfect mouth twitched again. "Not as frequently."

"I don't understand how it could ever work."

"Allow an example. In our fifteenth year, I was assigned to represent House Illcord. We who came from 12Fam never dueled for our own families, of course. Nate was my opponent, representing House Arkan and my father's claim. There were still objections to the match. Some thought our personal alliance too close, that nobleborn Ken'ri should only take assignments off-world, never duel for the Houses—"

"Nate, as in Illcord Natoth?"

"Yes, *Nate*." He gave the name an odd emphasis, I thought. And his uncanny eyes seemed to be assessing me for a reaction.

I rolled my own. "Did you know *her* too? Starfire?"

"I did." His tone dropped like we were conspirators. "Did you know that they married?"

"At fifteen? Seems a bit young." Wouldn't have been surprised. Everyone knows Terrans are brutes.

"Lee and Nate married *later*. But at fifteen, I won a duel in favor of Illcord Nextel, who is Nate's father. Nate fought on behalf of us—I mean, for House Arkan. Father had asked me to lose that duel as a personal favor, but Nate and I followed our Elders' orders, and so I was proclaimed victor." His voice hardened. "One Standard turn later, five Aemercy Associations expanded settlements into the Third Ring, establishing colonies on Unity worlds."

"So?" I'd taken to staring at the path before us while he talked. Hypnotic, I thought, the way the grass moved back and forth.

"So, their ships came from *Illcord* shipyards. Shipyards that House Illcord won because of me."

Was it me, or had the princeling veered wildly off course? "Does this tale have anything to do with our job?"

"Perhaps... no. I merely thought you'd find it interesting." From the man's injured tone, I'd insulted him.

"Well, I don't." *Nate. Illcord Natoth.* That hero Kamen-lord had pulled entire warships out of orbit during the Aemercy conflict. Smart smugglers did their best to stay in systems where a man like that was not. "Your Teapot machine told me that he's invading planets. With flying people?" I scoffed, but Davad's serious expression didn't falter.

"Yes. You understand why he must be stopped?"

Because of the flying people? I choked back a laugh. "Sure, but—" And then I recognized the look on his face. Fixed. Fanatical. Therion had looked similar when he lost our advance playing Venus Hold'Em—hoping for just one more bet on zed before our ruin.

Ken'ri Davad plans on taking out Illcord Natoth. I was suddenly as sure of that as I was of my own quim. And while a dead princeling wouldn't pay me anything, a man nuts enough to take on the most infamous living Kamen-lord in the Milky could be desperate enough to hire the likes of me.

I grinned. "You know, if you'd killed Nate in that duel when you were kids, he wouldn't be invading planets now."

Ken'ri Davad's voice flattened. "We were trained not to kill."

My ire about poor Hana, which had been simmering for some time, finally flared. "Oh, yeah? Were those golems your kind flew over Chessna and Kaushik dropping *friendly* cluster bombs? And don't get me started about how many folks died on NewLaramie. Those bases on Neskey were *occupied* when you Kamen-lords broke 'em to pieces—"

"Do *not!*" Without warning, the princeling tipped my chair forward, making me scramble. At the same time, his hand clamped down on my freearm, wrenching me to face him.

My false courage trembled. "Ow!" I might've whined as his fingers dug into my freearm. Maybe there were tears. Perhaps I even wailed. "Let me go!"

He dropped me immediately. I stumbled off the path to the grass. Behind, the man kept muttering, half to himself. "—like talking to a child. The Aemercy were worse than anything you can imagine."

I turned back from the safety of several meters. "Cowcrap, that's true!" Before Centauri wiped 'em out, I'd screwed a few Aemercy. Nice enough folk. Fond of guns. A lot like the people back home, actually, save for the atheist bomb-worshipping, and their pilots being Guild heretics. "Knew a Centauri trader on Neskey. Used to look her up when we ran supplies to NewLaramie."

"Through our blockades?" I'd startled the princeling. His eyebrows shot up. "You're lucky to be alive."

I crossed my arms. "Well, I am an ace pilot. That's why you're hiring me, isn't it?"

"Of course." He paused. "What kind of supplies?"

"Didn't get paid to check. Weapons, maybe? Food? Black market meds?"

His face darkened. "The galaxy burned, and your Syndicate profited."

"Don't moralize at me," I growled. "Or I'll—"

"Or what, you'll refuse my payment?" The princeling turned his back on me. My empty chair lifted and began following his broad-shouldered, indurate back.

"Don't be such a goon!" I yelled. The chair and my captor receded. The fake sky beamed down. "Go to hell!"

A smarter pilot might've lain low next. Davad had said he couldn't manipulate organic material. I recall thinking that maybe he couldn't see it, either—with whatever magic sonar Kamen-lords used to launch bolts at starships or shake Aemercy strongholds into dust.

"You ream of gob guts!" Hardly inconspicuous, I was still yelling when he disappeared over a hill.

· · · ●·●·● · · ·

(I'd like to blame Teapot's drugs for my loss of control, but I can't ignore certain patterns. Perhaps even without the Feldelroyan cliff, another stupidity would've begat an equally cruel fate for Registered Smuggler Polla Ottrava—and then this tale would be told by an entirely different soul.

Regardless, *you* have no room to be critical.)

· · · ●·●·● · · ·

More than ten meters away, my captor reappeared, cresting the same hill he'd vanished behind, and then I felt a tug somewhere on Second's wire, like a warning hum inside my skin. I think I screamed. Only a little. Not for pain. The princeling hadn't hurt me; he was far too careful for that. But for fear of what could be.

He advanced with that stone chair bobbing behind. His voice had darkened, those lovely features turned twisted and mocking. "You're not entirely immune to the kamn, not with all of that metal in your arm. Did you know, when we entered the war, every Aemercy commando with a gram of sanity removed their cybernetics? The Associations were forced to lure us underground into battles with wooden arrows and spears of bone. They used biologics to slaughter our soldiers, poisons proscribed for centuries. Of course, their *pilots* were still easy targets, and the Kamen Company crumpled their ships and trapped them in vacuum like rats—"

"Get screwed!"

I'd like to think my voice didn't waver, that I stood brave before him, but that's a lie.

The Kamen-lord continued, "My father changed the main doors. They were metal before. He's changed so much of the preserve. I hadn't been back in years."

"So?" Adrenaline and anger carried me forward. "I don't care about stinking doors, or Kamen, or your cowcrap life! If you touch Second again, I'll—"

"Call me more names?" That stupid chair was still bouncing behind him, looking like the perfect thing to bludgeon me with. His voice sharpened. "Tell me again, Pilot. How did you know those doors were wooden?"

The question was insane. "How didn't you? We've been here a year. You never used the front doors?" They'd been painted wood. Any child could've seen it, I thought.

"Mureen and I take the servants' passageways. Much faster." Before I had a second's pause, the princeling set his hands upon my shoulders and pushed me into that chair. I collapsed like a broken marionette as he rattled on. "Foolishly, I thought you would enjoy the gardens. This was supposed to be a pleasant walk for us."

To spite him, I slid off the seat again, misjudging my vector and nearly landing on my face in the grass. "Your gardens are lovely," I spat from the ground.

"I could send that chair higher, with you in it," the man retorted. "High enough that if you fell, you'd break a limb. Or worse." Another tug on Second, one that rattled my nerves through my arm and through my skull. I even felt my navvy stir as it registered the threat—but dimly—like poor Second were underwater.

[Error,] the poor thing whispered.

"Second can throw an arc at you," I warned, having no idea if it would. "Keep torquing me, and it won't be on my conscience if you get electrocuted."

The thin smile that made Davad's face a rictus did not dissolve his beauty. "My kamn channeled a particle cannon over the Neskeyan moon, bombarding the Aemercy settlements at NewLaramie into ash. There is nothing your symbiote can do to me." Another tug twisted the metal inside my limb sickeningly. "The same is *not* true in reverse."

I clamped back a scream.

· · · ● · ● · ● · ● · · ·

(My Aemercy pal Hana Stubblefield had been a blast. No pilot, of course, but a good sport, granting me screws and free drinks while my ex, Therion, did his best to scam her pals. One day, her comm went dark, and then the news rolled in about NewLaramie. A glorious Unity victory thanks to their brave Kamen Company, the one led by Ledas Starfire and Illcord Natoth.

Therion and I had given Hana a pilot's wake like she was our own—her and the rest of the Aemercy freedom fighters.

After that, we avoided the red patches on the galactic map. We weren't the only ones. By then, anyone half-sentient knew the Unity and their pet Kamen-lords would win that war, even if the Aemercy Associations were too pigheaded to surrender.

In the end, the Aemercy did surrender. Most died anyway—along with more than half of the Unity's own fleet.

I know the tale's grain to Feldelroy, but I thought you could use the reminder about how murderous, craven, untrustworthy, and completely insane Kamen-lords can be.)

· · · · ● · ● · ● · · ·

The Feldelroyan Smuggler's Handbook notes that effective negotiation depends on equal standing or a good trick. That day in the meadow, Ken'ri Davad showed me we weren't equal. Which left the trick—and it was more of one than he knew.

"You need me and my Second to fly," I said. "Give me one good reason we should."

His lip curled. "I find it increasingly likely that you're incapable. Piloting any hyperspace craft, especially a bloodship, requires reserve. Logic. Clarity. Precision."

I exhaled slowly. "Then fly yourself."

He gave me a mocking smile. "If I could, the Fringer colonies at Ilko and McPhee5 would still be intact. But they were ravaged by Nate's bloodships months ago. While you slept."

I knew the planet Ilko quite well. Its system was on the Tempest Trade Route, and there was a decent bar on one of its orbitals that Therion and I used to frequent. A joyboy named Emile whom I liked for the kip... Perhaps the loss of Emile calculated into my fury, but hindsight makes me doubt I was so civic-minded.

"If you're trying to convince me I'm special, I'm flattered." I bared my teeth. "But I don't care. Get another pilot."

The air was windless and too clean. I didn't like it. Didn't like *him*. Didn't like being frightened, most of all.

· · ● · ● · ● · ·

(I wasn't yet used to it.)

· · ● · ● · ● · ·

There was a long silence. Then: "We've invested nearly a Terran year in your rehabilitation." Davad's words dripped ice. "You are presently on 12Fam property—*Arkan* property—where my father is both master and employer to all. Do you think he will have another use for a criminal from the colonies who refuses to follow simple instructions? He'll have you killed by drones. They're monitoring us now."

I looked up at that fake sky and saw nothing. "One, our Fringer planets are not Terran colonies. And two, you're bluffing!"

"Oh?" He sneered. "All I want is to pay you. Isn't that in your smuggler's creed? That you take payment for services? Satisfy contracts? We established an agreement."

"Mureen said I didn't sign anything." But he had me. In truth, he had me six ways hogtied 'til sundown. I couldn't run, I didn't have a slug to my name, and I wasn't sure I could make it ten yards on my wobbly legs, let alone find an exit. Oh, Pollie, I imagined Ma saying. *How do you find these scrapes?* "You agreed to pay me if I met your ship." I swallowed, feeling my fingernails dig into my palms. "Killing me was never on the table. I'm too much of an *investment.* So stop bluffing."

Incredibly, he looked pleased. "And have you met *Bedalia*?"

"Haven't had the pleasure." *Bedalia* must be the bloodship's name. Could she talk? Did it matter? I just needed to collect the initial payment and move on… unless this princeling was lying about setting me free, and I'd surmount that obstacle later.

"Because you must see Father first." He lifted the chair again, lower this time. "Sit."

I stepped away from his proffered hand while the chair shuffled toward me, scraping the ground like it was chastened. "I don't have much choice, do I?"

"Execution by drone strike can be painless."

"You'd sure know." I sat in his stupid chair. I liked to think I'd never paid much attention to their endless war, but of course I had. *Golems*, the Aemercy used to call the Kamen toys that rained death from above. *Hellbots. Deathbringers.*

He nodded. "One of the first innovations I suggested when we joined the Unity's war effort were humane projectiles designed to eliminate suffering."

Humane? I was suddenly too frightened to crack another joke. Second jangled alarms across my retina, didn't hear when I answered, and I'd never felt so alone. I sank back in the floating chair, cowed as an autumn lamb. *Five million in currency*, I reminded myself. *Imagine it. Imagine a bloodship called* Bedalia. I did like her name. These fools were giving me five million just to say hello to a blessed miracle. And if I took the job, Davad had said she'd be mine.

I looked down and noticed that every blade of grass was identical to its fellow. Same length, same taper, same height. When I looked back, the place where I'd been lay undisturbed as if I never were. There was a *wrongness*, but one I possessed no words to define. When I rubbed my addled eyes, the stalks surrounding our stone path swayed, even without wind.

Five million in currency. The princeling paced ahead and my chair followed, driven by his will. My life had been entirely upended, but I clutched to the thought of that five million like a babe's suckling toy.

· · · ● · ● · · · ·

(Lost as I was in those first, desperate days, I had to cling to something.)

CHAPTER 6 ✳ BATHED

I heard about what happened to the *Unity Ascendant* a month after I got home. Heard it from our neighbor Doc Sahara, who'd started hanging around our parlor ostensibly for my welfare, but also, I think, because he'd taken a liking to Ma's excellent lemon pie.

"Terrorist attack!" Doc told us with bloodthirsty glee. "Earffers tried to keep it quiet, but news leaked to the gray bands this morning. They're calling it retaliation for Starfire." He grinned. "Good riddance to Terran scum."

"You know those Terran scum saved my daughter's life?" Da snorted. "Show some respect."

Doc waved him off. "Those tyrants occupied our skies for two months! Flex your fingers, Pollie. Are you doing the exercises I showed you?"

"Yes." But I lied. With no Second, I wasn't sure why it mattered if my hand ever worked again. But at Doc's direction I wriggled my scabbed starboard fingers and thought about Ken'ri Mureen, and her midnight eyes, and all those nights she'd crept in with me as I cried. "All hands lost?" I asked. I think I was sad, thinking of her probable demise, but the memory's colored by what I've learned about the woman since.

Doc Sahara said no, just a few hundred dead.

Then Da asked what kind of explosives could blow a clean hole through one of those Unity-forged hulls... hypothetically speaking, of course. Recall that hand-carved grenade case Da gave us for a wedding present, Sam? Some retired pilots take up knitting... And then there's Da and his love of explosives.

(I'd crack a joke about how well he'd get along with Ledas-stinking-Starfire, but that's no longer funny.)

• • • ● • ● • • • •

WE'D TRAVERSED NEARLY THE entire field before I mustered the courage to speak again. I vowed not to let nerves or the man get the best of me. *Oh, Pollie,* Ma used to say. *Catch flies with sucre, not knives.*

I shall be nice, I promised myself. *And not afraid.* For Ken'ri Arkan Davad had something I wanted.

"Are there a lot of kamntouched princelings?" my nice self asked sweetly. I was under the impression there were not. Kamen sorcery coupled with 12Fam arrogance. What could go wrong?

"No." Davad slowed to walk beside me, his own voice so pleasant that the previous threats seemed naught but a distant summer breeze. "Our Circle was an anomaly. Beya used to say the Elders put the 12Fam novices together so they could train the others in peace. I don't think she was wrong."

I'd only asked to be polite. "I had a cousin named Beya, but she's dead. Yours was a princeling, too?"

"Feldelroyan." He frowned. "I mentioned her before."

"The one you didn't marry." We'd ascended another slope and come to what looked like an edgeless lake, perfectly reflecting the sky. "So you were a freak among the freaks?"

He chuckled. "Not how I'd put it in front of Father. Watch your tongue with him. It would be best to stay quiet... if you can manage." His tone implied I could not.

I laughed back. "Oh, I can be sweet and quiet when I'm paid. But you haven't paid me yet."

"If you repeat your performance in the meadow, I won't have to."

"Then you won't get what you want."

His expression turned feral. "Neither will you."

"Was it only two princelings in your Circle?" I inquired to change the subject. "How many Kamen in a Circle anyway?"

"Three," he said, so sharply that I jumped in my chair. "I mean, six or seven, if you count the bastards. Fifteen is the standard number for a complete Circle, although it varies—"

"So you're not *special.*" My odd, brittle anger was back. "Not one of a kind."

He looked startled. "I never said I was."

The baths were accessed from a low-arched structure that rose out of the lakefront at the base of what looked like a miniature (and inactive) volcano, facing away from the water. We descended into a primitive tunnel lined with actual, primitive torches of fire. They created a flickering light, which painted the man in front of me in shadow. I saw no sign of tech—no security scans, no android or drone checkpoints—or even human guards, the kind I knew the Families employed, or indentured, or enslaved.

"Sure this isn't just the family crypt?" Looked like one.

"That is on Mars." He didn't even break stride.

We arrived at a formal antechamber tiled in variegated stone and glass with walls so smooth that I suspected Kamen shapers had built 'em, much like it was rumored they'd built the Grass Priests' catacombs back home. A circle of benches sat beneath a domed ceiling. A tiny artificial sun shone down through painted glass. We were, by my reckoning (hard to do without Second counting for me, but I still had a sense), about a hundred meters off the entrance waypoint, meaning we must be under the lake.

And beneath that artificial sky, my escort was stripping off his leathers. All of 'em.

I closed my mouth so as not to catch flies. Funny, because instead of admiring the beauty of his creation, I felt a chill.

Ken'ri Arkan Davad cleared his throat like he'd deigned to notice how hard I was trying not to stare. "Do your people have nudity taboos or not? I believe I asked before."

"No!" I was sitting, and he was standing, which made it worse. I cast my eyes as far as my neck would crane, trying to look at the ceiling. How could the man be freckled everywhere? I'd thought speckled pigmentation had something to do with solar radiation. "It's fine."

"You must remove your garment. A sign of trust." His voice lowered. "This is our Family Bath, where we hold no barriers and no defenses. My father is allowing you to enter his innermost sanctum. You can't possibly understand what an honor he considers it—"

"Did Mureen get honored by your father's bits too?"

"What? No!" He was scowling again.

"What makes me so special?"

"The fact that you can fly our bloodship. Bringing you here is not an… intimate proposition, and to even suggest—you have no idea how offensive Father would find the inference. I have cousins who died for much less—never mind what he would do to a servant." Davad loomed over me. Naked, he was all lean muscles and manhood. Diverting my gaze landed me on his bare arm.

I swallowed an indrawn breath.

My captor had been gloved, and so I hadn't seen the scars before: neat and even slices on the underside of his starboard forearm, culminating in a familiar pattern on the back of the hand. Unmistakable. But how did a Kamen-lord get a pilot's scars? There was nothing else they could be.

My mouth opened to make a bad joke about gelding, but the evidence before me made me think better fast. My fingers fumbled at the ruffled thing I wore. "Fine." I ripped my ridiculous garments off and let 'em fall. I held his gaze as I stepped out of the shortos and straightened. We were more of a height than I expected. "Let's go."

"Try not to stagger. He will be watching for weakness." Davad's eyes stayed locked on mine. "Answer his questions honestly, with no Fringer digressions about what you think of our politics or history."

"I've got nothing to hide," I said, gesturing rather pointedly at my skin.

He gestured toward the archway, letting me enter first.

 •　•　●　•　●　•　●　•　•

(On Feldelroy, they say curiosity's the Original Sin—the one that first sent the Blessed Twins out of the Garden and into the black. Curiosity's what made humankind look beyond ourselves, made us build shells to travel the stars, made us create computers to calculate the impossible. Curiosity drove us to find the mysteries of the gods in the first place.

I'd like to say I only followed Ken'ri Arkan Davad because he had a pretty face, or a noble cause—didn't even know his cause—or because of his threats, or that I was doing it for currency. But the second I saw those scars on his arm—things changed.

Truth, we learn from the Grass Priests, is a certainty. Indivisible. But circumstances are fickle, and sometimes certainties break. I followed Davad for the currency and the threats, sure, but from that moment on, curiosity took hold, and the urge in my heart of hearts was to know how a princeling became a Kamen-lord, and why a Kamen-lord would dare become a pilot. The Pilot Guild tells us that kamn touched never walk between stars for the same reason they never learn to combine elements or split atoms: such things are heresy.

Such things make them gods.)

 •　•　●　•　●　•　●　•　•

The Arkan Baths were pillared and ancient. I saw the telltale glints of force-fields preserving faded mosaics and buttressing claustrophobic walls that arched far above our heads. Water dripped from the ceiling, and the air smelled of sulfur. I'd caught a whiff coming in, but now the stench was a full-on frontal assault.

My legs wobbled and my skin pimpled as I moved into the dank, toward a round pool of water with the bulk of a flesh-colored figure on the other side. An old-looking man slumped at the pool's edge, surrounded by what looked to be priceless antique statuary.

The head of House Arkan was a barrel-chested porcine figure, with a bloated version of his son's perfect mien and a head of cropped red hair that looked brightly artificial. He sat between a painted statue of a curly-haired god who held some kind of tame ape, and a golden abstraction of a beast with long ears straight from my childhood nightmares. A few stylized nude sculptures lay behind him on plinths, forming a ragged tableau of white stone and bronze metal. Everything seemed collected from entirely different Terran eras, but I was no expert. Everything looked like a priceless artifact—and ugly—as if, I thought, to make the ruin of the man seem more attractive by comparison. My gaze lit on a rough stone chair, a near twin to the one that'd carried me here, set in the middle of the splendor like an afterthought.

The chamber was lit from above with another one of those artificial suns. I stopped just short of the pool, peering across at the aristo.

"Closer," the man wheezed, beckoning me with a ruddy, gnarled hand. "Come closer, girl."

I stepped into the pool, descending a short run of tiled steps. The water was flesh warm. About five meters away, the man's legs dangled in front of me, the furry rolls of his thighs affording the view some modesty, at least. The water only came up to my knees as I began to wade across, my disused muscles protesting every step.

"I have a name," I said.

"Irrelevant." His voice was colder and deeper than Davad's, as if the son were an echo to the man. I wondered why, with all of his wealth, he chose to look this bloated and ill. "You are the pilot. You will fly the bloodship. You will take my son to Nuala Erta. After that..." The head of House Arkan shrugged. "I will never see your face again."

"Fly to where?" I'd never heard of a planet called Nuala Erta. Odd, considering I'd spent my errant youth poring over star charts and stories, and what I didn't know, Second mostly had imprinted in its circuits. "I've never heard of it. Is the name code or something?"

Not every pilot has a solid map of the Milky, but I possessed Da's old charts, which made me somewhat a princeling among smugglers—at the time.

"Hah!" The man turned to his son, who'd waded in behind. "Still confident, Davey?" The man's eyes were just as gray as Davad's, but even colder. "Surveillance recorded that unseemliness in the meadow."

Davad reached my side. He glanced at me and then back at his father. "It was managed."

"I see the right arm has the symbiote well installed, at least." The head of House Arkan waved a hand at me. "Turn around. I want to see the repairs I've paid for. The finest vat-grown flesh, gene-mapped from your own stem line. Davey insisted. We could have made do with synthetic, but he wanted everything pure. Did he tell you we had to regrow one of your legs completely? The entire stub was sour, and that alone took another four months—far longer than the hole in your skull. A prosthesis would have done for that leg, but Davey insisted we make you whole. Only the best! And all the while, you remained mindless, a drooling vegetable—"

"Father!" Davad interrupted. "She's perfect now. As I promised."

I didn't like this. "Wait. What happened to my leg?"

"We wasted it," the old man hissed. "On you."

"She needed to be whole." Might've been heartening, the way my captor was defending giving me medical care, if he hadn't used his own round of threats on me mere moments ago. "And she is now, more than we'd hoped."

"Whole." The old man cleared his throat, leaning forward and spitting a glob of something into our bathwater. I tried to imagine it was chaw and not a piece of lung. "You said you needed a season to perfect her," he groused. "I have given you a year." His eyes raked over my body until I felt like he could see my bones. "She still looks like she'll collapse in a faint breeze."

However I looked, what I was was increasingly torqued off and knee-deep in a pool of hot water that might've been pleasant if they'd both dropped dead. I cast my eyes heavenward to the Grass Priests, hoping for a miracle, but miracles, as Ma always said, only happen to those who help themselves.

"She's perfect," Davad repeated—and damned if I weren't confused instead of flattered. I was far from my best. I turned my head and found him staring. His eyes flickered to the old man, and then back to me.

I thought I understood. The enemy of a business partner is a profitable opportunity, as our Smuggler's Handbook says.

Davad wanted me on his side against this quez?

He *was* paying. But I didn't like this.

"Perfection was not required. Stand up straight, girl. Keep turning." The hair on the man's chest was reddish mixed with gray, and his skin was scabbed and scarred with solar damage. I'd heard tales of impossible beauty being common with the Twelve Houses. Arkan Davad personified that. Despite the resemblance between them, his father did not.

I lifted my chin. "You dance first, ser. Just let your son blindfold me so I don't puke."

The quiet that followed was exquisite. I bent my knees and sank back, letting the warm water embrace my limbs, dunking my head until their voices faded. I kicked my scrawny legs in the air, wondering which was newly grown. The water was salty and scented with something that smelled clean. I closed my eyes and floated, letting their voices dissolve to insignificance. The sensation felt familiar as a pilot's dreaming. For a moment, even if I were beset by a pair of slavering pack wolves, I felt myself free.

"—stronger than she looks," Davad was saying when I lifted my head again from the water. "She can fly the bloodship. I'm sure of it."

I was glad he was confident. Might make for a funnier moment when he realized I couldn't even launch a skyskimmer without a working navvy. At least the last thing I'd see before a Kamen-lord killed me would be his surprised disappointment... but a part of me clung desperately to the idea that Second and I could resync. Plugging into a navboard might help. We'd be on the same plane then, at least. Stars, if I *could* fly this legendary bloodship, that'd be a coup I could hold over every crime lord in the Fringe.

• • • ● • ● • ● • • •

(Hope, as they say, springs eternally from fools. No doubt you're familiar with the expression.)

· · · ● · ● · ● · · ·

Arkan Genghis coughed. "As sure as your ability to manage the rest, Davey?"

"We procured Edat from NewPrinceton, didn't we?" Davad's voice hardened. "With no help from you."

"No help? I told you where it was. Make sure to finish *this* job." The old man's tone was acid. "I suppose we shall hear if you succeed. At least indirectly. A sudden absence of supply chain disruptions, a lack of newly contaminated planets..."

"If we fail," Davad told him, just as bitterly, "you'll not lose anything new."

His father lifted a heavy brow. "If you fail, the crypt will be symmetrical. *Two* white feathers, one on each side of the scarlet."

Davad's sharp intake of breath indicated a hit. I'd scrambled back to my feet when they were talking, now I looked over to see him looking away from both of us, his scarred hand clenched in a fist. "By the way, Father..." He bit the words like they hurt. "I need more funds."

"For me," I chimed in.

The old man laughed. "Both trusts were liquidated years ago, Davey. You may recall, something about donating my blood money to the Aemercy war effort?"

Davad's voice dropped. "I'm not asking for anything you'd notice."

The response dripped venom. "Boy, I have given you *everything.*"

I knew some families had problems, but I'd never heard anyone speak to a blood relative with so much raw contempt. If the topic of discussion wasn't my pay, I might've felt sorry for the princeling. Or perhaps I did, because I broke into their headlock with the grace of a hessi cut loose in a reliquary. "What's your called name, Ser Arkan? That I should call you now we're pals? Genghis, right? After the general who led Luna's Rebellion? Are you and Davad both clones of his? You look alike, except you're ugly."

Davad nudged my elbow. I elbowed him back like he was Cousin Sara interrupting me on a trawl.

Sadly, Arkan Genghis didn't look shocked like I'd hoped. Or even amused. He just blinked at me like I was a new specimen of cheese on his breakfast tray. "Certain traits are impossible to extinguish," he said. "There is one week left, Davey, before the Mortons branch comes to use this preserve for their spring hunts. I trust you will be gone by then."

Water splashed as the princeling took a sudden step. "You said we could stay at least another month!"

"I had not calculated your Aunt Cindee into that equation. After a Remembrance, my sister likes to hunt, and she has land rights—as I was reminded only yesterday, when her guest list arrived. Objections would cause questions. There is only so much I can do before our Board raises an inquiry, and Davey, if they vote against me"—his eyes had narrowed to slits—"if I lose control—"

"*Noted.*" The princeling cut in sharply. I glanced over in time to see

Davad's head drop, as if the old man had defeated him. "You've made your point. I will fix this, Father. I promise."

His father grunted. "Disrupt Illcord dominance. I go along in the hope you'll do that much. The rest of your claims are ravings. Natoth has caused devastation, yes. Outlived his usefulness, yes. But krov infestations are a Fringer problem. If anything, his predation only draws more colonies under our skirts. As for your outlandish theories regarding humanity's *doom*"—he made a rude gesture—"they're poppycock!"

I felt the princeling beside me tense. "But you've seen the reports from Carolina Station. The footage from Ilko and McPhee5. The reports of smaller settlements wiped out, the missing convoys—"

"Fringer concerns. Natoth remains his father's son. He won't attack 12Fam interests."

"Not before he can win. But every planet makes him stronger."

"For that possibility, I've indulged your experiment. But if you're not gone by Septday, your Aunt Cindee will arrive, and I will have no choice but to alert the authorities... for you and your gentle Ken'ri companion. The Fleet marches in step with the Circles now, and I know you're aware how Glos handles betrayal. That's not a fate I'd wish on a dog, let alone my son." Arkan Genghis raised his hand and pointed at me. "And Davey, that *thing*—"

"Would the Earff Unity give me a medal if I turned you both in?" I interrupted.

"Don't," Davad whispered.

"Glos would give you a crown, girl." His smile was hideous. "A crown of stone deep in one of their vaults. It would be a mercy for me to put you out of your misery instead." He coughed again. "And I would be well, *well* within rights."

"You don't seem like the merciful type, though." My voice sounded funny to my own ears, high-pitched and too sharp. "Are you?"

"Clever chit. You're right, I am *not*." He chuckled, a wet and burbling sound that turned into another cough.

My gaze had wandered, again fixing on that small stone chair, which sat next to a spotted clay horse. The chair really did look like the one that'd brought me here. A twinned reminder, I thought, of how barbaric Terrans were. More than half the population of Earff lived like Preflight Luddites under 12Fam thumbs. Their pet Kamen stole kids from their own families. The so-called "Human Unity" was naught but a fleet of thugs, forcing their trade routes and tariffs on every planet under their boot. Slags like this old man couldn't even be loyal to their own *kin*. Folks back home might hate their families, but they'd never sell 'em out.

On Feldelroy, we'd never betray one of our own, I thought. *Never.*

· · • •· • • · · ·

(Hindsight shows my opinion to be a rosy view of my planet fellows, but it would be some time before the denizens of Feldelroy disenchanted me, and some might argue that by then, I had it coming.)

* * * * * * * * * *

Remarkable how easy I found getting over a nudity taboo when angry. My wet skin prickled and I heard my voice harden. "What kind of da threatens his own kid? Think you can make another squaller in a vat 'cause this one didn't suit?"

One eyebrow rose, like a twisted version of his son's expression. "Get it out of my sight," the head of House Arkan hissed.

"Oh, we're leaving." I waded across and clambered out of the pool, naked and dripping and too torqued to be self-conscious, no doubt mooning 'em both. I walked along the water's edge, approaching the old man, who blinked balefully back, and then walked past him to that pile of art—or garbage—and turned the little stone chair to face him. I picked up the spotted ceramic horse and set it on top. I turned the horrible gold sculpture away from the one with the man and the monkey. I set two sealed enameled urns in front of an armless marble lady, then stepped back to admire my handiwork. "What is this pile of crap, anyway?"

Behind me, a silence grew.

I wondered if I should've gone with my first inclination, used the little stone chair as a bludgeon to smash everything delicate, everything fine. I realized I was panting, having had more exertion in this enterprise than in the last year. I eyed that marble sculpture of an armless woman and thought about setting her atop a long block of hammered metal that could've been forged from holy adamantium—but decided I'd done enough.

"I said, get it *out* of here, Davey!" The old man broke into a coughing fit, wet and bubbling and raw.

Everything felt too hot and too close. I rested my head against a large granite pillar. Even without Second speaking to me, its sonar alerted enough that I thought "Davey" had crept up from behind.

I turned and saw I was right.

"We should go," he whispered, gesturing with his scarred hand. Gently, like I was a wild thing.

"Sure." I held my own hands up so he could see I wasn't gonna try anything else. I felt my lips curve. "'Davey,' huh?"

His mouth twitched. "I hated that name as a child. Only the Old Man would dare."

I nodded slowly and lowered my arms. I felt very strange. Davad took my hand in his and led me away.

Behind us, the old man wheezed and gobbled. Laughter—or sobs. *Cry-ing? I recall thinking. Is the old spew actually weeping?*

Neither of us looked back.

· · • ●·● · · ·

(Choking on his own bile? I imagine you asking. Sadly, we were not so fortunate as to have the shock of my poor manners prove fatal for Arkan Genghis. Then again, time has passed. Perhaps he's expired by now.)

· · • ●·● · · ·

I tried to make sense of things *een root* back to the Arkan castle as I was floated in my chair. "So *Davey*..." I began. "Your da seems lovely. Mind if I ask him out for a drink?"

Davad walked beside me now. He snorted. "He'd have you murdered on the spot, but it might be worth it for the look on his face."

"Wouldn't want my death on your conscience. No Grass Priests here for the confess."

"You are unexpected." His hand hovered for a moment above my shoulder, and I feared he might give me a companionable pat.

I looked up at his lovely face. "So you're wanted," I began. "You and Mureen? What'd you do?"

His expression hardened, princeling arrogance fast replacing what had threatened to be a foray into melancholy. "Nothing Fleet Command has real authority over. Now, the Glos Circles... they could be a problem." The princeling picked up his pace, and I suspected he was making my chair jostle back and forth on purpose to shut me up. Then he added, "Mureen is blameless."

"Oh? Did you start your plea for her help with a kidnap and threats, too?"

He stopped walking. "Of course not!"

"So I'm special."

"You are a pilot. All we need is for you to fly the bloodship."

"To a place called Nuala Erta."

"Yes." His perfect jaw jutted out stubbornly.

I had an irrational urge to punch it. "Ever been there? Because I've never even heard of it."

"I have, yes." His words were clipped, proud princeling accent more pronounced than ever. "I have a rough triangulation of the coordinates for your symbiotic navigator as well, but it is the bloodship who knows the route. She is the *only* ship who knows the route—outside of Nate's own fleet."

"Is it a nice place?"

"It was supposed to be paradise."

I waited, but he didn't elaborate. When I glanced up again, all I could see was a wall of reddish hair, the tip of his perfect nose poking out, his limbs moving smoothly and easily across the grass while I floated like a broken thing beside him.

"Your da didn't mention our return trip."

He laughed. "How could I pay you if we didn't return?"

"My leg... was it really amputated?"

"As Father described. You were little more than a corpse." He stopped abruptly and went down on one knee before me, placing us at eye level. I boggled as he brushed a few strands of hair from my forehead, staring into my eyes with an expression I couldn't parse. Even his eyelashes were perfect, I noted with envy. A muscle in his cheek twitched. "I thought you were dead." He blinked. "I'm glad you're not."

"Oh. Uh, thanks for the leg, I guess."

Davad didn't move. His solicitude was as eerie as that garden. No wind, just flat water and grass. The castle looked like a child's sketch in the distance, and the edges of the horizon—where I imagined the dome ended—were covered in a gaudy mist, so fluffed it looked artificial. I cleared my throat to break the oddness. "Why'd you think we'd need another month if all I have to do is tell the ship to go there? Me and Second?"

• • • • ● • ● • • •

(With all the threats of death and being turned in, I managed to keep glossing over the fact that Second wasn't speaking to me. We hang onto what we can in adversity... and in the rosy-fragged dawn of my rebirth, it was the prospect of *less* adversity in the future that fueled my jets. That, and that kind of blind, heedless optimism usually seen in saints, fools, and babes in their mangers. *You* know what I mean, I'm quite sure.)

• • • • ● • ● • • •

"Teapot advised another month for your physical rehabilitation." Davad plucked a blade of grass and fiddled with it. "Mureen agreed. And I confess I was looking forward to more time. I've enjoyed these last few months more than I thought I was still capable of, and I wanted more time, even a few more weeks, before"—he shot me a conspirator's grin that was practically shy—"before fate sends us back to the fray."

"More time with me?" I was being sarcastic, but when I saw his gaze rest on the castle, the rest became clear. "Or wait—it's not me at all!"

"Your recovery is crucial to our success." He plucked a few more strands of grass, twisting them in a nervous knot. "That has been our singular focus."

"But it's Mureen you're after? You two an item?"

"We are not." But his color darkened, and his jaw twitched, and abruptly he was no longer beautiful—he was just another poor slob in love with a body who didn't know or didn't care. Galaxy churns, but that story's always the same. "That would be completely inappropriate! She is my guest. An ally."

"You *like* her." It was strange how much I enjoyed needling my captor. "You really like her." For a sec, I was thirteen again, mocking my cousin for one of her crushes.

"I am *impressed* by Mureen." He scowled. "If something came to exist between us, you would not be my choice of confidant."

"Do Kamen-lords even screw?" They did on Ma's show, I recalled, but so did everyone. *The Hook and the Rod* characters would put even pilots to shame, were they not fictional.

"Ken'ri do what we wish," he snapped. Oh, but I'd rattled him. "Of course, *most* choose to do as little as possible. Mureen is different." He straightened. "Time to go back."

But I had him in my crosshairs. "Is that why you tried to become a pilot yourself? To impress Mureen? Or because you thought Kamen-lord princelings could do anything?"

"What?" The princeling froze. A common expression, but I found myself chilled, as if the temperature around us had actually dropped.

"You've been here long enough to get a navvy implanted." I pointed at his arm, now gloved again. "Was I your second choice for a pilot—after your own self?"

He swallowed audibly. "How—"

"Your scars. *Gelded* scars. On your arm."

"Gelded?" Oh, his pridefully injured look was worth the humiliation I'd endured in that bath. "No one would dare!"

I started laughing. "If you'd ever been a pilot, you'd know what I mean. Which you weren't, because Kamen-lords can't be pilots. Didn't take, right? The navvy? Of course not. You've got kamn magic. Navvies can't mix with your Kamen cells. Your medics fixed my leg, your da said. Built it up from cells? You know what cells are?"

"You ask too many irrelevant questions." He grimaced. "The answer to most is 'none of your business.'"

I heard my voice clip. "Wrong. A Kamen-lord trying to be a pilot is every Guild member's business."

"The scars are nearly five years old. I keep them to remember my past mistakes."

I recalled Second screaming as I'd thought we lay dying. I remembered thinking at least we'd go together. Yeah, they were just machines, but they didn't really get that. We felt the same things... usually the same things. Thinking of Second made me frown, recalling how stuff stood between us now. Like we were calling on two different channels and it had my volume all the way down.

If slotting into the ship didn't fix that, what would?

"Did you hear your navvy when it died inside of you?" I asked Davad.

"The symbiote?" He stared down at his gloved hand and flexed his fingers. "A little. It happened very quickly—during the operation."

"Probably didn't feel much, then. They use our nerves. Yours hadn't had a chance to grow into 'em."

"As you say." That gloved hand trembled when he used it to smooth back his hair. Then, as if he'd noticed me watching, he shoved the hand in the pocket of his ridiculous coat.

What was it with navvies and this man? I'd just shaken him in a way I hadn't before. Felt some triumph, although also, inexplicably, blue. My sadness seemed even more odd since he was my stinking captor, not to mention Ma had always claimed I lacked a sympathetic nature.

"Time to go back." The Kamen-lord lifted my chair again, so fast that I almost tumbled off. "Apologies," he added softly.

"For what?" I clasped the chair's sides and hung on for the ride.

"You must think us strange. This all must seem quite strange."

"Not really. Everyone knows Terrans are barbarians." Flashed him a smile.

He gave me one back. "Everyone is correct."

My chair started up again. Thus we returned to the castle, both lost in our own thoughts.

Chapter 7 ✳ Exercised

You may recall the day I was mucking out the old compost, Sam. Hard work for an invalid, but I'd been home for nearly three months and Ma wanted me to stop moping and earn my keep. I had a floating screen with me because I couldn't stand the quiet in my skull, and the newscaster had just announced that the planet Ilko was under attack by a mysterious fleet. I had a friend there, Emile, and I was just wondering if I should worry about him, when you came over the crest of the hill. Seeing you, I put down my shovel and shut down the screen, which was showing screaming people covered in a green vapor that didn't look ethical.

You let me stammer out two whole apologies before you took my battered hand and asked me not to send you more flowers. You'd left your topknot loose, and an errant strip of wind blew dark strands across your eyes. I couldn't see your eyes, but your lips had turned up, and I garnered your intentions from that sweet, smiling mouth. "No more canyon runs for us, either," you added.

"I'm not allowed to drive for another year. Health and legal reasons." I flashed the Guild-installed tracker on my scarred wrist. You didn't flinch. Bad as my arm is now, it was so much worse a year ago. Everyone flinched back then. Even Ma.

"Do you want to talk?" you asked. "About that night? Or… anything, really."

I already was: "—even when I'm walking, it's hard not to check for sonar, or blink and ask some silly question just to hear Second yell back at me—"

"I know." I thought you looked sad. "I mean, I can't know, but I read."

"You read about navvies?"

You flipped your topknot back and smiled. "Polla Ottrava, would you like to have supper with me?"

I nodded, and then we kissed, and I'm not even sure why I'm writing this part down... except you were there, Sam, and we never will be again.

· · · ● · ● · ● · · ·

BEING TOLD WE ONLY had a week left caused Mureen similar consternation to what I'd seen with Davad, which made me wonder if she possessed a similar motive. I spent the next few days trying to needle her while she attempted to teach me a series of calisthenics that I'd learned with my grandparents on Feldelroy when I was three.

"It is important not to overtax," Mureen said, as I sat on the floor with my legs at angles and my back straight as a pin. "The stress of hyperspace... I wish we had longer to get you into peak physical condition."

"I'll be in better condition when I see that vault statement. Five million wired into my account. Today was the deadline?" Davad had promised over an awkward breakfast, but I had some concern his word was space dust—being was a wanted man.

"I do not understand matters of finance," Mureen admitted. "I realize mine is a privileged point of view."

I scoffed. "Not hard. An exchange of goods and services. My time's both."

"Don't slouch." The metal stick she'd introduced at our last lesson nudged me in the back again. Then Mureen paced around to my front, frowning. "You do look better."

"I feel better." Amazing what fresh air and proper clothes could do. Teapot had given me my own set of custom underwear, molded to fit so exactly I thought I'd never go back to buying from a catalog printer, and a flightsuit over that made of pure organics, plus boots fashioned from real leather with soles of wood. The machine even did my hair in what passed for Feldelroyan topknots—although it offered several unsolicited opinions, and even had the temerity to call me a brute. I felt a bit like a brute, actually, wearing Unity white with half my garments formed from real leather and vat-grown bone... especially when I put the fur robe I'd found in my overstuffed closet 'round my shoulders late at night and paced back and forth in my room, trying to assess my appearance in the reflection of my bedroom window—actual mirrors being nonexistent, because 12Fam were nuts.

"Left leg higher." Mureen's metal stick tapped my starboard. Mureen was wearing the same rumpled suit as yesterday, hair half falling in her eyes as it escaped whatever substance she'd oiled it with. It occurred to me she might be very pretty—perhaps even a match for the beauty in love with her—if she gave a damn.

I respected her more because she did not, but that didn't mean she was off my hook. I stretched my leg and took a breath. "Must've been hard for you two to get back to Earff... Davey being a fugitive... me riding along in a stasis tank?"

Her mouth pursed. "It was." That stick of hers went back to floating in mid-air as she paced to my other side.

"Guess the pilot who flew us here must've handled the face-to-face with customs... ground clearances, *eet seterray*... They take off already?" I leaned over my leg like she'd instructed, trying to work stiffness from my limbs.

She looked pleased. "You're curious."

"Just trying to make sure you didn't kill your last flier before I take the job."

"We did not! Our previous pilot is currently with the ship—ships, I mean. We came here in a corvette-class carrier that Lieutenant Navigator Sai flew quite capably. The craft you will fly, *Bedalia*, fit easily inside."

"The bloodship? I'll need to talk to your lieutenant. Not another Kamen-lord, right? Your guy?" I was leading to something, but her expression didn't get it.

"Kamen can't pilot ships." Her voice was dry.

"Well, Davad sure tried!"

Mureen blinked. "What?"

"His scars! On his starboard arm? You never noticed 'em?"

"Oh!" Her eyes narrowed. Had I ever checked her arms? I stared at her hands, now gripped around the metal rod she held. The long sleeves of her tunic were rolled up to the elbow, her skin completely unmarked. "I did not know Davad had... had tried."

"But you're not shocked."

"No. Davad fought with the Fleet for years against the Aemercy. His Circle tried several things. Experimental procedures." She lowered her voice, leaning closer. "You must know how science is forbidden to us? Well, his Circle convinced the Unity's admirals to let them initiate drone fighters. Davad even helped design them. Jumping through hyperspace must have seemed like a... logical progression."

I didn't care to rehash that decade-long war the Unity liked to call "Aemercy Aggressions," or learn more about how Ken'ri Arkan Davad helped invent the golem patrollers whose unfair predation had killed poor Hana Stubblefield and left many a scavenger dead in space and waiting for a free trip to jail—and so I changed the subject. "Is Davey watching us now? Is that why you're twitchy?" I tried to raise one brow like Davad did, but both denuded ones flew up. "Or his da?"

"I'm not twitchy."

"Then why are you whispering?"

"I-I'm not." She straightened, then gave an embarrassed laugh. Her cheeks were flushed. "Not on purpose. We Ken'ri are conditioned not to speak, or even think about your... *science*. Even here, with you... I suppose that must seem foolish."

"Seems suntouched. Maybe not as much as 12Fam hating mirrors, but close."

"We agree." She took a slow breath. "My training has left its scars... but I can assure you, we're not being watched. Davad is away, attempting to get your first payment." A pause. "It's a bit complicated. Whatever you said to Ser Genghis caused the old man to leave, too."

Her tone was polite but I knew better. "Don't blame that on me! That guy hated my guts."

Mureen nodded. "I've heard he can be very unpleasant. And it isn't your fault, but now Davad has to navigate the Arkan bankers himself, without his father's shell accounts. An added complication."

I scoffed. "He should've taken me along. Earff must have gray bankers—I know how to look."

"I'm sure you're quite capable, but the situation is delicate. Davad said he told you we are... refugees." She hesitated on the last word like she didn't buy it any more than I did.

"He swears you're the innocent one."

Her lips pursed. "Hardly. But Dav is a wanted war criminal, listed in the top ten on the Unity's kill list. There isn't a planet or a station that could offer him legal sanctuary. At least, not in civilized space."

Her tone was so matter-of-fact that for once I didn't correct her about whose space was civilized. "A Unity war criminal? What'd he do?"

"Three years ago, he was on the Unity dreadnought *Happy Elyse*. Representing the Kamen Company for the Aemercy Accords on Roe."

* * * * * * * * * *

(I have never found a more ill-named ship than the *Happy Elyse*.)

* * * * * * * * * *

I scoffed. "You're saying *Davad* made the Centauri suns go nova, not Starfire?"

"No." Mureen flipped that metal rod of hers and started spinning it, so fast the metal blurred. "But he was on the ship."

"You knew her, too?" I'd asked before, but even as early as that, I'd noted that Mureen's answers were not always consistent.

The Kamen-lord righted her stick and slid into a warrior's stance. I tried to match it and felt outmatched. "By reputation." She shrugged. "Not really. They were older. Off fighting in the Kamen Company while my Circle was still training on Glos."

"I was on NewBern when Centauri happened. My cargo got spoiled." Seemed petty and sad compared to millions dying. Had taken less than nine minutes, the shocked newscasters told the galaxy. Nine minutes of watching the sky catch fire on Roe, a bit more for the other two, Gryffon and Otwombe. A few ships made it to jump points. Precious few. There was a list of Kamen among the dead before anyone knew anything, and then the same Kamen presumed alive and traitorous—but I'd never paid attention to more, being (at that time) there was no reward given for war criminals, and Kamen-lords were dangerous... and smugglers... well, we had people to do.

Mureen tapped her metal stick against my ankle, and I began jumps of jack while she continued. "As an Arkan, Davad has a trust. Those assets have been frozen for years. We expected Ser Genghis would offer a loan against their worth, but since he is gone, Davad has to retrieve your payment from the Arkan vaults."

"Thought Kamen-lords weren't supposed to own anything."

Mureen opened her mouth to explain Kamen weren't lords (again), and I laughed. Obviously, Kamen princelings possessed their own rules. Not so different from Syndicate muckities, Grass Priests, Guild representatives, and Ma.

"By the way..." I was trying to work the point in casually. "Why was a war criminal like Davad out drinking on Feldelroy with Unity troops the night of my accident?" My memories were as spotty as spring showers, but I thought I remembered Mureen. Not so much for her face, but for that small, slim figure in beige fabric standing out among the wall of white uniforms. Davad could've been one of those Fleet soldiers... but that made less sense than pie on gravy.

Besides, the truth had been there in his pleased smile, the one that dared me to call his bluff.

Mureen shrugged. "Shore leave." She paused. "Carefully guarded shore leave. Of course."

"The Unity always gives its top-ten war criminals shore leave?" I stopped even pretending to do her silly stretches. I felt *fine*. "Hey. Did you know Davad's in love with you? Is that what this is really about? He's a wanted fugitive, and you're gonna run off to Nuala Erta together because Kamen-lords don't have babies?" I made a rude gesture that was banned on a few planets—like mine—implying a few implements would also be in the mix.

Mureen froze.

I smiled.

She blinked. "No, don't be silly. That is *not* what this is about." Two spots of red now burned on her cheeks.

"Oh?" I plucked a towel from the fluffy pile in a wooden basket by the door and wiped my face.

"All you need to do is fly our ship." My stars, but she looked torqued. "Our personal relationships are not your concern."

I shot her a glare as I wiped more of me down. "Lies are. Your man claims he was there the night I got hurt. You said he was there, too. But he wasn't.

I'd remember. Fancy man like him doesn't exactly blend."

A pause. I could practically hear Mureen's gears spinning. "Foolish of him to lie," she finally admitted. "And foolish of me to corroborate his falsehood. We didn't want to worry you."

I snorted. "Go ahead. Worry me. I'm already your prisoner." She looked away at that, and I continued, a little out of breath, and now relentless. "I am, right? Even if I refused to fly your ship, you wouldn't let me go?"

Mureen shook her head. "*After*, of course, after our quest is complete, of course we shall release you." She wore that fake smile again.

Breathe, I reminded myself.

"Davad was imprisoned aboard the *Ascendant*." Mureen folded her hands into her sleeves and then pushed the sleeves back. I'd definitely rattled her. "We took him into custody a week before your accident. He and I had the opportunity to speak. I told him about you... perhaps in so much detail that he imagined the scene."

"Do I seem stinking stupid, Mureen?" Davad had given the impression he'd seen me crashed and broken. Hadn't he said that? I felt suddenly disoriented. *Hadn't he?* I heard my voice crack. "Why are you lying for him?"

I thought you were dead. He'd said those words to me like a threat. Or like he cared? Bugged me that I couldn't tell which. Bugged me even more that I wondered.

"I'm *not* lying for him." Mureen gave me such a fierce glare that I thought she, at least, believed it. "Davad wanted to atone for his actions during the war. It's true he wasn't on Feldelroy the night of your accident, but not so strange to think he might have been. He was something of a... folk hero aboard our ship. Very loosely guarded."

I snorted. "That's cowcrap. Know how many times I've told a port cop I was returning the contraband in my hold 'cause it was wrong of me to have it?"

She shook her head, looking puzzled. "I'm sorry, I don't follow."

"Never! Because cops aren't stupid! Oh, but they'll pretend to be for the right incentive. Priests know I'm really trying here—with you—but it takes a bribe before a port cop even pretends to believe whatever stink I'm trying to sell. And you still haven't paid me!"

"What?" She looked confused. "I'm not sure I follow. We were speaking of Davad. As I explained, he genuinely wants to atone for his mistakes."

Everyone said the Kamen were naive, but I'd never known how naive before. "You don't get it. His business is none of my business. You're *paying* me for it to be none of my business."

"You inquired." Her tone sharpened. "So permit me to finish the tale. Davad and I came to a mutual agreement not to wait for his trial." The metal stick floated in midair again as her fingers plucked at her sleeves, but I'd seen it float so many times that I hardly flinched as she continued. "We constructed a plan to repair his mistakes. We recruited Rathe. I recruited you... but then your health took a turn for the worse, and we agreed to wait until you'd recovered."

"Rathe?" She'd just mentioned him. Another pilot. The one I hadn't met.

"Why haven't I met Rathe?"

"Rathe bunks with our ships, *Great Escape* and *Bedalia*. Security on castle grounds is tight, and he prefers fewer restrictions. As you pilots do." Mureen looked up. "You'll meet him soon."

"So, you're really Unity traitors," I marveled. "Don't get me wrong, I don't care."

"Good," Mureen snapped and plucked that metal stick of hers from midair again, prodding at my leg. "Because all we need is for you to fly the ship, Polla. Get us to Nuala Erta. Then this ends for you."

Like Davad, I noted she hadn't mentioned the return trip—the one where we were the heroes who'd saved the Milky.

"Then we're through?" I asked evenly.

"Yes."

"And I really keep the ship?"

She nodded. "If she will fly for you."

Too much. The amount they'd offered for a one-way trip was brutally excessive. To add a priceless, mythical ship to that tally—

"If she won't?" Second not speaking to me seemed an insurmountable problem.

"We'll find another pilot." Mureen smiled. "You'll remain here. Then, with your deposit of five million sharins, you may hire—or purchase—any ship you like."

"Davad's da is kicking us out."

Her smile froze. "Of course. Well... we shall find you a place to stay if it comes to that—but it won't."

"You could buy my silence," I offered.

"We *have*." That furrow was in her brow again. "All anyone knows is that you left *Ascendant* with us—left Unity custody with known traitors. If you were to be captured before our mission is complete, the consequences for you—" Mureen went into a great deal of detail, but I'd stopped listening, already convinced she'd overplayed her hand.

She's a liar, my conscience whispered. *Folks only promise the moon when all they've got is a handful of dust.* "Oh," I said aloud. "Maybe I could bunk in one of those sex resorts orbiting Proxima Spar—the expensive ones where everyone wears a mask. They have shuttles from Earff. Totally anonymous. Only take hard currency. Saw an ad once."

Mureen nodded brightly. "An excellent idea!"

More lies, my conscience mocked me. *She's desperate. She'll say anything.*

• • • ❶ • ❶ • ❶ • • •

(So it was that I decided curiosity had kept me long enough. I thought I had a week to escape this palace of cowcrap and find my own way home.

I didn't expect it would be easy.

I never imagined I'd fail.)

Chapter 8 ✳ Crowned

I think I rolled my eyes at you too much, Sam, but your obsession with Illcord Natoth confounded me. After the invasion of Ilko, breaking news about Illcord's "quest to avenge his murdered wife" played constantly on every newsband. Listening to the bands, you'd think that every missing colony, every lost ship, and every kitten up a tree were victims of his Living Fleet.

And according to you, he was a god. I'm sorry I laughed when you first said that over the breakfast table. But when we were kids, you believed every cowcrap story about Saint Bene of the Stars, Saint Polla of the Spindle, and Saint Jean of Terra... even the ones Sara and I told you about holy Saint Uranus of the Plunger, whom we'd made up completely.

Now I feel terrible for mocking you because you were right: Illcord's a god, just like his spacedamned wife. Our gods are real, Sam. You were right as an Aemercy oracle.

But those two were never saints.

· · · ● ● ● ● ● · · ·

I HAD FOUR MORE days. Days of being exercised, pampered, and fed like a fatted calf. When Teapot wasn't massaging, or Mureen poking, or we weren't strolling across that unnatural lawn, I was locked in my room. I couldn't roam free because of those drones, Mureen said. Since I didn't have the right biomarkers, they'd shoot me on sight. Couldn't pick the lock to my room without Second's help, either, although I sure tried.

Davad stayed scarce, responding to every question I asked about funds by leaving the room. Mureen apologized every damned time. I began to suspect that if she wasn't blinded by love, she was a doormat. Either way, the two of 'em turned my craw.

Maybe this mysterious pilot of theirs would be less cagey, I thought—but best if I fled before meeting him. They'd both said nearly nothing about Lieutenant Navigator Rathe Sai, yet I possessed a growing suspicion that they wanted me to ask.

But I had other things on my mind.

· · • · • · • · • · ·

(Despite rumors to the contrary, we pilots are not *always* distracted by the promise of a ready tail or the intrigue of a new flying partner.)

· · • · • · • · • · ·

On the fourth day, Arkan Davad came to see me at breakfast.

"Here." He dropped a cheap plasti sack on the table, right between my oats and the tea. Something inside clanked. "This collection would be priceless on the open market. Far more than the value of your down payment, even using criminal channels."

"You shouldn't have, *Davey.*" I was already peering inside. A tangle of varicolored metal and gems met my eyes, along with some small-looking round things that I assumed were legendary Terran pearls, preserved from a time when Old Earff possessed oceans. "Jewelry?" I breathed. "Was cash out of the question?"

"I could hardly apply for a loan. Even my shell identity has been flagged," Davad said coldly. "Mureen mentioned you know about my difficulties."

"You being a wanted war criminal? Yep." I beamed and extracted a long rope of Terran pearls from the bag. They were a pinkish gray that reminded me of lungfish soup back home—unsavory—but they were beautiful, and I looped them around my neck, then reached for a pair of hoops. I affixed those to my earlobes. An enormous faceted gem caught my attention next. Then a tiara made of filament wire that looked delicate as a star's web. I hooked it over my topknot.

"Got a mirror?" I asked my captor, just to nettle.

"We don't use mirrors," the man wearing a gold vest with red piping and a hat made from actual feathers said. "You look absurd," he added (perhaps because not having mirrors gave him no standard to judge). "Those gems were Mother's. You should never mix metals or wear the tiara with anything besides its accompanying bracelets."

I fished in the bag again and found one bracelet that seemed a match. "Are there supposed to be two?" It was comically large on my bony wrist.

He shot me a disdainful glance. "I had limited time robbing the family vault. As it was, I was seen. Even an Arkan company town has some Unity presence. Teapot arranged a diversion, but they will be on us sooner rather than later. We're leaving today." His irritated look deepened. "I'm sure Father will be pleased he left earlier. Now he can plausibly deny he knew we were here."

"Sure he didn't turn you in?"

"Not entirely. But you won't get the rest of your funds if we're captured. Remember that."

"You mean if you're caught. I haven't done anything—"

His mouth twitched. "You're holding a priceless pile of stolen jewelry. Do you want to give it back?"

My fingers tightened on the pearls. Davad smiled.

But inwardly, my gut sank. I was no closer to escaping than I'd been three days prior. And without Second speaking to me, I couldn't pilot us out of a jewelry sack, let alone lift an alien ship from an unfamiliar planet. "Mmm." I tugged at an earlobe. "So, I'll be flying us off good old Earff in this bloodship... today?"

The earring I'd removed dropped into my sleeve.

"Earth," the princeling corrected, with a frown. "And not alone. Rathe's excited to meet you."

"*Earff*," I repeated. "'Course your Earff pilot wants to meet me. I'm an exciting person." I flashed a grin. I also captured the pilfered earring between the fingers of my navhand and tucked it in between Second's weaves. "Probably boring being a Unity pilot. Is that why he decided to desert?"

"Mmm." For all of my efforts, my captor wasn't looking at me at all. Instead, he was staring at a long, flat box he'd produced from a vest pocket. "I have something else to show you."

"More jewelry?" I laughed like a rube. "Davey! You shouldn't have!"

"I did not." His features looked carved from stone. "This piece isn't for you to pawn. Or keep. Consider it your final... screening... if you will."

Inside the box lay a net made of stars. I gasped. "Is that a real copy?"

"Not a copy. It's the real Crown. Made from star rubies formed on Ararat. Nano-linked and strung together by some of the same filament wire the survivors salvaged from the *Grand Jest*. This artifact belonged to the first pilot in the Arkan family. Her name was Bene Dix." He sounded smug.

"Like the *monk*?" Saint Bene of the Stars. Martyred by gods, it was said, for daring to don their crown. A crown of star rubies woven by gods-touched wire. "You're related to her?"

"Probably not." The man shrugged. "Put it on."

• • • • ● • ● • • •

(For all of your learning, you wouldn't know the *true* story. As the Grass Priests say, in the days of the Second Exodus, pilots only lasted as long as their meat. When flesh failed, the techs would peel whatever was left off their chair and throw in someone new. That terrible fate was why Saint Bene Dix of the Stars got canonized in the first place. Stories like hers gave those poor slobs hope in the Dark Age of Spaceflight.)

· · • • · • · • · ·

"It's not the real one." I held it. Strangely heavy and cold. "It can't be!"

He chuckled. "Can't it?"

"But the *Grand Jest* was the Unity martyr ship." Silly to feel reverent about hunks of stone and space-hardy twine, but I couldn't help it. "If it is real, these rocks must be fifteen hundred years old!"

"They're rocks," he said wryly. "So far older, but the Crown... yes. Half an eon, more or less. Some of the other pieces in your sack are Preflight, but they don't have the same provenance. This artifact has been with House Arkan for seven generations. Brought out as an ornament on private occasions—but it had a true purpose, once."

I knew I was expected to ask what the purpose was, so I did not. "Thought Kamen-lords kept all the artifacts we got from the gods in their bunkers."

"They do. My Arkan ancestors stole this one."

I looked up at his face, which held a smug grin. "Following family tradition?"

Davad laughed. "I suppose."

I was already discarding the tiara and pulling on the Crown. The snood part fell over my head, hanging down past my eyes like a veil before I lifted it back. I gave him a smug grin. "Got a mirror? Do you turn to stone if you look at one, or is it that you don't have any reflection?"

"With your hair dark like that, it looks like the rubies are floating in space." Davad ignored my taunts. He didn't move, but I felt the Crown move as his kamn magic adjusted it. "There."

"Seriously, not one mirror?"

No response. His gaze felt like ants on my skin. I glared back for as long as I could stand. Then broke the silence. "Are you giving this to Mureen? Proposing?"

"I doubt she would accept. I am not giving it to you, either. I merely wanted to see... if it fit."

"How could it not fit?" I adjusted the band that fell across my forehead. The wire was colder than any wire had a right to be. My pilot's hand twitched. And then I felt tears prick the corners of my eyes, sparked by a sense of loss that I couldn't articulate.

[Second?] I blinked. [Second? Is that you?]

No answer. Just the echoing silence of being alone in my head. So *alone*— I felt that prickle on my neck again.

"Nothing." Davad frowned. "You sense nothing. I can tell by your face."

I'd been practicing my poker face since I was nine. Now I used it not to show pleasure that it worked. "You know, Saint Bene of the Stars wasn't even a pilot when she used the Crown to jump."

"That is what killed her."

"Yeah. Not like the Grass Priests make *living* saints. Seriously, no mirrors?"

My question earned a heavy sigh. "I believe Mureen told you we don't use them. It is quite rude to keep asking. If Father heard—"

"He'd have me killed?" The suit Davad wore probably cost more than Ma's new harvester, and we'd gotten so close that here I was, finishing his threats for him. "You know... if I'd your looks, I'd never stop admiring myself."

"I believe you." He smirked. We had another long silence, during which I pondered that I was wearing a priceless artifact on my head and he'd said I couldn't keep it, but he hadn't taken it back.

"What'd you expect when I put this on?" I closed my eyes. The blinking light that was Second had reactivated, as if awaiting instruction. [We're wearing the Spacer's Blessed Crown, you dumb navvy. You should wake up for that!]

Second didn't answer. *Nothing.* Like I needed a reminder that flying today was impossible.

"Nothing," Davad echoed unknowingly. "You may remove it now. Careful. The wire is fragile."

The Crown was heavy like it didn't want to let go. Its magnetized pieces clung to Second.

[Error,] my navvy whispered suddenly. [Prime?]

[Right here, you silly knot. Can you hear me?]

Silence. I opened my eyes and peeled the Crown off my navhand. "Did I pass?"

"It doesn't matter." He shook his head.

"What were you expecting? That I'd see a map in my head? Start speaking the gods' tongues? Thought you said I was the one from the superstitious, back-beyonder planet!"

He'd muttered words to that effect on more than one occasion.

The princeling gestured, and the thing floated up, taking that cold and heavy strangeness with it. The Crown landed in his hand neatly, coiling like it belonged there. Odd, but nothing involving Arkan Davad was ever normal.

I needed to focus. He'd said we were leaving. I'd gotten paid. We were out of time.

He folded the Crown into triangles, fussy as an auntie with a napkin full of scraps. He'd said it was fragile, and I saw a few places where the wire was already torn. I cleared my throat, smiling like a hapless, helpless fool. "Get me anything useful, like a gun?"

"A... *gun*?" The way he pronounced the word made it sound like I'd asked him for a fission bomb, or a cake made from cowpats. "You won't need to be armed."

I started taking the rest of my well-earned jewelry off, shoving it into my pockets. I left the necklace of pearls. It covered the horrid shunt on my collarbone. "We might get boarded, or when we land—"

Davad raised an eyebrow. "A gun won't help on Nuala Erta. The krov consumes everything metal."

"Guess I'll be beholden to your charms while we're there," I drawled. "What is it we're doing again?" I'd learned by then that nothing sent him or

Mureen away faster than me asking about their strange planet, Nuala Erta.

"I must go." He folded the net carefully and returned it to its box, then tucked the box carefully in his robes. "Mureen will escort you." He glanced at the writing desk they'd given me and the stack of archaic wood-pulp sheets and inkstick. I'd written Ma four letters that Mureen had mailed, but it would be weeks before she'd see 'em. Lately, I'd been using the paper for other things. I watched Davad's eyes go to my latest sketch.

"Is that a... cow?" he asked. "Mounting Father?"

"Bison," I told him. "Cow would have spots."

His mouth twitched, and then he turned to leave.

Heart in my throat, I stood, trailing after. My hand curled around the earring I'd palmed. Too light to be gold, which was good. Gold would be too soft.

Davad pressed his hand against the blank wall. Door's mechanism had to be coded to handprints, or a gene lock. Stars knew I'd tried everything to open it.

"Wait!" I said as the door whirred. He turned, and I grabbed his scarred hand with my pilot's one and squeezed them together. "I-I want to thank you properly, Davey."

"You don't—"

I didn't let him finish. We were of a height, so it was easy to plant a hard one on his lips. Open-mouthed. Lots of tongue. The kind they always say is "passionate" in the drames. Meanwhile, my freehand wrapped around his back, bumping into the doorframe and scrabbling desperately to shove the pilfered earring into the thing's electronic eye.

I expected a reaction, some kind of a reaction to my inopportune advance—disgust or desire. Either would've worked. (I had my money on the first—for all his stares, the man never seemed like he wanted me.) But Davad just froze. Even his mouth felt cold. I might as well have kissed a statue.

I withdrew, willing my expression to look ashamed, my cheeks to blush, but that kind of thing only happens when you *are* ashamed. I was wired, adrenaline pumping like a madwoman's. "Oops. Sorry. Thought the jewelry... that naked bath we took together... you showing me off to your da... Was this not what you meant?" I fluttered my lashless eyelids, which was probably overkill.

"No," the Kamen-lord said woodenly. He backed off, with me still standing in the doorway. "Mureen will fetch you soon. It is past time for you to meet our ship."

"Should I pack to leave for good?"

From the hallway, Davad turned his head toward me, taking in the empty room, the table, and the pile of jewels laid out on the cheap sack. He shrugged, aristo's nostrils flaring. "Teapot attended to the clothes already. You have nothing else."

Under his fish-eyed stare, I stepped back as the door apertured shut. Then counted to twenty. For some reason, I found myself gasping for breath, on the edge of hysterics. I grabbed my fortune off the table and stuffed it down the front of my tunic. Bounced a few times up and down on my toes.

The previously unbroken line of wall had a hooped earring shoved in it lengthwise. I knew my room was monitored, so I didn't have much time—no time, really. There might be alerts that showed the door wasn't locked. And Teapot was lurking someplace—the nurse android had an uncanny habit of popping up unexpectedly.

I approached the door, setting my portside foot almost against it, steeling my weak legs to prepare for a sprint. I tugged the earring out. The mechanism froze, then opened wider—and my freehand shot through. The door tried to close on my arm, but the fail-safe kicked in, this time allowing me to get a shoulder in. Then a leg.

The entire thing oscillated open, and I bolted through.

I knew what lay portside: the office, the stairs, more rooms, and probably the kitchen. From there, the main exit opened onto that long stretch of lawn. Far too exposed.

Something urged me starboard, the way Davad and Mureen had never gone. Pilot's intuition? The suspicion we'd never gone starboard because there was something they didn't want me to see? Perhaps something useful. An armory, a vault. A garage full of ground transport options to sell later. In my head, I was already imagining the tale I'd tell Ma. *Got captured by a 12Fam Kamen-lord! Tried on Bene Dix's Crown, and got jewelry. They made me do calisthenics, but I escaped—*

My feet pounded down the corridor. In an open doorway, I glimpsed an android that could've been Teapot—or just a regular household drone carrying a pile of bedsheets. I recalled Davad's warnings about drones shooting unaccompanied visitors, and a new blast of fury sped my steps. *Undoubtedly more lies.*

From its exterior, the castle had appeared symmetrical. The same inside. Ahead, there was a spiraling staircase, twin to the port one. I heard Mureen's shout echoing below. *They'll be watching the exits*, I thought and took the stairway that wound up instead of down, leaping the stairs two at a time. My rubbery legs burned. Three flights. *Five.* I pushed myself harder, to the top, to where I expected to find a corner tower.

The door opened at my touch as I gasped for breath.

I'd hoped for an armory. A treasure trove. A secondary set of stairs, a secret passageway. A hovercraft launching pad. *Magic beans.*

• • • ● • ● • • • •

(Or perhaps that's hindsight. In the thick of it, I don't think I knew what I wanted, perhaps something inarticulate and ineffable, something that went with that feeling I'd had when I put on the Crown, when my hand brushed that perfect grass outside. A *rightness.* A path forward.)

• • • • • • • • • • •

What I found was a child's playroom, covered in layers of energy shielding like it hadn't been used in some time. Dolls and furry animals lined the curved walls, all encased in a shimmer designed to keep them dust-free. Two beds were built into the masonry, each on an opposite wall. Two round windows, one above each bed. And another door, opposite the entrance. That door was made of transparency, and I saw my freedom beyond the rails of a balcony. Green grass, that impossibly blue sky. From this angle, the dark shadow of that volcano's lake spilled blood on the green. They'd said we were under a dome, but from the tower, the horizon looked infinite.

The wall surrounding the door was painted with a mural that seemed stylized and primitive: a painting of two red-headed children, one gray-eyed, and one green. Identical in size and dress. Green eyes held a toy sword, and gray clutched a stuffed creature. Green's face was a little rounder, the nose a little less delicate, like the painter had missed a stroke when he did that one. But even stylized, both faces held that same, eerily perfect symmetry, that fierce beauty that first struck me about Davad.

In the next second, I got who they must be: Davad and his twin brother, cozy as peas in a pod.

But he'd never mentioned a twin. Perhaps it wasn't him. Perhaps another Arkan set of princelings. Perhaps House Arkan possessed entire racks of Davads locked in towers, scattered over Terra like seeds. I didn't give a crap—I just needed a way out. I went to the transparent door, still feeling like I was in a dream. A smart smuggler would hide or run, look for a place to go to ground, search the room and find something—a weapon, a ladder, a clue—but me, I stepped onto the balcony.

Below, I observed a lively search scene. Small globular drones hovered like crop dusters. The green grass was lit with 'em. I'd have to reach the dome's wall, keep going 'til I found an airlock. Parts of this planet were uninhabitable, I'd heard: too much radiation, not enough oxygen, extreme temperatures, storms… but I could lay a trail and loop back. Davad had once mentioned underground passages, servants' corridors. A compound this large would have supply routes. Just logic and a bit of luck to find 'em. I could figure how the garbage got out, first—

My thoughts spun. I peered over the railing's edge. Another balcony below mine. For a second, I imagined leaping to it. *No, that's insane. Sheets,* I thought, stumbling back. *Sheets could work. Make a rope—*

My eyes fell on a box bolted to the tower wall and marked with the symbol for emergencies. An evac route for princeling kids. A ladder, or hover lifts inside—maybe if I was lucky, even a gun. I'd never shot an actual person. My hands trembled as I fumbled with the box's lid. In the drames, Kamen-lords stopped bullets in midair.

The lock was an old-fashioned metal ring. I screamed for Second in my head to spark it. Nothing. I needed to find a key, a brick to smash—

A voice spoke behind me, metallic and cold. "The Young Lord thought you would try the service tunnels," Teapot said. "The Young Lord and the Great One are looking in the sublevels. But I knew better."

"Teapot." I turned around slowly, pasting on a smile. "Loha! I was just exploring—"

"Always curious." The nurse android sighed. That triangle flashed its smile. "So curious, about the wrong things."

I edged away from the android, trying to angle toward the door behind it. "What is this place?"

Teapot flashed its eyes. An appendage extended and the symbol on its chassis went jagged. "This is a room where we were not. Upon waking, you mustn't say you found it."

I stammered something, but a pinprick lit upon my shoulder. I saw a yellow dart embedded there. My knees buckled. The stone floor rose with the inevitability of hyperspace, the wash of waves, and somewhere, like memory, a child's tears.

Grass, I thought oddly, and then for a time I thought no more.

Apologue 2 ✲ Departure

NATE'S SOFT VOICE CALLING her name intruded on yet another nightmare as Lee opened her eyes to darkness and the scent of roses and rot. The moss of her bed was cold, and a fur had dislodged itself from the nest of woven down feathers and sweet rush she'd layered on top. A salt wind buffeted her curls, guttering the fat candles she'd lit to mark the hours before departure. Such timekeeping was necessary, for upon their sunless planet, diurnal cycles were quite random, guided entirely by the capricious will of Nuala's sovereign.

"You were dreaming." That sovereign's voice was a murmur, his shape a black outline in the dark doorway, dimly illuminated by a few phosphorescent blooms from the vines twining overhead. In dimness, Nate was all broad shoulders and loose hair, the flat planes of his face giving way to the glint of a smile.

Lee was still half asleep, so much so that her estranged husband's presence barely triggered surprise at first. "I'm cold," she grumbled. "Did you have to bring the wind?"

He shrugged. "It followed me."

"All the way from Sheris's bed?" Her eyes opened a crack wider.

"Yes." His tone was amused.

With less than a meter between them, Nate's body felt like a furnace. Lee wondered if she dreamt still. Some bad ones began this way, pleasingly warm before the sky caught fire.

"I thought the wind was mine," she said. An old joke.

"Perhaps you summoned me with it." His head tilted as if appraising her mood. Vinelight glinted on his skin, dusting it silver. He had flowers in his hair, yellow ones, opening and closing like mouths.

"Come here." Lee drew back the furs. Even if this tryst turned back into a nightmare, she'd had worse.

• • • • • • • •

Some hours later, staring at his sleeping face, Lee mused that the war at the heart of her marriage had nothing to do with his concubine, the insipid Sheris. No, it was stone against blood, a conflict as old as the first spark. Things could hardly be otherwise as long as Lee ruled the stars and Nate held dominion over Nuala Erta. The stuff of stars and the stuff of life might be the same at their core (a fact no one knew better than she, Lee considered bitterly), but a star cannot rest planetside, and from the ground, that same star appears sterile and cold.

In the two years since Centauri, she and Nate had grown apart. Had they been ordinary 12Fam aristocrats like their parents, his adultery would have been dealt with efficiently with a gift of poisoned chocolate or the placement of a discreet, extremely localized bomb. But Lee and Nate had *evolved*. And so, when her interest waned and his eyes strayed, the two arranged terms in a manner that would have made their diplomatic Kamen Elders proud... had not those same Elders been allied with what remained of Fleet, and actively hunting them down.

Compared to Aemercy genocide, Nate's affection for his concubine was an insignificant mote. Just as meaningless, Lee reminded herself, as his unexpected appearance in the vine-covered doorway of her bower. Measured against saving humankind, both jealousy and need were but motes of dust. Measured against immortality, love and lust were a millisecond's weakness—facts Lee's own murdered mother would no doubt agree with, were she not dead for those crimes.

Lee sat up, pushing tangled curls from her face. Shadows now winked at the slips of the rising borealis, which sparkled through the leaves above them. The relentless piping of the bloodbirds was a familiar, if grating, tune. Their cacophony deafened the sound of Nate's lazy chuckle, but Lee still felt his laughter along her hips, where his warm weight pressed.

"Did you sleep well?" His voice was a warm rumble.

"Yes. Did you?"

"Extremely. A momentous occasion, returning to your bed." His finger slid teasingly up to the nape of her neck, toying with the symbiote's connection that nestled beneath the weight of her hair.

Lee looked down. Nate's eyes were now slit-pupiled like a cat's, but still the same clear brown as when they'd met as children, long ago on Glos. She'd found Nate refreshingly ugly that first day, with ears that stuck out too far from a shaved skull and a blunt chin too big for the rest of him. He'd grown into the chin, and the rest of his features had settled into bland 12Fam symmetry. Only the color and shape of those eyes remained: common and slightly downturned, giving him a perpetual air of melancholy that she knew he used to advantage—even with her.

"If you like my bed so much, I'll leave you to it. I have to catch my ship." But a thought intruded, irritatingly logical. "Nate? How did you know?"

"How did I know what?"

"When you came to me last night, you said—" She hesitated.

"Go on, Lee." Nate's voice was a dark purr. "I want to hear you say it."

She felt her skin heat. "I was dreaming about us. And you knew?" Nate held dominion over this living world, a power that had once both delighted and terrified them both. Yet if her estranged husband had evolved enough to hear her very thoughts...

Their eyes met. "Ah." His lips brushed her cheek, light enough to make Lee shiver—or perhaps that was a spike of reason finally needling through her brain, reminding her how precarious her position was—but then his voice sharpened. "Yes, wife. I *knew*." Nate's gaze had wandered to her body, but his expression had grown less seductive and more strained, like he was avoiding her eyes. "Your dream last night was more pleasant than most. I wanted to share it."

She suppressed a shiver, forcing her voice to remain light. "What else can you see in my head?"

"Quite a bit," he said. "You shouldn't feel guilty."

"I don't." They'd both learned the futility of regrets.

"You shouldn't," he repeated. "But you do. You always will."

Lee sat up, warily surveying the view of his rippled torso and the tousled sheet half covering his charms. She heard her breath catch as she noticed that the dark pelt sprouting halfway down her husband's thighs had thickened and now ended in a pair of hocked, cloven-hooved legs.

Nate chuckled. "I can also see you *hate* my new legs." One hoof twitched as he raised it for her inspection, but her eyes went to the ruin of his right arm—the one he tried to hide behind his back. That stench, roses and rot, it came from there. Of course. Where metal met skin, krov always burned.

Lee felt her voice harden. "The necrosis around your symbiote looks worse. Get Sheris to see to it. Or one of the Faege healers at Landing."

Nate snorted. "I also know you prefer I not see Sheris at all."

"I don't care about your whore." She used the Aemer'yc word, the slur.

"You do." Far from being insulted, he spoke gently. "You keep yourself apart for no purpose, Lee. If you joined the rest of us—"

Join the krov and lose everything. Lee sometimes wanted nothing more. Her voice felt brittle. "The medics at Landing possess formal training Sheris lacks—or do you have another goal, training your concubine to be useful?" *Replacing me, perhaps?* But no, that was laughable.

"I have many goals," Nate hissed through broken teeth. His teeth were always first to go. He was in the midst of regrowing them again, replacing decay with clean bone.

Shaping stone with kamn was simple, its results eternal, but molding a body with krov was as ugly, and messy, and brutal as birth. At times Lee wished Nate had never begun these "improvements." Sometimes she regretted encouraging their Company to bind themselves to the krov energy of this planet, following the example of the shapeshifting Faege, whose Aemercy ancestors had first crash-landed here three centuries past.

Well enough for these Faege to be bound to one planet. Most had never seen the stars—could never see them—not in a human ship, where the krov inside of them ate metal and rotted every seal. But isolation chafed for Lee and Nate's brave Kamen Company. And for their leader, who now bore the burden of peacekeeping an entire galaxy with an ever-shrinking network of spies.

Two years ago, Lee had made Alpha Centauri's binary sun go nova. Now, her doctrine of fear lay grounded on the premise that she was a monster, a galactic scourge who would burn any system whose inhabitants manufactured war machines or raised arms against another.

It was a doctrine of lies. Lee thought that she would rather surrender herself to Kamen justice—have her head entombed in stone for centuries—than cause more suffering. Still, as long as humankind believed her vengeful, she was bound. Sometimes she wished she could grow wings or gills, let her mind become wood or fungus, let her feet root in the fecund soil of this hidden green planet. Surrender all to krov as so many of their former soldiers had. But someone had to stop the galaxy's brushfires. Once there had been two of them to do it, but now—

Now, Nate was staring at her breasts. Lee wondered if he could sense envy as easily as he sensed desire—if he still cared for anything beyond Nuala's skies. Nate had once cared for everyone, and taught her to care, too.

Once they'd been one soul in two bodies, commanding entire fleets through the infinite. Now Serpent was a festering sore, Petal long past her prime, and Lee and Nate—

Well, they'd *evolved.*

Nate stretched as if to give her a better view of his redesigned lower half. One cloven hoof nudged her ankle, canted at an angle that made the limb look broken. "I thought you were leaving, wife?" He grinned open-mouthed with those brutal teeth, and Lee tried not to shudder.

"My brother's expecting me, and the jumps are quite tight," she said.

"Of course. Promise me you'll have the ship jump alone." His playful tone had turned serious. "No piloting, you're too far gone for that."

"Of course." Slipping into the pilot's death called deepriver would be an ignominious ending for rebel Ken'ri Ledas Starfire, the woman who had destroyed an entire civilization in the name of peace.

"No *jumping,*" her husband repeated, softer.

"I won't!"

"Will you kill him or not? I can't tell."

"Dee's letter claimed he just wants to come back."

Nate shook his head. "A lie. I should come with you."

Lee scoffed. "In your current condition, you can't even leave atmosphere—" She gasped as he wrapped both arms around her waist, pulling her back down into an embrace that was more battleground than hug. Retaliating, her elbow sank into his side. Sank, where it should have met cartilage and bone, rather proving her point. Beneath a krov-shaped crust, Nate's body was still half-formed. Dangerously vulnerable.

There was an audible, sickening pop when she pulled away.

"You can't go offworld until your new bones harden. Not even to Skye." She poked an exploratory finger back into his side. His flesh had, she thought queasily, become a bit like the dough they'd kneaded as children when assigned to the kitchens at Glos.

"You underestimate me." The warm brown of his irises abruptly went black, even to the whites. The krov energy consuming him flared hot. Before their arrival, Nuala's cycles had waxed fat with each new sacrifice, then waned as it drained them dry. Before their arrival, the position of planetary sovereign was a seasonal—inevitably fatal—position. Ruler for a day, a week, a year—and then the krov made another choice.

But Nate's godhood held reserves beyond anyone's dreams. From the day he drew the seed, their hidden refuge had prospered, producing fat harvests and plump babies beyond any historical precedent. Within a year, every desert on the planet went green.

Yet with that growth, a hunger grew.

Uncontrolled, Nate would swallow stars. *And I am all that stands between,* Lee thought. How long could she? Two years already felt like an eternity.

She forced her voice to sound jovial. "Perhaps we underestimate each other. I don't require an escort to meet Dee."

Nate scoffed. "So you think. If it's a trap, I'll avenge you. Probably."

"You won't." Lee stood. From her new vantage, his arm's rot was on full display and one of those monstrous legs was larger than the other. Nate was a Faege Pan, adding perversion to go with his adultery, and the sight of him in full daylight filled her with a furious remorse. "If I don't come back," she told him, "do *nothing*. Recall our agents, bed your mistress, and get fat in paradise."

Her husband extended that twisted leg. Its joints popped back into alignment with a sickening crackle. "We don't have that luxury. We'd have a fleet above our heads already if your brother could find us himself. Your bloodless little war must be driving the Unity mad. They will find us, Lee, and when they do—"

"You're wrong." He wasn't. Her bare feet sank into soft moss as she walked to the doorway. "I can manage my brother. Just keep Sheris out of my bed. I dislike fleas."

"She matters?" He raised an eyebrow.

"Earlier you claimed to know my thoughts?" Lee made them barbed, and saw his lips tighten.

Ridiculous. Nate held dominion over their sunless world, and Lee controlled the stars. Yet they warred over infidelity like primitives. Lee recalled the tales they'd learned as children. Preflight gods were as capricious as the mortals they served. But jealousy had never stopped Zeus from steering humankind, and adultery had never kept Mayahuel from service. Upon the island of Glos, Lee's favorite tutor once told his class of twelve-years that the Earthen gods were figments, symbols manifested by human need... but now that she'd tasted immortality, Lee found it more likely that the gods were formed *from* need. Made flesh by the same list of sins the hypocritical 12Fam used like an instruction manual: lust, avarice, anger, doubt, gluttony, sloth—

Pride.

Pride had once led Lee to think stone could contain blood and kamn could forever leash krov... yet here they were. She, hanging on by a thread, and Nate growing goat legs.

"You trust *him* over me." A cold wind rose with Nate's voice, blowing curls in her eyes.

"You're wrong." Lee trusted no one. In childhood they'd been trained to watch for blades in the shadows, to sound no alarm until the knives fell. Was that still love she saw in Nate's eyes? What did he see in hers?

Husband or brother. One she would betray. With the fickleness of a Preflight Shiva, or a Tiamat, or a Jean... she had yet to decide which.

Chapter 9 ✳ Bound

I didn't understand your faith in krovlords, Sam, but the day New Liberty Syndicate repossessed *Dancer*'s engine, you let me cry in your arms for more than an hour, and never once reminded me I was lucky to be alive, like Ma did, or lucky not to be officially shot for oath breaking, which was Da's opinion. 'Twas a mystery to all of us at the time what made New Liberty Syndicate back off so easily, but I've figured it out since.

This is where Captain Wade Skybourne comes into the story I never told you, although I suppose it's fair to admit he was there from the start, Sam: the pretty blond pilot sitting next to me at your bar the night my world ended.

Just like they say in the recruitment holos, the Pilot Guild takes care of its own.

• • • ● • ● ● • •

I AWOKE BOUND LIKE a prisoner, propped up on a moving platform. I had to admit the bondage wasn't a total surprise, considering I'd just broken my contract with a 12Fam House and two rebel Kamen-lords. Hell, if I'd done that to Brahz at New Liberty... My mind avoided finishing that thought because of course I *had* betrayed Brahz, and that was why I'd been hiding at my parents' farm on Feldelroy in the first place.

Numbly, I stared at the solid boulder where I should've seen my feet and wiggled my toes. My legs were encased to midcalf. My hands were stuck behind my back and felt similarly bound. Hell of a thing, having limbs caught inside rocks. Everyone in the Milk knew Kamen could do that, but seeing it in the flesh, feeling it on *my* flesh—

Of more immediate concern was the fact I was choking on lungfuls of ash.

I'd been wrong about where the spaceport lay, relative to the dome.

We'd left the dome far behind. Without an artificial atmosphere, the famous blue sky of Earff looked gray with a bilious yellow tinge. The ground was covered in grit—and so was I. The air smelled like an overheated engine.

I struggled in my bonds.

"The patient is awake, Great One," Traitor Teapot announced somewhere on my right. "I will reapply her oxygen mask."

"Not yet, Teapot. Try not to breathe deeply, Polla." Mureen's voice came from behind me, sharp and echoing oddly. "You won't want to scar your lungs."

I craned my neck to look back and saw the impossible. While grit coated me and every other surface on the hovercraft—for so our conveyance was—Mureen was surrounded by a bubble of air. I'd seen Syndicate scouts use tech shields in bad atmosphere—such protection wasn't cheap—but I knew that this was different.

Kamn. Pure Kamen magic.

"My precious patient requires a mask!" Teapot chided. "Her health is delicate!"

Mureen sounded brittle over the wind in my ears. "What if she'd escaped in this storm? She wouldn't have lasted an hour!"

"I would never let her expire, but she is too old to learn wisdom now," the android groused back. "And far too stubborn. The barbarities she must have absorbed!"

They said more, but I'd started coughing by then, alternating gasping for breath and trying to follow Mureen's instructions not to inhale more crap. I'd been in low ox plenty of times. Even seen a few sandstorms before, but this was bad. Pilots have tricks to handle bad atmosphere, but they require a working navvy.

Second stirred. [Prime? Hostile atmosphere detected!]

"Is she turning blue?" Teapot sounded alarmed.

[Prime? Saturation levels in the body are suboptimal. Initiating dormancy—]

My lungs seized. My body shook, and I fell sideways as Second tried to shut it down. Teapot's metal voice cut in: "No, Great One! You will *not* kill my precious patient!" Then something hard clamped down over my face. Air hissed. I took a bitter, medicated breath that opened my airways. I blinked my stinging eyes open to Teapot's ovoid body hovering over mine, clucking concern. "If you have harmed her in any way, Kamen..." It shook a retractable appendage in Mureen's direction. "I have been trained to deal with your kind! I possess wooden darts armed with a biologic sedative!"

"You were *made* for her, Tea." Mureen again. Flat and angry. "Why weren't you monitoring her location? What if she fell to her death from that roof? Or jumped?"

Roof? It hadn't occurred to me to climb onto one, or leap to my death from anywhere. No, I'd been thinking I could flit from balcony to balcony.

That thought made me giggle.

"I did not say my patient wished to end her life!" Teapot whined. "Perhaps she was on the roof, which is the place I found her, looking for a maintenance ladder or a ventilation shaft."

Would've been a good idea, had I been on a roof. But Teapot had found me on a balcony. "Didn't find me on a roof," I said—or tried. From Mureen's lack of reaction, she couldn't hear my voice behind my hissing mask. "Balcony isn't a roof."

[Saturation levels returning to baseline. Prime? Why don't you answer me?]

[Why can't you hear me when I do?]

Something buffeted my body, and I opened my eyes to see that the world had cleared. The grit in my mouth and nostrils vanished. The breathing mask fell off, its seal automatically broken. I took a clean breath.

"My precious patient is fine now," Teapot said to Mureen. "See? She is laughing."

[Corpus stabilized,] Second murmured. [Prime, where are you?]

[Right here.] I rubbed my eyes and realized the bubble that enclosed Mureen now enclosed me, too. "That's a neat trick," I muttered.

The Kamen-lord glanced down at me, her mouth twisting oddly. "You must learn. Actions have consequences."

"Yeah." I glared back. "They do." I had a moment of meaningless triumph when Mureen looked away first.

"Running was foolish." Her hand tightened on my shoulder as the hovercraft glided through a hellscape of rock and twisted earth. "You could have died."

"Didn't," I snapped.

"Because we shut down the defense grid to save you."

I didn't bother responding, just stared at the view, taking breaths of cleaner air while I tried to calculate our vector. Based on the pale disk of sun, and what I knew of Earff's rotation, we were... somewhere.

• • ● • ● • ● • • •

(Being as my sainted ancestors fled Terra, I've never bothered to study maps of your Original Garden.)

• • ● • ● • ● • • •

Ahead loomed an enormous insectoid structure of a kind familiar to smugglers everywhere: a prefabricated shipping hangar. We went through its open doors. My smuggler's brain noted we skimmed above the easily circumventable security marks. Could've gotten all sorts of contraband in—or out—of this facility, which had no guards, drone scenters, or animal sniffers.

For all I knew, we were.

"The *Great Escape*," Mureen said, gesturing toward the clumsy hulk of a patinated hull. "The ship that brought us here. Your living ship, *Bedalia*, lies inside."

Layers upon layers. Like NewOrion boxes in a drinking game. "What's inside *Bedalia*?" I croaked.

"Us," Mureen said. "Soon, I hope."

At first glance, the aptly named *Escape* was crap. Corvette class it might be, but only among bantams. Its hull was brutally blunt and battered, its form snub-nosed, with an old-fashioned solar mast lying horizontally across its back like a vestigial spine. It had various call signs and rubbed-out military marks stamped along its flanks, a few of which I'd never seen—and a few that made me wish I possessed a working navvy, because they might prove useful to know for some job or another later.

"Nice boat."

A man—too tall and too lean to be Davad—waved at us from the *Escape*'s loading ramp, brandishing a buffer hose in his free hand.

I was still operating on adrenaline and blind faith that I could get out of this job. If Second worked, I'd be able to fly, but, well, if hessi were horses they'd still be carnivorous, as the Feldelroyan saying went. "Where's Davad?"

"Inside." Mureen removed her hand from my shoulder. "I'm going to free you, but I hope you realize how futile another escape attempt would be."

"Sure." I'd bitten my lip sometime during the excitement, nearly hard enough to bleed, and it felt hot and swollen. I sighed meekly to appease my captor. "I get it. You're a Kamen-lord. I'm your prisoner."

"*Why* did you run? We had an arrangement." Her voice shook like she was taking it personally.

"Forget it." Answering wouldn't improve my lot. But as if I'd won her over, the restraints on my bound arms crumbled away. I tugged at my legs, and the stone surrounding them turned to powder, too, falling away like sand.

"Neat trick." I brushed the dust off, trying not to think about what else Kamen-lords could make crumble to dust. *Mountains. Metal ships. Build-ings—*

"I hope we don't have to restrain you again," Mureen said.

"My patient will be *good*," Teapot clucked, as if daring me to object. "She may be a barbarian, but I detect capacity for growth."

I didn't detect the same from this Kamen-lord, as she was now set to trust the registered smuggler she'd threatened... but these Kamen-lords were lucky I had a good heart and a healthy sense of self-preservation.

· · · · ● · ● · ● · ·

(As you know, a lot can go wrong in hyperspace when a pilot and their navvy are all that keep a ship and its cargo from the black.)

· · · · ● · ● · ● · ·

At least the wiry figure ahead of us in Unity white looked normal. shock of dusk-blond hair and a grin on his face that widened as we drew closer. Cautiously, I raised my newly liberated pilot's arm and waved back.

"Lieutenant Navigator Rathe Sai," Mureen said. "Acting captain of the *Great Escape* and your copilot."

"Don't need one." In the legends, living ships were small.

"That remains to be seen." Mureen straightened, brushing imaginary dust from her robes. "Rathe has a rapport with *Bedalia*. He helped repair her systems after the crash. Without him, neither ship would run at all."

"Copilot's a demotion for him, if he can handle a ship as big as the *Escape*. Why'd he agree?"

"He believes in our mission." Her tone was irritatingly pious.

"I might too if I knew what it was," I lied.

"Your mission is flying," Mureen said. "I thought registered smugglers don't ask questions?"

She had me there. Still, if Lieutenant Sai had flown this lot of wanted criminals here, his navvy must be working, which might prove handy when mine didn't.

I cleared my throat. "We still have a few. Your lieutenant soloed this hulk all the way here?" That was impressive. Normally, a ship the size of this corvette would have at least four pilots meshed intandem. "Is he another deserter, like you?"

"Rathe is a patriot," Mureen corrected me.

I rolled my eyes. "A patriotic *deserter*."

She sighed. "We paid—"

"Paid me to fly, no questions. Right." I'd already noticed that although I still wore the lungfish pearls 'round my neck, the rest of my horde had vanished from my person. But I'd worry about that later, for here was a fellow pilot who might have answers, even if he'd been indoctrinated by a bunch of Unity dogma. "Hey!" I called out.

The man turned, switching off the hose. "Yo."

"Yo," I echoed. "'Loha."

Navigator Rathe Sai possessed none of Arkan's terrible beauty, but he wasn't bad-looking, if a little skinny for my taste. He had tousled hair, a stubbled face, a long nose, and a pronounced chin. When he approached, I saw that his eyes were the colors of a Feldelroyan orchid, a pale blue laced with gold. He was garbed in a white Unity flightsuit that looked twin to the one I wore: molded tight to his skin with the starboard arm bare, exposing a gleaming navvy wrapping around his lean bicep, and braided across the top of his hand.

"Look who finally joined the party!" He gave me a lazy smile, one I recognized from using it myself, the automatic appraisal for the new stranger in port. "Why, Pilot Ottrava, you look much better when you're not unconscious and bleeding on a canyon floor."

"You were there when I crashed?" Unlike Davad the liar, I believed he could've been. One of those figures in Unity pale—not the pretty blond—but one of the others.

"I carried you to the med-evac." Rathe's easy grin was fixed, but I watched his eyes size me up and down with a navigator's precision. His brow furrowed. "You know, that guy of yours almost shot me."

"Guy?"

"The one on the bike with you. He got off easy, but you…" He shook his head. "You look a *lot* better now."

"Sam was really okay?" Mureen had said it, but I still found it hard to believe.

"Okay enough to tell our entire trauma team we'd have your Syndicate after us if you died." The lieutenant grinned. "Funny now, but at the time he almost got himself arrested."

I snorted and slid off the hovercraft. As a bartender, Sam must know his way around a crime lord or two, even if he'd never gone for the smuggler's license. "Sam has more sense than that."

"Well, he was worried and… uh, it's good to see you awake. Really good." The lieutenant flashed me another grin before turning to my companion. "Finished prep," he said to Mureen. "We can leave as soon as I give Captain Bike Crash here the tour."

"I see Davad already briefed you." Mureen stepped off our conveyance. "If *Bedalia* won't fly, we'll take the *Escape*."

"Sure." The man's smile on me didn't falter. "*Bedalia*'s a sweetheart, but she won't lift for me. You're some kinda bloodship miracle worker according to Mureen, so we'll see how it goes."

My heart sank. "Never even seen a bloodship. Thought they were a myth."

"Not sure that matters as long as she likes you." His grin stayed even. "And you're all set up so she'll like you."

"I guess we'll see." *Set up?* Sure felt like one. "If she doesn't like me, I'm free to go."

He snorted. "She's funny. Davad told me she was funny."

"I'm a hoot." This was not.

"We'll need *Bedalia* to get through Krovworld's net, but Davad thinks that's the easy part," Rathe said. "The *Escape*'s a yar boat, but she can't cross the biofilters."

"Right. The *biofilters*," I echoed, cursing my employers, who kept handing me pieces of what I needed to know like I was their stupid pet. "Need *Bedalia* for those biofilters!"

"Krov scum," he added and spat on the ground.

I spat too—just to be polite. *Krov who?*

"Davad spoke to you regarding the route?" Mureen asked.

"He did. We have a few options. Depends on *Bedalia*. If she'll do it, we can take her straight across. Flying the *Escape* gets trickier. We'll need places to refuel where we won't get arrested." His mouth twitched. "Again."

"I don't want a repeat of NewPrinceton, either, but Dav doesn't think Polla's ready for the bloodship." Mureen sighed. "We'd expected a few more weeks."

"I know." During their entire exchange, Rathe barely took his eyes off me. Now he shot me a wink. "We'll manage. I'm not objecting to more time flying."

No pilot would.

"Bloodships are really undetectable?" I asked. So the legends went. That was how Saint Bene Dix had gathered a fleet of 'em in Mars orbit a millennia ago before anyone noticed.

"Yeah..." Rathe was staring at my legs. I pivoted to give him a better angle. The tailored flightsuit flattered their length, even if their current lack of bulk made 'em feel spindly and unfamiliar. "But our *Bedalia's* a stubborn lady." His gaze traveled up to my face again, giving me another approving look. "Doesn't want to do what she doesn't want."

"I feel the same way," I said.

His mouth twitched. "I'll bet."

"Really? What odds will you give me on getting her off this rock today?"

His grin faltered. "This is too important for wagers, Pilot Ottrava."

Mureen broke in. "We shall leave today regardless. Davad's concerned that we've already been compromised."

"She keeps saying that this is urgent," I told Rathe. "I went for a walk and she had her android shoot me!"

"Objection: I am not the Great One's property. I belong to all of my precious patients!" Teapot chimed in from my port. That made me jump, for I'd thought the android was still aft. "I restrained you because I did not want your beloved corpus damaged!"

"Huh." His smile didn't budge, but something in it hardened. "Davad mentioned trouble."

Mureen sighed. "Polla agreed to help—"

"No, I agreed to meet the ship!"

"We'll get it done. Don't worry." He sounded sure.

"Good." Mureen gave him the same sympathetic smile I'd seen every time I asked to comm my folks, every time she'd brought me paper and stylo to write them more letters instead.

That smile reeked.

"It'll be okay. We pilots get used to anything," Rathe added, softer, to me. "Right?"

"Sure," I said. "Get used to being forced to fly an experimental rig with some Unity navjob you just met. Why not?"

That open expression on his face chilled. "Hope her flying's worth it," he told Mureen. "I said bringing in a civilian into this was risky. Especially a criminal."

"Yeah?" Pride overtook my reason. "I'm no criminal; I'm a registered smuggler. And the best pilot you've ever seen."

"Maybe the best from back beyond," he shot back. "'Course, you've never seen *me* go. Davad said he had to pay you off just to agree to help us. Saving the galaxy's not enough?"

"Saving the galaxy?" I snorted. "From what?"

Behind us I heard Teapot sigh. "I will be leaving now, dear precious patient," it announced. "It seems the Great One has the matter clearly in hand."

"Bye," I snapped.

"We should be fine from here, Teapot." Mureen sounded distracted. "Thank you for all of your help."

"I am leaving this instant," the machine continued. "For I must supervise the preparations for the estate's incoming party. The Mortons have several young ones it will be my pleasure to care for. Try not to damage the corpus I spent so much time and effort to restore. I consider her some of my finest work."

"Stars, thanks," I offered, startled. "Um... you too." I watched the android glide away. As Teapot vanished around the curve of the *Escape*'s hull, I had a funny feeling, even if it had shot me with a tranquilizer an hour past.

"Glad that thing's not coming with us," Rathe said. "He gives me the creeps."

"Teapot has served us well." Mureen forced a laugh. "But I admit, I'm not sorry to see him go, either."

I cleared my throat to remind them both of my invaluable existence. "What are we saving the galaxy from again?"

"Illcord Natoth?" My prospective copilot had wrinkles on the sides of his eyes when he squinted. "The Living Fleet? Ring any bells?"

"I was in a coma for the last year."

"And I've been stuck here, hearing about my mates dying..." Rathe looked increasingly torqued. "The war's been going on for over a decade! You didn't notice?"

"Not the same war all this time. And not *my* war. I'm a Fringer."

"Polla's an independent, Rathe," Mureen said softly. "Her home system is off the main trade routes. Even before her accident, she had little cause to follow events happening on the other edge of the Way. Davad and I thought it best for her recovery not to share too many details. The captured footage is quite graphic—"

"Plus, Kamen-lords don't believe in holo screens," I broke in. "Did they try and sell you that crap, too?"

He frowned, still staring at me. "But when Pilot Ottrava agreed to the operation—"

"*Agreed*—?" I began, only to be interrupted by the woman I'd once considered shy.

"I've focused my efforts on restoring her physically," Mureen said primly. "The Living Fleet's invasion is a classified Unity matter. The data we possess is highly sensitive. It wasn't my place to disseminate restricted intelligence, especially to a noncitizen—nor is it yours."

"Wait. There's an entire *fleet* of living ships?" Seemed important intel—so much so that I didn't wonder why a fugitive would care if it was classified. Would an entire fleet out there make me owning one worth less? "Living ships that fly themselves? All undetectable?"

"Ask the refugees from Ilko, or McPhee5." Rathe's skin flushed red. "Those systems could be under quarantine for centuries, and there's no telling the mutations the survivors will have. That stuff twists—" His voice cracked. "It twists people. Animals. Everything."

"Illcord Natoth has bioweapons?" That was like something out of an old morality play the Grass Priests might put on to scare us submissive. "Those are against the laws of gods and man!"

His words dripped bitterness. "Maybe someone forgot to tell the krov."

Despite myself, I shivered. "Stars. That is bad."

"Yeah. At least when Starfire was alive, the attacks were targeted. She might have been a genocidal bitch, but she didn't mutate planets. Or attack civilian settlements."

The stations on Neskey moon hadn't been civilian settlements exactly, but— "Except she did, a few times," I pointed out. "Like at Neskey and NewLaramie. And Centauri."

His face hardened. "Thanks for the reminder."

A glint at his neck caught my eye; Rathe had a circular patch of membrane on his breast bone, a little too light to be flesh. A feeding shunt there, pilot's kiss, just like mine. How many jumps does a military pilot do? Sometimes dozens in a day. Even intandem they burn out quickly, and Rathe didn't look green. His time had to be running low.

The pearls around my neck hid my own port. I fingered them self-consciously and wondered if he knew I had one. Having a kiss wasn't a sign of weakness—if anything, the opposite—but it was a warning, and one I hadn't earned.

"This war has exacted a cruel toll," Mureen sighed. "Upon all of us."

"But Feldelroy's okay?" I had a sudden shot of paranoia that Mureen wanted me to write a letter home because she knew I couldn't call—maybe because she knew I had no home left.

"So far." Rathe sounded like my lack of enthusiasm was getting on his nerves. "Would you be more willing to help if it wasn't?"

"For revenge." Half of our songs were omertà ballads, and I'd heard more Grass Priests sermons on taking eyes than I could count.

"Well, that's how I feel about McPhee5. I had friends there."

Our eyes locked until it was me who looked away, feeling oddly guilty. I cleared my throat as I searched for rebuttals, taking a second to examine the fascinating hangar floor. "So... we're off to Nuala Erta? Just us four? I'm a great shot, but we'll be outnumbered."

"That won't matter," Rathe told me. "Davad says Illcord's death will shatter the Living Fleet." He looked resolute. "We're going to Nuala Erta to kill him."

"Ah." I nodded.

They looked expectant.

I used my poker-playing smile because what else could I do? Four of us against the most fearsome Kamen-lord left alive in the galaxy? I recalled hearing that Illcord Natoth had once ripped an Aemercy flagship from high atmosphere with his Kamen-lord magic.

Should I care that my employers were insane?

Not if I could survive them.

"Is Illcord not too busy to wait for us to assassinate him?" I waved at the ceiling of the hangar, to the stars beyond. "Isn't he off attacking planets?"

"Dav says Natoth returns home every few cycles," Mureen said. "The beating heart of the krov is on Nuala Erta. He needs to stay close to it when he replenishes his strength."

"Davad says the krov have a symbiotic relationship with their planet," Rathe added. "It sustains them and they sustain it."

Davad had said quite a lot. Enough to make him sound like some kind of krov expert, which seemed dodgy to a simple Fringer criminal like myself. "But Nate's wife, Starfire, wasn't killed on Nuala Erta. Right?" I frowned, still trying to put the pieces together. "How was *she* killed again?"

"That was before, nearly a week before your accident," Mureen said. "We were celebrating the night we met you on Feldelroy."

"If you'd told me, I would've celebrated too." Maybe saved myself from a near-mortal head injury.

"You looked pretty celebratory that night with my pal Wade. You were sitting on his lap half the night."

"The pretty blond?" I frowned. I was pretty sure there'd been a song. "*To the end of the war!*" Someone had toasted that, I thought.

Apparently, ending the war hadn't worked out.

"Pretty?" Rathe snorted. "Sure. I guess Wade's pretty. You two togeth-er—" He gave me a slow grin. "You know, have a nice voice."

"I do know." Ma had wanted me to go for the Priests, but Da put his foot down and said I should follow my natural inclinations as long as they didn't lead to me getting knocked up by a first or second cousin.

• • • • ● • ● • • • •

(If only. Now I face an even worse fate.)

• • • • ● • ● • • • •

"You were singing along with him." Rathe shrugged. "Hard not to notice."

"I'm hard not to notice." I didn't have but a nub of a topknot to toss flirtatiously, so I just grinned.

"You're a pilot, so that goes without saying." He winked.

I winked back.

• • • • ● • ● • • • •

(Pilots... We have our reputation for reasons. But I was so full of myself that I didn't even notice Mureen had never answered my question: *how was Starfire killed?*)

· · • · • · • · ·

"Father has a saying: 'You can't sell the same moon twice.'" Davad interrupted our little gathering. I turned, and there he was, poised at the top of the landing ramp, like a voice from on high. "Nate would never fall for a trick used on Lee."

"Were you hiding back there this whole time?" I marveled.

The Kamen-lord shot me a smug look. "To answer one of your questions, Pilot, there is a barrier around the krov planet. It shorts ships' hulls, fries their circuits and sensors. Mechanical craft attempting to land on Nuala tend to disintegrate in the upper atmosphere." Davad wore a red robe with an orange scarf half draped over his head and looked every centimeter the Kamen princeling. I'd never seen him in boots I could prove were stone before, but the ones he wore now looked blocky and gray like they could've been. I'd heard all sorts of ridiculous, impractical legends about Kamen, and yet I'd only seen Mureen in sandals like a normal person, so I knew the legends didn't have to be true. "Only living bloodships can land on Nuala Erta," he continued. "The krov protects its own."

The scion of House Arkan approached us at a slow walk, commanding every eye in the room with his very existence. Quite a trick. If he was torqued I'd tried to escape, it didn't show. In fact, he was smiling. Upon closer inspection, I could see his boots were definitely stone, just like legends promised. I didn't want to admit I was awestruck (as well as my body having that all-too-familiar terrified response to his proximity), so I just grinned back, ignoring my racing pulse.

"We need *Bedalia* to fly us to Nuala's heart," Davad continued. His gaze locked on mine. "And so we need you, Pilot, to fly her."

"You repossessed my pay—" I broke off then because he had just pulled out my bag full of jewels like it was an apple and I was his best pony. He jangled it, and my hand stole to my neck, twisting the pearls as I tried to raise one hairless brow back.

From his puzzled expression, I'd failed. "Fly us there on *Bedalia*," he added. "Please. Then you may have your fortune. You have my word. Fly us in and you shall be free."

"And I keep the ship? Really?" Bioweapons were abominations. But the threat of me having a ship full of 'em might keep my Syndicate off my back.

"Yes," Davad agreed. Too fast, like Mureen, before. "*Bedalia* is yours."

"*Fine.*" I rolled my eyes.

· · • · • · • · ·

(Curiosity, they say, is the death of worlds. On Feldelroy, Curiosity's twinned sin is Pride. Back then I was proud enough to think that I'd get out ahead—no matter their play. *You* have no room to judge.)

Chapter 10 * Led

Those two months on the *Ascendant*, Mureen barely left my side, but when she did, it was my Guild representative, pretty blond Captain Wade Skybourne from the bar, who slipped into the recovery room to offer his official condolences.

Should've told you about Wade from the start, Sam, but I never thought you'd care, and I never expected to see him again—

$$\bullet \cdot \bullet \bullet \bullet \cdot \bullet \bullet \cdot$$

AT FIRST GLANCE, THE Unity corvette *Great Escape* had the deserted look of a barge where some sad lieutenant navigator had been living by himself for months, with its surfaces scuffed and full of half-completed projects. I'd been told we were leaving immediately, but my fellow pilot didn't seem rushed as we strolled through the corridors of a fighting vessel designed for a crew of fifty.

Rathe pointed out the improvements he'd made and took time to show me all the features built into a military-grade craft with which I had no experience: two backup life support arrays, twenty torpedo chutes, and five sets of retractable cannons fore, aft, and belly as well as the standard starboard and port.

The man didn't rush, yet covered everything from environmentals to the hyperdrive core's fusion reactor in less time than it'd take me to explain what those systems were to a dockside trawl. Despite surface clutter, every system was primed and immaculate. (Later, when I grew to know Rathe better, I'd learn he'd had the ship prepped to fly ever since they'd landed—and that being prepared came as natural to him as breathing—if not more so.)

I became aware of his quiet approval when I asked the right questions—and his impatience when I missed something he considered elementary. We even had a spirited discussion about how I'd managed to get my flying credentials without a working knowledge of commercial hyperlanes in the Unity's First, Second, and Third Rings.

"Never used *commercial* routes," I said, deciding not to mention that most of my forays into Terran territory had been on behalf of its underworld wanting alcohol or guns.

"*Bedalia* doesn't like the Kamen," he told me when we'd come to near accord again, our steps echoing in a hall built to fit squadrons. "Mureen says it's because of the krov. Kamn and krov powers are opposites, she says. Like scrambled polarities. They don't mix."

If I spoke Terran nonsense, that might've made sense. "Sure." I whirled around for the tenth time since we'd started the tour. Kept having the oddest feeling that someone was watching.

Only blank corridor returned my stare.

"You okay?" Rathe asked.

"Yeah, just..." I waved at the corridor. "Bigger than she looks." I'd called the *Escape* a bantam before, and that was true among warships, especially compared to the Unity's dreadnoughts. But you could still fit ten of my *Dancer* inside of her. Damned impressive that he could lift solo.

· • • ●·•●·• ·

(See, the bigger the ship, the more mass you need to fold, so the more engines you need to keep ticking, and the more pilots you need to corral the energy. Once you've made hyperspace, most systems revert to automatic, but you won't get there if half your ship's bent around an asteroid.

No doubt you've heard this before.)

· • • ●·•●·• ·

"The *Escape*'s a good ship," Rathe continued. "It'll be a crime to scuttle her."

"Only if you do it in Unity space. Fringers don't care what you dump as long as you do it away from population centers."

He snickered. "Davad was right about you being funny."

I hadn't been joking.

"Let's hope she likes you." Rathe opened another door to show me what should've been another medic's bay, except it was stripped nearly bare. "*Bedalia* likes me and Sexy well enough, but she won't fly for us."

"Sexy your navvy-name?" I didn't try to hide my smirk.

He shot me a grin. "Don't judge. I was young."

I shrugged. "No skin off my arm. By the way, how does Davad know so much about this bloodship?"

"He knew her before. The ship can't remember, but he says *Bedalia* must have a sense, and that's why she's—" The Unity lieutenant paused, scanning my face. His brow furrowed. "Blast, they really didn't tell you anything?"

"Nope." I drummed my navhand on the railing, guiltily remembering I hadn't exactly given a full disclosure myself. [Second? You're gonna have to wake up or we're doomed!] No response, but now that we were in range of a starship's quantum transponders, at least I could feel the poor thing again: a solid lump all hunched and miserable, curled in the corner of my brain.

Rathe shook his head. "Me, I'd try and impress you by telling you everything. Maybe looking like he does, Davad doesn't bother."

"Are you trying to impress me now by pointing out Davad's looks?"

"Should I?" Eyes light as his looked unnatural, but that smile was the most genuine thing I'd seen since my awakening. "We'll be flying together. That can—"

"We'll see." I shrugged like I didn't give a damn. Flying together could get funny, depending on sync. Was one reason I'd been over the moon about Therion as long as I was—even if he'd turned into a louse who wasn't fit to clean my ship's privy. Navvies are just machines, but Therion's Pokey and my Second had meshed *really*, really well. And that was stinking rare. More precious than 12Fam jewels.

"Right." Rathe went back on track like the military man he was. "So... the techs on *Escape* scrubbed *Bedalia's* working memory banks—but thank Griz they didn't wipe the rest. In terms of finding Krovworld, *Bedalia* knows the route."

"You mean Nuala Erta?"

"That's what the Kamen call it. Not me."

"Why'd they scrub her banks?"

"Uh, beyond my pay grade. But if I had to guess, I'd say it was so she didn't try to run after being captured." He frowned. "She's still confused."

I nodded. "So, we've a scared bloodship who knows the route. But you need me to fly her?"

"She doesn't need a pilot. She needs a reason. Trust me, I tried everything, but I'm not the right fit."

"How sweet you think I am," I drawled.

He gave me an odd look. "I don't just think—you're a fit. We're sure. But go easy on *Bedalia*. She's been through a lot."

"Okay." That might prove to be an advantage, as I was gonna have to go easy on Second, too.

But questions lagged my steps. Why did they need me at all? Most living ships did fly themselves, if the legends were true. A fleet of empty sentient ships, deadly as drones and capable of navigating hyperspace—that was what the First Unity Martyrs had encountered long ago, when space was new, and that was how they'd become the First Unity Martyrs. Then Bene Dix and her Crown harnessed those ships and saved humanity. If Illcord Natoth had a fleet like Saint Bene's, he could make a lot of martyrs.

In the year I'd been unconscious, perhaps he had. According to Mureen, 12Fam didn't believe in newsfeeds any more than they did mirrors, so I had no way to check.

• • • • • • • • • •

(Hindsight brings so many obvious flaws to the tale I was told that I find myself scrambling for excuses to justify my own credulity. Yet perhaps the truth is simple. Perhaps in ignorance I was all too ready to find bliss.)

• • • ● • ● • ● • •

Rathe and I came to an open stair, with a galley above and a long line of metal steps that led below.

"This mission time sensitive?" I asked.

"Thought it'd take a few months and it's been a year." He gestured toward the stairs, wanting me to go down first. "I think you were sicker than the Kamen expected."

"Not my fault." I whistled a shanty to cover my unease as I descended, glancing back only to see another empty white hall. My eyes scanned for security cams and finally spotted one, built nearly eye level, on a clever patch of alloyed wall with a transparent inset. Maybe, I considered, the feeling of being watched came from *being* watched.

I made a rude gesture in the camera's direction.

"The longer it takes us, the more planets go dark," he added. His voice dropped. "Hey. Are you all right? You seem jumpy."

"I'm fine. What do you mean 'go dark'? Is Illcord blowing 'em up with planet-killers?"

"No." He gave me another concerned look. "Starfire was using her bloodships to blow up munitions depots, shipyards—even sabotaged a few military academies—but after she died it got worse. Illcord's using those bloodships to infect systems with some kind of biophage. It wrecks circuits, transmissions, everything tech. We can't get probes close enough to see anything, and no one can get out, so—" His navhand jerked, and I watched with more than a little envy as he blinked back. Then his eyes refocused on me. "Sorry, Sexy's monitoring alerts. Fleet's been doing flyovers above this continent all morning. That's not unusual, but the timing's suspicious."

"McPhee5 and Ilko were hit, Teapot said." The android had also mentioned flying people, I thought, but maybe that was just my brain's addled memory, fresh from its coma.

He nodded. "Seven months ago for Ilko. Five for McPhee. Those were the largest targets. But at least one civilian convoy's gone missing since: a freight hauler with five chained ships. He's hit prospecting stations, too, and some of the Cargo worlds. Last week an entire Fleet class vanished on a training run to Viragio—we can't know for sure that was him—but if he's picking off our recruits it's only a matter of time before he invades Unity space."

"Oh." From Rathe's glower, my nervous laughter was a bad response. But I didn't like his insinuation—that the waiting was on me. They could've found another pilot. Why hadn't they?

"Guess we'd better hurry," I added.

"Yeah." My copilot cleared his throat a few times. "So, your plan is, after... Davad told me you're going to keep *Bedalia*?"

"Why? They promise her to you, too? I don't like to share."

"No. But the ship's special. You'll have to take good care of her."

"I take good care of every ship I fly. Why're you looking at me like I've got six eyes?"

He snorted. "Maybe I like six-eyed women."

"That proves you aren't blind." I grinned back, although my heart wasn't in the game. "They kidnapped me. Mureen and Davad kidnapped me. And you helped. Why?"

"Wasn't like that." His eyes were heavy-lidded. Under different circumstances, I might've called them sultry, despite their funny color. "You agreed."

"When? I was in a fragging coma!"

"Not the whole time. Wade said you were in and out." Rathe frowned at my blank expression. "You don't remember talking to Wade after your surgery?"

I shook my head. "Wade who?"

Both of his brows shot up. "Captain Wade Skybourne? The guy you were friendly with?"

I hooked a finger over my flightsuit's belt. "You'll have to be a lot more specific."

That made him grin. "The night at the bar? Before your crash?"

"Oh! Blond? Lighter than you? Pretty?"

"Yeah." His lean smile widened. "Very pretty. Knows it, too."

"I do recall Wade from the bar." I rubbed my forehead. "A little. Then everything's a blank 'til I woke up here."

"You don't remember spending two months aboard the *Ascendant*?" That seemed to trouble my fellow pilot. "Wade said you seemed fine, considering your injuries."

I felt suddenly uneasy. "No. But *you* do. Tell me what else I said."

He shook his head. "I never saw you, but Wade told me about you. And Mureen—"

"Wade told you about me and Mureen? Where's Wade now?"

"Blast, stop confusing things! Wade told me you were going to be fine, but Mureen said you relapsed after your navvy was reinstalled. You know, we took you off *Ascendant* in a stasis tube. Unconscious."

"Abducted me," I corrected, even as my mind puzzled over the words "reinstalled" and "navvy." Queasily, I stared at my arm. Second being reinstalled might explain how our wires had gotten crossed. "You abducted me in a stasis tube while I was unconscious."

"You'd already agreed—"

"I don't remember." I closed my eyes. Canyon wall. Screams. Pain. That was it.

"If that's what you think, do you want to leave?" When I opened my eyes, the man's posture had shifted. I tried to tell myself those lines tugging his mouth into a scowl and the hand hovering near the holster on his hip were just annoyance and not a potential threat.

"Just give me facts. Where is this Wade guy now?"

"If I know my pal, raising hell to hunt me down. I lifted his access codes to get us off *Ascendant*, and he'll know it was me—" Rathe shook his head. "Look, you cracked your skull. It makes sense you're confused." Several expressions seemed to cross his face at once. At the time, I didn't know him from the Original Adam, but I could still recognize at least one was guilt. "I'm sorry."

"You seem reasonable for a Unity job. Does this smell right to you? Any of it?" I waved my hands at the empty ship around us. "You really think us four can kill Illcord Natoth?"

"It's not ideal," he said slowly. "But we agreed to try. Davad's giving you everything he has. Do you really not want to help?"

"I don't care a crap about Illcord!"

His tone grew strained. "I get that. Find it hard to understand why you wouldn't want to take out a monster, but I get it. You're not the first smuggler I've come across—but you took the deal."

I shook my head. "Even if I did, I need more facts."

"I can't give you that. For your own protection. None of us knows more than we need to. That's standard."

"Standard for smugglers, too," I muttered. Half the time, Therion hadn't told me what was in our cargo hold—if he even knew.

That earned me a nod. "See? We're not so different."

"I'm prettier."

He laughed. "Not going to argue with that." The lieutenant turned on his heel and started down the stairs. "Come on."

I followed. "Why does the krov planet have a bioshield? What the hell is a krov?"

"Don't worry about it." He sounded serious when I caught him on the next landing. "Maybe that'll help with *Bedalia*, you not knowing anything. It was hard for me at first, and she knew it. Wade and I lost our entire squad at Centauri... You won't have the same problem. I admit, I wasn't crazy to hear she'd recruited a civilian from the Fringers, but Mureen swears you're our best shot."

"Recruited? I was a corpsicle!"

"Does that mean you want out?" A muscle twitched in his jaw. Was it paranoia that made me note he was armed? His hand rested on the railing—nowhere near his gun.

I shook my head. "No."

"So you'll help?"

I folded my arms. "I said I'd fly her. I can fly any ship."

· · ● ● · ● · ● · · ·

(Pride. Curiosity's twin sin.)

• • • ● • ● • • •

A trace of a smile crossed his lips. "So we're okay?"

I nodded slowly. "Just like all the facts on a job."

"It's for your own protection, I told you before."

I snorted, because I doubted anyone in the Unity would buy the excuse that a registered smuggler was only following orders. After all, their planetary officials imprisoned and sometimes executed my kind for doing just that.

I took a breath and tried not to stare at that pistol on his belt. "Look, you're a deserter, right? What's that, a permanent freeze for Unity soldiers? They'll only unthaw you if they need help with some medical experiment. So you have nothing to lose, and those Kamen-lords up there..." I recalled Mureen's face when she leaned over me in the hovercraft, mask finally off, and what lay beneath had been desperate. I recalled Davad's expression when he threatened me with a drone strike. Fury there, too. Directed at me? His father? Or the fabled Illcord Natoth? "*None* of you have anything to lose," I finished.

From the look Rathe gave me, I'd landed that one a little too neatly. "Thanks for the reminder." We'd reached the bottom of the stairs, and he punched the door mechanism, hard. "Here she is. *Bedalia*."

The door apertured open and there she was. I blinked. Everything I'd objected to washed away in wonder.

There she was.

"Still want out?" His voice was low, smoldering, like he knew every thought in my head. He did. Seeing her, no pilot could think of anything else.

The Priests of my childhood claimed bloodships were blessed miracles.

They were right.

"No," I choked. "I'm in."

"Sexy says you're not connected yet," he added as I fought the impulse to fall on my knees and genuflect like a kid, or scream, or laugh—or weep. He tapped his bare navarm. "Time to suit up, pilot."

"Oh." Reality came back as the gates to the Garden slammed shut. I needed my navvy to fly. "Yeah, just... give me a sec."

"Sure." Rathe's voice softened. "She really is something, isn't she?"

The living ship wasn't large, maybe built for four passengers—or none, as the *Twenty Books of Revelations* foretold. But she took up most of that small hangar, forming a solid wall of what looked like speckled flesh and bone. There were uniform, rib-shaped grooves along her side, and orb-shaped patches like two eyes above her long nose. She stank, but not a bad smell—something like a cross between stable manure and the sea. I'd seen pictures in Da's copy of a Preflight Bible of a Terran whale, a leviathan. *Bedalia* looked a little like that long-extinct creature that had been prone to swallow fisherfolk and lawyers. A standard airlock door was impressed into her side. The flesh (or bone?) around it was red-tinged, scarred like an old wound. She had no call signs at all—not even her name scribed upon her side. Of course not. She was no creature of anything human.

She was a thing from the uncharted expanse. *Alien.*

She took my breath away. I blinked my eyes twice, the movement in the right one activating the switch in my brain. [This is Prime. Second? Respond.]

[Prime?]

I felt a surge of relief.

· · · ● · ● · · ·

(In those days, I was like a Preflight timekeeper who kept kicking a broken clock and thinking it'd be right again. That this one last time would be the final charm and Second would finally hear me. Now I can almost hear *you*, parsing that Preflight clocks don't work like that. Really? Well, go to hell.)

· · · ● · ● · · ·

"Sexy says your navvy's come online. 'Second,' that's what you call him? Mureen told me, but I didn't believe it." Rathe paused, looking at me.

I shook my head. "Second's just a machine."

He looked startled. "Second's not a real name, it's the—"

"Default moniker, straight out of the tube. What of it?" I raised my hand to let him know I was busy, blinking my eyes like a happy fool. [Second! Thank the Priests you can hear me, you silly sack of wire! Listen, everything's fragged. We've been in a coma—]

[Prime? Where are you? Ping loc!] My hand jerked as it tried to plug into something—anything to get a feed on where we were. [Prime?]

A pause. Then: [Oh. It's just you again.] Second's wave of disappointment washed over me. [Hello, Lia.]

I blinked. [Who are you talking to, you piece of string? I'm right here!]

He frowned. "Sexy claims your Second's confused. She says even *Bedalia* senses it." He cocked his head and blinked several times quickly himself. "Oh! So that's..." His eyes unfocused and he went quiet again, blinking and twitching, communicating to a voice that only he could hear.

"Crap," I muttered. When he wasn't paying attention seemed a good time to confess. At least I could practice the speech. "That's what I wanted to talk to you about. Thing is, we're having some trouble, Second and me."

"Mmm..." My new copilot's eyes had closed completely, but I could see his orbs moving beneath the lids as he talked to his navvy. "Sexy says your connection's fine—" He held out his own navhand. "May I?"

I nodded.

"How about we continue this inside?" Rathe enlaced his wired fingers around mine. I felt the connection thrum up my arm. It was pleasant.

"Might be best," I agreed, trying to ignore the buzzing warmth between our hands.

He tapped on the airlock door, less a knock than the brush of his freehand fingers. "Lia? Can we come in?"

As if in response, the door retracted, and a portal opened to the wonders inside.

Chapter 11 ✳ Introduced

Funny, Sam, You asked me out when Ilko fell and we had our wedding-bless two months later, when McPhee5 did. Those lost souls got more footage out than the ones on Ilko—horrible stuff. Maybe bigger planets take longer to go dark, or maybe the McPheeans got desperate after seeing what happened to Ilko. I bet they knew they had nothing to lose.

STARFIRE'S HUSBAND CLAIMS MCPHEE5! The chyron scrolled across our parlor window, backlit by spattering rain outside. Springtime, and our fields were floods.

Me, I was damned enough to laugh. "Ill-crap Natoth?" I poked Sara, who'd just come from NovyiKorogod for our party.

My cousin started to correct me—Starfire's ship had crashed on her home planet, so she considered herself an expert. But then the newscaster came on with an explanation of what krov sorcery did to bodies, and Auntie Meta switched off the feed. Cousin Sara and I tied more ribbons 'round the traditional sugarspun candy gonads in the shocked silence.

"Kamen-lords are crazy," I muttered, thinking of Mureen.

"Natoth's a krov-lord," she said. "They're calling them krovlords now. Why are you really marrying Sam? Ma thinks you're hiding from the Syndicates."

"Your ma's an idiot." I waved my scarred arm and felt an odd satisfaction when she flinched.

Motherhood had rounded everything about Sara except her tongue. "You can't go on like you're still a pilot—not in Derra City. I hope you know that. Sam's doing grass rings for you, but it's not what he wants."

"I want things, too," I snapped. My eyes threatened to fill. At the time I thought learning to live without a navvy would be the biggest test of our union, Sam, but I hadn't factored in Kamen-lords, not to mention the rest of the Milky—

• • • • ● • ● • • •

I DIDN'T HAVE MUCH time to examine the airlock, or the sides of the ship, or the parts that looked normal, parts obviously cobbled from nonliving ships and installed inside *Bedalia*'s form. We passed across a loosely plated floor, through jointed walls of tubing meant to withstand multiple Gs, and bypassed two octagonal doors that looked like they'd been shoved in haphazardly. One was crooked. Rathe pulled me past, straight to *Bedalia*'s heart, which was a space most decidedly alien, with walls coated in grayish, shimmering flesh. Every surface was curved and carved and polished to a low sheen.

A pale, wave-shaped deck looked to be made of bone, and was split into two raised chairs at the center of the room. It looked like an organic version of a standard double pilot's dock, lying below two enormous dark blotches on the ceiling that I thought corresponded to the bloodship's "eyes" outside. A standard-issue viewscreen was bolted to one of the pilot docks, rather crudely. That inorganic piece looked dead and terribly wrong amid the flowing lines of our surroundings.

"I was using that screen to patch into *Bedalia*'s diagnostics," Rathe said. "You can speak there if she denies you a direct link, or if your Second won't tell you what she says. You really need to quiet that navvy of yours. It thinks you're in trouble, and it's threatening to alert local authorities. House Arkan has a lot of ice. I don't think your Second can break through, but if it does—"

"About that..." I began. "See, the thing about me and Second is, it's gone kind of deaf to me. Or I have to it."

"Deaf? Sexy says it's the loudest navvy she's ever seen. She claims it's been talking to *Bedalia* for months." He blinked a few times and then laughed at something I couldn't hear. "I thought we had a ghost! Sexy said she'd seen it too, but I didn't believe it was a real navvy. Sometimes there's... static. You know."

In fact, I did. Ghosts in our machines. "I'm glad someone can hear Second. But I can't. Not since I woke up."

"Ah." He frowned. "Guessing that's a problem you didn't share with our Kamen friends."

"None of their business."

"It will be if the two of you can't fly." He took my navhand in his. "Connections are fine," he murmured. "Second's right there. You're *here*—"

His Sexy felt like cool water and rocks in a running stream. Rathe himself was the smell of damp leaves and ozone—better than it sounds—tannic and wild and new.

"I feel you," I whispered. "Both of you."

"You taste like campfire." His lips quirked. "But sweet. Second feels like broken ice. And vinegar. Bracing little navvy, isn't it?"

"Yeah." My eyes were teary because he'd got it exact. "Gravel and snow," I whispered. "That's what I thought when they hooked us up."

As if on cue, the comm Rathe wore on his freewrist crackled. "*Everything fine down there?*" Davad, of course. "*Something's hitting our House security walls. Couldn't pick a worse time—we need those alerts.*"

"Sure," I replied, before my copilot could. "Everything's great! Hey, why does the bloodship not like you?"

A long pause. Then: "*This isn't the time. Can you fly her or not, Pilot?*"

"We've barely met—haven't met at all, actually. Just got inside."

"*What have the two of you been doing?*" Davad's exasperated sigh crackled through the comm. "*Never mind. Rathe? Can our pilot fly or not?*"

"Forecast's cloudy." Rathe's eyes met mine. "Right now, Polla's helping me pack."

I nodded, grateful he hadn't ratted me out.

A pained sigh crackled over the comm. "*Hurry. We'll secure things up here.*"

"Relax, Arkan. I already ran preflights." My copilot flashed me a conspiratorial wink. "Won't take more than a minute to lift."

I rolled my eyes as the green lights on Rathe's wrist comm flickered out, Davad having disconnected without even a farewell. "Yes, Lord Arkan. Whatever you say, milord princeling."

He snorted. "Oh, come on. He's not *that* bad."

"Did you say that about Starfire and Illcord too, back in the day?"

"Arkan always swore he'd introduce me, but I never had the pleasure. I served with him, though. On and off for years. The commanding officers brought him in whenever they wanted our squad to pull off a miracle."

"Had a lot of miracles?" I didn't want to ask if he'd been at Neskey and NewLaramie—I liked him too much.

His grin flickered. "I lost count."

"Oh yeah? Where were you when they did Centauri?" I'd meant that to be light, but I knew it landed bad by his hard exhale.

"Someplace else." He looked away too fast.

Centauri. Mureen might pretend familiarity; Davad came to it naturally. Me, I couldn't help remembering how it was the day the broadcast came in at NewBern. All flights grounded. Stars twinkling in the night sky. Would be ten thousand local years before the rays of that supernova reached NewBern, and so the sky had been peaceful and ageless. I'd tried to imagine the devastation, the destruction of three planets, everything in their wake, but my mind kept skipping past it.

"You never met them, Lee and Nate?" I asked. "Not even once?"

"I only knew Davad. They weren't all stationed together."

"But *he* knew her." The man had practically bragged about it. "He ever say why she did it?"

"Because she lost her kamn-blasted mind." I watched my copilot's shoulders straighten, his head turn back toward me, and a forced grin cross his face. "Get Arkan drunk enough, he'll talk your ear off. Now, come here." Rathe patted the raised cushion of gray that was slightly higher than the one he'd perched upon—roughly the right shape and position to be the main pilot's chair. "Still no Second?"

"Nothing." My head might as well have been gelded. "Can the bloodship hear us talking?"

"I don't think so." He swung his legs over and leaned back in his seat. "Honestly, it's hard to tell."

I frowned. "Davad said you're the one who fixed her. What went wrong?"

He shrugged. "Gravjocks brought her onboard with a high tractor. The whole time she was trying to rip a hole through our bulkhead. She nearly broke out of the beam. The Guild reps got her quiet somehow—I wasn't invited to *that* party, but Wade said they did it by wiping her short-term banks—and don't ask me how they knew where those were, because I've got no idea. Considering how long these ships live, she could've lost days—or centuries." He patted the ship's wall, tracing a hand down one of her ribs. "If I'm being honest, I don't know how I got her working. Sexy and I slotted in one day and we all"—he shrugged—"we just talked." He laughed nervously. "I'd never seen tech like her before in my life."

I hadn't either—and yet the room felt familiar. Maybe it was the shapes of the chairs, designed from flesh to look like our navchairs. My *Dancer*'s cabin was about the same size. She even had a few cheap manual terminals like the one bolted into *Bedalia*. The way the ship seemed cobbled together from spare parts and a prayer was almost ordinary. I'd been around ships like that my entire life.

That must be it, I thought.

"Sit." Rathe patted one of the chairs. "She's curious about you."

"Mutual." I sat and *Bedalia*'s chair breathed beneath me, adjusting to my form in a way that made my skin crawl, even as I felt my muscles relax into its form. I closed my eyes and reached out. [Second?]

Shivers danced up my spine, but the black remained. No flashing red light, no portal to the infinite.

[Second? Where are you?]

My arm buzzed warmly and I felt it lock into place, felt the chair connect exactly as any other Guild-designed chair would, but the black remained. I was connected—

—yet entirely blind. I had the sensation of being trapped inside a deep crevasse, buried alive in stone. *Containment*, I thought oddly. *Do no harm*—

Gasping, I opened my eyes a second (or an hour) later. My arm was free, the dock quiescent. From Rathe's calm expression, I surmised barely any time had passed at all.

"Nothing." I wiped my face with the sleeve of my freearm, trying to hide my fear. "I couldn't see anything."

"That's okay. You did good." My copilot stood over me. He had something in his hand that took me a second to recognize: a bag of orange goop with a tube at one end. "She's letting you stay on her, at least. Mureen tried sitting there once, and *Bedalia* threw her right off." He chuckled. "Ever seen a horse? From one of those farm worlds?"

I tried to match his jovial tone. "I've ridden a horse on one of those farm worlds. Feldelroy, remember?"

He grinned. "So you get it. *Bedalia* bucked Mureen right out of the saddle. Sent her spinning on her ass."

As if it could hear him, the seat rippled beneath me. Was a little like the hide of my old mare, the first Dancer. Shivers ran up my spine again, but this time not unpleasantly. *Easy now*, I thought, patting the side. *There, there.*

"How long was I out?" I eyed the feeding pouch Rathe had extended to me, for that's what that orange goop was. I felt my face wrinkle with disgust. "I don't need *that*."

"A few minutes. But Mureen said that android made us promise to get kilocalories into you every day until you're back to a fighting weight."

"I can eat real food. Second and me, we're not some old grist out on our deepriver runs!"

He shot me a rueful smile. "Have you seen yourself since you woke up? Really looked in a mirror?"

I rolled my eyes. "Of course not. 12Fam don't believe in mirrors."

"Funny."

"Yeah. They're funny all right." My stomach rumbled. "I'm starving. Is there any actual food on this ship?"

"We don't have time to go poking in the galley. Come on." He gave me another pained smile and pulled another pouch from his suit's pocket, popping open the seal. "I'm having one too."

I nodded reluctantly and Rathe fumbled with my necklace, exposing my port. "Just a sec, connector's a little ragged... there." The line snapped into place, and I felt an alien, almost nauseating coldness move past my breastbone as the feed began to run into my guts, bypassing my stomach completely. I'd read about this feeling, and it was as bad as I'd expected. Easier to bypass the upper guts, the Guild had found a long time ago.

"You're young to have a shunt, Polla." His hand brushed my hair absently, and then he sat back down next to me at the copilot's station. Our faces were very close. "How many jumps have you done?"

"About a thousand."

His brows drew together. "That's not very many—"

• • • •• • • • • •

(One thousand jumps in seven years was about average for my occupation. *You* wouldn't care about Guild Regulations, but our reps advise two or three jumps a week, with breaks to reconnect with the real world and our five other senses. In high seasons we all pushed the limits—and some always took it too far. But I'd always enjoyed reconnecting, enough that I took my breaks, spending the time screwing, or gorging, or dancing.

Close to the river, that changes. By the time a navvy and their pilot are ready to cross the Sticks, nothing in the galaxy has any flavor—not food, nor drink, nor sex. By then, nothing except dreaming has color or feeling left.)

• • • ● • ● ● • • •

I smiled back. "Didn't even have a kiss before the accident. The medics put it in while I was under. What about you?"

Rathe settled back into his chair, attaching his own pouch with a practiced ease that made me sickly fascinated. "Always one more, I hope."

I chuckled. "That's the dream. But how many?"

He tilted his head back and placed the pouch on his stomach. "Fifty thousand, give or take... but a lot were intandem. You're just a kid." His head turned toward mine, our faces close enough for me to see the creases at the corners of his eyes. "And it's an old port they used on you. Unity medics can be cheap bastards. We should get it replaced."

"Eww." Made my empty stomach churn, thinking of used medical equipment nesting in my guts, but then the rest of what he'd said hit me. "Fifty thousand jumps? Do you have a death wish?"

Rathe chuckled. There was a hollowness to his easy smile that tugged at me. "Helps with the soldiering."

"But fifty thousand—how old are you?"

"Not here." He turned on his side, and his navhand lifted across to touch mine. One lazy finger traced the place where Second's braid fused into my wrist. I felt that familiar buzz. Second was in there somewhere, but it was the unfamiliar sense of Rathe and his navvy that came to the forefront of my awareness: rich and heady like the taste of a foreign liquor in my mouth. I sighed. It's a pleasant feeling when our navvies sync.

If it weren't, we wouldn't do it.

"Let's go inside," he murmured. "Easier to talk there. We'll sort out your navvy. I'll introduce you. Okay?"

"Yes." I had so many questions.

"Relax." His fingers brushed mine, and I felt Second linking us perfectly.

I felt the brush of Rathe's navvy, and then something bigger, something immense behind it, but my eyes were still open in the real world, staring up at the domed expanse of ship above us, and I—

"Shhh," my copilot said. His hand had withdrawn, sunk back into his own dock. My eyes were blurring, but I watched as gray flesh rose from the chair to enclose him, wrapping 'round his form like muscle or wire, and my vision blurred as a warm rush shot through my corpus, and I felt the same happening to me, and I—

I—

I *was*—

[Hello.] The ship's whisper went into my bones. [I am Lia. Your navvy's very excitable. Tell it you're fine, please. It keeps saying you're not.]

[Is Second here?] I couldn't feel it.

[Rathe told me your name. But I need you to say it. Initializing for input?]

[Polla. I'm Polla Ottrava.]

[Good.]

The living ship took me inside. She was a sweep of gray, the sound of waves, a taste of salt, a wave of incandescent happiness, and a surge of indescribable grief.

"Hello, Polla Ottrava," her voice said, laughing. Her laughter was sunlight on water, ripples across stones. A butterfly's wings on an alien moon, half across the Milky. "I'm Lia."

Chapter 12 * Shipped

Sam, you may recall it was three weeks later on the morning of our wedding breakfast that the Biscayne newscaster broadcast the *Unity's Most Wanted* list.

News in Fringer space was getting bad. Illcord Natoth had started hitting Syndicate convoys by then... yet I was more concerned with my bare foot exploring the upper reaches of your thighs (well-hidden by the tablecloth, because neither of us were raised by pack wolves), than someone else's doom.

We watched the news about Cousin Beya Ottrava being identified in some footage at McPhee5—with green hair and a sword, no less—and you cracked a joke about how all the interesting criminals came from my side of the family. I couldn't laugh or the paint on my face would crack.

 At Ma's direction, our android Bolts clanked over to turn off the broadcast, but I yelled to stop him, for another name had popped onto that screen, one that made my blood run cold: KEN'RI MUREEN OF GLOS, the chyron read, beneath a holograph of her big-eyed, button-nosed mien.

"Mureen? Wasn't that your nurse's name on the Earff ship, Pollie?" Cousin Sara called out from the doorway with more pancakes. "You never told me she was a Ken'ri."

"She asked me not to tell anyone," I said.

By then, the room was starting to get packed with relatives chattering about Beya, whom we'd all thought dead at Centauri. Uncle Daigri lay the Unity's odds of getting a free Fringer citizen like her father to pay the survivor's benefit back at fifty-to-one, and a surprising number lined up to take that wager, including Uncle Absolm himself.

I might've cared to bet too, except I was distracted by her face. Mureen looked like a saint: driven, desperate, and more than a little insane.

Two days before, she'd been spotted on the duty-free planet of NewPrinceton. Footage showed an industrial complex in ruins, a plasticrete bunker that'd been pulled nearly out of the ground with its roof peeled back like a pot of Ma's preserves. The freckle-faced beauty they showed next didn't look familiar (not that I looked close), but the 12Fam moniker "Davad Arkan" circling his form made our relatives explode into a history lesson about corpro-cat princelings and Terran tyranny,

If you want to pick a moment when my obsession with treacherous Kamen-lords began, Sam, that was it: in Ma's crowded parlor, ten minutes before the Grass Priests blessed us and we burned the effigies—

· · · ● · ● · · ·

I awoke in our shared dream on an ancient sailing ship. The call of seabirds and the rocking motion of an ocean beneath our hull told me that Rathe was a traditionalist, envisioning the space between worlds as a Preflight ocean. I smelled salt, and my projection of *Dancer*'s metal ceiling melted away, replaced by a clear blue sky. The dream was beautiful, with a vivid clarity of sensation I'd never seen outside of a training sim. In training, the computer codes everything into a static, immutable reality so it can be shared by all users intandem. But this was wild space, unfettered and unchained.

It should've been a muddled mess, but was not.

"Hello again." Lia giggled. She'd hooked her heels around the rails, perched there like a seabird herself. A cloud of black curls tumbled over her shoulders. She extended a tanned, almost greenish hand and met my gaze squarely with eyes as clear and deep as an ocean. "You look different here, Polla Ottrava. Much better than when you're that broken thing in the cold world."

I was too amazed by her presence to be insulted, and so I shook her hand, warm and calloused, as normal as any hand anywhere. "Thanks. You... you're beautiful in both places." It was true.

"I like your hair." Lia smiled. "And your face. You feel nice." She raised her voice. "Doesn't Polla feel nice, Rathe?"

"Sure." His voice came behind us. I turned. "Bedamned if she's not the lady I remember from the bar." He grinned at me in a way that made us both in on the joke. "Stacked like a Venusian tower. Pushing face with my pal Wade and making her own guy jealous as hell."

He was so over the top that I laughed, stepping back so I could see them both. The tail of my topknot fell half across my face. I felt so relieved to have it back.

"Don't look half bad yourself." It was true. The lines of strain he'd had in the real world were gone. Rathe was well formed in our dreaming, hair longer, maybe even a little plump beneath a ridiculous costume that could only have come from some Preflight drame. He wore a striped shirt and trousers that barely extended to his knees. His feet were bare, hair bleached near white in parts, and his skin was gold and sleek in the sunlight.

"You don't have to be in uniform," he chided. "We're not flying. Hell, you're a civilian anyway."

"Uniform?" But I looked down and discovered I was wearing the same stupid Unity flightsuit Teapot had selected for me that morning. I banished it immediately for a plain jumpsuit—my favorite—patched at the knees and elbows, with a bit of Ma's lace sewn along the bloomers for color. I might've even been wearing it the day of my accident, but in that moment, I couldn't recall.

"Pretty," Lia enthused, and then she was wearing its twin. I couldn't remember what she'd had on before. The dreaming is like that—edges you don't focus on grow dim. Shared dreaming even more.

· · • · **•** · **•** · • · ·

(Real world is like that too, isn't it? A lot on the margins you don't see.)

· · • · **•** · **•** · • · ·

"To answer your earlier question, I'm thirty-seven." Rathe cleared his throat. "Last month. Terran Standard."

"Thirty-seven with fifty thousand jumps?" I was tactless. "No wonder you're going gray."

"Thanks." He snorted.

"You look good for an old man."

"I know." His eyes crinkled at the corners. "And I've seen your chart. So I know you're just a kid. Twenty-eight?"

"Terran Standard, maybe," I corrected. "On Feldelroy, I'd be twenty-six..." Except that was a year ago.

"Does it matter?" Lia asked.

"Not really." Rathe stretched his arms behind his head, exposing several centimeters of tanned midriff between his shirt and his pants that I was positive he'd displayed for my benefit.

· · ● ● · ● · ● · · ·

(*Pilots. We're not all shameless flirts of Babylon and NewSonora, but it helps.*)

· · · ● ● · ● · ● · · ·

"Sorta," I told Lia. "Sorta matters. Not a lot of pilots make it past forty." Retirement had always seemed like an abstract to me, but staring at Rathe's easygoing face, I felt a sudden pang. "Almost none to the half century."

"Why?" Her voice was curious.

"Don't have it in us." My copilot shrugged. And then to me: "Had your kids yet?"

"That's personal." I had not, despite Ma's gerning. Fringer religions encourage us to do our part to spread human biodiversity across the stars. A lot of pilots get that in early. My future prospects might be better, I supposed, being as I'd be rich as a princeling, but I was in no rush. "You?"

His eyes creased. "One son. He's at the Calabran Flight Academy on Dims VI. I went there too."

"Legacy brat?"

"Like me." He snorted. "Grandmother was a rear admiral."

"Fancy." I rolled my eyes. "My grand was a grass farmer."

"Well, my mother grew apples." Rathe smiled. "And she was a pacifist."

"I like apples." I'd never heard of a flight academy on Dims VI, and my knowledge of Unity training academies came mostly from what I'd learned in smuggling school, which was to avoid their ships and give fake comm codes to their pilots after screwing 'em in seedy portside notells.

"I like apples too." Rathe walked over to the rails next to Lia and sighed. "You made a beautiful day for us, Lia. Thank you."

"I know you like suns filtered through atmosphere, dear Rathe." She beamed, bright as stars. *Stars.* It hit me that I was dreaming with a living ship. Looking at the two of them, I didn't get the problem as to why *Bedalia* wouldn't fly for this man. They seemed close enough that she could've been his navvy.

"So..." I realized I'd forgotten to ask about my own prodigal. "You've seen my Second, Lia?"

"It is very young." Her lovely face turned serious. "And it thinks you're dead."

"Sexy's with it now." Rathe grinned. "Sexy took it to look at the dolphins."

"The dolphins aren't real," Lia added, to me. "I made them to keep it occupied. It likes to sing. Loudly." Emphasis on that last like it was my fault.

"What's a dolphin?" I asked.

"A sea mammal from this world, now extinct." She nodded at the sea, and I noticed a smaller boat far off on the horizon. "Rathe likes them. And Second is very upset this rotation. What happened?"

"I—" A small sharp agony stabbed between my eyes, making me wince. "There was an accident."

"Second gave me a detailed account. You were intoxicated and trying to impress a potential mate. You almost killed Second and your passenger. But it says you died in the crash."

"I was unconscious for a long time. We got separated."

"It says everything is wrong." Lia frowned. "I don't understand. You seem normal. From your navvy's account, I expected a monster."

"Told you she was yar." Rathe's voice was light and easy, like he was gentling a wild mare. "Didn't I?"

Lia furrowed her heart-shaped face. "You told me you thought she'd be an acceptable companion. But that was months ago. More recently, you told me she'd probably never wake up, and then you attempted to flatter me into navigating hyperspace for you and your monsters—and I told you I would never go back to that terrible place with those other monsters—"

"Hey now." He laughed. "No need to tell Polla all of my secrets. Look! I was wrong, wasn't I? She did wake up."

"But without her navvy." Lia tilted her head, frowning. "It does not want to come to you, Polla. It says you're not real."

"Hold." I was getting fed up. "How long have you been speaking with my navvy?"

She blinked. "Since we arrived on this planet. Of course, I wasn't aware it was *your* navvy—not until today, when I met you. But we were both alone so much of the time that we began to speak. It helped because I was in an accident, too. I lost my pilot, too. Rathe helped me get better. They scraped out my memories, but I remember she died." Lia's voice was steady, but I could almost feel her sadness, buried not very far beneath the water, an iceberg of boreal grief. "Rathe's lover died, too, and so he understands. Who died for you?"

"No one." I felt weirdly guilty. "I mean, some relatives did. They got old, and then..." I waved my hand. "The Grass Priests came."

In a different context her wide-eyed expression might've been funny. "Are the priests made of grass?"

"No."

A soft rain started to fall. The wind picked up. I shivered.

"But who died for you, Polla?" the ship repeated. Now her words held a darker note. "Second is sad because you died, but who died for you?"

"No one." Was this the depressed survivor's club or something? "Did Rathe explain what they want us to do? You're the only ship who can get through some bionet, so they want me to fly you to this mysterious planet."

"They want me to go home. But my pilot is dead." The wind picked up and buffeted me with a face full of imaginary hair. Imaginary salt stung my eyes. I tasted it on my lips.

"We could fly someplace else?" I offered. "Try that out? You and me. Or you and me and Rathe."

"No. I cannot fly. My pilot is dead. I cannot fly without her."

I shivered. Hadn't Rathe said the ship didn't remember her past? I grasped for something to say, for something that people said. "I'll light a candle for her, okay?"

Lia's voice dropped to a whisper. "I think it happened inside me. I think she died inside of me. Her blood was on my floor. Her bones are inside of me." The boat rocked back and forth, pitching as the water roughened. "Second said it would light a candle for me, too. And it made the same joke you did, about the priests not really being grass. It said that too."

"Silly navvy." I felt my lips try to grin. *Blood? Bones?* Had this ship killed her own pilot?

"I guess you are Second's pilot," Lia added. "You sound the same."

"Yeah." I walked to the rails and looked out. The other boat was closer. Two figures on it, etched in silhouette. One was as familiar as my reflection. Second and I raised our hands at the same time, and I felt both of our relief sweep through me like a tide. "I am."

"I would fly. But my pilot ordered me only to fly for her. And then she died. There was blood, and—"

"—and bones. You said before." I felt sick. "Hard to live without your bones. Least for us humans."

"Please try, Lia?" Rathe's voice, soft and soothing. The same one he'd just used on me. "Just try. Polla and I will help you. And Sexy and Second. We're all friends here."

"She ordered me to stay with her when the flock left. I was First. She finished my doors, and added machines, and she carved her home inside me. She made me *First*. I cannot leave her bones behind. I will not take another."

Was it my imagination, or was the wind picking up?

"And she is with you always. Like Opal is with me, remember?" He ran his hand along the prow of the ship. "We've all lost someone, Lia. We carry their memories inside. But we go on."

"No." Her beautiful face turned to me with eyes as blank as mirrors. In them, I saw my own reflection, distorted and terrified. Pale as salt. "I do not. She did not allow it."

"The hell with her!" Wasn't my imagination. Definitely a wind now, making my angry voice lost and shrill. "Who was she, telling you what to do? She didn't own you!"

"She made me with her own blood." The wind blew Lia's curls flat against her skull. My topknot whipped forward. "Who made you, Polla Ottrava?"

"My parents?" The Grass Priests would prefer that I said the gods, no doubt, but they weren't here to give me ten lashes.

Lia nodded. "And if they said not to leave them?"

I tried to laugh. "Hell, they packed me a bag. Ma converted my room into storage before I even graduated from Smug—"

A sharp pain impaled my side, staggering me with agony. A piercing torment between my eyes flared my vision to white. I heard my voice cry out.

"Polla?" Rathe was there, hovering above. He pulled me upright. His clothes had shifted into a Unity flightsuit, as if he'd put his professional uniform back on. "What is it?"

"She is remembering," Lia said. "It isn't good to do that, Polla. Not here, where memory shapes. Would you like to go swimming?"

The waves looked choppy and cold. You couldn't drown in the dreaming, but engaging in risky activities might trick your meat body into having a heart attack. "No." I took a deep breath, felt my side throb in agony. Then the front of my skull went numb.

At Lia's nod, Rathe released me and stepped away. Her voice was a whisper. "I think she used to take me swimming, my pilot. There was a world that was mostly sea. Just for us, she said."

The storm came with gusting waves—and suddenly I couldn't see the other boat at all. A gray wave of water splashed into us, soaking me to the skin.

"Lia!" I screamed. "Our navvies are still out there! You need to calm the water!"

"No. They need to *learn*." Her voice was dark as the deep. "Second needs to learn alone. Like I did."

"It's not the same thing! Navvies aren't like you. They need us! They're nothing without us!"

"I am nothing without her and Petal. You are nothing here. We are all ghosts." She shook her head slowly. "Can you not see that?" Her gaze went to Rathe. "Even him."

I turned. My copilot swayed easily while I foundered and Lia raged. I was aware he was watching me, watching us both, but he said nothing. Dispassionately, I realized that whatever this was, it had to be part of their experiment. I knew that thought should hearten or torque me. Either way, make me stronger.

It didn't. I think I sank to my knees. And the storm grew worse, sleeting out everything, hammering my skin with stones. I could no longer see Rathe at all. Lia herself was a blur of black locks and sodden limbs, looming over me like an elemental force—yet clinging to my knees and weeping like a child—both and the same, all at once.

The ship's voice became a scream that rent my bones. "I needed you and you never came! Rathe told me you're supposed to fly me, you and your Second." Her words became a wail, and her phantom grip on my legs tightened. "He wants me to go home, but I cannot! She told me not to leave her—to keep her inside of me—but they took her out—"

I closed my eyes, feeling my phantom lips move. Didn't have to scream, because none of this was real. Still, my words felt like a ragged whisper, like I'd been screaming all along. "I'll help." I tried to make my voice compassionate, my thoughts kind. I tried to becalm the storm that had wrecked over me, but the ship was too strong. I felt myself shake with the cold, felt my feet slip on the phantom deckplates.

I felt myself flail.

I felt myself fail.

I felt myself fall.

Again and again. Broken on a cliff face. Burning from the stars.

"You are *lying*!" Lia hissed, and I almost slipped overboard, the rails banging into my injured side, another breach that tore another howl from my lips. "You don't want to fly with me! You want to leave me!"

She was right, I did want to leave.

· · • ● · ● • • · ·

(In a classic setup, your ship doesn't have separation anxiety and it can't kill you. Your ship's a machine with a very, very clever abacus. You and your navvy shape what you see in that abacus and chart a path across the deep. You convert the calculus of interstellar travel into a map that your navvy transcribes through your nervous system, one that ends up translated by your own subconscious into something like the sea and the boat we were on.

Normally, what you see—what we call the *dreaming*—is a side effect of the whole kaboodle. Usually a pleasant experience—too pleasant, some doomsaying Luddites or Unity scolds might say—but also, mostly, uneventful. Don't bother to parse this if you've heard it before: what Lia was doing was dangerous. She was shaping this dreaming without any input from Rathe and me.

And her shape wasn't human. Didn't need the things we required.

So much can go wrong between the folds with interstellar travel: irregularities in the weave, rips in the continuum, a slip to the wrong coordinates and suddenly you and your ship are entombed in an asteroid. The dog's the least of it, really. When it's just you and your navvy—or you and your copilots intandem with their navvies—you've all learned the same controls. There are safeties in place, so you don't put your crew out an airlock or accidentally depressurize your own bridge.

But to add in a wild ship like Lia... She could've ended us both with a mere half blink of one maddened green eye. Overloaded our bodies or sent us all spinning through the quantum of space, to be lost forever in the black.

Of course I was terrified. Any sane pilot would be... which does, of course, exclude *you*.)

· · • ● · ● • • · ·

I felt my panic spike and knew I couldn't help but have the sensation carry into the real world, where my real body now had every muscle tensed, its heart pumping frantically, all its glands primed for fight or flight.

Lia's voice broke through me like thunder, like a god from on high. "Go away!"

And just like that I was out, shivering and alone in a meat body caked with sweat, lying back on a chair that had grown ice-cold, its former softness replaced by slick and slippery bones that rippled angrily beneath me.

This same chair had bucked Mureen off, Rathe had said. I jumped off, making a slobbery, weak noise that I didn't want to hear come from my own throat.

My fellow pilot was still slotted in, wrapped in gray flesh and comfy as a dream. Between the chair's strands I could see his eyes rolled back in his head, his mouth slightly open. Faintly snoring, a little drool. We don't look our best in the chair. That's one reason that piloting is such a private thing. Rathe's skin had a pallor in the real world. *Fifty thousand jumps.* I remembered how he'd touched my navarm, the crinkled corners of his eyes.

The cord of my feeding tube bumped against my arm. I ripped it out. That turned into a messy mistake, with nearly a meter of slime-coated silicate pipe ejecting itself from my port and me coughing and gagging. By the time I'd cleaned up, the comm on Rathe's wrist was beeping, but he was still gone. I hesitantly reached for his freehand, the only part of him not wrapped in the chair. His skin was ice-cold. I noted the faint tinge to his fingertips. Cold extremities weren't a great sign for us. *Fifty thousand jumps.* Why was he still doing this?

I raised his wrist to answer his comm. "Yeah?"

"*Will she fly or not?*" Davad didn't bother with niceties.

"Things started out great." I forced enthusiasm into my voice, because I'd be damned if I'd admit failure. "*Bedalia's* very sweet. But we're gonna need some time. By the way, did someone kill her pilot?"

A pause. Then: "*Where is Rathe?*" Davad sounded irritated. "*Why are you answering?*"

"He's still under. I'm taking that as yes, someone killed her pilot? Do you happen to know... did they kill her in the ship?"

"*Her?*" He sounded distracted.

"The pilot. *Bedalia* mentioned there was blood in the ship."

"*Does it matter? Those memories were wiped.*" Davad's tone crisped into ice, which meant he was torqued. "*Get Rathe out. He's needed.*"

"Not sure I can get back in." I'd never been kicked from a shared dream before.

"*You got in?*" I heard him sigh. I heard Mureen say something garbled in the background. She sounded pleased.

"We met, but Lia didn't let me stay." My pilot's arm was all prickled and cold. I wriggled my fingers to force circulation.

"*The next time will be better. But I need Rathe. SecForce just came through the Lunar Gate. Ten ships. Father's castellan warned me.*"

"Sure they're here for us?" Seemed to me that Unity Security Forces probably popped through gates all the time, what with them being so controlling.

"Yes." Davad didn't elaborate. "*Exastim's in a cabinet. If Rathe is in the secondary chair, that would be to his left along the wall. You will see a panel. Press on it.*"

I did and discovered that most of the medical supplies I'd noticed missing from the *Escape* were tidily packed in *Bedalia*. The exastim ampules were lined up neatly in the front, with an entire row missing, which made me wonder how many times they'd had to drag Rathe out of the dreaming in the time he'd waited for me to wake up.

Fifty thousand jumps. What we'd done didn't count as a jump, but Rathe spending a lot of time slotted in wasn't healthy.

His body jerked when I jabbed his portside shoulder, and he sat up fast, eyes a little wild, flecks of drool flying everywhere. We're not at our best, dragged out from dreaming. For a second, he looked through me like I was a stranger. Then: "Oh." His lungs took a heavy breath, and he fumbled with his port, his mess of tubing. The comm buzzed like an angry, mechanical bee as Davad filled him in on the details.

I leaned against a protrusion in the wall, watching my copilot dispose of our pouches through a circular aperture in the floor, and then wipe his face with a towel. He was expressionless, nodding slowly as Davad went on about Circles and Unity warships, then about both of us flying—

"We'll be right there," Rathe interrupted. "But I'll be running solo. Polla's not ready, and I don't want her first flight to be outrunning Fleet starrunners." His pale eyes met mine, mouth twitching into a weary smile.

My pride pricked, but he wasn't wrong. Without Second, I couldn't navigate my way out of a hat.

Davad's voice crackled with impatience. "*Why not? Her records say she's never flown anything the size of the* Escape, *but she claims to be expert at evading our*"—I caught his indrawn breath—"*their blockades.*"

"I've flown lots of ships!" I hadn't. Nothing nearly so big. But it torqued, hearing the princeling say I could not.

"I'll be fine alone." My copilot told the princeling. From Rathe's troubled expression, I got it. The dog was literally on his heels. He'd been grounded for nearly a year. A long respite helps, but there's no cure. *Fifty thousand jumps.* Deepriver wasn't something we talked about with civilians. *Maybe he hasn't told them,* I thought. Usually the ship's okay when deepriver comes for its pilot. Usually the ship pops out of hyperspace with all systems intact, even when its pilot's been reduced to a mass of organs not even fit for auction.

Usually, but not always.

"I'm sorry," I whispered. "I can try—"

Rathe shook his head, still talking to Davad. "Polla needs to see what we're up against. I know we talked about heading straight for Moonbase Celestean, but it's a long haul. I'll take us through the Abomination again for our first waypoint. You can show her everything."

"*Not a bad idea.*" Davad sounded impressed—or not as disapproving as he was with me. "*Fine. Get up here. Bring her. Hurry.*" A click, then the comm shut off.

"We'll take the lift up, it's faster." Rathe straightened, looking steadier than I felt. "Brought you down here the long way..."

• • • ● • ● ● • • •

(At this juncture, you may recall the original terms of my fool's bargain: I'd met their stinking bloodship. I'd tried to fly her. I'd come to the realization that I didn't want to be within fifty light-years of a bloodship ever again. You may wonder why I didn't broker another objection. You may wonder why I didn't make a polite excuse, slip off to a lav, find a ventilation tube, and climb out of that cursed ship. Time wasn't on their side. They were being pursued, not me. I could've hidden until they had to flee. Flee—or be captured themselves.

In hindsight, I wonder too. Not that my efforts would've gone well. If I were lucky, such a course would've found me merely dead in a sandstorm, asphyxiated on some bleak Terran plateau. Unlucky and, well... I'm sure you've imagined that fate.

Imagine going into it unknowing.

Imagine being innocent—if you still can.

No high-minded reason I didn't run. Sympathy for Lieutenant Navigator Sai? Of course. Sympathy... and attraction. But he'd made his bed and I had no illusions about saving him from it. Hell, even if I'd wanted to, I couldn't fly.

So why didn't I run?

You've never asked, you *cannot* ask, but I imagine you asking all the same, you with your cold voice and your unrelenting, *useless* logic: *Why didn't you run? You owed them nothing. Even then, you knew they were liars, and traitors, and thieves.*

I didn't think of it. That's it. That's the entire reason. I *didn't think.*)

Apologue 3 ❋ Wedding

PROPERTY OF PILOT GUILD. DO NOT OPEN.

Words scrawled on the cover in Guildsign: *Don't be stupid, gremlins. Leave this shit in the Starfire archives where it belongs.*

Never thought my best girl would leave me to swing, but life's an empty docking bay and sometimes you're just the fool with a cold cubic from Wada's, left freezing your ass off on a NewBern station as you stare out into the black.

The Milk's not a nice place. I told my Pollie that a thousand times in the seven years we flew together. *Take what you can get,* I warned her nearly as many times as I told her not to forget to flush *Dancer*'s tubes before liftoff, and how to keep two sets of books, but only one for Second. Navvies record lives, but they can't translate 'em. They collect our memories, but they don't understand a space-damned thing.

Treat 'em like a partner, I told Pollie. *Never tell your navvy what it don't need to know.*

The Grass Priests on our home planet say navvies are lost souls. Of course, those same Priests claim Feldelroy was formed by an alien saint with a magic wheel, so I always sussed their facts with a few hectotons of granulated salt. I had an old boss once who swore that Pilot Heaven was no more than some kind of alien entertainment system. Had a pilot lover who swore our Guild runs the galaxy, of course, Lireen was close to the river, raving and incontinent when she came up with that pickle.

I saw Lireen's betrayal coming a quadrant away. So I betrayed her first.

But Pollie caught me blindside. I never believed my best girl could leave me to swing.

Brahz took my knees the night I was caught. Hung me upside down and pulped my patellas himself with a nice rebar. The metal replacements worked okay—as long as I stayed away from magnetized engine cores. That was easy: when you're a pilot chained intandem to seven other fliers on a Syndicate high cruiser, you don't go near the engines. Not a bad life 'til you burn out drooling. Better than maintenance—half the slobs our Syndicate sticks in its boilers don't even have frontal lobes left.

I should've known I'd gotten off too easy.

· · · · ● · ● · · ·

One day Brahz sent for me and told me to go to Pollie's wedding. He kicked things off by handing me back my own gun.

"Make sure to give Polla New Liberty's regards." His eyes flickered up to my branded face. "Can I trust you to get it done?" he added, in a voice as silky as my Pollie's cheeks. "I think so. You must want revenge as badly as me."

I *didn't*. I wanted to burn out drooling in the black. I mumbled something to that effect.

"Cold feet?" He chuckled. My feet were always cold. I had hinges for knees, the skin below mottled as the Crab Nebula. "Not like you need anything below the waist for the chair." His bejeweled teeth flashed. "I could chop more off... right after I take care of your family on Feldelroy. What's left? One brother? Two elderly parents...?"

"Thanks for the opportunity, ser," I said.

"Make sure not to miss when you blow her brains out." Brahz handed me a second gun. "This one's better from a distance. See? Nice holographic scope—"

I hadn't been home in almost five years. Not since my sister's passing, and then just to watch her body burn. I had no invitation. I had metal knees and a brand on my forehead with the Syndicate rune for "failure" embossed like an Original Sin. On some planets, that brand would draw curiosity, or sympathy, but nobody on Feldelroy likes a failed smuggler. Brahz's crew had to paint my face like a torch singer just to hide the brand. They did other things with me too, to pass the time. Jolly crew... I asked one favor in return for mine.

Wedding present for my Pollie.

Pollie and her broke bartender had rented a shoddy event inflatable on the edge of Derra City for their nuptialisms. I'd been worried the staff wouldn't let me in, but one look at my painted mien and the bouncer opened the door with an ugly smirk. Torch singer at a pilot's wedding? What's the expression: grain to Feldelroy? I was just one more tear in the ocean.

My navvy, Pokey, he was always slow, but he had a mean streak and he didn't like tears. By the time we got inside, his thoughts were a clean targeting reticle driving us forward.

I had my wedding present wrapped in chill-paks and tucked under my arm. Chill-paks had been her idea on our last job. They'd have gotten her killed but for me. Sometimes I'm another kind of man and I leave her sobbing by that locked cage. I could've run. But Pollie, she always made me soft. I thought I knew her mind as surely as I knew every other orifice, but that day on NewBern, she proved me wrong.

Maybe no one ever knows anyone.

On her wedding day, Pollie was beautiful. Like a blue lily from a NewBern mountain. She'd let her hair down, and it fell loose to her shoulders. Her dress was marked so low that I knew she was blushing beneath that blue and silver paint—for all her claims that we were pilot jezebels, my Pollie was an Olden Church girl. She and her groom had kept the custom of painting their skin for modesty, and that was how I saw I wasn't the only one who'd been butchered. Her naked starboard arm was a mess of raised scars poking through that paint like the worst geld I'd ever seen. Loss churned my guts, mixing love and hate and pity until I felt Pokey tamp my emotions back.

[Target in range,] my navvy whispered now. Flat as prairie.

"Oh, happy to oblige, as soon as I find a good spot." I scanned the room. There was a balcony in the back, built along the curve of the inflatable wall. It looked promising.

Polla didn't look happy. Her teeth flashed and her voice rang out, cheerful and Pollie-shaped, but I knew in my balls she wasn't happy. She wasn't happy, and I was just one more white-robed torch singer walking at the back of the hall toward the stairs as her new guy said his vows. Not even a pilot, that guy. I heard two graybeards mutter something about him tending bar. His name was Sam. Or Clam. Does that matter? Pilots don't need vows or bartenders. We bind *minds*.

Something of me still burned in her. I swore I could feel it, even if she couldn't.

[Kill,] Pokey whispered.

I successfully avoided the flock of Grass Priests, all eyeless and chanting. Feldelroyan weddings are loud, and everyone's drunk. The chaos made it easy to drop off my gift, then slide up to the balcony. A few celebrants were already groping in the corners—Feldelroyan weddings aren't as carnal as Feldelroyan harvests, but folks like to have fun. I stepped quietly past 'em and made my way to the railing. A good spot—nobody but me was up here for the view.

I watched an eyeless Priest touch Pollie's forehead with a simulacrum of the Holy Spindle. I pulled out my gun and set it on the floor, that pistol was a tiny thing. Brahz's was better, with a sniper's scope that snapped out, self-targeting and good for fifty meters. Pollie was twenty to my fore. The wedding guests wore white, and she wore blue. Silver-painted, her lovely, treacherous mien was a moon. Like my doom.

Like the bad song the band played.

Poetry's got nothing on a bullet.

[Eliminate!] Pokey was triumphant.

"Preacher's choir," I muttered back, setting the muzzle on the rail. No security, as the Ottrava clan were so large and trusting—and armed. I wasn't gonna make it out alive. I'd known that going in, but I still had to take a breath to steady my nerves, and then I felt Pokey dump a whole lot of calm, freezing my soul.

Pollie used to laugh and say I was paranoid when I told her navvies control us. Pollie was a stupid stupid quim-canted slob. Our navvies learn from us until we're the *same*.

Now Pokey used our sweaty navhand fingers to tighten on that trigger. Pollie looked so happy next to that Clam guy. I'd never imagined the two of us on a grass stage before, but suddenly I did. In that instant, I forgave everything. I'd only lost knees. She'd lost her *soul*.

I hesitated, and lost more.

Pokey's sonar registered movement on our aft. "Sorry," a tenor voice whispered from behind me. "You look busy, Pilot D'Cainen, but we need to talk."

[Error!] my navvy said, as that voice whispered a code in my ear. My kill switch. All Guild pilots have one.

"I can't let you shoot." The voice rattled off another string of numbers, and the starboard side of my body went numb. My portside vision pixelated. I felt Brahz's gun fall with a clunk to the carpet next to my adamantium knees.

I heard a metallic cluck as the stranger picked up my rifle. "Did you know you left the safety on?" The voice sounded surprised. "Almost like you didn't want to go through with this. But Pokey sure did. Whistle had to freeze your navvy, and he's not happy—" The voice chuckled. "My little Whistle *likes* Pokey. Shame we didn't meet on better terms, Pilot D'Cainen. We'd have fun... but I can't let you kill sweet Polla Ottrava. She's the bull's-eye of a very classified Guild investigation, and if I told you more, I'd have to kill you"—the voice chuckled again—"faster, and we don't want that, do we?"

A strange navvy's touch shoved into my head with a stench of burnt oil and scorched skin. A pilot's metal hand gripped my wired elbow. I felt pinpricks along my spine. The rest of my body went numb, and alarm died in my deadened throat. Around us, moans and soft sighs. The rhythmic slap of skin on skin. I tried to turn my head, but I couldn't move, couldn't see my captor's face. I wasn't sure if the noises were something he was doing to me, or the sound of lovers behind us who hadn't noticed the beginning of my murder.

With Pokey cut out, my head felt hollow. "Guild?" I managed. "You're Guild, ser?"

"Ser?" the man said scornfully. "Don't be a bootlicker!" He nudged my ribs with something that felt sharp. I felt the fabric of my robe tear. The sharp thing moved unsettlingly close to the base of my skull. "I'm Wade," he added. "Captain Wade Skybourne. I'm your Guild representative. Do you understand what's happening now?"

"Yes."

There's a saying we have about Pilot Heaven: *may you be there forever before your Guild representative finds you dead.* They can pull us out, erase us from existence. They can take us before our time.

They can save us. If I *had* shot my Pollie, her Ottrava clan would've burnt me and Pokey alive.

Skybourne's rough face pressed close to mine. Stubble scraped my cheek and I saw a glint of the man's hair, pale as stars.

"N-nice to meet you," I managed. I thought my teeth were chattering, but I couldn't feel them.

"Is it?" His breath was too loud in my ear. His body embraced me like we were just another set of lovers above the stage. Some men get off on fear; they think it's power. For me, at the end, it was hope. I'd missed Pollie's wedding vows. Now, cheers. The ceiling opened, exposing stars. Sparks of muzzle flare lit up into the Feldelroyan sky. Below us, my Pollie's smiling face lit up like a supernova, and I felt a funny relief that she had a Guild rep on her side, someone our Syndicate wouldn't cross.

There she was in the candlelight, grinning back at her ma like a calf in clover. *Safe.*

"By the way, pet..." my Guild rep continued. "What was in that package you put on the gift table? It's not setting off any sensor alarms. Chill-paks? Tell me it's no bomb."

"N-no." My voice felt funny. I felt a wet trickle down my ear, something wet pool above my breast. "Just ice cream, f-from Wada's. P-Pokey—" I stumbled. "Pr-promise you'll t-take Po-Pokey t-t—"

"—to Pilot Heaven?" Skybourne's breath hissed. "Of course."

"Th-th-*thank* you."

"Of course! Now your Polla..." His wet mouth closed around my ear, teeth scraping cartilage as my Guild rep gave the lobe an exploratory nip. "Does she like ice cream?"

My outside senses ebbed. The world twisted and my body rocked beneath his bonesaw. The lovers' noises around us had gone—or maybe we'd moved. Logic says he didn't geld me atop that balcony, but I had no way of knowing time by then, no way of knowing if my navvy was still recording, if we were still breathing.

A proper Guild doc does a geld with careful tools in a surgeon's suite, leaving everything clean. Pollie's arm had looked like someone had tunneled Second out through her skin, strand by strand. Bad, but at least they'd left her whole, at least they'd closed up her skull when they finished.

When a Guild rep gelds you in the field, they don't care about anything but getting their property back.

The quiet whirr of Wade's saw whispered sweet nothings along the bones of my deadened skull. I felt, or imagined, a soft wind on my face. With the ceremony over, the rest of Polla's wedding party would be outside. Visions of the Priests I'd disavowed danced beneath my eyelids: harbingers of both life and death. Pokey was as quiet as my grave, and I wondered if he was still recording this, if Pollie would be happy with her bartender. I had no more questions. Registered smugglers, we don—

—*Final transcript of Symbiote ajei51554639, alias "Pokey"*

Chapter 13 ✳ Identified

I wish we'd talked about Captain Wade Skybourne when we had the chance. The man's a cant-cocked bastard, but all we did when he dragged me into that locked lavatory at our wedding reception was talk. I couldn't say no to a formal inquiry from my own Guild rep—or tell a civilian. You should've trusted me, Sam. I've done a lot of crap I'm not proud of, but I didn't screw my Guild rep on our wedding day.

Wade wanted the names of every Kamen-lord I'd met on the *Ascendant*. He didn't believe me when I said it was only Mureen; that I'd only caught glimpses of the others: the fat man who'd watched her change my bandages, the tall woman behind him who'd yawned, and that crowd of beige-clad whisperers, some barely more than kids, who'd passed by my room in favor of something more interesting down the hall. Kamen wore beige, I told him. That's how I knew what they were. Everyone else wore Unity white.

Wade was sweaty and desperate that day. When he pushed his hair back, I saw a streak of blood darkening his temple. He claimed he'd cut himself, but that didn't explain the blood under his nails. He claimed he was on Guild business, but he sure didn't act like it. Whatever fueled his jets was personal.

Maybe that's true across the Milky, Sam. These things we call business? They're always personal.

· · · · ● · ● · · ·

WAS PROBABLY GOOD FOR my psyche that I caught the first glimpse of my undistorted reflection in the mirrored door of the *Escape*'s lift, and not the reflective wall of a toilet, where I might've had time alone to reflect and therein lose my crap. True, my employers and I had other matters to struggle with—our possibly impending doom, the approach of a Unity Security Force, a mad bloodship, and the fabled villain Illcord Natoth—but I had my own vanity, too.

Vanity, Feldelroy's Fifth Sin, was, with my reflection, smashed to smithereens and destroyed all over the elevator floor.

"You asked if I'd looked in a mirror lately, Rathe." I licked my lips, and the hideous crone in the mirror did the same. "I hadn't. 12Fam don't believe in 'em."

"Oh," he said. "Well, if you can still make jokes, it's not that bad."

Our eyes met. Mine were bloodshot black pits, sunken and lashless. His were heavy-lidded and lazy and an unnatural blue laced with gold, like a Feldelroy orchid.

"Right." I muttered a few quiet prayers while I gazed at the emaciated stick standing next to Rathe's reflection. I'd thought he looked unhealthy... but the lieutenant was in the pink compared to this stranger with my face.

Hells, even my *face* didn't look right. I touched my brow to make sure my reflection was real. Had those bones always lurked beneath my apple cheeks that Ma loved to pinch? You could cut knives on 'em. I'd always gone sallow when I stayed spaced for too long, but now my skin was nearly translucent, so pale I could see the veins beneath. I also appeared hairless, except for my head (something I'd noticed in the bits and pits regions before but hadn't expected to extend to my face). I missed my eyebrows, had gone through a phase at Smuggler's when I kept 'em plucked and precise as Kynler arcs... but now my visage appeared blind and rather a lot like a rumpled newborn rat's. At least the flightsuit hid what had happened to my rack... although if my copilot hadn't been there, I might've pulled the fasteners apart and had another look at that too.

Rathe's hand touched my back. "You're okay."

"Yeah?" My eyes seemed enormous—had they always been so far apart? Was it lighting that made my skin so pale? "Didn't know I looked this bad."

"Well, it isn't... You don't look *bad*." He cleared his throat. "You're young. You'll bounce back."

"I don't even recognize me." I leaned forward and pinched my cheeks. The reflection did the same, giving me a death's-head grin. "Did they feed me *anything*? I must've lost thirty kilos!"

"You were pretty messed up." He started to reach for my navhand, as he had on *Bedalia*, and then obviously thought better of it, professional courtesy taking over now that he was on the job. "You..." He stepped closer and lowered his voice. "You do know about the leg?"

"Yeah. Davad's da rubbed my face in it. Made me meet him in their *Family Bath* so he could get a good look at what he'd paid for."

His tone darkened. "Haven't had the pleasure of meeting Old Man Genghis, but if I ever do, I'll punch him."

"Thanks." Our eyes met again in the mirror. "Uh, do you know which leg it was?"

He seemed startled. "You can't tell?"

"No—" But then the lift doors opened to the bridge.

"There you are!" Mureen exclaimed.

Rathe was immediately all business—heading past Mureen for the central, coffin-shaped chair at the bridge's point. I hung close on his heels, trying not to gawk at the splendor.

The *Great Escape* had eight berths for pilots, more than any ship I'd ever seen—except the time I'd been on a Syndicate high cruiser. Its gleaming banks were no doubt full of the latest tech. Unity dreadnoughts, I'd been told, could hold up to fifty berths for fliers. With that many pilots slotted intandem, their clumsy hulks could cross quadrants in days, and turn on a nail in a fight.

I was still staring in wonderment when Rathe pushed the hood of the central chair back and slipped inside.

"Luck," I said faintly to the Earff-enriched air.

A shaded screen of energy popped over him, which was a nice touch, I supposed, so one didn't have to be drooling and farting and (sometimes) crapping and pissing and puking, all in the middle of the bridge. I could still see the outline of Rathe's form beneath the shield as he sank deeper into the chair—and I felt a guilty feeling that was both envy and pity the moment his body stiffened, then went lax; he and Sexy now meshed with the ship's drive.

Beneath our feet, the engines surged. The *Escape's* anterior windows paled to translucent, and we lifted out of the open hangar gate, skimming across the surface of blasted Old Earff and angling toward the sky. On our port, I caught a glimpse of what had to have been the Arkan dome—farther away than I'd expected—and beyond the lights of what had to be a nearby company town. The vista vanished as we gathered speed, and then there were other lights and a few tracers of local traffic as we merged onto the atmospheric byways.

"Polla? You'll need to sit down." Mureen's voice interrupted my view. She was seated at one of the ship's banks, wearing what looked to be a white Unity captain's coat with a boxy white coif covering her hair. It was a uniform she had no right to (unless I was way off about what Kamen did), and it was too big for her. She looked ridiculous.

"Don't you look nice." I sounded like Ma. "Didn't you pack any normal clothes?"

"What?" She seemed distracted. "Did you and *Bedalia* get along?"

"Sure," I lied.

The floor tilted, and the transparencies flared with real liftoff, backlighting Mureen in orange. Damn him for a Unity pet, but Lieutenant Navigator Rathe Sai was a smooth operator. I could've put a split of full prosecco glasses down on that operations board and not one would have spilled, so gentle was he, climbing us into the high blue, and at such a pace to keep us keen. Meanwhile, good old Sol was setting outside. I realized I might never make it to the cradle of humankind again, and so I bade it farewell with a few choice Feldelroyan sayings.

I turned back to Mureen, nodding at her new uniform. "That's a lot of stars on your lapel there. Should I call you Commodore-General, or still

Ken'ri?"

"I may have to speak on the comms. They could request a visual." She shrugged. "Sit, please."

"Maybe I could do comms," I offered. "Aren't you a wanted fugitive?"

"I'll manage." She gave a polite smile. "Secure yourself. Any station is fine. We'll be going up quickly in a moment."

"You need to secure yourself, too!"

Mureen shook her head, and then we tilted full skyward, pressing into the Gs. As I finally took her advice and grabbed the nearest chair, I saw her coat flare back. Beneath, she wore grayish boots like Davad's. Stone boots, just like the tales. They attached her to the floor even better than mags would, even shifting with her posture as she leaned forward, like a racer on an uphill ski.

I'd sat down just in time to have the gravity drive me back into my chair's pneumatic embrace, and then we were both silent, watching Rathe's expert skills take us up and out of the world.

"Where's Davad?" I yelled over the crush and the engines' roar. Her shoulders twitched like she'd heard me, but then, with a hum, the i-dampeners kicked in, right before my vision tunneled. If we'd had that split of prosecco, it would've spilled.

In another few seconds the ship leveled out, angling into the black at a comfortable thirty degrees. I jumped up from my seat, leather soles of my shoes clattering in the sudden quiet. Unnerving, how big this bridge was. It occurred to me that a ship this size didn't have all those spaces for crew because they liked the legroom—there were probably vital systems being overlooked right now, with only one pilot, and us hapless passengers.

A gloomy thought, but not one I could help. The banks for manual command might as well have all been engineered for gods as far as I was concerned. There were rows of blinking lights and levers, and seats enough for twelve. I knew Unity hacks spent a decade at their naval academies just to learn half of it—

• • • ● • ● • ● • •

(In the Fringers, Syndicate high cruisers have what some might consider a tidier solution, relying on what they deliberately don't call *enslaved* labor to handle operations. More benevolent cargo haulers chain sails, relying on a centralized board, usually hidden on a ship someplace in the middle of the train, and actual Cargo skimmers, of course, don't even fly... being as they're carved from wood, or sand, or whatever their Cult disciples can find... Why digress? Well, while I'm sure *you* consider yourself an expert on Unity vessels, I'd like to leave a reminder that no one knows everything... some folks just think they do.)

• • • ● • ● • ● • •

"Davad needs the quiet." Mureen waved toward a glassed-in section at the bridge's very prow. The VIP room, I assumed, where brass could go for the view when they didn't want to mix with the plebs. Syndicate high cruisers had 'em too.

"Prepping for another grand entrance, is he?"

That got me a faint smile. "No. He is... with the kamn. Forgive me, I don't know how to explain it to a layperson."

"Communing with your Kamen-graced gifts? That might be what he *says*, but he's probably hiding so he can impress you in a few by marching in to announce something or other, maybe scare me, glower more..."

"You know him well, Polla. But we expect pursuit." She gave me one of her patented too-bright smiles. "No need for concern. We three have been in worse tactical positions."

"Like when we escaped from the *Ascendant*?"

"Yes." She beamed. "They fired on us full bore that day—and yet we survived!"

"Crap." Suddenly I was grateful for the size of this ship. A smaller vessel would disintegrate under the impact of serious fire, taking us with it.

"Six months ago, the three of us raided a munitions base at NewPrinceton," she added brightly. "Rathe evaded our pursuers quite capably. This flight should be tame by comparison."

"Where was I?"

"Oh, we left you with Teapot." At my look, she laughed. "Don't worry! We've changed the ship's registries since then!"

• • • ● • ● • ● • •

(No doubt you'd ask a relevant question, like why raid a munitions base? Still the clever one, *you*. Me, I was staring at the pretty lights, my mind on her forged registries and how good they'd have to be to pass muster.)

• • • ● • ● • ● • •

"Even with fake registries, this is still the same ship. Have they been looking for it this entire time—?" My gaze wandered. A holographic bank on my port plotted our trajectories with colored symbols, not so different from a smuggler's array. We were pitched very tight—sharper than I would've cut with this much bulk in orbital traffic—and veering away from Luna, Earff's solitary moon.

According to the map, we were merging quickly into the most crowded cluster in the Milky: Earff's high-speed network of shipping lanes. Rings of highly regulated traffic that encircled the planet in all directions, so dense that they formed their own habitat. Except, if the displays were right, the lanes were empty. Dead as dust on our scanners. Just a few blips marked as exporters and a few more flagged patrol.

The comm station buzzed, and this time Mureen ignored it.

I'd expected Rathe to decrease our ship's speed to merge, to try and keep a low profile, but we seemed to be speeding up. At our present vector, I thought we'd slice through the marked lanes—and anyone on 'em—like a driven knife.

Without a link to the pilot's output, it's hard to tell how fast you're going, but Da always told me to listen to the engines. Even when you can't hear, there's a vibration in the air around the deck plates—and right then I was pretty sure it wasn't my imagination telling me we were accelerating way too fast.

"We're running straight through?" Hells. I was impressed by Lieutenant Sai even if he had a death wish. "Okay... change the registry. Say we're a sanitation barge that's lost control."

Mureen shook her head. "We don't resemble a sanitation barge—or any local traffic. Davad did alter our registry today. We purchased a library of false codes from one of your kind, and we make good use of them... but... your planet believes in prayer?"

"Yeah." A bit too much, really.

She sat back down in her chair, gesturing until I did the same. "Say some now."

I didn't gauge we had time, and frankly, her weird fatalism was depressing. I heard my voice rise. "Look, do you know about fake registries? It doesn't matter what we look like. No bureaucrat is gonna look at the live feed for every barge on the town—" And then the obvious smacked my face. According to the map, we were the only barge-sized ship in sight. "Wait. Where's the rest of the traffic?"

Mureen gave me a death's-head grin. "The entire spaceway is in lockdown. A broadcast just came in across the beam about it." She tapped the earpiece in her starboard ear.

"Blessed stars, but planetary patrollers must've been pulling ships for a while for it to be this dead." I'd seen stuff like this before. Didn't like it. "They're culling so they can isolate what they don't recognize... Okay, they'll have realtime visuals—"

"Correct." She looked brittle and tiny, her mouth set in a furious line as her fingers moved over the controls. "You grasp the problem very well."

"So that's why Rathe's ramming us through—" Our ship jolted as we collapsed across several lanes of floating markers. I watched, stunned, as a hapless transport too slow to get out of our way seemed to give up on momentum and physics and careen to safety a second before we plowed past.

That shouldn't have been possible.

"Is that Davad—?" I didn't finish, because the same thing happened again, this time with two small ships coded red for Security Forces, both of 'em propelling up our y-axis to the traffic lane above—and again careening away unharmed.

Those ships were *heavy*, and the range—just how far away could a Kamen-lord be and do that? No wonder I'd been terrified of Davad when we met. Like my pilot's intuition had known. "Kamen magic can do all *this*?"

"More." She kept smiling as if to reassure me. "You're frightened."

"Of course I am! If he can do that, he can do anything. Can *you* do it, too?"

"Not as cleanly." Her head bobbed like she was being modest. "But those vessels were already in motion, and altering the trajectory of any object is easier than launching from a stillness." She shot me a sideways glance and I had the odd thought she found my discomfort amusing. "You're frightened of *Davad*... but not our pursuers?"

"Yes." Any sane person would be.

"He is trying to save lives, as well as save us. Did something—" She paused and seemed to gather herself before continuing. "Did something... happen when you were linked to *Bedalia*?"

"No." I became as small and blank as a gambler holding a pair of twos. "Why?"

"The bloodship was damaged in a crash," she told me. "But it is a good sign that she allowed you access. A very good sign."

"Less of one if they catch us—" I began, but she held up her hand.

"Wait. Incoming—" Her voice shifted, affecting a meek cadence I'd never heard before. "Yesss, I read you fine, sir. But we have orders from Naval Authority at Stockton Center—Yessir, I'll give a visual of our instructions... Incoming... Authorization code C-D37. House Singh approved... No, I'm afraid I can't hold for confirmation, our pilots are priming for the jump now... Why, yesss, perhaps it *was* premature, but we weren't expecting a planet-wide blockade in the middle of our time-sensitive mission—"

My eyes went to the map's display. We'd cleared the lanes, but three blinking red lines were now set to intersect our vector. I watched our screen simulacra swerve in a clever roll as I felt the ship shudder beneath my feet, torque bleeding through our dampeners. The lines followed our movements with uncanny precision. Kamen-controlled drones? Auto-targeted torpe-does?

I had a vivid imagination and nothing good in it. "Uh, Mureen—?"

Still speaking on her comm, she waved me quiet.

"What kind of torpedoes are those?" I pointed to the display. Didn't have to be a pilot to see an intersecting course, but being one gave me too good a line on our odds.

She waved me off again. "Yesss, we received your rerouted coordinates, but I'm afraid our pilots haven't responded. We may have a technical issue with the internal arrays... No! Please don't fire on us... A Circle? Mercy! We're a transport barge. Fugitive Kamen? On our ship? Heavens, I don't think so... No, I cannot hold for a Ken'ri Elder! This is House Singh business!"

Whoever was on the other end of that line wasn't buying a damned word of her sale. I glanced at the pilot's pods again, and then to the closed-off bow of the ship, where Davad was presumably performing miracles.

There's still too many, I thought. Visions of the defenses the Unity would have surrounding their Original Garden danced through my head like catastrophic checkpoints... EMP torpedoes to send us falling from the sky, shockmine nets if they didn't mind smearing us across the horizon. Railgun slugs that would cripple our engines if they wanted larger pieces. Boarding spikes filled with drones. Or worse, armored paratroopers blowing us open with exploding rounds—

"Stars-rot-it!" Mureen threw the earpiece on the ground and took off at a run toward the captain's quarters.

In the time it took me to blink, the area was open, and Davad met her halfway. "I know," he said as she practically hurtled into his arms, stopping just short. "I was trying to be subtle at first, but they've got a Circle tracing us now."

"They wanted *me* to hold for Ken'ri Elder Tiff." She lowered her voice, but I heard her quite clearly. "What if they know everything?"

"It won't matter." Davad leaned closer to her. "There's a thousand routes. Fleet won't know where to follow."

"You're sure?" She sounded tense.

"I'd have to be, wouldn't I?" He looked past her to me. I saw him swallow before setting that perfect jawline into the rictus of a grin.

Next to him, Mureen's profile looked carved from ice. "Then we go full Centauri."

"Full Centauri? You mean—" The princeling was still looking at me. I waved back as his face turned stony. "No," he said to her. "No. We can't."

"Not *that.*" Her voice gentled. "The other thing. Remember?"

"I thought you were joking." His mouth twitched. "We were drunk."

She shook her head. "No, *you* were drunk. Rathe was asleep. I was quite serious."

He frowned. "Can she manage it?"

"Standing right over here!" I called out. "Just ask."

Mureen shot me a distracted smile. "Polla studied acting. There was some kind of religious retreat the children of her planet attended every summer."

I didn't recall ever talking to her about Strangways. I assumed it must've happened in that lost time, shipboard.

• • • ● • ● • • • •

(Technically true.)

• • • ● • ● • • • •

Davad's voice dropped even softer. "Are you sure? It's not too late to claim I abducted you and surrender."

She scoffed. "They *should* thank us."

"They won't." He took her hands. "They won't ever thank us. We knew that going in."

Mureen looked down at their clasped fingers. She nodded. "Full Centauri, Dav." She brought his hand to her lips and kissed it, staring up at him. "*He* will know we're coming, and the Circles will know we've gone. None will be able to stop us."

He smiled. "You know, a large number will be too frightened to try."

"That is the crux of 'Full Centauri,'" she said.

When we'd first met, I'd thought Mureen had the profile of a saint. At that moment, she sounded like one. Driven. Holy. Maybe insane.

• • • • ● • ● • • • •

(You live in a house of glass yourself, so don't start.)

• • • • ● • ● • • • •

Trying to plot a contingency, I bent over and palmed the earpiece that Mureen had thrown on the floor, only to straighten and find 'em both staring at me like I'd grown wings and a tail. The communicator I'd nicked sparked in my hand, suddenly red-hot, forcing me to drop it again—while also introducing me to another application of kamn magic: making things get hot.

"Ow! I was gonna help!"

"You will, Pilot. Follow my instructions carefully. Sit... ah, there." Davad gestured at the formerly glassed-off section of the bow. As he stared, another set of walls retracted into the floor, revealing the *Escape*'s command chair, a rather ostentatious, low-backed piece of sculpture, plated in what looked like actual aurum, next to a low console gilded with the same.

I spied the telltale circle of an emergency escape pod hatch just beyond. What could they have in mind? Jettisoning me as a distraction? "Look, when I said I'd help, I didn't mean I'd die for you!"

"Don't be absurd. Put this on." Davad stripped off the white officer's coat he'd been wearing for some reason and tossed it at me. "Yours won't fit," he added to Mureen, who'd started to take off her own. "Too narrow in the shoulders."

"Do you want me to pretend the Commodore-General-Empress here went mad and I'm surrendering while you both run to the escape pods? Because you'll need to bail me out later." The Kamen-lord's coat fit me perfectly—almost. Absently, I tapped the seal that would tighten the fabric at the waist and straightened the epaulets.

"No." Mureen ignored my attempt at humor and shoved her hat unceremoniously upon my head. "Just speak into the communicator."

"As a Unity captain—?" I glanced down at the insignia on the coat. "What rank is two stars and a squiggly thing?" At that moment, the *Escape* bucked, and I was suddenly reminded that we had no time. A second later, our deckplates began rattling, a sound that'd make any rational person run to an escape pod immediately.

As I backed away in the direction they wanted me to go, I judged my odds of making it to an escape pod were poor.

"That Circle," Mureen said to Davad. "Which is it? Clarnesse?"

"Maybe. Or Ippa. Does it matter? They've got golem spears on our aft. They're using my own invention against us!"

"Have faith," Mureen said. She'd moved next to me, and her hand rested on my shoulder.

"What am I doing, exactly?" I asked as she shoved me into the aurum chair. "You haven't said."

"Speak into the flashing light." She spoke slowly as if to a child. "No introductions, Polla. Speak into that board and tell them to stop."

"She has to open it first—that blinking port, there, in the center," Davad added. Even in stone boots, he'd flanked me so silently that I nearly jumped out of my skin. "That one gives a line to High Command, not the fools chasing us. Don't wait for the admirals to talk. Just tell them to call off the attack by your... ah, by the order of House Illcord. Keep repeating that. House *Illcord*," he said firmly, glancing at Mureen. "It will work."

She nodded as the rattling of our ship's plates increased and Second flashed alarms across my eye. "Yes. Tell them we're on an important mission by House Illcord's orders. Repeat those lines until we jump to hyperspace. Buy us time. *Bluff*. You learned to bluff at your Smuggler's Academy, yes?"

"Yes," I said dully. I'd never felt less canny.

"They may try to confuse you." Davad's face had gone taunt with strain and Mureen looked almost white. I felt chilled. *Kamn magic*. My companions were using it right now out there in the black—but so were the folks chasing us. "Don't let them speak if you can help it, and... don't listen to anything they say."

"If you let them talk, they will lie to you," Mureen said. "Undoubtedly, they will lie to you. They may even call you names. Ignore them. Speak over them. Be assertive, Polla. Strong, like the warrior you are."

She'd moved to Davad's side and now she reached for his hand. "Did you feel that last wave? They're trying to force a mechanical failure, cripple us. I'm holding shields as best I can—"

"I know." His voice had gentled, staring at her. "You're so brave. And strong."

"I'm not a warrior." My words fell on empty air. "I'm a smuggler."

"Focus," Davad murmured. He stepped back, pulling her with him. "Keep those barriers. Rathe's got the course. We're almost through."

I adjusted the lapels of my coat and tugged the hat more firmly on my head. "House Illcord. Important mission. Stop attacking. That's all?"

Seemed thin.

Later, I would make time to ask questions about why I'd had to impersonate someone working for the very Terran house we were supposed to be on a quest to destroy—not that I'd ever get answers. But as those deadly red vectors approached and our ship shook, I knew we were out of time.

Kamn was doing this. Kamen-lords. A *Circle*.

I slid into the chair. It molded to my bim like an old friend. I thumbed on the holographic screen Davad had indicated and saw a row of unfamiliar faces projected before me. Four of them, so alike in expression that their features blurred.

· · · · ● · ● · · · ·

(Later, I realized I didn't notice age or gender or any other descriptive characteristics. Dressed in identical hats and collars, the four heads simply were. You would know who they were, no doubt. Me? I still don't care.)

· · · · ● · ● · · · ·

"*Ready to listen to reason yet, Arkan?*" one began. "*Surrender now, or we will have no choice but to... to—*" The expression on the first holographic face looked shocked, and the voice stuttered silent.

All four heads were staring. I recalled my haggard reflection in the mirror, but I'd look worse as a corpse in vacuum, and there was a high-pitched, mechanical keen in the air now, just within my hearing. Da could've said which vital system was failing. Me, I just knew it was bad.

"Call off your attack immediately!" I slammed my pilot's hand down upon the board for emphasis, hard enough that the resulting pain nearly made me bite my tongue. "House Illcord! Call off your attack!"

"*What—?*" To my astonishment, they looked shocked enough to listen. I had a millisecond's wonder about why Mureen hadn't gone with this House Illcord play herself before I waded back in.

"House Illcord is important! I'm telling you! Off!" I slammed my hand down again, a little softer this time.

"*You!*" one said.

"Illcord!" I repeated. The rattling had increased. Our deck now felt like we were in a groundquake. I noted from the corner of my eye that Davad and Mureen had fallen to their knees, holding each other's hands. A faint glow emitted from their bodies—or my eyes were playing tricks?

Second screamed errors on my retina, and for a second I swore I could feel the kamn myself, coalesced in a pool of power around us, and another pool of it outside our hull exerting force in the opposite direction. Our poor ship was caught like a bone between dogs. When I blinked, I swore I almost saw everything, outlined in an abstraction for which I had no voice.

"Mission! Important!" I cried.

"*You're dead!*" one fellow had the audacity to growl. Threatening *me*!

White-hot rage surged within my breast. I can't recall the precise words that came next (or perhaps I'm embarrassed), but it's possible my speech went something like:

"Silence! All of you." I rubbed my forehead, which had developed the odd ache again between my eyes. "Close your stinking maws, or I will call Nate to finish this himself. Kamen-lord Illcord Natoth? Do you think he would countenance this obstruction of his own ship on its *extremely* clandestine and costly mission for House Illcord? Because I do not think so. I think he would... not."

All four looked even more polearsed.

"*Traitor—*" another began.

"Calling me traitor? How dare you?" I felt offended they'd even suggest it, forgetting that in normal times I'd be even more offended if they thought I was loyal to their precious Unity.

An alarmed series of chimes began, as the four began tracing frantic symbols in front of them, communicating with stars only knew who. I crossed my arms and glared like I was Ma, and these commanders—or had Davad said admirals—were just some tweeners I'd caught drinking inside our best barn. "Well...?" I tapped my pilot's hand slowly. I might've emitted a cackle or two, just to show I was working with the bad guys. "Call off your nest of vultures. Now."

"*Done,*" said the first one, still gaping.

The forces shaking our ship stopped. I sank back down in my chair. I felt very strange.

"*We underestimated you,*" a brave one muttered. "*It seems.*"

"Indeed." I smiled, trying to make my voice drip ice like a Grass Priest in the confessional.

"*But,*" another whispered, "*this—*"

I raised a threatening hand. "I issued a plain and simple order, Ser! Did you not hear me?"

"The... *audacity of*—you—" The one on the far right cracked, his face twisting into a mask of hate. He turned to the others. "*Order the Circles to launch drones! Cripple that ship! They're heading for Telamon Jump—six dozen waypoints from there and beyond—*"

"Silence!" I intoned, slamming my hand down again. "I said silence! Are you refusing a direct order from House Illcord? Has it escaped your notice that I also speak for Illcord Natoth and the Living Fleet?"

"*Vadim!*" another shook their head. "*Scouts were spotted two days ago near the Canus Daya waypoint, within two jumps of Sol. He could be close. She isn't bluffing!*"

"Trust me, I am no one's... bluff." They teach acting during Strangways, and I fancied myself rather good at it. Now, I put those skills to use. "I am Captain Polla Ottrava from the planet Feldelroy. Acting on House Illcord's orders, and he ordered us to do this—thing, and..." My voice faltered, as pilot's intuition made me think I could actually hear the shift in our engines (impossible), the sound of small-arms fire crackling against our shields to weaken them (also impossible, even if we hadn't been in vacuum), and a sinking sensation in my guts that I suspected was someone trying to cripple our dampeners and force gravity to fail.

"Stop hitting my ship!" I thundered. "Now." I stood, and at that moment the ship rocked back and forth—nearly sending me sliding before I locked my pilot's hand onto the chair's arm. "If you continue your aggression, I shall make Nate send an invasion your way that will make the battle of NewKalnik look like a tea party for your orphaned children. I shall demand enough retribution to make Centauri seem like a light solar breeze—"

"*Standing down.*" It was the one who'd stood up to Vadim, before. Blinking at me with something like horror. "*Lady—*"

"Third Ranking Lieutenant Captain Polla Ottrava to you," I snarled. "Excellent. Good. Excellent work, Vadim. And... and... you, the Other *Vadim*, do not think I shall forget your insolence." I curled my lip exaggeratedly, really getting into the role now. "I guarantee this act will never be forgotten, and when I tell Nate about this infamous day—well..." I chuckled. "Let us say that if you *ever* fire a missile at me again, I will personally request that Nate shove it so far up your own orifice it never see daylight and then, after that I shall deal with y—"

The world rocked. My head spun, and suddenly I felt Second close, like warm breath across the top of my skin. The startled faces before me froze and then winked out. Rathe had made the jump to hyperspace.

[Error,] Second whispered

I let out a breath, and my legs wobbled. [Silly string?]

[Prime? Where are you?]

[Second! I'm here.] I closed my eyes, collapsing back into my seat on legs made once more of rubber. Across the void and in my head, I reached out and almost felt our fingers brush.

Then its voice again, plaintive and frightened. [Prime? Lia says you're right here, but why can't I find you?]

[I am here!] We were as close as we'd been since I'd woken up—both of us feeling the loss of being on the wrong side of a pilot's chair in hyperspace—but still so far away. [I'm right here, you silly bunch of wire.] I stroked my arm where the connections met.

[She says we're broken,] my navvy whispered. [Lia says we're broken. Like she is.]

[No.] Maybe it couldn't hear me, but I blinked to soothe it anyway. [We are not.]

[We are not,] Second echoed, whether because it heard me or we held the same thought, I will never know.

Outside of my control, my chair swiveled 'round, and I looked up to see a Kamen audience of two standing over me like justiciars. In the holographic spray from the command banks their expressions were wreathed in shadow. I swallowed hard. "Look, I know I went a bit out the airlock there. Just... I didn't know any other names from House Illcord besides *Nate*, and they were threatening me!"

"You were fine." To my astonishment, Davad closed the gap between us and embraced me, pulling me out of my seat and squeezing hard enough that I thought I heard my ribs creak. I boggled as his triumphant smile emerged to blind me with its splendor. "*Better* than fine, Pilot. Catastrophic."

"Hey!" I pulled back.

"You were terrible," he choked out. It took me a few seconds more to realize he was shaking with laughter, and not rage. Behind him, Mureen was wiping her eyes, but her expression made those tears look like mirth. "Truly."

"Was it too much?"

Mureen broke into her own high-pitched laugh, shaking her head. "No."

"We're not actually working for Illcord, are we? I don't care if we are..."

Mureen wiped her eyes. "We are most definitely not working for House Illcord, and certainly not for Nate."

Davad seemed to have developed a case of the hiccups. "But Unity Command will think we are. And if they think the rest of Illcord works for Nate... that should delight Father... And when a recording of that speech leaks, as it inevitably will... *Nate*..." Davad shook his head. A wicked grin I'd never seen the like of before stole over his face. "Dear Nate will have no idea what to expect." He stepped forward and planted a kiss on my forehead, right between the eyes. "You are a kamn touched miracle, Pilot."

"I told you, Dav." Mureen beamed.

I pushed the princeling away, as he looked in danger of hugging me again. "Kinda familiar for someone you didn't want to kiss this morning." Had it only been that morning? It felt like a century ago.

He scoffed, stepping back. "This morning you were a stranger." I suspected his easy grin could melt stone. "Now you're one of us."

Oh, you, I thought. Something twisted in my chest. Not desire—not even desire's drunk second cousin—but the feeling held an intensity of emotion that still made my eyes prick. "Okay, Davey, or is it Dav, now..." I meant to use the pet name Mureen did as a joke, but the word made my voice crack. "Dee," I tried again. "Okay, Dee."

His easy grin froze. "Where did you hear that?"

"Dee? From Mureen. Just now. Do you prefer Davey?"

"No." Somehow he made that short word echo.

Behind us, Mureen was still snickering. I don't think she'd noticed our last exchange. "Oh, I think you make a lovely couple—"

We both turned at the same time. I laughed to break the ice. "I'd rather suck a waste tube."

"The pilot and I agree," Davad added. Whatever had shaken him, he recovered quickly. "Mureen. You too were magnificent." He brought her hand to his lips, staring deep into her eyes. "A goddess. The way you raised our shields against the Circle—"

"Full Centauri, Dav. No coming back now." And then Mureen went into his arms, pushing him against the wall with an urgency I'd have never expected from her. He said something back, low and husky and wild, and I thought of Ma and how this was *exactly* how Kamen-lords behaved on every episode of her favorite show.

I turned to give them privacy. Spent a few minutes blinking, trying to get Second to speak again—but in vain. Finally, the quiet was too much. "What now?" I said to thin air. I looked back to see if they were done with that passionate embrace and felt my face heat. They were... not. After fifteen seconds of watching the two of 'em reenact a morality play about star-crossed lovers chained together until the end of time (by their lips), I averted my gaze to stare at Lieutenant Navigator Rathe Sai's pod, instead.

Usually, a comms officer or an apprentice pilot would set up a link so we could reach him in the dreaming. But there'd been no time. Rathe had been alone for this entire near-death experience—just him and Sexy.

I thought about those fifty thousand jumps and wondered if he'd noticed. I stared at his silhouette and tried to ignore the rustling noises behind me. To the Kamen-lords' credit, they were pretty quiet, but I had no idea if we were five hours out or five days. Hell, for all I knew, the dog could've taken Rathe to the deepriver and I was staring at his mindless shell. The readings blinked green on the side of his chair, but that didn't have to mean anything.

I perched on the pod next to his. The odd pain between my eyes had started up again. "How long does it usually take you to finish? And how long is this jump?" I called out. Silence. I glanced at the navchart projected over our heads and noted no one had actually bothered to note our course. Where we were going was all in Rathe's head.

Criminally dangerous... but, of course, we were criminals.

I thought I saw a shadow move out of the corner of my eye. Craned my head around. Nothing. I tugged my hair as if that would make it longer. I mourned my lost eyebrows and wondered what Ma would think of me now. I heard the walls move up behind me, giving my Kamen companions a private bower for their carnal acquaintance, with eight plates of military-grade clear between them and the black.

I raised my hand in a backward salute. "Take all the time you need."

There was a long pause, and then a speaker crackled. "You could pick out a set of quarters, Polla," Mureen began brightly. "If you like. Rathe's are in the Blue Wing. Two flights down."

"Thanks!" I called out.

I had so many questions. Questions best answered not by selecting my own bunk next to Rathe's, however convenient, charming, and all-too-suspiciously symmetrical that might seem.

No. Questions to be answered with a lockpick and a prayer.

Chapter 14 * Schooled

Once I started looking into the conspiracy, I fell into a wormhole. I was braindeep in Kamen-lords, reading everything about 'em that I could find, even those Grass Priest pamphlets that claimed a kamn touched soul would lead the bloodship invasion of Feldelroy, the one prophesied in the *Twenty Books of Revelations*.

When you saw those pamphlets, you joked that I'd finally gotten religion. Bene help me, Sam, in a way I had.

The Pilot Guild makes us swear loyalty to our Guild reps first, employers second. They don't recognize marriage, which makes spouses, at best, a far third. I'd learned Cousin Beya was a wanted war criminal. I'd learned Mureen was on the *Unity's Most Wanted* list—and on our wedding day, Wade told me that Second's removal was "under formal review, pending a terrorist investigation." I wasn't even allowed to tell Da, and him a gelded pilot, with his own connections.

But I should've told you. I told you about Pilot Heaven on our honeymoon—cried on that windswept beach for the reward my poor dead Second would never see.

I should've told you everything from the start, Sam. Not like I hadn't broken oaths before.

$$\cdot \ \cdot \ \cdot \ \bullet \ \cdot \ \bullet \ \cdot \ \cdot$$

(You're the expert:
How long does it take two Kamen-lords in the full flush of their health and beauty to realize their unrequited attraction was, in fact, 'quited all along?

At least one year.
How long does it take them to consummate that attraction?
Less time than I liked.)

• • • • • • • • • •

I located Davad's sleeping quarters (unimaginatively at the prow of the ship, one deck below the command center—first place I looked) and nearly sent myself back to heaven trying to short out the lock without Second. Just when I was about to give up, the door cracked open enough for me to squeeze inside. I glanced around, belatedly thinking a security cam might've recorded my incompetence. Saw nothing.

My sack of jewelry was set upon a night table. I reclaimed it.

Finding nothing else on my first sweep was profoundly disappointing. Davad's room contained no secret data screen with a galactic wideband unit—in fact, no data terminal at all, not even one for prerecorded entertainment. He had no interesting weapons, no stacks of currency or codes for mysterious bank accounts. Dozens of garments, although I should say costumes. Barbaric Terran finery in his wardrobe, with nothing but expensive lint in all of the pockets. One pair of normal shoes, proving that the stone ones were just for showing off. A battered copy of an agricultural almanac, of all things, tucked into one of the shoes. I thumbed through it and dislodged a small packet of seeds. *For Dee*, the inscription read. *Our First Creation*. Some sentimental trinket, I thought, so I put it back.

Under the mattress, I found a half-full bottle of five-hundred-year-old whiskey with a label from the failed Mars orbital. Worth a small ship... if genuine. Took a swig to check, decided it wasn't, and so I reached to return it. The bottle clanked on something.

My freehand closed over what felt like a hard rod, roughly phallus sized. I began to snigger—until I brought the stone thing out to the light.

A stone knife balanced perfectly in my hand. One tip was honed to a diamond point. I touched it, and immediately yelped. I'd cut myself, which was even more disturbing when I held the weapon up and realized, in addition to my blood, the... thing... the *spike*... held an unmistakable brownish stain from a previous use.

I didn't like holding it. The response crept from some animal corner of my brain, made my navhand shake, but for some reason, my fingers 'round the hilt didn't budge. I bent down to put it back, lifting the mattress, and came across its twin.

I pulled the second one out without thinking, and then I was holding both, one in each hand. The second dagger had a larger bore and was stained further, as if its bite had been deeper, nearly to its narrow hilt. It was shaped differently, more violently, somehow. Less a knife than a stake.

No mistaking that brown stain.

I recalled the slaughterhouse where Ma used to drive our cattle, back when she kept a full herd. That same color, soaked into its concrete floor, that smell of iron and rot and an animal's fear. I recalled Da dressing a trawler deer in our hunter's blind, and me trying not to be sick.

I started shaking.

I slipped the first knife in my pocket and put the second, the larger one, back beneath the mattress. I scarcely knew what I was doing. The day thus far had been an overload of shocks. Instead of questioning why I'd just pocketed someone's filthy dagger, my mind kept stuttering excuses as to why Davad would own two bloodstained knives in the first place.

Maybe this wasn't as bad as it looked.

He'd probably killed someone. He was a Terran princeling, and they did that. He was a war veteran, too—and people died in wars. But I'd worked for murderers before. And if the princeling were planning to kill me, wouldn't he have done it already?

Maybe these weapons weren't even his: perhaps they were Aemercy war trophies he'd taken as prizes.

But if that were the case, wouldn't he have cleaned them? What kind of freak kept old bloody knives under their bed?

Kamen freak, my thoughts whispered. *A Kamen freak who can push ships out of the way with his mind, and has threatened you, more than once—*

I shivered, suddenly freezing.

Maybe the spikes had belonged to the guy who'd lived in this cabin before. Maybe the princeling didn't know they were here.

But I was truly shaken, in a way that seemed disproportionate to my smuggler's brain. So what if Davad collected used murder weapons? Why should I care?

[Second?] I reached out for comfort, a cry in the dark.

No response.

I glanced at the door, feeling like someone—or something—was hovering there, just out of reach.

Nerves, I thought. I refused to have a guilty conscience. I wasn't the one hiding murder weapons under my bed! But those nerves sent me to the lav, which was dismayingly basic, with a hole in the floor and another in the wall. Also, I noted, with some irritation, a *boma fiday mirror* bolted precisely to the wall, with a neat shelf below that held a tube of facial delip, and a tooth wand.

My hollow-cheeked ghost blinked back back at me. I bared my teeth and didn't recognize myself. My hairless mien looked lean and feral, practically dangerous. Cold comfort, swimming with Kamen-lord fugitives so far out of my depth.

I was just getting around to tapping the walls for loose panels when my Kamen-lord employers finally appeared. Mureen's short hair was disheveled, which gave her a ruffian's beauty, and Davad looked immaculate, which figured.

"Trespassing?" the princeling deadpanned.

"Mureen told me to pick quarters." I shrugged. "But I don't like these. The door doesn't lock."

He raised one enviable eyebrow. "To be fair, it did lock this morning."

"I only came to retrieve my jewels." From the corner of my eye, I watched Mureen cross the room and sit primly on the bed. Davad didn't budge and was now blocking the doorway.

I looked into his silvery eyes and tried not to flinch.

He blinked coolly back. Silence passed between us. "You're bleeding," he noted finally. "Your hand."

I raised my freehand and saw it was true. The place where I'd pricked myself earlier had bled a surprising amount. Glancing down, I noticed I'd left a bloody handprint on my flightsuit too, which faded even as I watched, the fabric being self-cleaning.

"Oh, that?" I feigned surprise. "That's nothing."

Another long silence came and I heard myself take an uneven breath. I knew it was completely irrational for me to be frightened. The princeling still thought he needed me, and I'd committed no crime.

· · · ● · ● · · ·

(Regarding the knife I'd stolen: on Feldelroy, absconding with an object that's been used for murder is considered a public service. Disarming a killer is always good civics.)

· · · ● · ● · · ·

"You must have questions, Pilot," Davad said finally. "You're not dim-witted." From her perch on the mattress, Mureen gave me a kind smile.

I had too many. They threatened to bubble out of me like lava and take down everything, destroy this fragile peace, and possibly my own sanity.

My voice trembled. "Why does the Unity want you dead? If you're trying to kill Illcord Natoth and the Unity's at war with him, wouldn't that make you on the Unity's side?"

"Ideally, yes." Mureen plucked at the fabric of one of her sleeves. "But wars are rarely so simple as to have only two sides."

Davad shot her an approving glance. "Nate still has allies left on Earth. Undoubtedly some within House Illcord, although Father could never prove it."

"And his allies want you dead, too?"

"Everyone wants *me* dead." He shrugged. "Count yourself fortunate not to be in the same position." The princeling joined Mureen on the bed with a careless shrug, gesturing at the room's only chair as if I should sit.

I folded my arms instead.

Mureen began rubbing his back. "He chose this, you know. Had Davad only waited for his trial, he would have received a full pardon."

His voice darkened. "I would give myself a Kamen execution before I took a pardon for what I did."

I tried not to roll my eyes. Should I be insulted to be too innocent for a kill list? Should I feel sorry for Davad, who'd turned down a pardon to stay on one? "That's one hell of a way to live."

He reached for Mureen's hand. "Surely, in your line of work, you've encountered other desperate characters? Smuggled persons as well as goods between jurisdictions?"

In my line of work, I'd learned you didn't have to be on a kill list to be a desperate character. Ken'ri Arkan Davad was so beyond desperate that I couldn't wrap my head around what he was. "None with a Kamen Circle and the Unity Fleet chasing them."

"More than one Circle." Mureen smirked like she was proud of it. "By now."

"They won't catch us." Davad's sudden grin would make angels weep.

"Then what's the hovercrash about Illcord Natoth?" I asked. "You Terrans fight all the time. Why's this different?"

"The 'hovercrash' is that Nate has the krov," he said. "We've told you enough already."

Mureen shook her head. "Dav, Polla proved herself today. She's earned the right to be curious."

"Has she?" The princeling's mouth twitched. "The stakes are high enough to burn the stars, Pilot. You'll see for yourself when we reach Carolina Station."

I was getting tired of his games. "You know your play's not that complicated? By making it look like we're working with House Illcord, you're making 'em seem like the real enemy of the other Houses. Why do we need to do anything at all? Let the rest of 12Fam tear 'em apart."

"Quite." Davad tapped one of his stone boots on the floor. My eyes were drawn to it. I realized the boot was bending in time with his foot, the stone itself temporarily molten, its grain shifting like watermarked silk with each step. He glanced at me again. "Except they can't get to Nate. Neither can Fleet. They can't find his planet."

"But you can?"

"Not precisely. I've been there, but it moves."

I stifled a laugh. Of course, I thought, the Kamen, not knowing science, wouldn't understand that all planets—indeed, everything in creation—*moved*. I'd deal with his ignorance later. "Then why not give 'em a rough location? Let your Unity Fleet look for it."

"Because the admirals would attempt a full-scale invasion. A bioweapon that feeds on energy surrounds the planet. Conventional assault would only make the krov stronger—" and before I could ask another question, he held up a hand to stop me. "And yes, I did try to convince Fleet Command to use a different tactic. For nearly half a year, I promised them coordinates that were as close as I could calculate. I warned them of the increasing krov threat, too, but being as I was already branded traitor"—he shrugged—"my testimony was considered... unreliable. Only the Old Man's intervention kept me from execution. It was he who arranged my pardons, contingent on... *terms*." He bit out that last word with such grim finality that I took an involuntary step back.

"Dav?" Mureen put her hand over his. "You're confusing her."

"You said she'd earned the right to know." He looked nearly as nettled by her as by me.

"Perhaps another time. I think it's been a long day and we're all exhausted." Mureen looked at me. "You look tired, Polla."

"I'm fine." Wasn't tired, but she was right about me being confused. "Who's the Old Man? One of the admirals?"

"*Father* is the Old Man. Our father." Davad looked at me. "But Mureen's right. There's no need to dredge up the past."

"Right..." I shifted on my feet. Shoved my hands in my flightsuit's pockets, and closed around a stolen stone shiv. *Our* father, he'd said. For some reason I recalled the painting of freckled twins in that tower and the room Teapot said I shouldn't see... and then my mind returned to the filthy stake, the one I gripped in my navhand. I had a sinking feeling that joining a war criminal's gang was going to prove detrimental to my long-term health. It also occurred to me that I'd just told some real whoppers to some high-placed Teran brass.

Worse, I realized, had I truly mentioned *my full name and home planet?*

Stars, I was pretty sure I had.

Sure, "Polla" was the second-most common name on Feldelroy, but it wouldn't take much to figure out which "Polla Ottrava" had last been seen with Terran traitors. Frag, I realized the Unity would have the *Ascendant*'s records. No doubt those admirals knew who I was already. And that would lead them...

Home, I thought bleakly. *Oh, Da will kill me if the Unity shows up on his doorstep. And Ma will be so disappointed—*

I realized Davad and Mureen were still looking expectant.

I forced a grin. "Sorry, missed that last bit... Second was talking... Is there any way I can get a message to my folks?"

"We're in hyperspace," Mureen said, like I didn't know how a quantum ansible worked. "And even when we emerge, the war has disrupted communications in Fringer space. But if you'd like, we may be able to arrange a courier."

"Letters would take too long!"

She gave me an apologetic shrug. "We'll have access to Arkan's network," Mureen said. "On a limited basis."

How? I thought. "Didn't House Arkan turn us in?"

She shrugged. "We're not certain. An alert was triggered from within the House security grid, but it appeared to be an equipment malfunction, or perhaps some failsafe we overlooked in our launch sequence, given the haste of departure. I suppose the events of the past few hours may seem chaotic to you—"

"To anyone!" But I recalled what Rathe had said about Second trying to get a distress call through House Arkan security walls—and decided to drop the subject.

Davad cleared his throat. "One bit of good news... the Old Man may not understand the krov threat, but he does want House Illcord destroyed. Your remarks to the Alta Admirals may have extended our credit with Father. Or not…" His mouth twitched, and I knew from his expression to expect another barb. "He does hate liars."

An unnatural cackle emerged from my throat. "Yet he loves you?"

His smile glinted. "By the way, I'm pleased you found the jewelry. I'd quite lost track of where I'd put it."

The bag had been lying in plain sight and the spike in my pocket was a weight I wished I'd never stolen.

"Why does your father hate House Illcord?" I asked. "Are they extra corrupt compared to the rest of your 12Fam?"

Davad's brow knit as his good humor faded. "Not really. It's… personal. I wish I could say I'm different than my father. That I'm like Mureen, doing all of this for the greater good… but I'm not. I never was."

"You are, too, Dav." Mureen looked at him with those midnight eyes and her sainted profile. Gazing at her, for a second I could've sworn harps sung.

"No." He shook his head. "My motives are selfish. Nate is of House Illcord… and so I damn them all. All of my Kamen training… and I'm still my father's son."

"What's the personal reason? He piss in your bed? Or were you two—?" I made a hand gesture representing an act you had to be married for at least five years to perform without witnesses back home.

He laughed sharply. "Personal means none of your business."

"Perhaps we've done enough for now," Mureen broke in.

I shook my head. "No, he asked if I had questions!" I jabbed a finger at him. "What happened to my eyebrows?"

"What?" The princeling's perfect mouth fell open.

"My eyebrows." I thought of his toilet mirror, wondering that he hadn't smashed it since 12Fam didn't use mirrors, and then my drowned rat face. "My eyebrows are missing."

"Oh, Polla! They should grow back," Mureen cut in, laughing a little. "Teapot had to use skin grafts on your face. But the follicles are fine—they will regrow."

"Not just my face," I muttered. *Skin grafts?*

"Your hair will return," she assured me. "Everywhere."

I rubbed my brow self-consciously. "And why does the ship hate you two?" The dagger weighed down my pocket like ballast on a deepriver run. "*Bedalia*, I mean. Why does she hate you?"

"She doesn't—" Mureen began too quickly.

I cut her off at the hyperlane. "Rathe says she does. He told me *Bedalia* bucked you out of the pilot's chair, Mureen. The ship hates both of you, Rathe said. Is it because of your Kamen powers?"

"You *know* why, I think," Davad said. "What did Sai tell you? I had eyes on *Bedalia*, but she scrambled my feed."

"He told me that you're a rat! Always spying on people!" I snapped.

"I never spy on *him*." He examined his nails, flicking off imaginary dust, and I suddenly wondered if he'd chosen that pose to give us—or maybe just Mureen—a gander at his extraordinary profile. "The lieutenant is an honest man, sometimes to a fault. I expect he told you about the leg. And about whose ship *Bedalia* was—"

"Dav?" Mureen's voice sharpened.

Rathe *had* said something about my leg. He'd asked if they'd told me about it. Of course, Davad's father was the one who'd mentioned it being replaced. They'd used my own stem line, the old man had said. Or stem cells?

Ma must've signed 'em out of storage, I thought. *Shipping to Terra must've cost a fortune.*

"Did you put a tracking device in my leg when you regrew it?" I asked. [Second! Scan for any foreign body—Second?]

My traitorous navvy remained as quiet as Ledas Starfire's stinking grave.

"No." Davad scoffed. "Why did you look under my mattress, Pilot?"

"Mattress?" Mureen laughed. "She was searching your room for valuables, no doubt. But what could she possibly find under your mattress? The whiskey?"

The princeling closed his eyes. The grooves around his mouth deepened, and for a sec I could see the old man he'd be if I didn't shove him out an airlock first—an echo of his father in those perfect features. All in the bitterness of his expression. "Can't you tell?"

Instead of lifting the mattress to look, like a normal person, Mureen's eyes unfocused. Then: "You *kept* them?"

"After we escaped, Rathe and I went inside the bloodship to assess the damage. *Bedalia* had already repaired the... grave. The techs had wiped the ship's banks to keep her quiescent, but they touched nothing else. I suppose the Unity considered the entire area a forensic scene for my planned tribunal." His eyes were blank, face a mask. "My gir was lying on the floor above the... place, where..."

Mureen sighed. "Oh. And then you took hers—from—"

"Yes." He took a shuddering breath.

"It doesn't matter. I think it's best if we leave more questions for another time." Mureen stood and walked over to me. "Give me the gir in your pocket, Polla. Please."

"The what?" I blinked to look innocent.

• • • • ● • ● • • • •

(As I was, not being a *princeling murderer*.)

• • • • ● • ● • • • •

"The gir," Davad snapped. "The stone weapon you found beneath my bed. The one in your pocket. It cut your hand."

I pulled it out of my pocket and passed it to Mureen. "I think your whiskey's counterfeit. I used to smuggle bottles like that, only when I was starting out. They were always counterfeit." My heart was beating too fast.

I had an odd feeling, like everything was hollow. *Bedalia's* pilot was dead. *Bedalia's* banks were wiped. But the ship still might sense something, the same way Second sensed me reaching out even when it couldn't hear me calling back. Or, I wondered, maybe Second was reaching, too, and I couldn't hear it?

I tried to listen, but only silence echoed in my skull.

"I stole the bottle from Father's private reserve." He shrugged, with a carelessness I knew to be feigned. "You could be right. The man never had any taste."

"Do you two want the room?" I stood. "Maybe there's time to have another screw before we jump out of hyperspace. How much time, exactly? Rathe said there's something for me to see. I wouldn't want to miss it."

"A few days, we think," he said tiredly. "Is there anything else?"

My voice felt too high-pitched. "Why are you going to kill Illcord Natoth? You said it was personal."

Davad's jaw tightened. "Haven't I said enough?"

I shook my head. "You were friends before. With Lee and Nate. Now you want to kill him. What changed?"

I'd surprised him. I could tell by the way those lines in his face softened. "He changed. They both did. Centauri was... excusable. I convinced myself Centauri was excusable, which was madness itself. But Nate had a way of making all of her schemes seem reasonable—even to her, I think. Without Nate, she'd have turned back long before Centauri, I think." A rueful expression crossed his face, and he gazed at me like we were the last two people alive. "I think she would have."

They. She. The truth was on the tip of my tongue. "You were friends with Illcord Natoth and Ledas Starfire." My brain finished the rest. *And then Starfire died. Just like Lia's pilot. And Davad just* happens *to have two daggers covered in blood that he just happened to pick up on our very own living ship.* I had to force my voice to stay breezy. "Guess you knew Lee pretty well."

"That wasn't enough to save her. I wanted to save her." The princeling paused. His voice wavered. "Are you sure you want to know what happened to Ledas Starfire, Pilot?"

I rolled my eyes, trying to ignore the funny feeling in my chest. "On Feldelroy, we always eat the apple. Snake's just another sin. One of the Twelve Original."

"Remarkable." He turned to Mureen. "She's spouting Fringer dogma at me! Like a trained parrot."

"Dav!" Mureen frowned. "Our Fringer pilot saved our lives."

"Tell me the rest of it." I barely recognized my own clipped tone for its high-pitched coldness. "You brought me into this, Kamen-lord. So tell me."

"Tell *you*?" Hindsight paints an eon's worth of regret in his voice. "My sister married Nate. Forsook our House. Renounced our name and betrayed our Circle. She took us all to war. And I followed. Even after Centauri, I followed... Nuala was supposed to be paradise." His face twisted. "Our *reward*."

"Why?" I thought of the tower and the painting. I'd thought the kids in that painting were brothers, but the piece was so stylized, and the kids so young, it scarcely mattered. One had gray eyes, the other green. I tried to remember what they looked like but couldn't, except for the freckles.

One held a sword. I couldn't recall which.

One could've been a girl, I supposed.

"We were trying to make a better galaxy," Davad said.

"How?" I stared at his perfect shoulders, his bowed head. My mouth was dry. The hair prickled on the back of my neck. I felt terrified, but more than that, I had to know. I had to know. "How were you going to make a better galaxy?"

"By eating your apple, Pilot." When the princeling looked up, his eyes were like riverstones. Cold and buried deep. "By using forbidden knowledge."

I raised my pilot's hand to my face, fingers cupped. I took an imaginary bite. Chewed. Took a breath. "And what was her name, this ruined sister of yours?"

His voice roughened. "Don't insult my intelligence. Or your own."

Twins, I thought. Growing up in that tower. Going to Glos. Then she'd met Nate. Somehow, they'd gone to war.

"Lee. Her name was Lee," I breathed. *Dee*, I thought. *Dee and Lee.* My vision blurred and I wiped my eyes. The fasteners on Davad's shirt were slightly askew—astonishing carelessness, for him. *Fastidious Dee, letting something like that slide,* I thought. I would've laughed out loud, but monsters aren't funny. "You called her Lee. And *Bedalia* was her living ship."

"Yes." His throat bobbed when he swallowed, his long neck was a vulnerability I hadn't noticed before.

The dagger had been so heavy in my pocket before he took it from me. "She must've trusted you, letting you in so close."

He nodded, lips twisting. "Of course."

"So you stabbed her." I kept my words even. "But there's two of those gir beneath your bed. Did she stab you back?"

"I think she tried." He exhaled. "She would have. I took hers from her. Then I stabbed her again."

I rubbed an itch above one of my nonexistent eyebrows. "You killed her. Then what?"

He shrugged. "I expected to die with her above NovyiKorogod. I knew the ship would react badly—and she did. I lost consciousness. I'm told the bloodship nearly killed me—I was quite badly burned. When they captured *Bedalia*, the Fleet saved my life." He drew a jagged breath. "Of course, I knew their ships would be there." He glanced at Mureen again. "I suppose I still held out some small hope."

She smiled back, sad and gentle as a dove.

NovyiKorogod was a one-spaceport town out in the Fringers, a little like Feldelroy. Unity patrols didn't go there. 'Koro didn't even have a tourist season. I knew it pretty well, because my cousin Sara and her family had emigrated there for the schools. If Feldelroy were a crumb in space, 'Koro was naught but a speck. "You knew the Unity would be there because you tipped 'em off?"

Mureen claimed Davad was a hero.

He was. He'd brought down a monster.

He'd killed his own blood.

"I told Father I would bring Lee. She and I had met in that system before."

"It was a set up?"

"I hoped for a better outcome." His eyes met mine again, silvery, lighter than his skin. In this light he looked blind. "I wanted my sister to help me kill Nate. She knew what he'd become."

I snorted. "Do 12Fam princelings not believe in divorce?"

That garnered me his faint approval. "They do not, in fact, but we Kamen aren't bound by 12Fam restrictions. Lee and Nate's union was all but dissolved. Lee was still herself, at least... physically. But Nate has not been human for quite some time. She agreed the situation was untenable, but not to my terms." He took another heavy breath. "Nor I to hers."

Twins, I thought. "So that's why there were two chairs."

"What?" He boggled. "Chairs?"

"In that dome. Two stone chairs. The one you carried me in and the other. Stuff behind your da in his bath was some kind of shrine? To Ledas?"

"Not just her. A collection for all of our departed. We were twins. Not in the... bodily way your Fringer planets define the term. But decanted on the same day, formed from the same branch. We looked alike. Both kamn gifted. Most Houses would be thrilled to have two Kamen, but Father was not. He lost two heirs the day we were tested. He had to commission another."

"Was that the..." I reached for a name, but it escaped me. "The one who was coming to use the estate? The one who had land rights?"

He raised an eyebrow. "Mortons Cindee? No. Mortons are a cadet branch. After us, Father's heir was named Peter. He died on Roe. I don't believe Lee ever knew he was there." His nervous chuckle sounded fake. "Actually, I have no idea who the official heir is now."

I was positive that wasn't true, but it wasn't my business. "Will you tell me why your sister blew up an entire star system?"

"Haven't you seen the broadcasts? Because she thought it was *right*." Davad kneaded his forehead. "Are we done, or is there one more question you'd like to ask?"

"Yeah. *Why* did she think wrecking an entire star system was right?" I could see from his expectant face that wasn't the question he wanted from me, but I had no other.

He exhaled. "You'd have to ask her. But you can't, can you, Pilot?"

"No." Not to mention, a genocidal maniac's reasons for murder weren't my problem.

Still, I felt a strange heaviness, which struck me as pointless. Knowing why Ledas Starfire made a supernova wouldn't bring Alpha Centauri's lost souls back.

Apologue 4 ✷ Death

Two ships hung in space above NovyiKorogod: one ship metal, one ship bone, tethered by an umbilical docking tube. Lee had to command Lia not to consume the metal and silicates that made up that tube, for her ship was starving and they'd parked on the dark side of the planet, hidden in shadow.

Nate had been correct about the risk of deepriver, and so *Bedalia* had navigated hyperspace solo through the black while Lee spent three days in one of the cramped cabins trying to read an oldbook about Mars settlements, and then one of Nate's old war diaries, sentimentally addressed to her. *Bedalia* wasn't happy, and her unease had spread to Lee's Petal as well, much to Lee's annoyance—an ire that was exacerbated by Nate's diary entries, which made their alliance with Fleet appear entirely too noble.

Now Lee leaned against one of *Bedalia*'s two piloting chairs, tracing her hand across the ridges that lined its surface. Normally the gesture would soothe both ship and master, but Lia's skin rippled beneath her fingers, skittish as a first-year Ken'ri.

There was the hiss of the airlock opening, brisk footsteps, and then another irritation arrived, dressed in cloth of gold and scarlet with a black leather cuirass and matching black boots. Lee saw that her twin wore Arkan colors, which told her everything.

"It's been too long," Dee's smile looked nervous.

She forced her voice pleasant. "Indeed it has. Have you finally chosen a side?"

"Good to see you, too." He gave an informal curtsy. "But this isn't a matter of sides, Lee. Father wants us both on Earth. He sent me with terms."

Amusing, that the Old Man thought his wishes were still relevant. "To atone for my crimes?"

Her brother's jaw worked. "He's offering a full pardon."

Her laugh felt like acid. "Impossible. The plebs need a show."

"Oh, Father's made one on spec. A public execution. I said I'd let you pick for both of us. Stones or hanging?"

Most murderers would never have the chance to witness their demise, let alone have options. Despite, or perhaps because of everything, Lee laughed harder. "How will he marry you off if you're dead, too?"

Her twin ignored the jab. "I saw test footage. The hanging's more convincing. Father's editors are terrible with blood spatter."

"Which piece of rock has the Old Man picked for my permanent exile?"

Dee brushed imaginary dust from one sleeve. "Minerva. Your ocean moon."

"You believe him?" Nearly an Earth year had passed since her brother left Nuala. Much could happen in a year. Another twenty of their former Company had gone to dirt. Her twin had grown his hair. It flopped like a cloud over his eyes.

He shrugged. "What do you think? He wants Nuala's location in return, of course."

Of course. A bargain Father knew she would never take. "I think you should come with me instead. Home to your *real* family."

Dee shook his head. "Look, you and I could leash him. Couldn't we? With your ships and your Crown?" He positively radiated sincerity. "It's a way to save the Faege."

She shook her head. "We don't need another House puppet." Nextel was hard enough to manage.

One of her twin's brows arched. "Oh? And how is dear Nate?"

Dee was reckless. Fencing like they were still children.

"Nate is perfect," she lied.

His lip curled. "The three of you must be very happy."

Trying to anger her did not make the tactic ineffective. Lee heard her own words sharpen. "Your former lover Aoife has shaped herself into something like an eel. I'm worried one of our fishers might catch her for supper."

He swallowed. "She always liked the water."

With kamn-enhanced senses, Lee could see her brother's ship next to *Bedalia.* A rich man's pleasure yacht, armored and expensive. Now, a cannon extended slowly from its dorsal plume like the legs of a barbed spider, swiveling to point at her ship.

"Nate is loyal to me," she added pointedly. *Probably. Like a mad dog.*

"Nate is lost," he replied. "A year ago, you told me that yourself. Now..." He made a disgusted face. "Have you seen a mirror lately?"

There was one in her cabin. Lee had looked at her face that morning. Unchanged. So much like Dee's... though she had always envied his more delicate nose. "I'm fine."

He shook his head. "You have flowers growing in your hair. And you're wearing rags."

"The flowers smell nice." Irrelevant, but Lee glanced down, noticing the white uniform she wore had stained black along its seams. Torn at the knees now with its leather-braced arm ripped halfway down the side. The suit hadn't been damaged three days ago. Lee would have noticed—wouldn't she? Hadn't the flightsuit been pressed and cleaned before departure? Hadn't she commanded someone—

Who? her mind mocked. *Who is left to do your laundry?* Her bare, freckled toes were dark with caked grime. She'd forgotten shoes.

[Alert!] Petal interrupted. [Neighboring ship charging plasma cannon. Lia requests we begin an evasive trajectory.]

"You actually stink, Lee." Her twin's delicate nose wrinkled as if they were six.

[Tell Lia to hold,] Lee instructed her navvy. "I do not."

Dee rolled his eyes.

The gir hung heavy in her pocket. In the stories Teapot told, one twin always died by another's hand. Those stories were lies, but Father had programmed their nursery android to tell them for a reason. Perhaps, Lee thought, for a time like this.

No doubt her twin saw his death in her face, just as she saw pity for her in his. He took a breath. "Look. Before... before anything... we were going to have lunch?"

"Of course." He'd come to kill her. And yet, Lee remembered when her brother had smashed every one of their toy spaceships because she cut her hand on one. For a moment, she doubted her own judgment. "*Could* I be safe on Earth?"

A smile thinned his mouth. "I'm not sure. Has Nate turned into a tree yet?"

"Worse." She felt the bleakness of her own grin. "He's grown hooves to impress a girl."

"I told you that woman was a mistake."

"Nate was in pain. The pain made him forget his humanity. Sheris... reminds him."

"Shouldn't you remind him?"

Only to Dee could Lee admit the truth. "Most of the time, I feel sick looking at him."

Her brother laughed. "Actual hooves? Like a centaur?"

"Only two. Pan, I think. Or maybe just a common faun."

"Not a common faun." He shook his head. "Nothing common about our dear Nate. Come to my ship? Or... I can have the food brought here, if you'd prefer." When she didn't respond, he continued. "Sharing a plate, Lee. No poison."

[Lia requests we raise shields,] Petal interrupted. [She doesn't like the look of that ship.]

Neither did Lee. [Raise them.]

Her brother's eyes flickered. He would sense the change in the kamn as the shields thickened over the bloodship's hide, just as Lee abruptly sensed the gir dagger in his right pocket, now sharpening to a razor point.

He still thinks he can win. Lee sighed. "The Circles won't take you back, but Father has. Did he promise you the Arkan seat if you bring me in?"

Dee scoffed. "Have you forgotten Father has an heir? Child of thirteen? Big for his age?"

Nik was nearly fifteen, but Lee felt nothing for the boy. "You should have watched over him instead of coming for me."

"His *parents* might have. But they chose a crusade against the Aemercy." Heat in his voice.

"You chose it too."

"I did." Her twin nodded. "More's the pity."

"Our Circle vowed to have none. Just like the Aemercy. Have you forgotten how Kaygaz used us?"

"I recall how Father called your bluff above Roe. You swore you'd back down if they agreed to disarm."

Too late. But she'd never admit it. The heart of a sun is a simple thing. Two suns make ending them even simpler, but it still takes time. A geomagnetic trick, making the work of ten billion star years happen in six Standard days. The theory of how to spark a supernova had kept the rebel Kamen Company engaged for months. Lee alone had possessed enough power—and the will to wield it.

"Father knew better than to cross me." Strangely, for an aberrant second, Lee remembered Nate and his ridiculous hooves.

Her brother sighed. "I know you didn't want to end them." His hand had slipped into his pocket.

"The Accord wouldn't have lasted a year. One or the other side would have found Nuala, too." Her words felt thin and cold. "Kaygaz was already in the right sector."

Scorn twisted his delicate features. "Well. You took care of *that.*" By his look, they'd finally passed the Rubicon. There would be no more talk of lunch.

Lee drew out the Crown. The alien metal vibrated beneath her fingers, strands brightening as her kamn awoke the energies within. Dee would never bring just one ship; there would be more waiting, either timed by jump points in hyperspace or concealed from her senses by the planet's bulk. Nate had been right: Father had gotten to Dee and this was always a trap.

But no trap laid by mortals can catch a god.

The Crown settled on her brow, its map of stars unfurling, dimming her brother's figure and their physical surroundings to motes in the cosmos. Lee heard her own voice echo like a celestial scream. "Because of me, a thousand worlds are safe."

He sounded tired. "Because of you, millions died in nine minutes. Put that away. I'm offering you Earth."

"Are you really?" Being a god on Nuala was tiresome. Being one on Earth, she thought, would be exhausting.

"Stars! I had a pardon, a real one. But I came back. I gave up everything for you."

"I know." She watched Dee's gaze shift to the viewscreen crudely bolted on *Bedalia*'s wall. Had he already commanded his crew to fire? Fool! She had the Crown. Now Lee drew on its strength. The viewscreen's image flickered with a blue haze and then sparked silent as her kamn crisped its circuits—not that either of them needed cameras to see beyond *Bedalia*'s hull.

"Did you get my letters?" He spoke fast, surely aware of his doom. "You never wrote back."

She'd discarded them like leaves. It had been Xeris, her secretary, who'd brought this invitation to her attention. "My couriers are very efficient."

"They'd have to be. No one's sure how you're still knocking off factories no matter how well they're hidden."

"I still have friends." Fewer every day. Picked off by Kamen operatives or gone to grass on Nuala. Everyone would go to grass eventually. Even her. "You were one, once."

"I never stopped being your brother." Dee wore House colors, black and red and gold like a painting of an old bishop.

No weapon on his ship could touch *Bedalia*'s shields. In the overlay, Lee saw the curve of NovyiKorogod beyond their ships. And then, stars. So many! Each the stuff of creation. Upon every living world, each life, fragile and precious, perfect and safe.

Safe—because of her.

"You're smiling like a madwoman," her brother continued. "And glowing. So I guess you've decided."

"I am sorry." Her twin should have ended his days on Nuala, growing roots in the sun. Almost absently, Lee sharpened the gir in her pocket. *The heart*, she thought. *Not the head.* Dee was stupidly vain. She would send his body to Father. The family could have their Remembrance, and then one golden feather for a hero beside her coward's white in a Martian crypt. Both would be lies. "I would have saved you."

He laughed and came closer. "For Nate to kill later? No. Have the decency to end me yourself."

"I'll make it quick." Her fingers closed on her gir, still in her pocket.

"Go on."

"I am." Did he think she would not?

Staring at his beloved face for the last time, Lee almost missed the warship that popped out of hyperspace. In another instant, manned fighters streamed from its bays by the hundreds. Sparks spread like fireflies to encircle *Bedalia*. Following after came Kamen-controlled golems, her brother's own creation. Their shape was originally inspired by the parachuting spiders Lee had thrown at Dee to make him scream—how old were they that summer?

Six. The last summer before Glos took them.

The Crown's overlay flared. Automatically, Petal began sorting its data.

[Sister?] Lee's ship interrupted, overriding protocol and buzzing through Petal's interface. [There is a big dead thing above us, and I do not like it!]

[I know. Hold.] Lee's vision splintered as vectors and probabilities diverged. Too much for a human mind. They threatened to overwhelm even the Crown's interface, but one does not need to see every water molecule to comprehend the tide. [Wait, Lia. More are coming.]

Another dreadnought popped out of hyperspace. Another Kamen Circle aboard. Two more, the same. *Fools.* With the Crown Lee had the strength of a thousand Kamen. And their ships were *metal.* She felt a brute grin part her lips as, in the cold of space, she felt that metal twist—

"I'm sorry, too," Dee whispered in her ear. Lost in stars, Lee almost missed the brush of his lips upon her brow.

At first, she barely felt the bright pain in her side, was startled by her body's sudden weakness. Her knees buckled. The pain grew sharp. Lia screamed in her mind; Petal, a weaker echo.

As children, they'd trained on Glos to miss vital organs with their weapons of stone... But in order to miss, they had learned to kill.

"End this!" His voice hissed raggedly in her ear. "Command *Bedalia* to turn to the sun, not the planet."

"You—" Her fingers scrabbled for her own gir. Beneath their feet, *Bedalia* bucked, diving for atmosphere as a stream of fighters gave chase. Bolts spattered harmlessly on Lia's hull, lightly, like spring rain. Lee realized their opponents weren't even firing live rounds.

Of course, she thought dimly. *They want my Crown.*

Dee plucked the gir from her fingers. She felt her body sag into his. "I'm here," he whispered. "I won't leave you."

Bedalia dove, and gravity failed. Orange curls enveloped her vision. His? Hers? Lee's hand tried to close on a weapon she no longer held, batting at her twin with clumsy fingers. Petal's alarms painted her retina, indexing her body's failure and the threats to their ship. Lee's vision blurred those readouts into a stream of red.

"I'm sorry," he repeated. She felt muscles bunch in his arm as he raised the weapon he'd taken from her, using it for the final blow. She heard his breath choke, his sob—

Light-years away, her Living Fleet woke: bulls trumpeting to rally the flock. With the Crown's amplification, their call deafened Lee's last seconds to insignificance; and in her ships' screams, both loud and fading, Lee realized she would never know, precisely, how her life had ended.

Chapter 15 * Horrified

Remember how we made Junior the old-fashioned way on that honeymoon? Alone under the stars and next to the fire. Thanks to Da's bribe, the Grass Priests had set up their chanting circle out of earshot. That was a good day, Sam.

. . . . ● . ● . . . .

The jump to Carolina Station took six days, three longer than projected, long enough for me to worry about Lieutenant Navigator Rathe Sai's well-being. Long enough for me to pick the lock to his bunk, too, which I regretted the moment I saw the smiling holographic faces of his friends and family, all tacked on a line above his bed. None of Rathe's pals looked like types who'd be low enough to pick locks and snoop in someone's room, making 'em all more upstanding than me.

The grinning kid standing alongside a relaxed-looking Lieutenant Sai in full dress whites looked old enough for me to figure Rathe had gotten him just out of secondaries, probably before he'd enlisted. Kid looked like a darker version of his da, although in one pic they were accompanied by a curvy brunette who had to be the ma. There were also pictures of Rathe with another black-haired woman, and with that pretty blond guy I might've kissed on Feldelroy, during the last evening of my normal life. Might've been my vivid imagination reading more into those smug grins, but I thought Rathe'd probably been doing all three of 'em (or none) before he took off with the Kamen-lords.

Not much middle ground with us pilots.

I found no weapons under Rathe's mattress, but he did have a saucy holo of the curvy brunette tucked there, wearing naught but shortos and a smile. I thought my rack was better (when I'd had my fighting weight), but hers wasn't bad.

I tucked the holo back.

In his closet, I found a decent-enough slug gun tucked in a pair of spare work boots next to a funny pistol, which seemed to be carved from wood.

The slug gun was charged and in immaculate condition. He'd probably want me to have it, I told myself. For my own protection, caught on a ship with murderers and thieves. I carried that sluggo for a good day and a half, still trying to shake the feeling someone was watching me, before guilt made me put it back.

My wardrobe had been stored in the room next to Rathe's. Although flightsuits are self-cleaning, I'd been supplied with a dozen, and then twice as many pairs of shoes, but naught else. The elaborate costumes fit for princelings had all been left on Earff, apparently.

Mureen moved in with Davad, which made searching her ascetic bunk a breeze. The door wasn't even locked. She had a collection of Terran books that might've been priceless or forgeries—all set with a fixative that made their yellowed pages indestructible as armor. Poetry, mostly, which surprised me. One poem that she'd marked with a piece of ribbon still sticks in my mind, although I can't remember the author's name or origin.

> *I was angry with my friend;*
> *I told my wrath, my wrath did end.*
> *I was angry with my foe:*
> *I told it not, my wrath did grow.*
> *And I watered it with fears,*
> *Night & morning with my tears:*
> *And I sunned it with smiles*
> *And with soft deceitful wiles...*

Then something about an apple tree and poisoning your enemies. Surprising sentiment for someone as mild-mannered as Mureen. I thought at the time that I hardly knew her at all.

I also found a torn, half-written note tucked into another book.

> *Dearest Beloved, I am sorry. But sometimes a cause takes precedence over the heart. If I succeed, you will be safe and never know how terribly I betrayed you—*

She'd left the note unfinished, like Mureen had lost her nerve about whatever she'd planned to tell Davad. I thumbed through pages looking for more. Ended up reading half of it. The tale of some poor demon who'd been tricked into moving to a strange land so two scheming ladies could steal his treasure or the dirt from his grave. It was written as a series of letters.

· · · ● · ● · ● · ·

(Preflight accounts of gods have always confused me. It's difficult to distinguish fiction from metaphor or satire. Even the Grass Priests struggle to do that, I think.)

* * * * * * * * * *

The rest of Mureen's collection was no better, dealing mostly with indecipherable ancient philosophers who made my eyes cross. I also found that bloodstained poniard Mureen had taken from me, washed spotlessly clean and tucked under her mattress.

Unlike with Rathe's gun, I didn't feel guilty when I stole it back.

Kamen powers being what they were, my employers must've known I'd taken it, but she and Davad never said a thing.

My quarters were small, with an entertainment display whose electronic guts had been removed. I wished I had pictures of Ma and Da for the walls. The feeling of being watched hadn't left, although I stopped looking over my shoulder after the second or third day from sheer stubbornness.

My companions seemed to get a fair amount of sex done, judging by the time they spent alone in his bunk, but they also spent a lot of time on the bridge speaking in hushed voices that stopped whenever I came in. Mureen insisted we meet for daily workouts. She also insisted we all take meals together. Her dogged determination to make me and Davad get along soured the pleasure I might've taken from the Unity's astonishingly good meal-paks.

The princeling himself just kept brooding and glowering while I kept snarling back. I think I called him a stinking murderer at least six times in the first two days of our journey, and every time he granted me another dead-eyed stare. Once he even yawned. Something about his demeanor made me think about how oysters make pearls—the irritant shoved between their skin keeps them constantly trying to smooth things over. Talking to the man who both terrified and enraged me made me feel a lot like an oyster would, I reckoned… if oysters were sentient and not just gene-modded crustaceans that corpro-engineers used to terraform polluted worlds.

To get away from the loving couple, all I had left was *Bedalia*, the ship I was supposed to fly. She'd already kicked me out once, and now that I knew the truth about her master, I didn't want to face her alone. Hard to reconcile Lia's laughing face with Ledas-stinking-Starfire, the destroyer of worlds.

But I did try. I tried twice. The first time, I stood for five minutes in front of her locked door, calling her name. Nothing. I slunk away like a failed lover, or an outcast refugee. The second time, I leaned against the door's cold metal surface. Inhaled that smell of hers, the mix of brine and space. Before I could speak, the airlock opened, so quickly I almost fell inside.

There were reminders of Rathe everywhere in *Bedalia*'s warren of rooms: half-finished mechanical odds and ends secured with cables for liftoff, and carefully packed supplies tucked in every corner. An extra box of exastim stashed beneath one of the bunks.

A mysterious, unopenable crate shoved in with the food supplies.

It was the size of a small child and coded "Rations, 2wk" in Rathe's handwriting, but unlike "Rations, 1wk" and "Rat., 3wk," the mysterious crate wouldn't open. I think I laughed out loud. I might've even clapped my hands together with glee and spent at least twenty minutes trying to open the clever thing, tapping the sides for a hidden lock, experimenting with various vocal commands—before I was rudely interrupted.

"Ahem," a familiar Terran voice clipped.

I looked up to see Davad standing in the doorway. "Didn't realize you were allowed back on this ship..." I began sweetly. "After the last murder."

His mouth quirked. "Trust me..." The princeling brushed imaginary dirt from his gilded sleeve. "There is nothing in that crate you'd want."

In my excitement, I forgot to be indignant. "You know what this is?"

"A thing that is not yours. Do we need to have another conversation about personal property?"

I was too excited to think of a comeback. "Where'd you get a Titan X-K anyway? Full chameleon plates, die-cast... I can't even find a seam!"

His brow knit as if he were astonished I'd mastered human speech. "*What?*"

"This is an X-K crate. Da had one of the X-Ls... used to fill it with liberated tigron fangs. Once he stuck a live quez in there—special commission—that was before they went extinct. I was a babe, but he told me about it..." I trailed off, noticing with some astonishment that the princeling's mouth now gaped open like an endangered pufferfish.

"You are talking about the container? Not the contents?"

"Yeah. Whatever's inside can't be cheap, but these chameleon panels?" I patted the top of it. "I'd sell my starboard teat for one. See how this crate looks like all the others?" I nodded at the other two I'd opened, which did contain rations. "Port sensors won't pick up anything except what's in the other crates. And the lock's set personal by the owner... no two alike. It's worth a fortune!"

"The crate was expensive, yes," he allowed. "I wasn't privy to Rathe's decision-making, only his receipts."

"Is this his payment for our job?"

"Rathe said it was needed."

"Can I have it when the job's done?"

"Perhaps you can purchase your own with the fortune I'll provide."

At that moment, I became convinced the box held Bene Dix's fabled Crown. The box was big enough to fit forty crowns. Perhaps there were more priceless artifacts inside. The File Broom, or Ashagre's piece of the True Cross, or the First Spindle... or the last.

"Hadn't pegged your crew for smugglers," I said. (Which meant they were either Centauri at it or exceptional.)

Davad shrugged. "You could ask Lieutenant Sai, but then you'd have to admit you've been going through his things."

"I would not! Most of his things aren't here—they're in his rooms."

"You're right." A smile flitted across his lips. "I might be forced to mention you broke into his rooms... By the way, you're very good with locks. Unnaturally good, some might say—"

. . . . ● . ● . . . .

(Was I?)

. . . . ● . ● . . . .

I waggled my navhand. "Just takes a little creativity with the wiring, but yes, I *am* good with locks. And you're very good at *spying*. How are you spying on me?"

He sniffed. "Mureen thinks you should spend more time with *Bedalia*. She's delighted you're here." Davad didn't sound delighted. I thought his tone implied *Bedalia* would be better off spending time with the *Escape*'s sewage reprocessing unit than the likes of me.

I countered: "How'd you get in? Didn't you say the ship tried to kill you before?"

"Have you tried the pilot's chair again?" Not answering my question like I wasn't answering his.

"Of course not!" Did my Kamen-lords truly not know how unsafe it was, entering a stranger's dreaming in hyperspace? I barely knew Rathe.

"Why not?" His voice was dry. He had to know, I thought, with all that time spent with pilots in the war.

I rolled my eyes. "Have you screwed a black hole lately?"

"Hrm." The Kamen-lord cleared his throat. "Mureen would prefer you take this time to establish a rapport with the ship. You could use the console to communicate, if you prefer not to use the chair. Mureen would see you try. Today." He examined his spotless nails. "She requested I pass on that instruction."

I was starting to think I'd learned enough of this man to note the choice of words. "Now that you have, what's your advice?"

A soft grin crept across his face, transforming it. He looked at me. "Don't."

I rolled my eyes. "Don't slot in?"

"Don't befriend *Bedalia*."

"Because she tried to kill you?"

He shook his head. "Because it isn't necessary. She'll fly for you, when the time comes."

"You sound sure."

"She is your ship." He paused, and I could tell by his expression he wanted me to ask why he thought it was that simple, or maybe ask again what was in that locked crate of Rathe's, or how he'd gotten in past *Bedalia*'s locked door—

"That's all?" I wanted answers, but I was sick of Kamen games.

"Is it?" A hint of teasing in his tone.

The door was metal. He'd probably just forced it open. For some reason,

I didn't like the thought of that. "You've obviously got more to say."

His eyes narrowed. I was already learning to recognize this, his lecturing tone. "I know a bit about bloodships. More than the others."

"So do I," I shot back. "On Feldelroy, the Priests say they have souls."

"Not human ones. The ship may seem human in your dreaming. Nate can seem human, too. But that symbiote on your arm has more humanity than either of them."

"Not planning on meeting *Nate*, so I don't care. When will we get to Carolina Station?"

"Coming from Earth took us three days before."

Had I known they'd done this before? Had I known why? Wasn't gonna ask and give him the satisfaction of seeing me confused. "It's been four now."

Davad gave an exasperated sigh. "Then your guess is as good as mine."

• • • ● • ● • • • •

(Getting my childhood pony, Dancer, haltered was easy, but the first time I tightened her lead line, she pulled me half across the paddock. The second time I kept the rope loose, and she circled, tangling my feet until I tripped. Third time, I fed the line out slow, giving her just enough so she had her distance. When she came closer, I reined the rope in just as delicate, and there we had it: balanced and in accord.

My recount of the tale makes me sound like a pony-training savant, but in truth, there were more than three times. There were tears, and scrapes, and lectures from Ma about how I was doing it wrong, and the back end of my naughty pony galloping away, the saucy swivel of her ears, the twist of her spotted neck as she looked back, that curious huff she made when she came 'round to me again. Her hay-scented breath when her nose ruffled my hair as I lay there kicking dirt and wondering how I'd done it wrong.

It occurs to me now that Davad danced me on a similar lead to that pony. Circling me forward, then reeling me back with the same lack of grace I'd shown poor Dancer—at least at first. He would improve—and I grow more trusting—but at the start there were many times when he'd turn and vanish, leaving me ruffled and alone in a crowded cargo bay, wondering when the nice human would come back with another treat.

I've seen how you treated your pets, so I know you understand.)

• • • ● • ● • • • •

I spent the rest of that day reading in Mureen's quarters—deliberately trespassing, just to show those smirking Kamen-lords that they weren't the lords of me.

There are, of course, no connections to ansibles in hyperspace, and so no live newsfeeds on any ship. Even the great vessels of the Unity Fleet rely on primitive semaphore blasts to redirect courses mid-flight, or send warning. But I couldn't even find an old feed downloaded on the *Escape*, which was odd, considering Rathe had lived on her for nearly a year. Did he not care about the outside?

Another bad sign for the river.

That thought made me rush to the bridge and fidget over his unconscious silhouette... but there was nothing I could do. The *Escape* had fancy Unity tech keeping him clean and fed—nothing like the bad old days with my first leased ship, where I navigated in a diaper and with a prayer, attached to an electrolyte drip. There was even a readout on the side of Rathe's coffin-shaped chair where I could check the lights that tracked his vitals, thankfully all blinking a reassuring green.

"Plug in and say hello if you're so concerned," Davad said when he caught me hovering on the fifth day of our jump. "Would certainly make monitoring you easier."

I knew he was baiting me, but I grabbed the worm anyway. "Gonna tell me how you're spying?"

"If I told you, the method would be less effective." He rested his long arms atop the curve of Rathe's chair and leaned over. "We're not really spying, you know. Merely monitoring your health."

I'd been on my knees, checking Rathe's readout. Now I stood. "If you're worried about my health, you wouldn't tell me to slot into a strange ship in the middle of hyperspace."

"Why not?" He raised an eyebrow as if his pilot's scars made him some kind of expert.

"Lots of reasons. Starting with, it's bad manners." Also impossible without a reliable navigator, which reminded me—

[Second?] I blinked.

[Error,] it shot back as I blinked again to reboot, over and over, until my vision tingled with spots.

Meanwhile, he began another lecture. "I saw someone go under in hyperspace. We were in the middle of an assault mission, boarding a hostile ship." His insolent grin made me want to punch him—or flee. "We breached the bulkhead just before they made the leap. At the time, Aemercy pilots had a tendency to send their ships into suns if they thought they were being boarded... so to secure the *Decameron*, we sent one of our pilots into their dreaming—"

"Not interested in your stories." Especially one that broke every Guild rule in the book. No Guild pilot I'd ever heard of would take a risk like that. Not only was slotting into someone else's dreaming uninvited bad manners, it was dangerous. If they didn't know you, or didn't recognize you—

At the least you risked permanent brain damage. If it went really bad, you could fry their cortex, too.

"Rathe's a good man," he continued. "I'm sure he wouldn't mind if you went in and said hello."

I boggled. "You don't break into someone's dreaming. Some things are private."

"Yes." The Kamen-lord stood.

I'd found my door's lock broken the second day after I moved into my room, with the threads I'd stretched across the doorframe still undisturbed. Couldn't tell if Davad had circumvented 'em or broken the lock as its own lesson.

You have nothing, he'd said back on Earff.

Now, under his obstinate, terrifying gaze, I fingered the Arkan pearls I'd taken to wearing around my neck, giving my best imitation of a bored glare back. "Are you still torqued about me searching your room, Arkan?" I raised one denuded brow. I'd been practicing only raising one in my lav's stinking *mirror*, and I'd gotten much better at it.

"I merely wonder what possessed you." He eyed me suspiciously, which didn't seem fair for a man who held all the cards.

"Greed. You'd taken my jewels." I kept them tucked into my flightsuit now, with me at all times.

"For safekeeping." His eyes narrowed. "You've gotten the necklaces tangled again. Some of the wire is quite fragile—"

"Fence will melt 'em down anyway." I grinned, and he glared.

"The emerald tiara was worn by an empress. The enamel work alone—"

"I think I preferred your boring war stories."

"Oh?" As if that comment had given him permission to continue, Davad launched back into one with more detail than I'd ever cared to know about a stolen Aemercy gunship—and what the Kamen had done to the prisoners they'd taken.

"That wasn't very nice," I pointed out, someplace in the middle.

He snorted. "Niceties did not apply."

"Keep telling yourself that and you'll justify anything."

"Yes." A smile flitted across his narrowed lips and died.

I wasn't sure if I wanted to laugh at him or run. On the trip to Carolina Station, the two of us inhabited an uneasy truce that way, balancing on a ripline between friends and foes. Not yet trust.

Alarms signaled our return to normal space.

Dropping out of hyperspace is a dance, one where you're never sure when the music will stop playing. It's easy to estimate the average time for a particular leap, but there's a lot of variation. I'd always prided myself on me and Second knowing all the mapped routes in Fringer Space—but I'd never heard of any Carolina Station there. Mureen claimed the system was someplace in the liminal between the Unity's Second and Third Rings, too remote to be useful for trade or habitation, a speck in the infinite among thousands.

In my current state, I had no way of telling. Old Terran sea ships could navigate from the position of the stars relative to themselves, it was said. So could a good navvy, but they had to be slotted in to do it.

And speaking to their pilot.

When the alarms rang, I hurried up the bridge to find both Kamen-lords already there and the portside windows still showing the matte black of null space. Mureen was holding that bottle of fake whiskey, and four glasses were set on the spotless captain's board, like she didn't care about spills, which I knew, having spent the past few weeks conscious in her company, was not true.

"A tradition!" She waved the bottle at me. "The three of us always have one drink when Rathe comes out. For luck."

"At this point it probably is luck, him coming out again."

"What?" She looked confused. Davad didn't look like anything at all as he had his back to us both, staring out at the black.

"Fifty thousand jumps? Ring a bell?" I walked over. She'd slicked her hair back again, was wearing a clean set of the tunic and trousers I was starting to think had to be some kind of Kamen uniform. "Rathe's gotta be close to deepriver. Rolling the dice every time."

"Deepriver?" Mureen looked puzzled, and I was abruptly reminded of the fact that Kamen-lords were, quite literally, raised under rocks.

"She means our pilot's neural interface may soon erode beyond repair." The princeling stared into the void. "In the Guild they call it 'going to the river.' An allusion to the mythical Styx, I believe. Should a pilot 'cross' deepriver, they never return."

"Usually the ship pops out of hyperspace okay," I added. "Usually."

"Oh." Mureen's eyes widened. "I had heard about what happens to pilots, of course. But Dav, you never told me Rathe was close to... that."

Davad turned to us, dismissing her concerns with a wave of his hand. "Sai's had months of rest. Most pilots have time to remove their implants before they go to the 'river.' Pilots have a charming name for it..." He raised an eyebrow as if to prompt me.

"We call it getting gelded," I muttered. "Time off is good, but days overdue on a jump isn't."

"Then how fortunate I found a pilot to replace our lieutenant," he replied. "If she will."

"Still the matter of the rest of the funds. Not too clear on how you're gonna come up with the millions as a wanted man—" My voice broke off as a twinge of intuition alerted me to the change in our surroundings a few seconds before the first pinprick of light appeared on our transparency. That dot of light widened to a crack, like we were on the inside of an eggshell.

"We're through." I turned toward Rathe's chair. Under so long, he'd need help getting out.

"Look first, Pilot." Davad commanded. "He wanted you to see."

I looked up. A vista of stars spread before us, unremarkable as pie, but ahead—

"Blessed hell!" I ran to the transparency, both of my hands landing on its curved surface as I gazed like a child at the impossible.

A glittering ornament made of interlaced star shapes lay to our port. The refraction seemed to be part of a fluctuating energy shield. That shield now pulsed like a heartbeat.

An ordinary station, bell-shaped and basic, the kind we used in the Fringes for temporary supply depots, shadowed the wreck's seething midsection. The glittering ruin looked like the crushed skeleton of some vast machine, spikes of its entrails spilling out over the spars of its bones. It took me a few more eyeblinks to note the clues of its origin in the shape: the bell-shaped curve along its dorsal piece, an unmistakable spiral transmission bar bent at a broken angle along the lateral.

The ruin was another space station, pounded nearly flat, like from a child's excited fist.

"Good. They're alone." I heard Mureen sigh with relief. "I thought we'd timed enough between supply rotations!" A second later, our comm board pinged, and she broke into a happy conversation with someone on the other end, full of "how are yous" and cheery updates about people I'd never heard of.

"—*pilot?*" I heard one voice ask, just as a feminine tenor inquired about Rathe by name.

"Yes—no!" Mureen agreed and protested at the same time, half laughing. "You're going to have to miss him this time, I'm afraid. We're jumping again as soon as Rathe clears the Abomination."

"*Oh, no!*" Someone on the other end sounded disappointed.

I tore my gaze away from the stars to ask Mureen if "this time" meant their trio were wanted fugitives who stopped in this Unity-controlled system a lot... only to find Davad lurking on my heels. "Sai will bring us closer," he said in my ear. "Come. There's a better view from the bow."

"Okay." Before the jagged thing we were approaching, my voice felt very small. I saw the *Escape's* solar mast rise on the holographic display. The image flashed, indicating the sails were engaging aft, cutting our speed. I followed the princeling to the bow, where all the walls were down. The commander's chair slouched like a golden egg. The board where I'd spoken to Unity Command was smashed completely.

I boggled.

"Never mind *that,*" Davad said, grabbing my freearm. "Look outside."

"Did you fragging melt it?" I was still gawking at the wrecked board.

"Mureen thought it wise. In case they had some way to track us through the console." His grip on me tightened.

I shook him off with a sharp jab to the ribs. "That's not how comms work. Even if you had a synced point, it'd be relative—" I halted. "You did all of that with the kamn?" I finished casually, so as not to sound concerned about what Kamen magic could do to a pressurized hull. But my guts curdled. The command board was flattened to the floor in spots like it'd melted after being smashed.

His tone was scornful. "A child could do that with the kamn. Look outside. The atrocity out there was done with the krov. By Nate and my sister."

I looked out onto hell. Rathe was speeding us through on sublights, bringing us in faster and closer to the shifting monstrosity than I would've dared. I had always thought of myself as a dare-bedeviled pilot, but Lieutenant Sai made me feel like a coward by comparison.

Hell was a glittering shield of energy, an impossible web, containing twisted, blackened lines that crisscrossed the ruins of Carolina Station like a drunk spider had woven them. Beneath the energy shield, the struts of the station had a peculiar opacity, with patterns and whorls that reminded me of an asteroid mining operation.

I blinked. "Is that... ice?"

"Yes. Here." Davad shoved a pair of binocs into my hand, then actually pulled them up to my own eyes. "Look."

The binocs were dialed to the highest setting. When I looked, I saw hell was inhabited—frozen bodies floated through spaces between the webbing. Some seemed to have extra limbs. A few had... wings?

"Statues?" I hoped.

"You know they're not." He stood so close that I could feel him breathing.

Somewhere in the background I heard Mureen cheerfully rattling on about how we didn't have time to stop, no, not even for refueling, not even for a local hour—

Great cracks in the wrecked hull were surrounded by more of that dark webbing, tubes of it. *Vines*. I saw the shadow cast by our ship pass across the ruin, our solar sail's bell-shaped shadow darkening that glittering web. Beautiful and terrible to be frozen in space. Familiar as a nightmare. Every spacer's worst outcome: cast adrift forever.

"Imagine," the princeling said. "Imagine this done to an entire planet. Imagine it done to every planet. Imagine the galaxy as you know it reshaped. Imagine everyone molded into beasts like those. Imagine our species' devolution."

I shuddered, still too busy imagining that hull breach to get the rest. "Why would anyone do this?"

"To make it better." His tone was mocking. "To eliminate inefficiency, to end suffering... but those reasons are lies. Because it *wants*. Because this is what the krov does. It shapes."

I blinked at the bodies as we flew past. A knot of them looked like they'd grown together before they'd been frozen. And then we passed another cluster much the same, branched and reaching, almost like a root.

"And that other space station, the one orbiting it?" Now clearly visible, the lights upon it twinkled almost cheerfully, as if this horror didn't exist.

"That's Carolina1. The energy shield is maintained by the Circle who live there. They work in shifts to keep the Abomination from spreading."

I pulled down the binocs to look at him. "A Unity Circle? As in, the Terrans chasing us?"

"Obviously not, we left the Circles chasing us on Earth." The narrowing of Davad's eyes told me that was his attempt at wit. "Glos has a long reach, but all Circles are not in lockstep with its dictates, especially since the war. Mureen served here before she was assigned to the *Ascendant*. They tolerated me, when we stopped before. Sai was quite popular." Faint amusement tinged the last. "Kamen were first assigned here to fix what Lee and Nate left behind. But kamn cannot fix it. Now they maintain that shield. Contain the contagion."

"Contagion?"

"Perhaps I misspoke. Spores. Seeds. I don't have the words..." He shook his head. "It was a mistake, what happened here. That's what I was told. In her manifesto, Lee called it a warning, but privately, she was devastated."

"You really knew her," I marveled. We were so close to a height that my eyes locked to his as I scanned that perfect face. I suddenly had the odd notion to touch his hand. Mine reached out and landed on a bare, freckled forearm. Davad only wore gloves for formal occasions, I'd learned. His skin was cool, like Kamen-lords ran colder than the rest of us.

· · · ● · ● · · ·

(That's true, isn't it?)

· · · ● · ● · · ·

"She was my sister." He glanced down at my pale hand on top of his golden one and swallowed. "My *twin*. Of course I knew her."

"Conscience bugging you for her murder?"

His eyes were so clear they looked colorless. "No. Do you think it should?"

"Dunno. *I've* never killed anyone." I pulled my hand back and tried to force a laugh as my conscience still thought otherwise, still thought about those poor kids on NewBern far too often for my taste. "But after she blew Centauri—"

He shook his head. "I was there for Centauri. Not for this. She and Nate did this alone. The rest of us were on Nuala by then. We didn't know."

"But you knew she'd do Centauri?"

"No. I knew she'd do *something*. The man I was... He couldn't have imagined it. Or this."

"And after? Did you have perfectly normal conversations about taking over the galaxy?"

He raised a brow. "I advised against that. She never wanted to rule. Nate was the autocrat; Lee just wanted peace."

I opened my mouth to laugh at the image of Saint Ledas, the *peaceful* genocide-bringer, but something held me back. "Why didn't you stop her?" I asked instead. "The Aemercy were *people*, they didn't deserve what she did to them, what she did to your own fleet—"

"I did stop her," he said sharply, "when I stabbed my gir through her abdomen, and drove hers through her skull."

"Oh." I felt dizzy.

Davad was still talking, words now coming out in a torrent. "If you're asking why I didn't do it sooner, that question is my first thought every morning and my last at rest. I dream and stop her a thousand times. But the best of intentions can end with the worst of results. We were fifteen when we left for Roe. Our Elders assigned us to a backwater planet because the corrupting influences we had at home were our parents.

"There was a man on Roe, and for a time he was the teacher we all wanted: kinder than our noble progenitors, softer than our Elders. He sold us on a dream, and when that crusade conflicted with Unity interests, we chose his side. We were his *swords*, fighting his people and our own... until the day we were not. And then we had to stop him. That took another decade, and cost nearly a billion lives."

"So?" By then, I was used to the princeling veering off course, just as he seemed accustomed to my jabs.

The wreck reflected in his luminous eyes. "So, at first our choices seemed like those pearls around your neck. Orderly and beautiful, one after the other, with everything in an obvious line. But..." He gestured out at the devastation in front of us. "War ends in entropy. Chaos."

I bit back a laugh at his unscientific explanation of entropy that came from pure nerves, because nothing about this was funny. "You're talking about that Aemercy general, the retired pilot?" My mind reached for the man's name, but all I saw was Second's flashing light telling me about my adrenals in overdrive, my heart racing. Hana Stubblefield, I recalled, had shown me a book of the man's poetry. "Aemercy pilots are all crazy, everyone knows"—I shook my head—"*were* all crazy, I mean."

"General Purcell Nikolai Amadeus Kaygaz," Davad said. He gestured back out at the black. "Just look at the Abomination, Pilot. I'm tired of stories."

"That's probably," I muttered, "because all of yours are so stinking depressing."

He snorted, and I tried to smile back. "Does Krovworld have creatures like those?" I waved at the wreckage outside. Davad had called the place Nuala Erta. I liked Rathe's more direct name more. "Shaped? By the krov?"

"Yes."

"They must be in agony." Ma had always said I lacked a sympathetic nature, but I felt sorry for those poor things, frozen in space.

"Not the ones on Nuala. It... wasn't a bad place."

I recalled what he'd said the day we met, kneeling on the grass before their childhood home. Speaking of about a power that could alter cells, alter genes, that could mold people as if they were trees—or make people *into* trees, he'd said.

I'd taken that speech for some kind of princeling arrogance. Now I shivered. "Are the things on Nuala... sentient?"

"They're human, although some have forms that you wouldn't recognize. Krov shape themselves like animals or plants, fantastical creations or monsters. We think they came from the Third Exodus four hundred years ago—one of the expeditions launched by the scientists on Roe.

"They've retained some Aemercy customs, and they speak a dialect somewhere between Standard and Aemercy. Kamen shape with the kamn. But the Faege use krov and call themselves krov and see no difference. Before we came, they had forgotten there was anything above the clouds of their world."

"They call themselves krov, or they call themselves Faege?" I was confused.

"Both. Either. Nothing at all. Lee and Nate thought they could use the krov—the power, not the people—to curb 12Fam greed. The Carolina Station hydroponics lab was supposed to be an example."

"Good job," I snapped. "Your sib blew up a solar system, then apologized with a minor apocalypse."

"It broke her, I think." Davad had edged close enough that I could count every freckle on his tragic face. "Centauri was a threat, intended to show what Kamen truly are. Carolina was supposed to show the promise of what we could be."

Distorted by the monstrosity before us, our reflections in the transparency looked the same. We could've been anyone.

"What are you?" I asked.

"Petty policemen who settle 12Fam disputes with duels. Clever machines who build or tear apart." He scoffed. "But Lee would hate that answer. Lee said Kamen were gods who refused to take responsibility."

"That's what I love about Kamen-lords. So humble." Wasn't a spark of lust in me for this lovely man, this wanted fugitive who still lied to me. And yet, my arm slid around his waist as I shivered, reaching out to comfort us both.

So cold in the black. *They should be free*, I thought. *Poor things.*

"In some ways life seemed surprisingly mundane, on Nuala Erta." I felt his own hand lock around my waist. "Pleasant, even. I met a woman, one of their shapers. We were... curious about each other."

"Mureen know?" I joked, glancing over.

His eyes glinted back. "No. One day my krov friend decided to... change. The being she became, I could no longer—"

"Screw?" I'd meant to be funny, but his body stiffened.

"*Love.* Aoife lost her voice and then her mouth. She shed her human skin and took to the sea like some twisted fable from our childhood—and I could not follow."

"Because you didn't have the krov to change yourself into a... fish?"

"Because Aoife made her choice, and I made mine."

"But she was important to you."

He shrugged, which I took to mean he didn't want to talk about it. "Some of us mastered the krov quickly. Nate did. He was one of the most powerful Kamen on Glos. He once pulled an Aemercy troop carrier from orbit."

"Heard about that."

"Everyone has. But when Nate turned to krov, he lost the kamn. Nate's power is tied to that place, but any world in the galaxy with life upon it is vulnerable to him."

"Or space station, apparently." I nodded toward the spectacle before us.

"If it has life upon it, yes."

I swallowed. "That's everywhere people live."

"Do you understand now?"

I didn't. I stared at the wreck. "What's he doing with the people? Does he turn them into frozen things like that?"

"I told you before. The krov *shapes*. It wants and it shapes. Planets.

People. Anything it can."

Planets. People. I shivered.

"Lee used to say the lives at Centauri weren't lost at all, merely transformed. She claimed that in ten million years, one hundred million, one hundred billion, they would evolve again, perhaps into beings like us." His lips twisted. "Better than us."

Your sister was a madwoman, and you're a hero for ending her, I thought, but what I said was: "That's an excuse for murder I've never heard before."

The hero laughed softly. "Your humor is appreciated. More than you realize."

I stared out at the black. "So, what happens to this wreck? Circle keeps it from leaking into open space? Why not blow it up? Or cut it down for parts?"

"This is a classified Fleet installation. Their scientists are carefully monitored and checked for contamination before leaving the system. The risk is high. Whatever life force exists upon that station wants to spread. These days, the Circle extracts samples for the researchers using drones. There's a smaller satellite for visiting scientists—you can see it there in the viewscreen, that shadow behind the first. It's usually unmanned. Most work is done remotely."

All that life, breaking down alone in the dark... I felt colder. To die in space was a pilot's worst nightmare—or as some of our more devout Guild fanatics had it, best fate. If you went past the point where you'd get gelded, pushed past the point where your mind broke... where else could you belong but the deepening black?

Cold heaven and hell at once.

Poor things, I thought.

Chapter 16 ✳ Toured

After our honeymoon, news kept coming about the *Ascendant* terrorists: where they might be hiding, how they might be working for Illcord Natoth. I couldn't get Mureen out of my mind. And Wade kept visiting Feldelroy every few weeks. To check on me, he said. He always brought ice cream—

· · · ● · ● ● · ·

"What's the buzz about Circles—" I broke off as Mureen gave a peal of laughter so unlike what I'd expect from her that I suspected a seizure.

"—and then Rathe—" She laughed again. "Exactly! You know Rathe!"

"Rathe said what? I'd like to speak for myself." His voice, a little hoarse and roughed with sleep.

I turned away from the hellscape.

Our pilot had come out of his chair with no ceremony, was now perched atop it with his legs slung over the side as voices chattered from the speaker built into its arm. Those voices sallied questions rapid-fire as Rathe replied with his eyes focused squarely on me.

"Got the second-best pilot in the deep with me." He winked. "Can't wait for you all to meet her."

"*She's awake?*" a male voice sounded startled. A pack of others asked who.

"There's no time to stop," Mureen said. "We'll have to jump as soon as we reach the point. Polla can join you, which should help any fatigue."

My copilot's easy smile didn't fade so much as stretch. "She's not ready."

"*You're really not coming?*" Someone sighed with girlish regret from the comm. "*Not even for half a day?*"

"No need to be hasty…" I wasn't entirely sure if I was backing him up, or protecting my own secret. "Don't disappoint your fans, stud," I drawled, walking over. "Need a break? It's space. We pilots call the shots."

"I'd never miss a chance to see you, Yurys," Rathe said to the voice on the comm. His navhand reached out and clasped mine. His fingers were ice.

Dimly, I felt our navvies touch, even felt Second's alarm like an electrical shock up my arm. Up close, his eyes were red-rimmed and bloodshot, pupils too small for the blue. My fingers tightened in sympathy.

"*Is that your new pilot?*" asked another. A deeper voice. Maybe older. "Hello!"

Automatically, I made my tone cheerful. "The name's Polla. Can't wait to meet you!"

Mureen frowned. "We've a few things to sort out, Ken'ri," she announced, leaning over the board. "Give us a moment." She switched the short-range communicator off, folding her arms and straightening her back as if that would increase her authority. In fact, it made her look like a ruffled chick, but I daren't laugh.

"Told your pals about me?" I asked. I was puzzled, considering we'd just met. Perhaps my reputation? Sure, I'd written all those posts on the Guild forums about the Biscayne race and how to chart it... those had made me pretty well-known.

"Told them we had you in stasis, prepped for surgery," he said. "Maybe mentioned what Mureen told me about your reputation..." He lifted an eyebrow. "Your *flying* reputation."

"Good things?" I eyed Mureen's expression from the corner of my eyes and saw the way her smile suddenly brightened like she'd swapped its lumens.

"You may have noticed our lift from Earth was more fraught than expected." Davad addressed us both and immediately took Mureen's side—unsurprising as the hens back home growing teeth every spring. "Carolina may no longer be the refuge it was. Not such a reach to connect Mureen to this Circle. We should jump as soon as we can."

"Was a blasted mess getting out." Rathe ran his freehand through his sweaty hair. "Torpedoes nearly fried us, and those hull plates were shaking like crazy." He gave Davad a rueful glance. "Now I know how those Aemercy felt."

"Hah." The two men exchanged tight smiles.

"You were incredible." I remembered those red lines on the screen. Rathe had made our tub of a corvette move like she was greased.

"I am amazing." Rathe gave me a careless grin. "I'll teach you a trick to boost acceleration in the next leg." His eyes seemed to take all of me in at once. "Passenger life suits you. Got some color in your cheeks. Guess they've treated you right."

"All we've had to do was sleep and eat. And screw, but Davad and Mureen didn't ask for company, so I just slept and ate."

Mureen turned an odd pink. I laughed.

Rathe laughed too. "It's about time. Have to dock now, Dav. Yurys owes me a hundred sling."

"Don't forget breaking into our rooms," Davad said coolly. He'd draped himself across the central pillar of the pilot's station like he was waiting for servants to lay down carpet, managing to make the simple act of leaning into a wall a formal exercise. "Our pilot is quite skilled with locks... Did you hear me before, Rathe? We can't stay. We'll jump again. Now."

"Huh." My copilot looked from me and then back to the princeling. "I see everyone's still getting along. And *Bedalia*?"

My voice felt small. "Haven't... I haven't checked on her lately." Hard to say there'd been no time when I'd just admitted to doing nothing.

A little of his cheer seemed to fade. "Damn shame. Hoped you two would be right by now." He moved stiffly over to the whiskey and drained his glass. "I'm not skiving off for the company, Arkan. I need a break, and it's not safe to anchor so close to the Abomination. *Escape's* not solid enough to maintain her own orbit. Those dorsal jets took a beating on that run. I'll need a day just to fix that. What's the harm? The Carolina route was scrapped from all the public maps. We've been through here twice already."

"*Twice*?" I echoed. That seemed awfully confident.

Davad looked at Mureen, ignoring me. "What *harm*?" He gave the last word an odd inflection.

She shrugged. "My Circle hasn't betrayed us yet." Mureen took a delicate sip of her own drink. "I told you, Dav, we share a singular purpose."

"You told me Ells and Solon thought you overreached."

"I told you they didn't think it would work. But it has." She set down her glass, and her small chin lifted. "Perhaps they *should* see—Solly and Ells should."

Rathe frowned. "No. Not Edat. I won't allow it."

"What?" I broke in.

"Of course not Edat." Davad brushed me off. "Mureen meant they should see our commitment of purpose."

"What's an Edat?" I asked, but by then Davad and Mureen had both begun speaking at once, loud and fast and over me and Rathe—and, I think now, not by coincidence.

• • • ● • ● • • •

(I recall their smug expressions so clearly. Especially *hers*. The way her fingers tightened on that fragile glass.

Pride's the death of worlds, and Mureen of Glos had it too—in hectotons beneath her fragile frame.)

• • • ● • ● • • •

"So it's settled. I'm steering us into their dock on manual," Rathe announced with the quiet authority our kind have by right (in space, anyways). He hobbled to the main board as if his joints ached. "Mureen? Raise the comm again. We need to make sure they open the tube clamps this time, we almost clipped the stabilizers before."

"You're sure the new pilot isn't ready?" Davad trailed after him.

"Right here," I snapped, pride pricked. "And I can fly anything."

[Error!] Second chimed in. Not for the first time, I wondered if it played me.

Rathe shrugged apologetically. "Sexy's sure. You know how navvies are." His mouth twitched. "Lia told me you went through my things."

I thought of the holo of the woman in his bunk wearing shortos and a smile. *How does Lia know?* Then I remembered the bloodship's own cargo bay. He meant his stuff there, probably. "Sorry," I told him. "Not like I want to disappoint you war criminals."

"You will be stronger soon," Mureen assured him, which was less than encouraging, considering she'd apparently just learned what deepriver could do.

"Does your symbiote think she's ready for the bloodship?" Davad was awfully twitchy.

Rathe shrugged, catching my eye. "Sexy and I'd both like to see Polla in a conventional craft first."

Mureen cleared her throat. "What if we use the science post instead of docking at the main station? Would it be large enough to anchor?"

"The substation?" My copilot looked startled. "Why?"

"Would Carolina2's structure suffice to maintain our vessel or not?" Mureen's tone had developed an edge.

"Should." His brow furrowed. "But—"

She held up a hand to cut him off and tapped the board to open again. "Solon, are you still there?"

"*Of course.*" The tenor voice brightened. "*What a shame you won't be able to join us, but our hectic station could overwhelm your new pilot, so recently recovered from her injuries. We completely understand—*"

"Have you not met pilots before, ser?" I broke in.

Mureen ignored me. "We've had a change of plans. With your approval, we'll dock at the science substation. Perhaps you could bring a small contingent to us?"

"I... see." There was the chatter of others speaking, with several insisting on talking to Rathe. Whatever else these Kamen were, they didn't even have Syndicate discipline. "*I'm so pleased your new pilot has recovered enough to join us. A pleasant surprise. We don't want to overwhelm her. Perhaps a limited audience?*"

"Wouldn't be overwhelmed—" I grinned.

Davad shot me a glare to freeze space. "We trust you, Solon," he said. "Just make sure you provide everyone with an itinerary before arrival."

"*We shall review the menu on the shuttle,*" the man replied. "*Of course.*"

"Bring variety for me!" I added. "Not too particular about bits, but I do like something protruding. It doesn't have to be attached—"

Mureen clicked the link closed with her hand, using more force than seemed necessary. Her hand went to her temples. "Done."

Davad walked over, began rubbing her shoulders. "Yes."

She sighed and leaned into him. "What will they think of you and me, Dav?"

He kissed her. "They'll say you can do better. Your Circle are a direct bunch."

"Guess it's a lucky night for everyone." Rathe's smile was lovely. I wondered if I'd imagined the doubt in his eyes before. He nudged my elbow. "Protruding, huh?"

"Something." I batted my lashes. "Or I could. Don't mind a swap in dreaming."

He snorted. "Want to sit on my lap while I bring the *Escape* to dock? Might give you an impression of what I've got."

I laughed. "Think I'll assess your docking expertise first. Don't want to rush into port with only a half-cocked clamping tube."

His yellow brows rose. "Oh? Everyone swears my clamps are always fully cocked..."

We went along in that vein (ahem) for some time while Rathe used the manual steering deck to steer the corvette around the Abomination to the dark side of its rotation.

Pilots and their sport. Didn't mean a thing. Docking the *Escape* was mostly automated—a matter of punching in coordinates and then having the ship's sail and thrusters shoot us into the clamps at the bay.

Three of our hosts met us after the airlock in a dusty bay: two men, one fat and one thin, and a woman who looked a lot like Mureen—at least at first glance. The latter hurtled herself into Rathe's arms.

"Hold on, Yurys," he said, laughing. "Don't knock me over! I'm fragile!"

"You look awful," the Kamen told him. "I thought you promised to take care of yourself."

"I am." He pushed her off, chuckling. "Really? Awful?"

"I hate beards." She sighed, seeming much younger than Mureen, for all that she looked older, having some lines on her face herself, skin a little "off youth's bloom," like Ma used to say. Her arms wrapped around him, and her head peered over his shoulder at the rest of us. Thought she gave me a nod, but it might've been for Davad, who was ripe on my heels.

"I'll delip, don't worry." Rathe's hand slid easily around her waist and pulled her to his side.

"Everywhere?"

He groaned. "Have a heart!"

"And this must be her," one of the men said—the thin one, smiling at us all like we were bringing blessed notes of enlightenment or church attendance bonuses. "We advised on your care," he added, pitching his voice high and loud like I was deaf. "I am pleased to see you looking so well, err—"

"Polla," I snapped, shooting Davad a dirty look for not giving me a real introduction. "Name's Polla Ottrava. Wasn't aware that Kamen-lords gave out medical advice."

"Hah." The fat man chuckled, joining in. "What Solly means is, we assessed the health of your symbiote. The Guild has us assist on its medical cases from time to time."

"Second's fine." I craned my neck 'round to see how Rathe was getting on. Mureen's look-alike (although now I'd come to see it was mostly the hairstyle and clothes which gave the resemblance—the other woman was lighter, her nose larger) was still all over my copilot, whispering something in his ear that made him laugh.

"Really?" He slipped his arm around her waist. "Tell Derien I'm flattered, but—"

"—wasn't expecting an accent." The thin man held out his hand like I was supposed to do something with it. "You speak very well, Polla Ottrava. Pilot Polla, is it? Does one use a title in your line of work?"

"All us Feldelroyans speak *well*," I snarled. I dodged his hand and backed into Mureen, who'd edged behind me. "You speak well too... for a *Terran*."

At that point, Mureen broke in with introductions, and those went on for an interminable time. If you'd quizzed me twenty seconds later, I couldn't have told you one of her fellow's names, a matter not helped when five more of 'em came through the aperture and repeated much the same dialogue. By the time I'd been told I looked very well by the third strange Kamen-lord in a row, a weird twitch had started in my starboard eye.

Second was a sullen, silent presence in the back of my head. On top of everything, I needed the lav.

"You seem tired," the fat man said to me, while Rathe, my hoped-for savior, flirted with three Kamen at once. They were all so... glossy. Not a hair out of place, and in immaculate garb, smiling like Eighth Day cultists before the Priests.

I realized they gave me the creeps.

"You look fat," I snapped back, shifting on my feet. I was vaguely aware that comment had stopped chatter in our immediate vicinity, at least for the nonce.

The thin man opened his mouth like he had something to add, but then, to my surprise, it was Davad who came to my rescue, stepping between us and slinging an arm over my shoulder while breaking into a laugh so strange that I almost elbowed his ribs just to make it stop.

"Our new pilot's just fine," Davad said. "She's put up with us this far."

"Remarkable," someone said behind us.

"I am fine," I said, giving Davad's ribs a warning nudge. "And I've always wanted to see a Kamen lair. Can someone give me a tour?"

"We don't usually come here," offered a pink-skinned brunette. "It's for the scientists."

"Of course." I rolled my eyes. "Can't mix with science folk. One of you might learn what a carbon molecule is."

"Our pilots need time to relax." Davad's elbow in my ribs was probably no accident. "Alone." He took my arm and started walking, forcing the crowd to follow. I did so under duress, craning my neck back and still trying to assess the scene. This station was tiny, three levels of narrow corridors and modular chambers. We passed a few deserted labs that looked subpar, even for the lowliest of Syndicate chemists. Then Davad paused again.

"Which way from here, Solon?"

"Lowest level," the thin man said. "We thought the pilots might appreciate privacy."

I snorted. "You really haven't met many pilots!"

"I expect propriety." Davad warned no one who cared.

"You can't blame the Ken'ri for curiosity." The fat man chided him like they were old pals. "You look better, Dav," he added gently. "Far more at peace."

"There's a fair amount of blame to go around, Ken'ri Ells. We're only here to make sure our pilots rest." Davad glanced back at Rathe, who was barely visible, surrounded by his throng of admirers. "And I do mean rest, Sai. Hear me?"

"Yep." Rathe stepped through a bevy of beige robes and caught up to us. "I know."

"Look after her. Understand?" Davad's silvered gaze turned to me. "This is a Kamen installation, Pilot. They have more than locks on these doors. If you go where you're not welcome, you'll be in for a shock."

"Sounds like a dare." I didn't like the way he was ordering my copilot around. The hallway we were standing in was bog-standard space station: plated walls a shade between brown and gray, that acid smell of recirculated air. It was cold and empty and dull as toast.

"She's like a child sometimes," Davad whined, addressing Rathe, maybe, or Ken'ri Ells. Somewhere behind us, I heard Mureen laugh at something someone else had said, bright and careless, like all of this was nothing at all.

"She's standing right next to you." Rathe chided, frowning.

"She has a *name*," I added, glaring.

• • • ● • ● ● • • •

(I think that was the moment I realized I'd never heard Davad say it.)

APOLOGUE 5 ✳ MUTINY

BEYA AWOKE TO FIND her cabin's porthole black with null space instead of overlooking the planet Roe. "Shit," she said.

"What?" Her bedmate lifted a tousled head and yawned, pushing back a fall of reddish hair.

Beya indicated the porthole. "The ship's jumped."

Sheris sat up. "What about your parade?"

"Guess Lee and Nate didn't think I deserved one. I shall murder her." Beya gave herself a few seconds of bliss while she imagined crushing Lee's gene-locked skull with a levitated boulder. *Battle humor.* Ten years of fighting Associations had made even the softest from the brave Kamen Company as hard as stone.

"Maybe it's a drill." Sheris was a new recruit, and sometimes her ignorance showed. She stood, a cantilevered marvel of pink and gold. Even her disappointed sigh was sensual—but Beya's ire against Lee was spoiling her pleasure at the view. Sheris looked like a shorter, paler version of Lee, which made Beya uncomfortable because she liked to think she had more motivation for choosing lovers than a *type.*

"No," Beya told her. "Hear the engines? That's hyperspace." The vibration was nearly inaudible to ordinary ears, yet unmistakable to Kamen. "Running hot. Burning stars."

Her lover sighed. "I'm sad we'll miss your parade. You deserved one after all your hard work!"

Deserved. Sheris didn't know half of what Beya deserved. "Is Lee trying to piss me off?" Beya paced to their discarded pile of bedding. Sheris's skin ran hot, and she was constantly kicking off the blankets.

"I'm sure it's not personal." That innocent expression meant the opposite, Beya had learned. "Back to bed?"

"No." Another noise had joined the engine's steady purr, perhaps imperceptible to anyone not trained. To Beya, the discordant hum of Kamen-braced shields flared like a roar. The boil came from the deck above their heads—and that meant central command.

"The manual said there'd be an alarm if anything went wrong with the ship—" Sheris's voice broke off as bells rang, signaling all hands.

"I swear by the stone, one of these days I will kill her," Beya vowed as she tore through the pile of bedding, looking for pants.

The second they reached the bridge, Beya knew she'd been right. The *Happy Elyse* had jumped to hyperspace during its sleep cycle, thus ensuring only a skeleton crew would be awake when the battered dreadnought folded its solar sails and tacked toward the jump points.

It was, Beya thought, fragging typical that Lee hadn't considered whether the rest of the Company might have wanted to stay and party. Indeed, the slight seemed personal. A parade down the main street of a blasted-out city wasn't Unity Purple, but the local Associations on the planet Roe had started calling Beya "the Butcher of NewKalnik"—and being Aemercy, they meant it as a compliment.

The air was thick with charged kamn, and Beya registered an unusual number of pilots standing around, at least half of whom should have been flying their dreadnought. But only one pilot's chair out of the forty was occupied. The tip of Lee's impertinent freckled nose poked out beneath its dome, along with a few red curls.

"She flies dreadnoughts *solo* now?" Beya heard her voice crack. Her glare went to Nate, who grinned calmly back from his command seat, which he'd detached from its base to hover a meter above the navpit.

"She insisted." Nate waved his metal-laced hand like he was showing off his own illegal symbiote. "Quite simple for us," he continued, bestowing his benevolent smile on Beya. "Lee and I find piloting a command carrier no different than a starfighter, truly."

"No fail-safes?" Beya turned to look at the pilots. "You let her take the ship?"

"Commander Illcord's orders." Ursin's voice was flat, his eyes shadowed from lack of sleep. "Lorimer and Ramsamy objected. He had Lavar throw them in the brig."

"Lavar *escorted* our friends to a secure location," Nate corrected. One knee was crossed across his lap. "I plan to let them out..."

"*Idiots!*" Beya stalked past the muttering pilots and the madman to Davad. "Don't tell me," she began as Lee's twin raised an eyebrow, "We're off to tackle injustice in the Fringers?"

"Commander Illcord hasn't informed anyone of the *plan*." Davad's tone was laconic, but every line of Lee's twin was tensed. "A surprise, he says."

"Is this a coup?" she asked.

"How can it be a coup when we're in charge?" Nate called from across the bridge. *Kamen hearing.* So few secrets lasted shipboard more than a deck or two. His smile was pleasant. Nate was good at smiling pleasantly, much better than Lee, good at suggesting they were all in their glorious cause together, but someone had to steer their course—oh, and with his leadership experience, he didn't mind.

Perhaps the lines worked because Nate's face lacked the off-putting beauty found in most 12Fam progeny. Or perhaps his gift lay in the sincerity with which he delivered utter shit. Right now, Nate grinned like he and Beya were the only two people in the room. Being Kamen, he didn't even shout—his voice was an intimate whisper, direct to her ear. "This is our reward, Bae."

Bae. Beya imagined how much fun it would be to crush Nate's head with a rock before she did Lee's.

"*Nae-toth?*" she directed her own voice back, sending an exploratory jab of kamn at his shields. Nate's grin widened, and the barrier flickered over his skin. Lee and Nate had become freakishly strong. Beya might have taken a symbiote too if she hadn't seen Davad's arm go black and him start screaming just before that drunk medic opened her skull—

She had no regrets.

Gods, Lee and Nate would now be called back on Beya's home planet of Feldelroy. Their Kamen Elders had a more accurate term, one Aemercy shared. *Abominations.*

Staring at Nate's placid face, Beya felt a chill. After Lee and Nate received the Purple, (an award that no one had offered *Beya,* even if she'd done as much for that peace as anyone), Lee had locked herself in her stateroom, not even emerging for meals.

I'm worried, Davad had confided. *Lee's stopped taking Father's calls—*

She's sulking, Beya had said. *She wants to pass this off as a victory.*

Victory. The word tasted like ashes. Even beaten, the Aemercy had won. Kaygaz and his merry crew had been pardoned. Beya thought it might take another decade, but she had no doubt their old chess master would try his invasion again.

For an Aemercy pilot, even a retired one, ten years was an eyeblink.

Still the party rolled on. Their victorious Unity Fleet sat in orbit around Roe. Outside the cordon, hyperspace by-lanes were packed with refugees leaving the system. House Illcord had made *personal* settlement offers for any Aemercy who wanted to leave their native system, giving the vanquished opportunity to settle under Unity skirts.

Typical Terran garbage—fist in a velvet glove, shit in a silk sack, Beya thought. Half the planets Illcord offered were former Unity worlds that the Aemercy had blasted to ash in the war, and those remaining required intensive terraforming, which the Aemercy were prohibited from doing themselves by the terms of the treaty.

Cynically, Beya was sure that most Associations who took the offer would end up selling their own kids to labor contracts by year's close. Anything for a better life... but ten years of fighting Aemercy had drained her of sympathy. Hate was refreshingly uncomplicated.

After ten years of war, they all hated Aemercy, but Beya thought the Houses might be worse. Dear Lee kept swearing that she and Nate would use their status for reform... yet here the brave Kamen Company flew (like thieves in the night), beating a hyperspace retreat from the cheers of victory.

Our Elders must be so proud, Beya thought, staring at her sleeping friend's spotted nose. *We've become just like them.*

To Beya's left, Sheris was still fawning over Nate—and she wasn't alone. Most of their newest recruits looked thrilled to be off on some unknown adventure. And Nate grinned back, cracking jokes as if this were a wonderful game.

"I want to hear from Lee!" Derien's heavy baritone cut through the din. "Pull her out."

"Don't be absurd!" Nate laughed. "We're in the middle of hyperspace!"

"We did it to Aemercy all the time," the other man spat. Derien looked frail compared to Nate's bulk, but the fool was squaring off like this was a show-ring duel.

"You want us dead in space?" Nate snorted. "What would that accomplish?"

"If I cut the power to her chair, it might make you take us seriously." Derien already had his gir out, and now he shaped the metal into a sword.

Nate's smile grew harder. "Try."

Beya rolled her eyes. *Bloody Derien.* Was the man stupid enough to think Nate would accept a formal challenge?

Possibly.

The pilots had clustered to one side. Rees and Faudra were blinking, their symbiote-laced hands half touching and their eyes unfocused. Rees must be furious. There was a lakefront orgy he'd been talking about for weeks. And Chedrik, who'd flown a hundred missions with Beya on wing, shot her a furious look that she didn't need alien telepathy to read. Their pilots knew exactly how dangerous little Lee's stunt was.

She had a sudden urge to laugh at Nate and Lee's utter *hubris*: pissing off the only people on their ship who knew how engines and life support worked.

"Explain." Davad's furious words cut through the rest. "Save your speeches for the admirals, Nate. Just tell us what's happening. Where is Lee taking us? And why?"

"A world called Nuala Erta." Nate was starting to remind Beya of one of those smug predators from Gryffon, a spliced tigron who'd overpowered his prey by sheer density. "You'll love it."

Behind her, someone else who'd taken Elder Tiff's class on Postflight myths and legends laughed, and Beya couldn't help snorting herself. "The Aemercy fairy tale?" she called out. "Oh, come on. If the two of you wanted a beach vacation, you could've just asked."

Nate's smile turned back on Beya. "Nuala's quite real. Lee and I found it months ago." The kamn coiled thick as syrup around him, but as she stalked closer, Beya noticed the sweat beads suspended in his shields and new lines of strain grooved around his mouth. Lee's husband might be playing cool, but his act had a cost.

"Why today?" she pressed. "Did you forget about my parade?"

His easy grin flickered. The closer Beya looked, the worse Nate appeared. He kept his hair cropped short—most of them did—but his skull was scraped bloody, like he'd shaved it with an unsteady hand. Now, Nate ran his left hand down the wires woven through his right hand's skin. He licked his lips before answering her, a crack in that vat-grown facade. "Nuala's our reward." His voice buzzed in her ear. "I promise you'll like it, Bae." He paused, then twisted the emotional gir, the one that worked so well on both of them.

"Lee thinks so, too."

Derien spat on the deckplates, an Aemercy curse. He had, Beya thought, always been a little in love with Nate, just like Beya with Lee—although as far as she knew, Nate had never reciprocated, unlike Lee, who'd only stopped for marriage. "Running away?" Derien mocked. "Do you expect us to give up the cause?"

Their self-appointed despot chuckled. "For now, I expect obedience. Lee will explain more when she emerges. You can try taking over the ship's controls then... but you'll fail." His mouth twitched. "And you know it."

"Oh, yeah? As soon as this ship gets out of hyperspace—" Derien kept blustering, but he'd lost. Kamen and pilots whispered like rats, until the din became so overwhelming that Beya raised auditory shields so that half the sound died.

"By the time we get to the Al-Murad jump point, none of you will bother," Nate's voice boomed. "Lee will explain."

Beya doubted Lee wanted to—the woman hated speeches. More like *Nate* wanted Lee to explain, which meant this was like the time she'd decided to hurl pieces of a moonbase onto unprotected Aemercy farmland. *Just a few, Bae, until they back down—*

Far from backing down, the Aemercy had ripped up the last of their treaties and started attacking civilian convoys.

"What has she done now?" Beya snapped. "Sabotaged the peace talks? Just say it."

Nate's smile finally died. "You wouldn't believe me."

"You think I lack faith in your wife fucking us over?" Beya spat on the floor just like Derien, but as it turned out, Nate was right. She wouldn't have believed him.

What Lee had done shouldn't have been possible.

Back then, Beya still thought her first lover had a conscience—or at least a line she'd never cross.

Chapter 17 ✳ Tested

I know you got sick of living with my folks, Sam. It seemed practical while we saved for our own place, but I know you wanted the buzz of Derra City. And driving a hauler must've been lonely after all those nights tending bar. Locked in your own head for hours as you traversed the Bogallino Crevasse? You and I have one thing in common, I think: neither of us have ever wanted the time for introspection.

I was blind to that about you, Sam. I'm sorry.

· · · ● · ● · ● · ·

(FROM THE NAVPOINT RATHE had jumped us through, there were thousands of unique destinations, several hundred of which must have looked far more promising for fleeing criminals like ourselves than the Unity-controlled black ops site of Carolina Station—or so my companions assured me. Later, we figured the Unity took no chances. Must've sent a squad of fighters to each of those jump points... because otherwise, surely, they would've sent more after us faster.

Or perhaps we were betrayed.

But I'm getting ahead. First on that dusty science station, we had two days of relative peace before the crap hit the hyperdrive. Who knew relative peace could be found on a half-deserted research station with a pack of stone-shaping hermits?

Not me. At least, not the woman I was.)

· · · ● · ● · ● · ·

With Davad's arm still locked around my shoulder, he and the fat Kamen took Rathe and me down a flight of stairs. The flickering lights and dusty air vents screamed of disuse. I tried to cover my unease with a remorseless stream of insignificant chatter, amusing myself with the way my folderol made Davad cringe and Rathe smile. Throughout, the fat Kamen-lord stared at me constantly—so much I half expected him to run into a wall. Something about his gaze raised my hackles, but I put that down to nerves... adjusting my concern up to raging unease when he touched in a code to a door at the end of a too-dark corridor, then gestured us to come inside.

"This your guest suite?" I tried to wriggle out from Davad's iron grip, but he held me fast.

"We thought you would be more comfortable in your own wing." The man had told me his name at least twice. I still didn't know it. "Pilots need rest."

I caught Rathe's frown. "They've done this before?" I asked softly.

Nearly imperceptibly, my copilot shook his head. "We'll be fine down here. Thanks, Ells. If there's food—"

"We'll chute some down." The man—Ells, I supposed—backed away. Davad followed without a backward glance. The door slid shut behind them.

I ran to it immediately. Locked. "Did they lock *you* in on Terra?" I asked Rathe. "Because they locked *me* in."

"You were hurt," he said, but I thought he looked troubled, even more when he reached for my hand and squeezed it, glancing up at the low ceiling. "You know, I could use a *shower*." His voice had pitched louder and strange.

"Think there is one?" I matched his tone, catching his exaggerated upward glance. *Looking for cams*, I thought. I knew how much Kamen-lords liked to spy.

"It'll be this way." He traced an unfamiliar pattern on my hand. No doubt Unity pilots had their own codes, just like smugglers.

Our eyes met and I shrugged, tracing a symbol myself that meant I thought I got it—with sheep.

His grin creased when he shook his head, laughing softly, and shrugged.

I laughed too, and let him lead me down the hallway, past a set of branching doors that led to like bog-standard bunks, and through a narrower corridor with the universal symbol for hygiene stamped above an arch in holographic blue. He didn't pause, just stripped to his skin as careless as Davad had been in those Arkan Baths.

I felt my cheeks heat. Davad was one thing. Rathe another. Leaner than I usually liked, but he'd looked skinnier clothed. He was all broad bones and angles, the planes of his chest flat and wide, tapering to a small waist and compact bim.

"Join me?" he said while I stared at the scars on his ribs. Two bullet wounds, and an old burn that could've been from lasers. I knew he'd flown in combat, but that didn't explain getting hit with bullets. A few of those scars looked fresh.

"I'm gonna check the bunks first." I backed toward the door.

He slipped into the stall. I heard the water start, and then his long sigh. "Feels fantastic!" he called, but I was already backing away, trying to sort out my next move.

The bunks were nothing special, four chambers with three beds each.

A faded picture of a Chessna starliner on one wall told me we weren't the only guests this station had ever seen, although it looked like it'd been some time. A light on the wall in that room was flashing, and I pulled open a cabinet to find a dumbwaiter with a domed tray and two cups of something warm. I took a swig and almost gagged at the bitter taste before setting it down. Paced back and forth a few times and stretched my limbs. Counted to twenty. I tried the locked door at the end of the hall again.

Still locked. Second could've shorted the lock (if it would), but I recalled Davad's warning about what Kamen could do to trespassers.

I considered that every time I started to become a trusting sort, my companions knocked me off-kilter.

For lack of a better plan, I stripped down to my undergarment and went back to the showers. The enclosure had been treated to not fog, giving me a good view, and just because I was there for nonsex purposes didn't mean I didn't take a moment to stare. A facial delip revealed the strength in Rathe's jaw, the cleft in his chin. His skin was goldish, hair only a little darker across his chest and down in a line that crossed his flat navel and went down to where his hand was methodically soaping his own hardened length—

I think I made a noise because he looked up. For a sec, he looked embarrassed, but then recovered, dropping himself and straightening to push the door open.

"Want me to strike a different pose?" He cleared his throat. "Or company? Or I can leave if you'd rather shower alone—"

"Let's talk instead." I met his eyes with what I hoped was unbothered sophistication.

He nodded. Rathe's face was far too drawn, but the hot water gave his skin a healthy glow. He touched the wall, and the water from the ceiling misted, steaming us both with a light rain. His pilot's arm gleamed, half-lathered, all metal and skin. I felt my skin prickle just looking at it. Hells, I felt more heat approaching that arm than I had staring at his cock.

Pilots... Outsiders never understand.

I stepped into the enclosure, which put us face-to-face. "Just came for a conversation. Figured we wouldn't be heard in here."

"I figured too." His mouth quirked, and he reached out to touch my custom undergarment, which covered a good sixty percent of my flesh. "This is something that you've got on."

"Teapot made it for me."

"A teapot made it for you?" His mouth curved up.

"No, Teapot, the nurse android at the Arkan estate."

He chuckled. "Davad told me it used to be his nanny when he was a kid. Thing's trained to keep a Twelve heir alive, so it can handle anything short of brain surgery."

"It seemed to think it could've handled that too. I guess Teapot replaced my leg and reconnected my navvy..." My voice trailed off because Rathe was staring down at my legs now. Under his frank gaze, I felt bare, even beneath the layer of fabric. My skin prickled with another irrational wash of desire. He smelled like soap and musk, the air was steamy, his navarm gleaming, those thick wires on his shoulder entwined like lovers with flesh and bone...

Pilots... I realized I was grinning and wiped my face. A tendril of hair had detached from my topknot and fell over my eyes, curling oddly. I pushed it back only to have it bob into view again, coiling like a rebel helix.

He cleared his throat. "You know, I can't tell which leg. Thought it would be paler or something. Of course, you're pretty pale all over—"

"Not when I get grounded on a planet with a decent sun."

He nodded. "Saw that with Lia. At least your feet are the same size. Hell of a thing if they weren't."

"I'd have to get custom shoes." Didn't understand where this was going. "Do you like feet? I hear that's a thing."

"Uh, I like a lot of things." He was staring at my face again, looking as distracted as I felt. He leaned forward and tucked that stubborn sprig of hair behind one of my ears, a gesture that sent another pleasant prickle along Second's filament.

"Me too." I meant for my voice to be husky and knowing, but it came out like a squeak. In that instant, I quite forgot that I'd just come in so the Kamen-lords couldn't hear us.

I took a step toward his arm—just as Rathe interrupted me like a dash of ionized water. "Did something happen on the way here? I don't think Davad and Mureen trust you."

I laughed. "Was your first clue when they locked us in?"

"Third time through Carolina, and the Kamen never wanted to berth on the science station before." His easy grin faded. "Do you really want to leave? I can talk to them. We can find someone else. It might take more surgery, but anything's possible—"

Surgery? "No!" I said. "No, I want to be here." Smuggling was stinking *dull*, not to mention, I didn't exactly have a job to go back to. And whatever else they were, this trio weren't dull. I met his warm gaze and felt myself smile. Second was quiet in my head, but its receptors buzzed. Some say the heart wants what it wants, but with us pilots, it's more like our starboard five-fingered appendage is in control. In that moment, I wanted nothing more than to feel our arms touch, interlace our piloting hands, and feel the heat of his wire on mine...

I felt my cheeks flush and knew he got the gist.

Rathe cleared his throat. "It's none of my business. But you're so young that I keep wondering why you're doing this."

"I am not young! Had my own leased ship for seven years. I've seen things. Been halfway across the galaxy." And back. And halfway across again. An endless loop. I'd seen the same six spaceports two hundred times. "Anything in particular you think I'm too young to do?"

"No." His expression wasn't flirtatious now. "But if I were you, I wouldn't be mixed up with us without a damned good reason. You've got your whole life—"

I held up a hand. "After we finish your job, I'll have my whole life, twenty-five million in currency, and my very own living ship. What about you—what'd they promise you?"

His voice dropped. "They didn't have to promise me anything. You know it's dangerous. We might not come back."

Really? Going after Illcord Natoth is dangerous? I tried not to roll my eyes. "I want to stop him too." Still wasn't clear to me why the four of us had better odds than the entire Unity Fleet, but they seemed so confident. "You wanted me to see Carolina Station, now I've seen it. You're right. This krov thing needs to be stopped."

"Yeah." Water rippled down his chest, darkening the hair there, outlining the flat planes of his body, the pale gold of his skin. "Now imagine planets like that. Imagine entire systems."

I'd been trying not to. "You wanted me to understand what we're up against? Now I do."

He nodded slowly. "Now you do."

There was a long silence while our eyes locked.

"This is bigger than both of us." I swallowed. "Look, I get that. Illcord's bioseeding planets. Even the Aemercy didn't pull that crap."

He cleared his throat. "Guess I'm old-fashioned, trying to protect the civilian."

"Guess you're old-fashioned," I agreed. "Don't need your protection, Rathe."

"I can see." His grin widened. "I don't trust Ells," he added. "Mureen didn't tell her Circle everything about our plans. We should watch what we say. But I'm pretty sure they can't hear us over the water."

I edged closer, purely in case of listening devices. "Got that much when you twitched like a tranked diver on the way in."

He chuckled. "Sexy says that your Second's still upset. Any idea why?"

"No." When I focused, I could almost hear it still calling for me. But the damn navvy refused to hear when I called back. "You gonna tell on me?"

"No." Rathe kneaded his forehead with his piloting hand as if his head ached. Long jump—it probably did. "We'll work it out."

"Maybe it was being unconscious for so long that split Second and me. Or the head injury."

"Maybe." He sighed. "You holding back? Sexy thinks you're holding something back."

"No. But *you* did from them. Mureen didn't even know you were close to the river! Hell, she barely knew what it meant!"

"Nice shot." He raised an eyebrow. "Polla, I'm *fine*. Just need you and *Bedalia* for that final push, so our sacrifice isn't in vain."

"Sacrifice?" I snorted. "I'm not sacrificing anything."

Rathe tilted his head back and let the water stream over his face. I wondered if he was doing it to shut me up, or to give me a good look at the lovely way water beaded on his lean-muscled skin.

"Let's not borrow trouble," he said when he finally emerged. His gaze met mine, steady as a course. "If this goes right, I'll get gelded, patch things up with my ex, and spend the next forty years needling my son to make grandkids. Maybe even move to a farm planet like yours. I grew up on one, you know."

"Which?"

His voice went soft. "Djenné."

"Oh! I'm sorry."

Djenné was among the first casualties of the Aemercy Aggressions, when a toss-up over grain rights between Aemercy colonists from the Seventy-Fifth Association and the Unity's agricore markets had turned into a minor riot, which became a ground war, followed by orbital bombardment.

· · · ● · ● · ● · · ·

(That was the first time the Unity Fleet called the Aemercy's bluff. Also the day everyone in the Milk learned that Aemercy don't bluff... but this topic is more grain to Feldelroy. Say, were you there? I'd lay odds on it. Some folks are catastrophic.)

· · · ● · ● · ● · · ·

"Nothing for you to be sorry about. My family gone... Djenné was just a place." His wistful tone said otherwise.

"You lost people on McPhee5 too, you said."

"Yeah. You know, when I said *sacrifice*, I meant wasting my last jumps solo—never liked flying alone. Now it's all I do."

"Judging from your fan club here among the Kamen, not all you've done—"

His lips quirked. "Jealous?"

"Can't be jealous of something I've got on offer."

"True, but if you're turning me down... Want me to save some Kamen for you?"

"I haven't decided." I took my time perusing his form to emphasize my point. "Not sure I'm keen on *Kamen-lords*."

Rathe reached out and traced a line down my pilot's arm, following Second's metal braid into the crook of my elbow. "Then slot with me." That damnable pilot's touch. I even felt Second respond like it liked him too, attuned to the merest brush of his thumb rubbing against its wire.

I pulled my hand away. "Don't know anything about flying a ship as big as the *Escape*."

"Easier with two." His voice softened. "We can do a mock flight while we're docked. We could do a test sync right here."

"No. When I'm actually *flying*, I like solos." Hadn't linked to anyone but Therion in a god's age.

He nodded slowly. "You're young. It gets harder, just you and your own life... out there in the dark."

I laughed. "This the sympathy play? You're not *that* old."

He shook his head. "Polla, I need you. Doesn't have to be about anything more than the flight, but I can't do this alone. Not anymore."

I snorted. "What do you need me *for*?"

"Whatever you offer. Like I said, it can just be about the flight. Or more." His mouth twitched. "I've got excellent references about three flights up."

"If I turn you down, you'll make our hosts happy?"

He matched my tone. "Won't you?"

"I haven't decided." I tilted my head. "Like I said. Barely got a good look at 'em." In truth, I hadn't been looking. Not at the Kamen.

"I'd rather fly with you." He traced my arm again, a feather touch, but it made a low urge coil between my thighs. My breath hitched, and he grinned at me hard, like he knew exactly what he'd done.

"I've got a broken navvy, and I'll have two torqued Kamen-lords when they realize I can't fly their ship..." I was babbling. I thought about that hologram of a topless lady Rathe had hidden under his mattress, the mother of his kid. Bet she never babbled. I thought of Davad on *Bedalia*, him telling me she'd fly for me no matter what. I wanted to recount that tale, but my lips came out with another question entirely. "Did you know they made me comm the Unity? I'm a wanted woman now."

He chuckled. "They could hardly do it themselves. We pulled that con in a few ports. Was it so bad?"

They could hardly do it themselves, he'd said, but Mureen had tried, hadn't she? Hiding under that captain's cap. She and Arkan didn't even trust me for that—not until they were desperate. "I told some Unity bosses I'd sic Illcord Natoth on the Unity," I said.

"Wait, what?" Rathe's smile froze.

"Davad told me to say we were working for House Illcord."

"Who, exactly, did you speak to?" Those lines around his kissable mouth were pulling it down.

"No idea. Four of 'em. Maybe five. One was called Vadim. I think." I thought back. "Or maybe two were called Vadim." At *least I'd called two of 'em Vadim?*

"Was one Alta Admiral *Ivo* Vadim?" He looked startled.

"Maybe. He was—"

"She."

"They were all only heads. Holographic heads." I pondered. "Wearing hats. White hats. Mureen made me put on one too."

"Huh." Rathe muttered what sounded like a curse under his breath. "House politics are above my pay grade. Davad must know what he's doing." He didn't sound sure, and then he added to my unease by returning to our original subject. "Let's try a simple link, you and me." His eyes crinkled when he smiled, and that kissable mouth turned back up with an optimism I didn't quite buy. "We can talk in peace that way. Away from Kamen ears."

True, as far as it went. But... "Slotting in won't heal your cortex."

His navhand tapped his naked thigh, jittering in a way I'd seen on other pilots before—and didn't like. His cock was down again, too, hanging like an afterthought. "Come on, just a two-way bridge—"

"—that mimics whatever you want it to. Might as well be a feelie sim." I shook my head. Therion and I... Toward the end, we'd spent more time linked like that than we had in an actual bed—or actually flying our ship. That experience still left a bad taste. I stared pointedly at his crotch, feeling my traitorous cheeks heat. "Don't need me for your feelie sim, Rathe."

His voice darkened. "Just to *talk*. This isn't anything more than you want it to be."

I wanted too much for my own comfort. I wanted him, and we both knew it, but what would I be doing, getting mixed up with a Unity freak? Screwing another pilot wasn't like picking up a dockside trawl, especially in the dreaming.

I dragged my eyes back up to his face. "You're close to the river and you know it. Hell, you shouldn't even be speaking to Sexy when you're not flying."

"At least my navvy's speaking to me." His smile was gone now, winked out like it'd jumped to lightspeed.

"Glad someone is." I didn't need more complications. I walked out.

"Polla, wait!" I heard the shower switch off.

"Get some rest," I snapped, not looking back.

There was more than one room in our locked quarters. I took some of the food and found the one farthest away. I stared at the door for a long time, wondering if I wanted Rathe to knock, wondering if I'd just turned down a good screw, or ruined something more serious, and, as a bonus, torqued off the only ally I had.

But my copilot didn't knock, and eventually I fell asleep.

That night I dreamed of oceans, darker and deeper than any I'd ever seen. We flew into seas like space, and I couldn't remember a time before when I'd been this free.

I woke in the strange empty room with dried tears on my cheeks, lips tasting of salt.

Mureen greeted me the next morning with the fat man, Ken'ri Ells, standing in the hallway outside my room like they were hunters lying in wait. She informed me that Ken'ri Ells would give me a tour of the station. Didn't see much I could say, so I went along, although I couldn't help noticing that the bunks we passed on our way out were all empty. I wasn't sure if I was jealous Rathe had found company or that, unlike me, he'd had access to leave the entire time.

"Where's Davad?" I asked as we climbed the stairs back to the station's main level. Wasn't going to ask about any pilots and their sleeping arrangements.

"Busy," the man told me, tone implying it was none of my business how. "Mureen? Ken'ri Solon wanted to see you this morning... Perhaps you can give Pilot Ottrava and me some time alone."

"Of course." But Mureen paused, looking between us, and I couldn't read her expression at all. "Do what Ken'ri Ells says, Polla. It is important."

"Not gonna kill a person," I said. "Or violate any commandments." I was joking, but there was a long and terrible pause. "A joke," I added. "Let me try that again. I'm not gonna kill—"

Mureen was already making her way back the way we'd come.

"Follow," the fat man commanded. He was smiling like I'd amused him, at least.

I think it was his smile that silenced me. We climbed back up three flights of stairs and then down another identical corridor. I realized what bugged me about the place. "Transparency shutters are all closed," I noted. "Not one showing the view."

Ken'ri Ells nodded. "There is an old greenhouse on the upper level, should you need to see. We Kamen do not. We can feel the horror of the Abomination with our every breath."

"Yeah. Well..." I shivered. "Guess I see your point."

"Do you?" The man's face was a blank moon. We'd crossed into a main room encircled by several couches, depressions in the seats and a few half-filled drinks suggesting it had recently been occupied.

"Where is everyone?" I asked.

"I sent them to another lounge two levels down." He sat himself, gesturing until I settled in opposite. "This sojourn is pleasant for the Ken'ri who accompanied us. Maintaining shield integrity requires constant concentration. Normally we have very little time to relax."

But he didn't look relaxed. The man stared at me like I was the last quez in the Milky, sprawled naked on a platter.

"If I'm keeping you from vacation—" I paused, because then he pulled two wooden boxes out of his jacket and set them down on the table. "What? Presents? You shouldn't have."

"I want to test your awareness, Pilot Ottrava." He tapped one of the boxes. "Can you tell me what lies within this box?"

I reached for the one he'd indicated.

"Without opening." His clammy hand covered mine and pushed it back. "Or touching."

"Well, no." Had an inkling of what he was about—and it was nuts. A vague memory. Hadn't been more than five, and the three boxes were colored red, blue, and yellow... "This is a kamn test?" Ma said I'd cried when I failed. (I didn't like failing, still don't.) "Some Kamen-lord tested me when I was a kid. Bombed it like Djenné."

"Close your eyes." He ignored me. "Reach out with your senses. What do you feel?"

My senses felt like this fat man had a lot of bad ideas.

I felt Second stir dimly at the back of my mind like it agreed. [Error?] It sounded almost hopeful.

[Second?] I tried thinking encouraging thoughts, but my navvy fell quiet again. I truly didn't like the glint in the man's eyes. Something hungry there. Expectant.

"Nothing." I shrugged. "Empty. Both of 'em."

"Hrm." He gave me a sidelong glance. "Are you sure?"

Suddenly I was. Tests like this were always tricks. "Slug's in your hand, and that's the worst game of two-box monte I've ever seen." Not that two-box monte was a thing. Binary odds were too basic.

Ells put a bullet-shaped slug of metal down on the table next to the boxes, and I realized the slug *had* been in his hand.

"Well, look-it that," I drawled. "The Priests blessed me after all. A stinking miracle."

"Hush." He didn't seem rattled. "One box is heavier than the other. Can you tell which?"

"That one." I pointed at random. "Or neither. Let's go with neither. They weigh the same."

His right eyelid kept twitching. Could be a tell, I thought. "Do they feel the same?" he asked.

"How could I tell from here? One's got a layer of metal?" That seemed like the kind of stunt Kamen would pull.

There was a long silence.

"Okay?" I yawned. Had been a strange night. I usually remembered my dreams, but mine had been formless and left me with a creeping sense of dread. *Oceans*, I thought suddenly.

"Both metal," Ells admitted. "Beneath the wood. What can you tell me about the metals?"

"Hard and smooth?" I snickered.

The Kamen-lord sighed. "Davad said you sensed wooden doors on Earth, ones that he assumed were metal."

Had I? "Couldn't Davad tell they *weren't* metal?"

"Not at first." His brows drew together. "Ken'ri are trained to act upon what we see with our eyes. To ignore all else. Can you imagine that?"

"No." I felt uneasy. "You don't *see* those golem spears you use in space. You don't see metal buried underground when you mine for it, either." Or a *stone gir in someone's pocket,* I thought. My hand closed around the one in mine.

"True." He looked like I'd pleased him. "And such work is dangerous. Some Kamen believe extending our senses has a corrupting influence, and we should not do it at all, even to help others. Did you *sense* those doors were wooden, or was it a clever guess, when you saw they didn't open?"

I shrugged. "I guess I guessed. But I could use a spectrometer. Got one?"

His eyelid twitched again. "And why do you carry a gir in your pocket? Why *that* gir? Did Davad give it to you?"

"I don't know what you're talking about." My freehand tightened around the stone. My poker face was good, yet I felt my cheeks flush. "Why shouldn't I carry it? No one will give me a gun."

"A gun?" Ells spoke as if the word were alien. Perhaps distasteful. His brow furrowed. "Do you prefer guns?"

Wouldn't anyone? "I was raised with 'em."

He pointed to the slug he'd set on the table, an ovoid chunk of ore. "Can you make this float? Or move across the table? Have you ever made your gir move without the use of your hands, or reshaped it, even a little?"

"If I could do crap like that, don't you think I'd be in a casino or locked up with you Kamen-lords already?" I'd never heard of people developing the kamn in later life... although I supposed anyone who did wouldn't advertise, since that'd get them locked up instead of being free to get lucky at casinos. "People don't just *get* kamn. You're either born with it or you're not."

His stony expression reminded me of Mureen's. "Developing a gift late in life is rare, but not unknown. You could have been tested too early before."

"Did I pass?"

"Some answers were imprecise. We would need three more hours of the same for a proper evaluation..." He paused, then shook his head. "But no."

"Because pilots can't be Kamen-lords." I tapped my navarm. "If I had your powers, Second never would've taken to me." I thought of Davad and his scars. "I know Kamen don't know anything about science, but the links we make with navvies can't work with your magic—"

"Not magic. And that is a lie." On another man, his round face with its smile lines and dimpled cheeks could be called jovial. "One your Pilot Guild chooses to disseminate. The practice is highly illegal, but Kamen have been pilots, even a few within recent memory."

"Well not me."

"No. Not you, Pilot Ottrava." The Kamen-lord sighed. "Show me the gir in your pocket."

I put it on the table.

Ells looked almost jolly. "Ah. And how did you acquire this weapon?"

"Stole it." I shrugged. "Why are you acting like it's gonna grow legs?" For he was. His grin couldn't hide the beads of sweat on his brow, or his sharp intake of breath.

The Kamen-lord exhaled slowly. "Do you know to whom this gir belonged?"

"Yes, Ledas Starfire. Can you tell by looking?" Maybe gir were all chipped with codes only Kamen could read. "Davad kept it. Sentimental, I guess. Did you know he and Starfire were twins?"

"I trained them both." The Kamen-lord picked the gir up gingerly, and I gasped, because in his hand the stone reformed, lengthening, until it was a two-meter-long staff, taller than both of us. The man stood, resting the staff flat on both hands, and pivoted, bending over in what looked like a formal bow as he handed it back.

I took it awkwardly. Too awkward sitting, so I stood, holding it in both hands. "Oh." I had an odd impulse to twirl the stick around in my hand, but when I started, of course it thunked onto the table, nearly overturning an empty bev. The table was made of some kind of alloy, and it clanged when the rod hit it, making me jump. "How did you make it so long?"

"I shaped the stone. The rod is hollow. See how light?" Invisible pressure tugged at the stick, as if to pull it from my hands.

I tightened my grip. "Stop that."

"Can you *make* me stop that?" That smile I'd taken for gentle wasn't, and his tone possessed a new ugliness. "The shiv is a coward's weapon. Her gir should not be shaped thus. My student was many things, but never a coward."

"And?" Why had Mureen left me with a madman? "She's dead, so who cares? It's the other one Davad and Mureen are stopping. Illcord Natoth. Do you know that?"

His lip curled. "Do you?"

I leveled the stick, only too aware this Kamen-lord could rip it from my grasp and wrap it around my neck if he wanted. *Stone-shapers.* Come to think of it, Kamen-lords possessed all sorts of ways to cause me bodily injury. Davad had said they grew up dueling. Running trials by combat for the princelings.

"What you lot do is none of my business." I kept my grip on the rod steady through sheer obstinacy. "Just here for the job."

He smirked as if I'd proven something. "Your form is terrible."

"Get screwed with a rusty." I dropped a hand, pointing the gir out like a sword in one of those vids. Waggled it from side to side, trying to straighten my back like all those exercises Mureen had shown me. Come to think of it, she'd used a staff too, only hers was metal. Did gir come in metal?

I felt ridiculous.

Ells walked toward the exit. "I'll be just a moment," he called as the door slid shut behind him. I heard the click as he locked it, probably using his damnable mind, and I stood, trying to twirl Ledas Starfire's fancy stick without hitting the wall or the table, which was harder than it looked. Impossible, really, unless I held my hand above my head, which didn't seem practical. Maybe Starfire had been taller. Or maybe the fat man had made it too tall on purpose, just to keep me off-balance.

I'd moved on to drinking someone's half-finished cup of caffeinoid by the time he returned, carrying another stick, also outsized. I'd put mine—hers—on the now-dented table. At his approach, I leaned back and folded my arms. "Not fighting you, ser. I don't have a death wish."

"And yet, you've agreed to a very dangerous mission."

"I'm just the flier."

"You sound quite sure." Ells stood, stick in hand, that rounded belly hanging over his belt.

I had an irrational urge to punch him. I'd never wanted to punch anyone besides Therion (and once my cousin Sara) before. My anger felt foreign, like a sick twist in my chest. Second registered alarm, and I tried soothing it, only to have my navvy's panic intensify fear in us both. My words came out terse. "I know my job. Do you know yours?"

"Yes." A gun floated out of his robes and onto the table.

I froze. The man had said he'd trained Ledas and Davad. He'd never said he'd trained them *wisely.*

"You prefer guns?" He gestured at the pistol with his stone stick. "Take it."

I did, stammering thanks, and fiddled with the magazine enough to see about two dozen flechettes, sharp and reassuringly dangerous. "This is very nice." It was. Da had nicer back home, but not by much.

"I'm glad you're pleased."

"Why?" I held his gift in my pilot's hand, still clutching the gir in the other, and tried to twirl the pistol in my fingers like I'd done a thousand times—only I nearly dropped it. "Davad said I don't need to be armed. I'm not going to assassinate any Kamen-lords or—"

"Illcord Natoth?"

I swallowed. "Right. Just flying the ship. Not getting within a thousand meters of him."

"Illcord *Natoth*," the Kamen repeated like a taunt.

"If he's responsible for that thing outside"—I waved vaguely with the gun—"then he's a Kamen-lord problem, not mine."

"A problem Glos has tried desperately to fix." He settled down on the couch opposite mine. "May I share something classified? Something even Davad and Mureen don't know?"

"Nice of you to ask first." I leveled the gun. Not directly at him, of course, but cocked at an angle above his head. "Shoot."

Ells grinned like he got the joke. "Within the half-year, Glos has sent more than a dozen agents to intercept Illcord Natoth."

"So you know where his secret planet is?" Nuala Erta sure seemed famous for a secret planet.

He shook his head. "Glos sends operatives to sites they predict Nate will visit. There were two on a supply convoy that vanished last week. They never report back."

"Perhaps Glos's agents aren't very good." My voice sounded cold in my own ears.

"Glos sends the best of us." He leaned forward. "But my former students were the best of us too, once. You have to understand, Kamen are vulnerable to the krov in ways you can't imagine."

"So it's hopeless." The Kamen couldn't stop Illcord. The Unity Fleet couldn't stop him, either. Nice of Ells to tell me I'd taken on a fool's errand, when my bim was already in the fire.

His face creased. "It may be very hard."

"That would be my employer's problem." I tried to twirl my new gun again. He looked mildly concerned when it dropped on the table. I picked it up fast, re-securing the safety, which I'd somehow knocked open. *Da, I thought, would kill me.*

"Do you know how your companions plan to stop him?" he asked softly. "I do not."

"Told you already, I'm only the pilot."

He nodded. "I have every confidence in their ability—"

"You don't sound like it."

He continued like I hadn't spoken. "—but if it came down to *you* to solve our problem? Could *you* shoot Illcord Natoth? The head would be best, I think. The brain. More than once. You'll want to do it from a distance. Perhaps from the back."

I tried to keep my poker face still. "Guns don't work against Kamen-lords. Everyone knows that." I thought about shooting at Ells to prove it, but you can train as much as you like in summer camp and Strangways, it's still not the same as actually taking what's been drilled into your bones as a deadly weapon—never a toy, not even when you're six and playing with a toy version—and shooting at a person. *Birds.* Da and I shot birds sometimes, but those you could eat. I'd always been too squeamish to go after Feldelroy's larger mammals. Always thought I could in a pinch, but—

But looking into the fat man's eyes, I became convinced that he could see the sum of me: all of my summer camps and hunting trips, that time I'd threatened a sleazy narc in a portside bar and then turned and ran, every time like that NewBern warehouse, all of those times when I hadn't been a hero, all written on my face, plain as day.

I'd never shot anyone. Like any good smuggler, I was a coward, not a killer.

I put the weapon down carefully on the table, trying to ignore Da's voice in my head telling me to check the safety twice. "Nate could reflect a bullet back. Don't you Kamen-lords do that?"

"Natoth is no longer Kamen. Do you understand?"

Like I cared about their philosophies. I checked the gun's safety. "Isn't krov the same thing?"

"Not for us." He steepled his fingers. "According to Davad, Natoth can no longer manipulate inorganic material. Ergo, you *could* shoot him with a metal bullet." There was a glint in his eye, a near childish glee. "He would never see it coming from you."

I snorted. "Especially if I shot him in the back."

"Exactly!" He beamed.

Again, I reflected on how much Davad seemed to know about our enemy, and how everyone kept taking his word—the word of a *boma fiday* twin-killing traitor—as gospel. "I'm not planning on seeing Illcord Natoth. I land the ship, then I take off. That's my entire job." Safety secure, I shoved the gun in my pocket. "But thanks for the piece."

He nodded at the gir I'd put on the floor, still shaped like a stone rod. "Humor me and take her weapon as well."

"Make it small," I shot back. "Not very portable like that, is it?"

"Pick it up and I will."

I did to shut him up, and he leaned across the table and knocked it out of my hands in a gesture too quick to even register, nearly hitting me in the face. It rolled across the floor, and the man stood, leveling his own. "Again."

"Get soldered," I shot back, sitting back down. "No." Drinking someone else's caffeinoid wasn't hygienic, but it gave me something to do with my hands after I flopped back down on the couch. My pilot's arm throbbed where his stick had banged into Second. And Second was utterly silent. If it knew what we were doing, it clearly gave no damns.

"Hrm." The Kamen-lord loomed over me. His kind face had turned blank and cold.

I glared back, wishing for Second to hear me so I wouldn't feel so alone. There'd been dark times with my Syndicate: times like those slave pens I couldn't bear to remember, and my last run, which I'd never forget. The run when I realized my entire haul was contaminated and my boss wanted it delivered anyway. A stock of expired antifungals meant for a colony where every third kid under five already didn't make it due to the crap in the soil. Not the first time my Syndicate boss had used me for a job shipping death—but those crap meds were just my breaking point, one that should've come five months earlier in the stockyard at NewBern, when I let Therion lead me away.

Still, in all my years smuggling, no Syndicate boss had ever pegged me for a button gal.

"I'm not gonna fight you," I said. My gir lay on the floor where he'd knocked it.

"So I see." His eyes looked like flat blue stones. "But you will shoot Illcord Natoth?"

"Absolutely." I flashed him a smile.

* * * ● * ● * * *

(As any Feldelroyan child learns on their first summer Strangways, when you're dealing with a moon-touched madman, it's best to agree with whatever they say.

The Grass Priests got a lot of converts in those summer sessions. At least for the duration.)

Chapter 18 * Confided

While you took more jobs off planet, my belly grew and I kept looking into more crap. Ken'ri Arkan Davad (aka Davad Arkan, or Arkan Davadius Mortons), was the name that kept popping up in conjunction with Mureen's. The bands claimed that redheaded beauty was the real mastermind behind the *Ascendant*'s bombing and the botched raid on a NewPrinceton depot. He was *also* Starfire's brother (increasingly rumored on the gray bands to be her murderer), and, by all accounts, had been just as much of a brute in the Aemercy Aggressions as Illcord Natoth himself.

The casualty list at NewPrinceton claimed Arkan was responsible for four hundred and three dead guardsfolk.

From the perspective of a forcibly retired Feldelroyan smuggler, the difference between Arkan and Illcord came down to tonnage and time.

And you called Illcord Natoth a god, Sam. Like being a *god* is some excuse.

* * * * * * * * * *

OUR AWKWARD DÉTENTE BROKE when the door slid open and Davad walked in. I watched the muscles in his perfect jaw twist as he looked from Ells, standing with his big stick, to me on the couch with my bev. Davad's gaze dropped to my gir on the floor, and the princeling's words could've frozen vapor. "What's this?"

"Your pal tested me for kamn." I put the bev down. "I don't have it."

"Of course not." Davad turned to Ells. "I tested her myself. I told you last night."

"You were vague," the fat man said mildly. "I needed to be sure."

"You tested me?" I broke in. "When, princeling? When did you test me?"

Instead of answering, Davad lifted his hand, and the stone rod rose from the floor, snapping into his grasp. He flipped it twice, and then in his hands it shrank, reforming to that familiar squat shape, that menacing daggerlike point. I was starting to feel like an old hand watching Kamen-lords shape their weapons, and I think I barely blinked at the sight of a murderer holding the very one he'd used to kill his own twin.

Our eyes met, and I fancied I could see that realization dawn on Davad's face. His gaze dropped to the floor. For a second, I actually thought he was going to hand me the gir back.

But then Ells moved. The staff he held twisted like melted wax until he held a *boma fiday* archaic sword, blunt and long and disturbingly sharp. One of his legs slid out into some kind of combat stance as he raised the weapon at Davad. "Precisely *how* did you test her?"

"I used an artifact." As I watched, my gir grew and flattened in Davad's starboard hand until it was a blade like Ells's. "Do I need to name which?" Davad's arm whipped forward. Their swords crossed with a dull scraping noise that set my teeth on edge.

"Thieves don't generally admit to possession." But Ells's voice had softened. The sword in his hand reformed to a shorter baton. He twirled it in one hand while Davad minced away from him in a series of almost comical steps, still extending his own blade.

"You'd have to take that up with my ancestors. I'm not the one who stole it."

"Oh?"

"Not from the Glos vaults three hundred years ago," Davad amended. His sword had shortened, developing a nasty-looking curve. He landed an uppercut on Ells's arm, fast enough to blur, but the blade rebounded, as if caught on an invisible shield. "Whatever else you've heard is true."

"Where is the treasure now?"

Wherever it was, speculating about its whereabouts and their rooster's contest had Ells's full attention, which was a relief for me.

I crossed my knees and leaned back to watch the show.

"Safe." Davad stifled a yawn and flipped the stone blade back and forth between his hands. I noted the edge had blunted again, although I supposed that could change in a heartbeat. "Where Nate will never find it."

The older man settled back down on the couch, resting his gir on his knees. If they'd proven anything with that ridiculous display, I had no idea what. Ells gave a heavy sigh. "If he recovers it—"

"Oh, it's not *here*." Davad gestured with his weapon, perhaps indicating the station, sector, or quadrant. Seeing his calm expression, I vowed to search his quarters more thoroughly.

"Are you sure your plan will work?" Ells asked.

"I fix my mistakes." Davad glanced from me to the floor.

"You've failed at least once." The Kamen-lord Elder looked just as unruffled as Davad himself. Considering the man's penchant for arming strange smugglers, I doubted that was true.

Davad shrugged. "I had an instructor who swore he'd give me another chance."

Ells leaned back with a heavy sigh. "We're sheltered here, but not blind. Incursions have intensified tenfold since—"

"We're not here for your blessing." The princeling's gaze slid to me and then back to his old teacher. "Mureen might think it appropriate to leave the pilot with you, but I hope you haven't confused her."

"He wanted to duel," I chimed in. "But I'm not crazy."

That comment earned me a smile from Davad, who'd shaped my gir back into a shiv before Ells broke in again. "Did you ever think of trying it yourself?"

Davad snorted. "I saw what it did to her before. Now..." He shrugged. "Inert as it was when Bene Dix pulled it from the wreckage."

"Oh!" I thought I understood. "You're talking about Bene Dix's Crown?" I recalled the net made of stars. "That's what you were doing when you made me wear it? Testing me for kamn?"

"And you felt nothing." Davad turned from me back to Ells. "So, as you see, Ken'ri—"

"Quite a risk—" But the fat man sounded approving.

"I was already quite sure."

"And where is the Crown now?" His tone sharpened.

"Safe." Davad's grin got glacial.

"Why did you think Bene Dix's Crown would work on me?" I interrupted. "I don't have Kamen powers."

"I knew it would not." Davad glanced between us both. "You felt nothing, Pilot, and I sensed nothing." His head lifted, that arrogant poise I both envied and despised coming to the fore.

• • • •●•●• • • •

(In fact, I hadn't felt nothing, merely nothing I could define. How do you describe an emotion you can't name? One without thought or form? Of course, hindsight, that wretched beast, makes certain things so obvious.

The sum of us is more than we ever dared think—)

• • • •●•●• • • •

"But why test *me*?" My words fell into a vacuum. Both men were staring at each other, with faces blank and empty as stone.

"Let's go." Davad gestured for me to stand and follow. "You may safely ignore Ells from now on," he added, casting the man a parting glare. "We shouldn't have come."

"Wasn't my idea," I snapped. "But Rathe needed the rest."

"We could have stayed on the ship."

"*You* wanted to show me atrocities. Got any more?"

"I hope not." One side of his mouth quirked, and I felt oddly pleased.

"I do wish you luck," the Kamen-lord behind us called. I opened my mouth, but Davad pushed me through the door before I could advise Ells where he could stick that gir of his—and his spacedamned luck.

• • • ● • ● • • • •

"Rathe was placed to watch you," Davad told me when we'd turned 'round the corridor's bend. "No need to introduce confusion—for you or this Circle."

"I'm not an idiot," I snapped. "I can take care of myself. Rathe was gone when I woke up, and Mureen left me with your old teacher. Why does he think I have Kamen powers?"

"He just confirmed you do not."

I decided not to mention the gun. This princeling showed no sign of returning my gir, and I didn't want to lose a weapon that could be useful. But Davad had sensed the gir in my pocket before. Did Kamen do that automatically, or did they have to try? Did me thinking about the gun make it more likely that he'd sense it? Of course, Kamen couldn't read minds—could they? I tried to distract myself by thinking of anything else—something absolutely filthy in case he could—but that only drove my thoughts back to the gun.

My freehand checked the safety again.

The princeling carried on, seemingly unbothered. "Ells still has ties to Glos, the others say. It's not my place to ask Mureen why she left you with him."

I frowned. "Not your place? Isn't this your plan?"

He laughed. "No. *My* plan was to put an end to my sister. I expected someone else would deal with the aftermath. I assumed *we'd* be dead."

"Cheery." I shivered, remembering the two gir under his mattress, both stained with a murderer's blood. "So Mureen planned everything?" She acted so meek and mild. If I were Davad and a suspicious person, I'd wonder if that meekness was an act—yet he preferred to cast his doubts on me.

"After my wounds healed, I was placed in a cell." He stuck his hands in his pockets and increased his pace, walking through the blank halls like he knew exactly where to go. "Mureen was one of my guards."

"Couldn't you just short out the cell's energy field?"

"Yes, and I did, when we escaped. But for a time, grief consumed me. The fact that my jailers considered me to be a hero..." He made a disgusted face, and to my amazement, spat on the floor.

I must have made some reaction, because his voice cracked. "I-I'm sorry. That was—"

"*Human.*" I spat too, to keep him company. "You killed your evil sister, and you were sad. That's *human.*"

I'd earned a smile. "It is crude," Davad said slowly. "Expelling saliva as we just did. One of the worst insults for 12Fam."

"Go on," I urged.

"Thanks to what I'd done, I was a lightly guarded prisoner. Mureen brought my breakfast trays. And one day she offered me a chance to... fix things."

"Romantic," I drawled.

The Kamen chuckled. "At its heart, her plan was as simple as mine."

"Kill this Illcord guy."

He nodded. "Nate is tied to the bloodships, just as my sister was. Without him—"

"Without him, some other slob will come along." Had Arkan Davad never seen how a Syndicate worked? Had my Kamen-lords never seen a drame in their lives? Hell, wasn't that how the 12Fam Houses worked? *Meet the new lord princeling, just the same as the old lord princeling—*

"No." He sounded absolutely sure. "After Nate there is nothing."

I waited for the rest, but it didn't come. His feet clattered on the deckplates. Those stupid stone boots. Ells wore them too.

"Plan isn't simple if Rathe can't fly us off this station." *Plan isn't simple if Second isn't speaking to me and I can't fly at all,* I thought. We both had our secrets.

He glanced at me. "*You* could fly us."

If only he knew. "Not alone. Not on a ship as big as the *Escape.* And Bedalia—"

"She frightens you."

I didn't like admitting it. "She doesn't like me."

"I told you that doesn't matter."

What did he know? I took a deep breath. "There's something else."

"What?"

"I—" I stumbled for a way to begin. "Don't be angry."

Davad walked faster, forcing me to match his stride. "What is it? Did Ells say something?"

Ells had said a lot. "He was cowcrap, but it's not that."

"He was my tutor when I was seven. Lee's too. For a time, he was assigned all three of us." He scoffed. "I thought he was so wise. Now all I see is a scared old man."

All three. The third being the man Ells wanted me to shoot. "What'd he teach?"

"Ethics."

My incredulous laugh clattered off the walls. "Really?"

"Lee was the favorite. What were you going to say?"

"Where are we going?"

"Here." Like a change in air pressure, I saw the open transparency beyond the bend, and the cold wreck of Carolina Station beyond that. Ells had mentioned an old greenhouse before, a viewing station designed to collect solar radiation from the light of this system's dim blue star.

Three rows of benches lined the view, surrounded by empty planters. From the look of things, nothing had grown here for some time. Davad moved to the center bench.

"Sit, Pilot. Circle members rarely come here, so we won't be interrupt-ed. What were you going to ask?"

I sat. Took a deep breath and stared out at the Abomination. The name fit. *Time for the confess.* "Second and I aren't working. It's not speaking to me."

"What do you mean?" He sounded confused. "Did it say something?"

"No. That's the problem. It can't hear me. I can hear it, but all it ever says is 'error.'"

"Ah." He nodded slowly. "How long has this been the case?"

"Since I woke up on Earff."

Those hooded eyes blinked. "I see. Go on."

For a while I couldn't. I'd expected anger, but he barely looked surprised. Silence stretched like an epoch. I detached myself from his cold gaze by turning to the view, but that was worse. All those lives cut off and alone in the dark—from this distance, the doomed station looked like the twisted branches of an of unholy tree.

I didn't have to see closer to know their end had been every spacer's nightmare.

I took a deep breath. "Ells told me they've been trying to take out Illcord for ages. They haven't done it. The Unity hasn't done it, either. What makes us different?"

"We do." Davad held out his palm. "You say your symbiote isn't working? May I see?"

"What are you going to do?"

"Check for loose connections."

I eyed him. "You can do that?"

"During the war I used to do it all the time for our pilots. Sometimes even minor repairs." He extended his hand. "Let me see."

I let the weight of my starboard palm rest on his. If he'd been a pilot, it would've meant something, but I felt nothing.

It only took a moment before he withdrew. "The symbiote is functional." His other hand hovered over my skin. "You're perfect."

I shook my head. "But it can't hear me. We can't fly."

He sighed. "Rathe must know."

I nodded. "Second talks to Sexy, but not to me."

"Too many secrets. I'm not surprised our lieutenant kept yours." One eyebrow raised. "He likes you."

"That's not the point." An image of Rathe in the shower rose, unbidden, to my forebrain. My face felt hot.

"And *you* like him." A low chuckle. "Have—"

"None of your business! I just told you my navvy's crap, and you want to know if I'm copulating?"

"Physical intimacy might—"

"*Don't.*" My face felt uncomfortably warm, quite unseemly for a jezebel.

"Why don't you go see him?" The unfamiliar kindness in his tone made that suggestion sound entirely too reasonable.

"Think he's occupied." I recalled the empty bunk.

"I don't believe so. He returned to our ship this morning to do the repairs."

"He's on *Escape* alone?" I frowned.

I was no expert on Unity corvettes, but the repairs Rathe had mentioned to our fellows hadn't triggered any maintenance alerts that I'd seen. I'd assumed he'd made them up to get the time off he sorely needed.

• • • • ● • ● • • • •

(Easier sometimes to tell your crew it's the ship, not the flesh. Less embarrassing that way. Less *personal*.)

• • • • ● • ● • • • •

The princeling pilot expert was still talking. "—I do know something about pilots, Pilot. The last time we were here, Rathe was popular." Davad paused. "Are you jealous? Your kind aren't known for it, but you come from a morally conservative planet."

"Don't be stupid, I'm worried. I don't think Mureen gets it, but you do. You knew Rathe was close to deepriver, but you still left him alone this past year."

"Incorrect. As much as possible, Mureen and I kept our lieutenant engaged. I encouraged outside interests. He went to town weekly. He had a lover there, and when that ended... Stars, I'd have bedded him myself if he wanted."

"You and *Rathe*?" I snorted.

"Neither of us had the inclination. But I know what physical connections mean to your kind. He would bed you... and you would bed him. You *like* him." This damnable Kamen-lord knew too much. "A mutually beneficial assignation. You are receptive—you asked Mureen and me intimate questions regarding his personal life."

"Rathe hardly knows me! Or me him."

"With pilots, that rarely matters."

My indignation sharpened. "You don't know a damn thing about us!"

"I know if you lose your connection to the physical world, you die."

He was hitting damnably close to the reasons I'd drawn away from Rathe in the first place—burying any attraction I might've felt for Lieutenant Rathe Sai under an ion storm of my own indignation. I forced myself to sound careless. "Pretty cynical for someone who waited a year to bed the woman he loves."

"A bit too soon to speak of love—"

"Oh, do you and Mureen need another year for that?"

"We aren't pilots, Pilot." His mouth tightened. "And there's no future for us."

"Obviously. She can do better."

"Undoubtedly." He let out a heavy sigh. "Your symbiote's fine. You control it. Keep that in mind."

"That's not how it works."

"I know how it works." He gestured at the hall, which continued past our viewing bubble into what I assumed was a mirrored layout of the way we'd just come, small space stations being what they were. "Go find Rathe. Oh, and tell him..." His voice hardened. "Tell him I need to speak to him alone when he can find the time."

Pride. Arkan Davad had it in spades.

"Find Rathe yourself." I stood. "I've got better things to do. Or better people. Some of those other Kamen looked interested. If I'm gonna screw someone, might as well pick a bedmate who isn't gonna cross deepriver before their next birthday. The way Rathe jacks in when he knows he's scrambled... I'm not even sure he'll last the week. Did you know that? You think you know everything about us, but did you know that?"

"Just how close is he?"

"Closer now than before that last jump." Cold extremities, weight loss, loss of interest in the outside world, loss of libido—the image in the shower came to me again.

Perhaps Rathe hadn't lost everything.

"How close?"

"How many jumps to your planet?"

"Not... many." Davad seemed to hesitate. "You'll be there. That will help."

"Not if Second isn't working!"

"It will." At least the Kamen-lord princeling who'd never flown a ship in his life was sure I could.

"He rested for a year and it's this bad. He didn't rest *enough*." I was abruptly sure of that. Solo, with the dreaming at his fingertips... No pilot's made of stone. "Every time he goes under—just being slotted in fries us, slower than flying, but it's not nothing. You said you knew pilots?"

"I knew one quite well." Davad's scarred hand tapped the metal bench. He was wearing gloves again, but I'd never unsee the scars on his starboard. "And I worked closely with others assigned to me during the Aemercy conflict, including Rathe. He was fine then."

"How long ago was this?"

"We first met nine years ago."

"Was it you who made him take fifty thousand jumps?"

"Is that a lot?" He sounded so dry I assumed he was joking.

"Most pilots retire before a third of that. How many did your best pal take?"

"With one ship?" He shrugged. "She lost count."

"Doesn't matter if you fly the same ship every time, or a thousand different ones. Each jump fries you a little bit more!"

"You misunderstand. She flew thousands at once."

She. An ugly feeling sank in my guts. What had Ken'ri Ells said about Kamen and implants? That some fool Kamen got wired to be pilots? And if that wasn't obvious *enough*, I was starting to realize that only one person in the entire Milky could put that tragic, fixed expression on Arkan Davad's face. The man had locked in on his own ghost again, was now staring through me like I didn't exist.

"Hey!" I elbowed him. "I'm talking about us mortals. Not your stinking sister!"

. . . ● . ● . ● . . .

(Some say the Guild are monsters who make pilots into lemmings, turn us into sea-rats who won't stop running at the cliff. It's true our lives are hard and fast. I've never regretted that, not really. Even now, I'm not sure I can. The Guild designs our navvies so we won't stop flying. They tap into our pleasure centers to keep us connected in the black.

The Guild does quite a lot we don't care to worry about. In fact, I'm a little surprised the Guild didn't have their rebel Kamen-lords killed, considering how many rules were broken—or did they try?)

. . . ● . ● . ● . . .

He scowled. "How did you know I meant Lee?"

"Your teacher." I threw Ells into a garbage lane. "He told me a few things."

He raised one eyebrow. "Testing you."

"Was it jumping that drove her nuts enough to wipe out Centauri?"

His smile tightened. "Some believe."

"No licensed Guild doc would put a navvy in a Kamen-lord—"

"An Aemercy drunk who didn't care why we'd asked and didn't know what we were performed the operation. Three symbiotes for ten thousand Earth solis."

Too cheap. Guild didn't install for less than fifty thousand, and that was only after five years of training. I felt sick. "He gave you rewipes? Wait, you said three?"

"That's what puzzles you? Lee, Nate, and I. We had a fourth, but she declined before they strapped her in the chair."

"Wise girl."

"Feldelroyan."

"We're known for our smarts." Yet my cousin had been dumb enough to follow this lot and die. I wondered if it was her he'd known. If so, at least Cousin Beya had been smart enough not to get a navvy from a rotting corpse... unlike these spoiled princelings.

"You're rich," I continued. "Why wouldn't you get new ones?" With all that Arkan power, there had to be a way around the Guild monopoly. Stranger things than unassigned navvies fell off the wrong lifter, as I was in a position to know. And there was a way around everything. Da had taught me that.

"Perhaps we could have. But Lee had a theory that a symbiote that was already broken would be easier to..." he frowned. "To *bind*? I don't know your terminology. She thought there would be less chance of rejection."

I felt ill. "We don't have terms for that. Only scavengers use rewipes. And you'd better hope your Aemercy drunk wiped 'em, because if not—"

"The symbiotes were erased before installation." That eyebrow rose again. I hated that the expression made him look wise. "I'm quite sure. Part of the arrangement."

"Guess we can't blame your stinking sister's war crimes on a new personality." I was joking, but the words felt flat.

He boggled. "What?"

I was treading on dangerous ground in terms of Guild confidentiality, but he claimed to know everything. "That's why scavengers wipe 'em—to get rid of the old pilot's memories."

"Oh, *that*." He dismissed one of the Guild's sworn secrets like he'd read it on a gossip plimsi. "Of course. I'm surprised you know about that."

"My da told me." Lee's and Nate's rewipes would've been stolen after extraction, or worse, ripped from their pilot's bodies and then erased. Whoever their navvies' original pilots had been, their souls were gone forever.

•‌•‌•‌•‌•‌•‌•‌•‌•‌•‌•

(It becomes easier to stomach an inevitable demise and/or loss of occupation when you think of your soul—or a decent copy—safe in a Guild vault. *Wiped* was an ugly whisper in pilot lore. A bogey out there in the dark. Only the Aemercy never returned navvies to the Guild. Aemercy pilots stuck theirs in a new body when the old one was through.

Centuries of memories made the Aemercy damned good pilots—although also, completely insane.

The Guild's biggest secret? I'm sure you know, but I'll say it—if only to twist a knife into your cold, black heart. The Guild's archives host our afterlife. Supposed to be secret, but we all know. The thought of Pilot Heaven comforts us, alone in the dark. It's why pilots always help a fellow flier, no matter their Syndicate or planetary alliance; why we're all bound to recover the metal when nothing can be done for the meat.

Guild Archives are the only version of heaven we pilots will ever get, unless the Grass Priests got it right... and I haven't bought into their crap since I was nine.)

•‌•‌•‌•‌•‌•‌•‌•‌•‌•‌•

"My father told us about symbiotes." Davad stared out at the black. "He thought it would keep us loyal, knowing what other Kamen did not."

"Did he teach your sister how to blow up a sun?"

"Hah." His chuckle came out strangled, and I considered I wasn't the only one trying hard to play it cool.

But I kept going so as not to think. Some things are too big to get your head around, and the Kamen-lord and I were dancing on the edge of a black hole. I recalled his da's fury. Had seemed personal, even misdirected at me. "Your old man shouldn't know. He's not Guild."

"The heads of 12Fam have access to secrets beyond your wildest imaginings, Pilot. Controlling information keeps them in power." My princeling paused. "Do you even know what your precious Guild is?"

"A voluntary organization of pilots, organized by pilots, advocating for pilots, with no allegiance to planet, station, or settlement," I recited. "Also, none of your business. They'd geld me for even having this conversation."

He chuckled. "Are you frightened?"

I glared back. "Gonna explain why that's funny?"

"No. Knowledge is currency, but ignorance is kind. Do you want me to tell you?"

He'd been the one to bring it up. "Screw you!" I glanced again at the mess of Carolina Station. The way the sunlight frosted the twisted shapes was beautiful, and that was terrible. I had a lump in my throat and an anger that wasn't all directed at the smug Kamen next to me.

Kamen weren't supposed to be pilots because being pilots made them into gods. *Power* had caused this, just like Centauri.

· · · ● · ● · · ·

(Had Illcord Natoth walked by in that moment, I think I could've put a bullet right into his brain.

You know, when given the chance, I *did* try.)

· · · ● · ● · · ·

I took a deep breath. "So Lee got a navvy, but yours died. What about Nate?"

"His operation was successful. My sister and Nate mastered flying small craft easily. They began scouting for Sub-Commander Vadim—" Davad broke off as a high-pitched voice echoed from the stairs, followed by the loud tramp of feet.

"—how?" The voice giggled.

"We're to fortify ourselves as needed. You heard Solly. He brought the *good* swill." A deeper tone. "And for you, a pilot's arms—"

Another laugh. "I'm not sure I can stand it."

"My dear, think of Dav—"

"Yurys? Is that you?" Davad's tone feigned an enthusiasm I'd never heard from him before. I knew it was fake because I could see his expression, still distant like his thoughts were caught up with that genocidal twin: Ledas-stinking-Starfire, the destroyer of worlds.

Chapter 19 ✳ Wagered

We had grass rings, Sam, you shouldn't have cared.

· · • · ● · ● · • · ·

The first Kamen-lord to enter the greenhouse was the woman who'd greeted Rathe upon arrival, the one who'd reminded me of Mureen. At the sight of us, she brightened like she'd plugged herself in. "Pilot Ottrava! Enjoying the view?"

"It's horrible." I stood up to be polite, only to have Davad try and tug me back down again, until I turned and shot him a glare.

"Mureen and Solon were just asking where you'd both taken yourselves," the woman added. "What a surprise, finding you here."

Davad didn't move from his seat, barely glancing in her direction. "Hello, Yurys. Is it just me, or has that thing grown?"

"Grows... shrinks... It is alive." She stepped between the front row of benches. Her hair was slicked back, her face a faint pink, eyes pale and colorless. "Sometimes I swear I feel it whispering. We can only do so much—"

"Careful," my princeling said.

She gave a laugh. "Advice about corruption? From *you*?"

"So devastating to see the Abomination in person." Yet the one who had followed Yurys through the doorway barely looked at the horror. Peering around Davad, I spied dark interested eyes and a flash of perfect teeth. The man was handsome in that way that sold a billion Unity war bonds, with features too even to be real. Slender, with skin only a few permutations paler than his black hair. They were both dressed in the same beige drab, but the man's garb seemed finer, perhaps measured to fit.

I leaned to get a closer look, only to discover the stranger's gaze had locked on mine. He smiled, and my heart might've skipped—save the man wasn't my first princeling.

"I am Ken'ri Virmarr." His accent was as clipped and proud as Davad's. "Have we met?"

"No." Given the man's looks, he and Davad had come from neighboring vats. "You're a princeling too?"

"He is." Davad sounded bored, which meant he was seething.

"Which House?" I asked.

"Foxconn." Virmarr sidled toward us. Ignoring Davad, I let him take my hand and raise it to his lips. "Honored," he murmured into my skin.

In response, I felt my knees bend like the curtsies I'd seen on Ma's show.

"You're doing it all wrong!" But he sounded delighted.

I straightened too quick, knocking my knees against the bench behind me. "I thought your kind were rare in the Kamen."

"Moreso every day." His gaze on me didn't falter.

"Marr, when did Solon approve your sojourn?" Davad sounded annoyed. "You weren't here last night."

"I didn't ask Solly. Merely secured a shuttle across from Carolina1 when I heard the rumors." The man's smile illuminated his mien... but I'd seen the sun before. In fact, seeing Davad next to another of his kind made me consider one could reach a place where all that preternatural beauty might become dull.

Virmarr continued: "Solon and Ells scolded me for coming, but I had to see for myself. You know, hearts broke last night when your little cabal chose to dock here instead of at Carolina1. Quite a few caps were set for Lieutenant Sai."

"The science station has the better view," Davad replied stiffly. "We docked here because I wanted our new pilot to see it."

"And now that she has, perhaps we should find something more pleasant for her to look at." Virmarr had such a rooster's sauce that I knew he was referring to himself.

"So far so good." I grinned, although it was more placeholder than proposition.

Davad frowned. "But why are you here at all? I heard you'd been assigned to the Boards."

Virmarr laughed. "Is *that* what you heard? Does Glos usually confirm its assignments with Lee's fugitive brother?"

Davad's lips thinned. "Just answer the question."

The other princeling shrugged. "I'm here because I want to be, the same as you. Clever of you to come back a third time... even Solly and Ells are in too deep to report you now. But Glos has gotten quite serious about your capture. Wideband alerts are out as far as the deep Fringers, and there are Glos-approved Circles back on every Fleet dreadnought." He was speaking to Davad but still looking at me. "You've no idea, the chaos you've caused."

"I can imagine." Davad's voice had gone flat. "You still haven't said why you've come, Marr. It can't be for us."

"Happy coincidence." Virmarr winked at me. "I wanted to see an Abomination, so I had Mater Foxconn put in a word."

Yurys broke in, too loudly. "You were unconscious before, Polla. You look much better now."

"When did you see me unconscious?"

"A medical consultation." Her lie wouldn't have fooled a sheep.

"Just how many times have I been here?"

"Once. When we returned, we left you on Earth with Teapot." Davad kneaded his brow, like my curiosity pained him.

"Was that the raid at NewPrinceton?" Virmarr's voice brightened. "Mureen looked lovely on the surveillance cams. So much footage! Were you two *trying* to get caught?"

"No," Davad's scowl grooved lines around his mouth.

"Oh, stop. I'm going to *weep*." Yurys looked more angry than sad, I thought, but then a glassy smile appeared on her face. "By the way, what was it you wanted from that parts graveyard on NewPrinceton, Dav?"

"A class-sigma cooling array for our ship. Ours was failing. Didn't Rathe tell you the story on our last visit?"

"He did." She smoothed the front of her robe. "I was just curious if you'd say the same thing."

"The place looked rather fortified for a parts graveyard," Virmarr added. "I suppose you've seen the casualty reports?"

"It's rather hard to find parts for our ship." Davad patted the bench next to him, and I sat down again, feeling rather buffeted by their exchange.

"Can't you ask your *father*?" Yurys giggled.

Davad looked unruffled. "With Illcord's chokehold on Fleet contracts, no."

"Are you blackmailing this entire station, Davey?" I broke in. "How?"

"Virmarr told you how." Davad sounded disinterested, which meant he was furious.

Virmarr snorted. "Like a true innocent."

"What?"

"Stop *baiting* her, Marr." Davad sounded like he was ordering soup from a serving android, which meant he was murderous.

Virmarr winked at me. "Oh, you think I'm baiting *her*?"

Yurys giggled, so high and sharp that I almost jumped. "I love your hair, Polla. So exotic. Do you enjoy being a pilot?"

I didn't like her. It wasn't rational, just something hard in my guts. "More than anything."

She nodded primly. "Different," she commented to the ether.

"From Rathe?" I'd seen how she'd grabbed at him. "There's a lot of differences between me and Rathe."

"Do you know if Rathe found accommodation last night?" Davad asked. His eyes were still on me, I thought, like a prickle on my skin. But I was staring at Yurys.

"Derien and I." Yurys's skin pinked like a virgin's. "He showed up just before dawn."

"Good. See, Pilot? Rathe is fine. Perhaps follow his example."

"I thought you wanted me to keep to my quarters." Now I was staring at his shoes. Those spacedamned boots. They all wore them.

"I may have been overly protective." When I looked up, Davad's gaze had gone to Virmarr.

· · · ● · ● · · ·

(Hindsight shows so many undercurrents in that conversation. But I bobbed above them all like a piece of jetsam.)

· · · ● · ● · · ·

Yurys giggled again. "Any of us would be delighted to spend more time with you." She'd perched on the bench in front of mine. Now she reached for my navhand. "We could find Rathe—"

I jerked Second's arm away. Maybe too quickly, because she made a noise like a stuck hen.

"No," I said.

Her face fell. "Is it me?"

Despite a professional reputation as a jezebel, I felt my face grow hot. "No." Davad had muddled me more than he'd helped—they'd all muddled me more than they'd helped.

But I was a pilot in my prime, and so I rallied fast, slamming a careless grin on my face and affecting my Fringerest drawl. "You know, I'll need to get my land legs back before I spread 'em... and I could use advice. Yurys, what can you tell me about everyone here?" My gaze lit upon my princeling. "Don't spare the particulars."

"Of course!" And she was off, with enough information to make a flesh-dancer wince. I'd never considered what Kamen-lords exiled on a remote station would get up to before, but to hear her tell it, they got it up *a lot*.

· · · ● · ● · · ·

(Hindsight suggests Yurys knew how sensitive such topics were for 12Fam, and poked a buried ant hill. In that vein—ahem—I suspect at least some of the feats she described were imaginary... and yet, who knows?

At the time, I expected Davad to stop her after two minutes instead of fixing his eyes heavenward, but now I understand. Sex is a fantastic distraction, and the game of two-box monte my princeling played was in full swing.)

· · · ● · ● · · ·

After Yurys had gone on for an epoch with enough detail to make a pilot blush, I broke in. "Yurys? Can I meet everyone? Last night was so rushed."

"*All?*" Her eyes widened. "I don't think Derien will suit—"

"Rathe can have Derien." The man sounded dull anyways.

Her smile faltered. "Now?"

Strangely I didn't feel a speck of lust, but I suspected my libido would rally for a willing partner. "Introduce me properly?"

"Of course!" she breathed. This time, when she reached for my freearm, I allowed her to take it.

Davad stepped aside. "Go on, Pilot."

"I am." I shot him a sideways glare.

"Then go."

"I am." Yet I expected an objection—or another cautionary tale.

"Wait!" Virmarr appeared on my starboard. "So few choices would be appropriate. You'll need advice."

"Don't be a snob." I laughed. "I come from excellent stock, and this is screwing, not breeding."

"I meant few here are as beautiful. May I?" The black-haired princeling indicated Second, hovering his palm just below its wires.

I was relieved he knew to ask. "Sure."

He kissed my knuckles between the wire. The touch sent a shiver down my thighs, one I'd noted had been entirely lacking in my interactions with Davad. "Pol-la, is it? Pilot Pol-la Ott-rav-UH?"

"We aren't big on titles. Just Polla is fine."

"Then I will be Just Virmarr." His perfect eyebrow arched heartrendingly.

"One more thing, Marr," Davad said. "Before you make off with my pilot, can you relay a message to the Old Man for me? I know you've got a comm smuggled in. You always do."

On my port, Yurys gasped with exaggerated shock. "*Savage!* He just comes right out and *says* it!"

Virmarr chuckled. "I see life as a fugitive has made you nearly as brutish and uncouth as your sister, Dav. May she *requiescat in pace*... What do you wish me to tell him?"

"Father owes me a moon for that departure. Tell him I'm taking it."

Virmarr shrugged. "Oblique. Anything more?"

"Earff military's after us," I added. "Can his da bribe 'em?"

From the pained noise emitting from his lips, Davad disapproved of the direct approach.

"Did you want House Arkan to bribe the entirety of Alta Fleet Command, or just the First Ring?" Virmarr made me realize how foolish I'd sounded. "By the way, Dav," the man continued, "have you heard about Glos?"

"I have to assume you're still Father's spy and not theirs," Davad said. "So tell me."

Virmarr rolled his eyes. "Why do I have to be someone's spy? Perhaps I'm just a concerned friend."

Davad lifted an eyebrow.

Virmarr sighed. "Rumors of a Guild alliance to destroy House Illcord? Do you know more?"

"As you said, Glos doesn't run their plans past fugitives," Davad said coldly. "Also, I don't care."

"Interesting." Virmarr stroked his small beard.

"There were Kamen Circles after us," I chimed in. "Back on Earff."

"Earth," Yurys corrected. "And we know. We have nearly as much to fear from them as you."

"No, 'earth' is what you call dirt," I snapped. "The Original Garden's *Earff.*"

Virmarr snorted. "Does she sound like Beya, or is it just me?"

"My cousin—" I began, but they all spoke at once, so quickly I could barely follow.

"—*finish.*" Yurys glared at Davad. I'd missed something from how quickly she'd gone cold.

"Either way, you won't see us again," Davad told her. "I promise."

"Do you think he knows what he's doing?" Vimarr murmured in my ear.

I think I laughed.

Yurys kept talking: "—Solly says we shouldn't ask, but I don't think he knows either. You could be working *for* Nate and he and Ells still wouldn't believe it—"

"After what I did, they know I'm not." Davad's voice had dropped, but I heard him.

"After what you *did,* what have you done?"

"Mureen seized an opportunity."

"Mureen." Yurys sniffed. "You know what they say—"

"I would be careful not to say it," Davad replied coldly. "In front of me."

"*Children,*" Virmarr broke in, and by the looks on their faces, I knew his attempt to annoy both had succeeded. "Is there a point to your knives? Your pilots need sojourn, and Yurys, you get to bed the notorious Sai. Meanwhile, our lovely Polla can be my guest."

"We'll see," I said.

Virmarr's hand traced the metal band along my wrist. Our eyes met. His were lovely, an amber brown that shaded dark at the center. His sensuous mouth curled, yet I recall being more confused than aroused—

• • • • • • • • • •

(To which hindsight adds guilt—)

• • • • • • • • • •

"Marr, tell the Old Man—" Davad swallowed. "Never mind."

• • • • • • • • • •

(And it may only be my wretched hindsight that puts a complete emptiness in my princeling's gaze, a void like space, remorseless and uncaring—)

• • • ● • ● • ● • • •

"Never mind—?" Virmarr prompted him. "Was there more?"

"I've told you it already." Davad turned to me. "Go with them. I'll check on Rathe."

"He shouldn't slot in," I warned. "Not even for ship's maintenance."

"I'll make sure he does not," Davad said. "See to yourself. Have fun. We'll be in the breach soon enough." His smile glinted at me, almost shy. "My sister used to tell me that constantly."

"She *would* quote Shakespeare." Yurys sighed with enough drama for two morality plays. "Such a pretentious twat—Lee refused to read anything more recent than the First Exodus."

"The Grass Priests have a sermon about breaching," I offered. "Once more unto the breach, dear friends. Once more? And then there's plows? Actual ones, not... *plowing*. You know."

Davad rubbed his temples. "Go, Pilot."

"Would you still like to meet the others?" Virmarr's hand had crept to the wires on my elbow. I felt Second buzz, but dim. "Or have you made your choice?"

On my port, Yurys patted my freearm. "I do love your hair," she cooed at my face, which had none.

"Show me the competition," I said to Virmarr. "And then we'll see."

• • • ● • ● • ● • • •

(Back then I still had the optimism of the damned and the blindness of a Priest.)

• • • ● • ● • ● • • •

At first acquaintance, the Circle members looked less overjoyed and more nervous when I graced 'em with my presence. It was, perhaps, the tension in the room that led me to open with a cheerful one-liner. "Who," I declared, "do I have to sleep with on this station for a decent caffeinoid?"

"You would sell yourself for a drink?" A rather dour-looking man boggled. He wouldn't have been bad-looking, packing a solid bit of muscle and a neat beard, except for the expression on his face, which resembled one of our pond bullfrogs back home. "There's no need. Any one of us would happily—"

"She's joking, Lavar." His companion beamed. She had hair like a sun, all in curls around her face, and two spots of red, one on each cheek. Her eyelids were painted blue. Among the drabness of the rest, she shone.

I would learn her name was Risa.

Lavar looked so confused that I instantly crossed him off the list.

"What do we call you?" another asked. His rangy frame reminded me of Rathe's, but he was shorter. He had light eyes like Rathe's, although his were more green than blue. Mine were drawn to the open neck of his tunic, which dipped lower than the others wore theirs, low enough for me to see his gold-fuzzed pecs.

"By her name, James!" The woman sitting next to him elbowed him sharply. She looked a little like home, with skin the color of good Feldelroy earth, but her accent was pure Terra. "Polla. Polla Otter—Ottravant—"

"Ottrava," I finished for her. "Registered smuggler, at your service." There were six all told, all sitting on two half-moon-shaped couches. I plunked down between the woman who'd known my name (I would learn hers was Elsa), and the dour-looking man. "My bev?"

"I'll get it." The light-eyed man with the pecs (James), got up and went to the neighboring wall, which held a small galley. He extracted a cup of something steaming from a bulky machine and brought it to me. "Here."

I took it and took a sniff, then a gulp. "Thanks."

There was, in my memory, a long silence, and then a barrage of questions. They wanted to know all about my trade, which seemed funny, then odd, and finally a little sad as their questions revealed their Kamen lives to be more sheltered than anything I could have imagined.

• • • ● • ● • • • •

(Or so goes *one* explanation.)

• • • ● • ● • • • •

"Not that dangerous," I amended, after a tale of my last run (rather heavily embellished) produced a round of oohs and aahs. "No one messes with registered smugglers. See, our goods are all chipped or watermarked—not like you can just sell 'em off." (Untrue, but I believed in keeping the mystery alive.)

"And your progenitors?" the dour one—Lavar—asked me. "Do you remember them? Were they proud of your criminal activities?"

A shocked silence followed. Someone gasped.

"Apologies for him." Risa wrinkled her painted nose and patted my freehand. "Don't answer that. We're not all rude."

I snorted. "My parents aren't dead. Don't you remember yours?"

She flushed. "Of course not!"

I'd stumbled across another one of their odd taboos.

Lavar looked guilty. "I thought it was polite to inquire," he muttered. "Some Fringer planets have strong bonds. Derien, you remember what you said about Beya—"

"That she'd be better off *dead*?" Dark-haired Derien scowled at Lavar, which was a pleasant change from him scowling at me.

"Beya?" I broke in. "My cousin Beya went to Glos. She died in the war."
Derien made an ugly noise in his throat.

Beya was almost as common a name on Feldelroy as Polla... but surely, I thought at the time, the galaxy couldn't be that small.

• • • ● • ● • ● • •

("Surely," the galaxy would soon reply, "you are a suntouched, stinking fool.")

• • • ● • ● • ● • •

"Beya was always talking about her family," Lavar said. "Feldelroyans do that. Wasn't she an Ottravant too?"

"*Ottrava*," I corrected. "If she's the same one. I only met her once. She came home from the Kamen on furlough. I was nineteen, she came to my graduation from Smuggler's—"

"Furlough?" Risa's laugh was too sharp.

"What are the odds?" The other woman (brown-haired Callie) laughed too.

"Remember that time she deserted and ran to her mother?" Yurys said. "When was that?"

"After NewKalnick," James said. "She lost half her squad. Lee tried to commandeer a full dreadnought to go after her. Xao had a fit."

"But did Lee go herself?" Callie asked. She was the only one with hair past her shoulders and had a pretty, ruddy face. "I can't remember—"

"No." Elsa shook her head. "She sent a pilot. I forget the name—"

"Erin," Derien said. "Lieutenant Erin Fow. She was at Centauri."

"*Requiescat*," they all said in unison—so unexpected that I nearly jumped from my chair.

They all stamped their stone boots and toasted. Those who weren't drinking tipped imaginary cups back and repeated it: "*Requiescat*."

Their movements held the pattern of a too-familiar ceremony. I felt suddenly cold. "*Requiescat*," I echoed a beat too late. My eyes went to Virmarr, the only person in the room who hadn't joined in. He leaned casually on the wall, twisting a pendant he wore on his neck. Meeting my gaze, he rolled his eyes.

"Beya remembered *her* family." Risa's voice held an edge I didn't understand. "She was ten Standard when Glos found her. Most of us don't remember much. Not if we're normal folk... the 12Fam have their own rules."

I'd heard that Cousin Beya had died in the Aemercy Aggressions. Her parents hung a Unity flag in their parlor window for months. Had to keep it in the window because if they'd hung it outside, someone would've set it on fire.

I wondered if they'd think the flag story was funny.

Lavar was still talking to Elsa. "—you said we were to make polite conversation until she picked one of us—"

"Hey!" I interrupted the man to put him out of his misery. "Does anyone have a transmitter, so I can comm home? No need for fancy. I don't mind a time delay."

He looked shocked at the very idea. "You can't call anyone!"

"Lavar!" Yurys gave me what passed on her for a kind look. One dimple flashed. "I'm sorry about him."

"It's fine." I waved her off. "But is there a way to make the call?" In the first week of my awakening, I'd written letters and Mureen had promised to mail 'em. My folks had to be wondering why the letters had stopped.

"We don't call anyone," Yurys said. "The Fleet severed the ansible to this system when they put up this base."

"Can't risk the Abomination infecting the nets," Risa added. "So they keep us isolated."

"But you have a comm," I called out to Virmarr. "You and Davad were just talking about it."

"I have a *device*," he corrected. "It won't transmit to your Feldelroy."

"How can the Abomination infect quantum ansibles in the first place?" I asked. "That doesn't make sense."

"It breaks down tech," Callie told me. "Anything metal, or manufactured."

"But entanglements aren't..." I started to explain about a typical void, using that common example from *A Child's Intro to Quantum Astrophysics*, but from their expressions, I might as well have been a Grass Priest preaching to the damned.

"It... wants to spread." The skinny man, James, was rummaging around the shelves for another round of refreshments. He glanced at me. "Can you feel it yet? We all start to. If you do, *resist*, that's very important."

"James!" Risa, again.

"Don't worry her." Elsa patted my hand. "No need to be concerned, Polla. They rotate us between atrocities every few years to keep us sound. Most of us are due for reassignment, but we're all perfectly fine."

"Especially *me*." Virmarr folded his arms and leaned against the wall.

"Spy." Yurys shot him a fond look.

"12Fam's bestboy," someone else broke in. They all laughed as Virmarr denied it.

"They call me a spy because I come from the Houses." He leaned over the couch to whisper in my ear. "Commoner prejudice. We nobles are always on the outside, peering like peasant children through a frost-covered window at the feast within."

"Feast days are for everyone back home." I couldn't tell if he was joking. "Where do they rotate you to?" Nowhere central, obviously. James hadn't known in which sectors of the Milky the Fringers began.

"Other alien sites." Lavar lowered his voice. "We've been exposed to the mysteries. Can't risk returning us to taint innocents back home—"

"Ken'ri!" Callie shot him a warning glance, then me a too-bright smile. "We do as needs must." Somehow in all the fetching of drinks and pastry I'd ended up between her and Elsa. "Do you have more questions?" she asked. She was leaning so close that I could smell the salty stuff she used in her hair.

I tried not to sneeze. "Yeah, that other guy, the..." For a second, the fat man's name slithered away from me again. "The bossy one, is he a bimhole?"

"Who?"

"The fa—Ells." His name came a beat too late. "*Ells*."

"He's one of the Elders." She giggled. "So yes."

"Ells and Solon are here as punishment because they trained us," Lavar added. He chewed with his mouth open and I pretended not to notice. "They still treat us like children."

"You act like a child," the blond snipped. "And you're forty."

"Oh, well for you to say—"

"Have you heard much about the war, Polla?" Yurys interjected. Her eyes were hard and bright

I nodded. "I lost a good friend at Neskey. And I was in NewBern when Centauri happened. Heard the first broadcast in a bar. No one believed it was real..." I began *that* tale, which had a bit to explain about port laws in NewBern first, but I was interrupted.

"Fascinating." Risa picked at her nails in a way that told me she wasn't fascinated at all. "Fellows? I'm out. After a while it's just not funny. Elsa can have my share of the pot."

"No—Risa?" Elsa grabbed her friend's arm and whispered something in her ear. They both laughed. On my other, Callie snickered like she was in on it too.

Suddenly, I felt less like a clever smuggler regaling a group of innocents with tales of my adventures and more like the last quez on Feldelroy locked in a zoo.

"Your Elder Ken'ri Ells told me he trained your two traitors." I cleared my throat. For some reason, I felt irrationally angry. "Lee and Nate? Then he tried to show me how to use one of your magic sticks. Why would he do that?"

"He offered you a gir?" Elsa's hand clenched around Risa's arm.

"He tested me for kamn."

Dead silence grew legs and evolved enough to invent hyperspace. They all stared, and my mouth felt dry. I remembered the time I'd said the sermon at church when I was twelve and everyone laughed. This was worse. Like any pilot. I liked attention—but not all of it. I cleared my throat again. "Guess what? I don't have Kamen magic."

"That's good," James said seriously.

"You don't want it," Callie said.

"You should enjoy today, lady." Virmarr inclined a hand to me for me to stand. "For who knows tomorrow?"

I took his invitation. A pleasant warmth tingled along my navarm's circuits as our fingers brushed before he politely withdrew. *Perhaps Davad was right*, I thought. *Should've trawled for Kamen before. Who knew they were all such jezebels?*

· · · · ● · ● · · · ·

(Only Ma and everyone else who'd seen *The Hook and the Rod.*)

· · · · ● · ● · · · ·

"Virmarr?" someone began. "That's cheating!"

"Please. Let him." Derien looked tired.

"Oddly appropriate." James tilted his head toward the ceiling with a heavy sigh. "I'm out. Elsa?"

"Hate losing to royalty," the brunette said. "But they look pretty standing there. Like something out of a painting."

"Guess Marr's really not a House spy," someone else snickered. "Or he wouldn't dare."

Callie scoffed. "You didn't even try, Derien—"

"He would be too frightened." James yawned.

"It's not fear."

I turned to my starboard to gaze on the notorious Derien. Black hair. Bluish eyes under a heavy brow. The man's glare could've dissolved stone. With him being a Kamen, that meant he was probably holding back.

"I will never be interested in you," Derien told me icily.

"Your loss." I shot him a grin. "Say hi to Rathe for me."

His jaw twitched and I knew I'd scored.

Virmarr was still chuckling. "This was the lady's choice." He held out his arm for me. "Shall we?"

"There was a wager?" As we walked out together, I could hear the others settling their lost bets like biddies cackling in the coop.

"There isn't much else to do in this sector." Virmarr kissed me on the cheek, which startled me more than a straight run at the crotch would have. His gorgeous eyes creased with laughter at my confusion. "Except keep the galaxy from its doom."

· · · · ● · ● · · · ·

(At the time, I recall thinking these Kamen all seemed too young for the age of their faces, as if the war had stolen adulthood—not innocence—from them.

But how many of those jokes were a performance for their audience of one?

I have no measure to mark their characters. I can only offer the last members of the Kamen Company my sincerest respect and eternal regard. Their names were Lavar, James, Risa, Elsa, Callie, Derien, and Yurys.

Every one of 'em deserved the Purple more than you.

Requiescat.)

Apologue 6 ✳ Flashpoint

WHEN THE COSMOS SHOOK a few days later, the *Happy Elyse* was still in null space. The force of the explosion made Beya drop her glass of whiskey. No one knew what had happened, but they all felt it. Risa threw down her hand of euchre, and Toma looked green. Sheris retched up bile on the common room's priceless Preflight rug.

Before any of them knew anything, they all knew Lee had done her *something*.

The bold Kamen Company met on the bridge again, although Nate had never left, was still hovering in his chair above Lee's navstation like a broody raptor. Beya wondered just how badly their self-appointed leader had to piss by now, but her eyes went to Davad. He stood apart, pointed at the transparency's view of null space like the rest of them didn't exist. Save for a slimmer hip, Lee's brother looked just like her from behind: the same broad shoulders and elegant neck, those same red curls, his fastidiously oiled down his back.

Most of them had given up on small vanities, but not the Arkan twins.

When Davad turned to her, the look on his face was so bleak that Beya surprised herself by taking him into her arms, awkward as that was with her head barely reaching his chest. Hugging him felt like embracing a brittle tree.

The others were still demanding answers, but Nate had said it himself: this had been Lee's play, she'd just left Nate to spin it, same as when she'd formed their damned Kamen Company in the first place.

Davad's expression looked like a piece of ancient porcelain about to crack. "Have we met?" he asked Beya. "The Fringer brute I know doesn't like my hugs."

"Maybe I'm bored," she shot back. Dav smelled different than Lee, like oranges, as if he'd applied scent. Lee hated scents. "I thought we agreed to warn each other if she went 'round the bend."

"'Round the what?" His chuckle sounded forced. "Spare me Fringer aphorisms. I had no idea."

"We both knew she was plotting *something*. Was it an Aemercy planet-killer on Roe?" That was the worst thing Beya could think of—for another five seconds.

Davad shook his head. "Nate says it was the *sun*."

"Oh." The scale was so impossible that for an errant second, Beya felt thankful that everyone they'd left behind on Roe was safe. "She used a planet-killer on the sun? Tell me she had a drone fly it—that she didn't send our own pilots—"

"Beya. *Stop*." The slight underbite the twins had made them look younger, but those shadows under his eyes had turned Davad's face into a skull. "She didn't send anyone. She didn't need to. She just"—he swallowed—"she just did it."

A bubble of hysterical laughter threatened to emerge from Beya's throat. "So her talk about giving land to the Associations who left—*that* wasn't a trap." She had bet Captain Frene it was, and now Beya owed the good captain two hundred chits of confiscated draal.

Captain Frene, whose cunt tasted like strawberries, and had last been seen on Roe, mustering the honor guard for Beya's parade.

"But Alpha Centauri has *two*—" Her grim joke died at the sight of his frozen expression.

Did they still have my parade? Beya realized she was holding back sobs, that the plasma wake of trapped emotions currently lodged in her throat could undo her completely.

Davad's voice had gone flat, like he was holding it in too. "Some of the others... they didn't just feel the suns go." His eyes searched her face. "A *lot* of people died today, Beya."

"Three inhabited planets. Plus the moons." Beya willed herself not to remember the Thirty-Fifth Association who'd taken them in when they were teenagers building irrigation canals on Otwombe, or the way the sun rose above the mountains on that planet. Not like she didn't have practice in the art of remove: she'd divorced sentiment from recalling Kaygaz long ago, and she'd replaced the Armery'c Mothers' songs with curses the day she bombed her first blood farm.

"Will it spread past the system?" she asked. Lee and Nate had taken actual astrophysics courses, studied that forbidden subject under Kaygaz himself before everything went bad, but Beya had never bothered.

"I don't know." Dav's teeth had been gnawing on his lower lip, it looked red and raw. "She made me *count*. Who stayed and who left. Every Association. Every name."

"Her census." *Busywork*, Beya had assumed at the time. Something to keep the Unity's military machine occupied while their accord negotiations tore it apart, something to keep Davad from doing anything rash like tell Old Man Genghis just how far his darling daughter had fallen off the map in those last few rounds of prisoner executions.

"I think at least five million. Maybe twenty. It's not like we ever knew their real numbers." He swallowed. "Plus our own *fleet*, Beya. Our own people."

Locked in a cone of silence, she and Davad could have been the last people in the universe. "They didn't warn *anyone*? Not even Xao? He loved them!"

"Every admiral. Nearly every subcommander. Our *officers* who *trusted* us—" His head turned toward Nate, who looked almost jolly if you didn't look close, holding court like this was a moot from their childhood. "It was his idea."

"Are you sure?" Beya was sure it wasn't.

"I'm not sure of anything."

Lee had left nearly every Unity officer to die, but not, Beya realized, the bulk of their military: those noncommissioned and conscripted. She knew they were safe because Lee had assigned her those rosters, citing cost overruns as the reason for shipping every petty, pleb, swab, and groundhog back to Fleet bases in the First Ring. Lee had even demobbed everyone from the *Elyse* who wasn't Circle or pilot, amidst much grumbling from their own about who would cook breakfast.

But Dav would blame Nate. Lee's brother had grown to despise Nate—Beya was one of the few to know by how much—but he'd never openly oppose the man his sister loved, any more than he'd ever admit Lee had crossed the Tharsis Divide with her war crimes years ago.

Before that last round of executions, Beya had been reluctant to admit it too. But Lee and Nate had been monsters for a while. Vat-born to the job, after all.

And what does that make me? The faithful ex-lover? Their fool? Suddenly Beya's conscience sounded too much like Ells, their old ethics instructor.

She buried her head in Davad's chest and his arms tightened, both of them holding each other while their friends fought. They didn't have to watch to sense raw kamn unleashed, feel its untethered kinetics coil and strike, lashed from dozens of minds like groundquakes.

To his credit, Nate harmed no one. He did nothing but maintain shields around himself and his wife's chair, and the others did nothing but try and shatter those shields. The floor trembled against the soles of Beya's stone shoes, but no one was suicidal enough to pull pipes from the walls or wrest pieces of deck from the floor.

Those from their Company who lacked a healthy sense of self-preservation had all died in the war's first bloody years.

"They must have planned this for months," Beya said to Davad, a few hours later.

Even stubborn Derien had backed off by then, his face drawn and exhausted. She was barely surprised when Nate ordered the mutineers to kneel like they were all trapped in some monarchist hell-drame. Sheris knelt last, looking a bit too much like she enjoyed it for Beya's taste. Nate held Sheris's hand longer than the rest, Beya noted, her irritation offset by the thought of how hearing about it would infuriate Lee.

"If he asks you and me to grovel, I'll assassinate his father," Davad muttered.

"He knows better." Their eyes met, and Beya realized he'd only been half joking. "It's an *honor*, being us, best friend and beloved brother... did you catch what Nate said to make the others shit themselves?"

"Something about iron jewelry."

"*Oh.* Hemagoblins." Beya felt sick.

"*Hemoglobin.* We all have iron in our blood, Beya. Not just Aemercy."

She shuddered. "Will she blow up another sun every time the Unity has a territorial spat with its own protectorates?" *Probably.* Lee was about as subtle as an avalanche.

Davad's face held a more delicate quality than his sister's. Now it crumpled. "I wish she'd never met him."

"Of course you do." Beya had tried for a long time to forget her own siblings—one of them had turned her in for floating a sock, after all—so she knew how little family meant, but a part of her melted at the tragic look on the softer twin's face.

Another part of her wanted to slap him.

Most of the others were leaving the bridge now, but Sheris was blushing, leaning on one of the navchairs to flash her tits like they were over a country fence.

Beya considered that her new lover was a social-climbing twat. That was an easier thought than facing the scope of what they'd collectively done, sticking their kamn into a war that might've ended in a year had they not intervened. That had been the Elders' prediction... although their Elders had underestimated Purcell Kaygaz.

We were supposed to tell them, Beya remembered bitterly. *If we saw anything untoward.*

It would be a few years before Beya realized that Kaygaz had won his war. The man himself would be dead, his civilization spacedust, but between them, his former protégés would manage to bring the Human Unity to its knees.

But that was later, and by then she'd switched sides at least twice.

Over a dozen Kamen and more than half the pilots left the *Happy Elyse* at Al-Murad. Given fuel and safe passage back to Ring Space, just like Nate had promised. Beya heard later that Glos took them back; that most dedicated their lives to containing Lee and Nate's *second* interstellar catastrophe: the disaster in the Carolina system.

Despite her doubts, Beya stayed on. For Nate was right, Nuala Erta was paradise.

A paradise Beya found she'd do anything to keep.

Chapter 20 ✳ Screwed

• • • • • • • • • • •

I HAD ONE PLUS a half-night with Ken'ri Virmarr, and both were unexpected.

The first strange thing was that he didn't want to bed me at all.

"Davad's more my type. Not that he'd give me a moment. But I didn't want you auctioned off. The others are beneath you."

"But—" I felt weirdly relieved. Trawling for Kamen had been unsettlingly easy. "Wasn't your choice to make."

"Of course." The princeling peered at me. "Would you prefer another? We can be discreet—I can tell you which ones are *genuinely* discreet. Elsa, perhaps. Not James. Definitely not Derien." He chuckled and stole another glance. "Watch out for Derien. He despises you."

"He doesn't know me!" But the thought of picking a Kamen lover like this was a Syndicate bordello had put me off my feed.

Virmarr shrugged. "The man is a little too fond of Lieutenant Sai."

"Lieutenant Sai's welcome to him."

"Yes." He flashed me a flawless smile. "Shall we?" He gestured at a table with a board of black and white squares. I'd seen a Preflight vid of fiction once, about a plucky young tweener who had to play chess against a team of invading invertebrate aliens, so I knew what the game was called, although that was the extent of my skill.

I recalled Ken'ri Ells and his tests. "I'd rather not. Have you and Davad ever screwed?"

He shook his head. "But our families have been allied for more than a decade. We were raised in the same Circle, there were summer retreats with our Houses... hundreds of informal duels..." He paused. "And, of course,

I followed them to war."

Them. I was heartily sick of how a dead woman kept inserting herself into every conversation—but I found myself asking. "You were friends with *her* too?"

"Ledas?" Virmarr shrugged, arranging the pieces on the board. "Not really. Shall we play chess? Do you know how?" His eyes searched my face. "I did know Nate. In fact, I knew Nate *very* well."

For some reason, I felt colder. "Still in touch?"

"What if I were?" A smile bent his lips. "Any message?"

I forced a laugh. "Depends. You princelings like formal announcements when someone's coming to kill you? Or prefer the surprise?"

His grin widened. "There might not be time for embossed invitations, even if we could find a decent printer here among the hinters—"

"Printer? To make the bullets?"

"The *invitations.*" He covered his mouth with his hand in an exaggerated gesture. "On paper. Sent by courier. It's... oh, never mind. I suppose you barbarians would just comm."

"I prefer surprises myself," I said and got up to rummage through his refrigeration unit, checking for snacks. For some reason, my hand trembled.

Behind me, he chuckled. "I have no idea if you're serious."

"As Centauri," I replied with an entirely faked cool, which made Virmarr break out laughing full bore.

We spent the rest of the evening watching old Unity vids, the kind they broadcast at home on Eighth Day after services. Wholesome, didactic, and surprisingly entertaining. At some point, Virmarr promised to share the proceeds of his bet if we continued our fictitious screws. His terms were good enough that I agreed.

Of course, circumstances intervened, and I never did collect.

Rathe was hollow-eyed and flushed at breakfast, sandwiched between Yurys and glowering, dark-haired Derien. He flashed me a too-bright grin. Was relieved to see him looking better, but irritation that he seemed like a calf in clover mixed a strange brew in my chest. My fellow pilot didn't look like *he'd* been up 'til three-before-rising, watching *The Terror of Sodenbad Mountain.* Marks on his neck spoke of more interesting sport.

"Having fun?" he asked cheerfully. "You look more relaxed."

"You too." I snagged a piece of burnt bread and crunched it. "I can see why you like it here. The whole gir thing? So many possibilities. I made some sketches of a NewCalifornian crankshaft, and Virmarr here just shaped the stone in five seconds, so then we both climbed on the ends—"

Virmarr laughed too loud. Ken'ri Ells got up from the table, looking green.

Rathe kicked me and leaned across the table. "Don't joke about gir." He winked. "But have fun. Things will get serious soon enough."

I rolled my eyes. Davad and Mureen were at a table by themselves in the corner. I felt Davad's disapproving glare on the back of my neck like a small sun, but when I turned, Mureen merely waved.

It was after lunch that Davad and Mureen accosted me, dragging me off to the *Escape* for private words with barely a by-your-leave for my Kamen admirers, who'd requested more stories. I didn't object. The day before had made me feel like a trained quez, and I was oddly relieved to leave the other Kamen behind—even Virmarr, who winked and said he'd see me at dinner.

We'd barely cleared the *Escape*'s first airlock before I caught the tense looks my companions kept shooting at each other.

"What's wrong?" I began. "Look, if you didn't want me to bed a strange Kamen-lord, why'd you leave me alone with so many?"

"Oh, it's not *that*." Mureen laughed, and then told me I should ask *Bedalia* to run a test flight, which gave me the opinion it was her idea—confirmed, I thought, by Davad's bored disdain. The princeling skulked against our corvette's inner bulkhead, while she rattled on about how they just wanted to make sure the bloodship was spaceworthy. "Orbit once around the station, then dock again," she concluded.

My eyes went to her companion, who was occupied with a piece of lace on his sleeve. Every Kamen on station wore flat beige, but Davad still dressed like the last crusader on a doomed barge. (I myself was garbed in a similarly-garish flightsuit of white wool and gold leather, since he'd provided me with no normal clothes.)

"It's simple," the foppish princeling added, flicking his lace. "Command her."

"Simple, huh?" On my arm, Second was so quiet it felt dead. I looked up at our corvette's empty stairwell spiraling above us, the slatted shadows from the steps casting my companions in an ominous light. Their air of expectance set my teeth on edge. "Where's Rathe?"

"Rathe is letting his cortex heal." Mureen began walking, making me quicken my steps to follow. "Davad told me about your difficulty with Second. Perhaps this exercise will help you reconnect."

I shot Davad a glare, which he ignored. I had a sudden, paranoid thought that this was a trap, a punishment they'd concocted for me lying about Second.

Does Rathe know? I wondered. Their smug looks reeked of conspiracy. My thoughts ran as I tried to talk myself back from a precipice. *Maybe they know what they're doing? We all want Rathe to get better. And Davad's the bloodship expert. Bedalia's his sister's ship—*

He killed her on it!

He doesn't seem concerned.

Indeed, the princeling could've been waiting for his land yacht.

I beamed back at his unsettling mien. "How about I try slotting into the *Escape*, first?"

"No." Davad made a show of checking his nails. "*Bedalia* is your ship."

"We could be on Nuala in days if she'll take your orders," Mureen added cheerfully.

I stopped walking on the next landing. I was tired of lies. "Favor for a favor." I crossed my arms and leaned against the wall. "Let me comm my folks."

Davad leaned on the railing opposite my wall and crossed his own arms. "No."

"Polla, there are no ansible points in this system—" Mureen began.

"Plus, the *war*?" As with Davad, we'd grown close enough that I felt comfortable finishing her excuses. "The war's disrupted every entanglement link in Fringer space? Every single one?"

"You can't comm anyone." Davad's tone was flat. "Accept it, Pilot. None of us can."

I wasn't about to. "Your pals said the Abomination infects the bands. But that's not how quantum entanglements work. Scientists transmit remotely from this station. You said that too. So there must be waypoints out there." I waved in the direction of space. "Just for once, stop lying!"

Mureen's gaze went to Davad, but he was staring at the floor. There was a long pause, and when he finally spoke, his words were clipped. "You swore to ask no questions."

"That was before I knew you were stinking *liars*—"

His gloved hand rose. "Stop. If you can't... *work*, we need to know now. Before"—he took a breath—"before we go farther."

My chuckle came out ugly. "Aren't I working now, here at your beck and call?"

"If you can't fly either ship, you're of no use. Better we learn that here than abandon you on some uninhabited asteroid later." His cold eyes met mine.

Once I might've quailed, or cracked a joke about how that seemed oddly specific, but by then I could suss his insults for what they were: spurs, meant to goad me to his trap.

"*Answer*," I snarled. "Are there working comm connections on this station or not?"

"Yes." Incredibly, he looked pleased.

"And Virmarr has one," I continued. "Otherwise, how could he send a message to your father?"

"Marr always has something. Ever since we were novices, he's flouted the rules. But it's Ells who monitors incoming broadcasts. The man has a real affection for drames." His voice went silky. "Did you want to know who won the Biscayne last week? After you fly *Bedalia*, we can ask Ells to check—"

"Stop steering me off course! Why do you keep lying?"

"We don't want you to worry," Mureen cut in. "The bands have disturbing reports. More planets attacked—"

"Feldelroy?" My blood froze.

"No." She gave me a level stare. "Truly, Polla. Your home is safe."

My mouth felt dry. "Then what? You made me talk to those admirals. They saw my face. I gave my *name*. Tell me they didn't go after my folks—"

"Hah." Incredibly, Davad sounded amused. "No. But our next stop is an Arkan installation. We can send your letters home there, if you like." He cocked his head, assessing my reaction. "Is there more?"

I gritted my teeth. "Why do you *keep lying*?"

Mureen sighed. "Dav, tell her what's happened."

"We discussed this." His voice had lost its humor. "It has nothing to do with her."

"She has the right—"

"She has *no* rights." The man was poised like drawn wire. Definitely goading me. So obvious that I just grinned back, a response that seemed to throw him into confusion.

Mureen gave a pained sigh. "Polla, the planet CanusDaya was attacked by the Living Fleet yesterday. I don't know if you've heard of the Canus system. It's in the Second Ring—"

Davad's voice strangled. "Mureen?"

Her expression was almost smug as she glanced between us. "I changed my mind."

·•••••••••

(Does hindsight add a rehearsed quality to their speech? Or was that the first crack? Stars, even now, it's so hard to know what was real.)

·•••••••••

"Of course I've heard of Canus," I said. "I have a pulse." Twelve terraformed planets. The industrial powerhouse of the Human Unity. Commercial ship-yards, factories, tech labs, dozens of free orbitals, the works. "Does Rathe know about the attack?" He'd be upset, I thought. *So why isn't he here?*

"Yes," Davad bit out. "And he agrees it doesn't concern you."

"It's the talk of the station." Mureen confessed like she was granting me a favor.

Talk of the station—except around me, I thought. Fury at being excluded fueled my words as I tried to repay them in kind. "Canus is a Second Ring dump. Why should a Fringer like me care?"

Davad smiled. "Because you have a heart in your chest, and when you lean against the wall pretending otherwise, I can hear its echo beating faster."

I stepped away fast. *Fragging Kamen tricks.* My voice wavered. "Are they all dead?"

"Minimal casualties," Mureen said slowly.

"Good?" I wanted it to be.

She nodded. "A targeted strike. His forces leveled one factory and then withdrew."

"A warning." The princeling's expression etched grooves around his mouth.

"Sounds like your sister."

Davad shook his head. "Nate was seen, rather deliberately, with a ground party. His ship, too, in low orbit. It's the first time anyone's seen the flagship. I believe it's the *Elyse,* our old dreadnought. We scuttled it on Skye, but he's got it spaceworthy again. That shouldn't be possible."

"What's Skye?" I asked.

"Nuala's moon."

"Minimal casualties is still good?"

Davad shook his head. "My sister never used the biophage when she attacked for good reason."

"Except here at Carolina." I corrected. "If by 'biophage' you mean the Abomination. Didn't one of the Vadims say something about Canus when you made me threaten 'em above Earff?"

"*One?*"

"Of the two?"

He gave an incredulous scoff that I ignored, continuing: "—and Nate attacking a Second Ring System—isn't that a declaration of war?"

His tone went boreal. "I had no idea you were so well-versed in our laws."

"Well, I've seen the newsbands talk about it—" My voice faltered, because I couldn't recall when. "—and Da told me," I finished.

· · ● ● · ● ● · ● · ·

(That could even be true.)

· · ● ● · ● ● · ● · ·

His gaze went heavenward. "Nate sent the Living Fleet to flatten one of the same factories that my sister attacked three years ago. Deliberate provocation. Like throwing a glove in dueling season."

"You throw *gloves?*" My laugh choked.

Mureen gave me her patented smile. "Polla, there are at least one billion souls on CanusDaya alone. Six billion in the system."

"Oh." I stared at the *Escape*'s plated wall while Second's readouts blared alarms about my adrenal spikes.

"Six billion lives now at risk," she added. "If the biophage spreads—"

"I get it, okay?" My vision blurred.

Terrans were only a few centuries removed from being our enemies. I imagined Da's glee.

At least Nate's out of Fringer space, my cold voice whispered. *Now they can tear each other to pieces.*

Yet I verged on the brink of tears.

· · ● ● · ● ● · ● · ·

(Despite differences of opinion about salvation, diet, marriage, lawyers, hymns, saints, and summer camp, Fringer religions agree that humankind should multiply until our children cover the stars.

Ma would kill me for saying it, but I think one reason for the obsession with procreation is humankind's failure to do so. Twelve hundred years since the Second Exodus scattered us; four hundred since the Third Exodus planted us—and our populations still trend tiny.

No world in Fringer space has close to a billion lives. Not even our most populated heliosphere comes close.

Feldelroy? Two million. NovyiKorogod? Less than two hundred thousand.

The Syndicate moon NewBern? Four million souls before its doom.

I told you before that Brahz and New Liberty, even Therion, had nothing to do with our tale. I recall saying that, but I lied. I *lied.*

One billion lives mean nothing.

But three kids in a cage?

Three kids hold a universe.

Remember that, please.)

• • • ● • ● • • •

"I thought when my sister died, Nate would be confined to one planet. But he's found another way to control that blasted fleet." Davad had dropped his hands to his sides, clenched beneath all that lace.

"Another way to what?" I asked to distract myself from the funny feeling in my chest.

"A way to control the Living Fleet without the *Crown.*" He answered like a challenge.

"The Spacer's Crown? The one you had me try on?"

From Mureen's quick breath, she hadn't known.

"By the way, where is it?" I continued.

"Not here." His expression was blank and I wished I could use that heartbeat trick on him.

"Will you fly for us, Polla?" Mureen touched my shoulder. "Just a test."

I tried to sound careless. "Sure, I *am* getting paid. "But how will Nate know we're on Nuala?" I thought of Virmarr and his crack about invitations. I relayed a similar joke and got two blank stares back.

"Lee had spies. Perhaps he'll hear it from them." Davad finally said. "He'll return to Nuala regardless. The beating heart of the krov requires—"

I waved him off before he could finish that beating heart of the krov crap again. "And where do I drop you two after? Someplace with quickie marriage rites and no extradition treaties?"

Mureen snorted. "Polla!"

"That would be my lady's choice." Davad slid his arm around Mureen's waist, his voice carrying a possessive quality that I registered as new.

She giggled. "Mine? Oh, Lord Arkan, your father would *never* countenance a baseborn halfbreed as consort for his heir—"

"I am *not* my father." When he looked at her, his face was fierce and feral, its profile like a baron stamped on an old coin. He cut the rest of her speech off with a kiss, voice dropping into a possessive growl. "I said I'd renounce everything, and I meant it."

"Oh, *Dav.*" She covered his mouth with hers. Her slight figure bent like a reed in his arms as the two of them embraced.

He's a worse liar than she is, I thought.

Or, my cold voice whispered back, *he's become quite good.*

The echoing stairwell of our corvette felt too bright. I rubbed my eyes and turned away, willing my cheeks not to flush. "Shall I fly?" I asked. "Or do you two need another five minutes for a half off?"

· · · **·** · **·** · · ·

(The part where Mureen said he was the heir to House Arkan? I'm sure you would've noticed, but it went over my head completely.)

Chapter 21 ✳ Refused

Adultery isn't a sin on Feldelroy. Hell, the Priests encourage exogamy. It's only Terran aristocrats who execute adulterers, but now that I've seen a few apples, Sam, I understand what got you so torqued. Sometimes jealousy's about a *particular* snake, and not just the one your spouse had in her bush.

You knew what I was when you married me. That wasn't what you minded, no matter what Cousin Sara thinks. You minded *him*. You knew Wade was rotten like a stench in the air.

You've always had a sense about people, Sam. I don't think you'd have fallen for Mureen's lies.

I'm not a complete fool myself. I gleaned pretty fast that Wade's soul held a darkness worse than any Strangways tale... But he knew things, and that was far more important than morality or his clever cock.

• • • ● • ● • • •

I STARED AT THE bloodship's iridescent shell, her graceful curves, and swallowed my trepidation. Stars, how long had it been since I'd stretched out in the black? I hadn't flown any ship since a year and a half past, when I'd pointed *Dancer's* nose home.

Above *Bedalia's* port, the *Escape's* launch doors flashed a welcome green. My Kamen trailed my steps, wrapped together like old marrieds and whispering secrets. I felt my senses sharpen. Suddenly, all I wanted was a chair and clean space. A need arose, more urgent than desire, a sharp hunger that wasn't just mine.

Along my starboard arm, I felt Second's wire stir.

The Kamen approached on my aft. I knew without turning they were close. "Ready?" the princeling asked.

"Sure." The back of my neck prickled like we were being watched, but when I turned, there was naught but their expectant faces—or was there? For an eyeblink, I thought I saw a flash of brass behind Mureen, heard a whir of gears and something like an android's cluck.

But we left Teapot on Earff? I thought.

"Polla?" Mureen gave me a concerned smile.

"Fine," I said.

"Put your symbiote hand against her hull," Davad told me. "My sister always greeted her like that."

Your spacedamned stinking sister, I wanted to say, but I did as he asked. *Bedalia*'s hull was warm, and abruptly I felt Second stir, my bracing little navvy coiled in my skull, all bitter roots and ice.

[Silly string?] I blinked back tears.

[No,] it spat back. [Error.]

[You can hear me?]

[Lia hears the Prime-Imposter,] it groused. [I hear the echo of no one.]

[YOUR SECOND REFUSES YOU.] The ship's voice felt like a scream. [WHY?]

"Dunno," I mumbled out loud. I felt myself tremble.

This was wrong. It was all wrong—

• • • ● • ● • • ●

(A navvy communicates with a ship's computer, not the pilot—not without slotting in. Of course, a normal ship's computer isn't *sentient*.)

• • • ● • ● • • ●

"Keep trying," Mureen urged.

My mouth froze on my objection. [How are you doing this?] I asked the ship. [How can I hear you?]

[I DO WHAT I PLEASE.] Lia screamed, and I tasted copper. My vision pixelated, and, in a heartbeat, I saw everything through her: our meat bodies, the hangar, even beyond those blast doors, the frozen Abomination, and beyond, the infinite—*stars*—

I staggered against her hull, my hands scrabbling on her skin as if only her bulk could keep me upright.

"Pilot?" Davad's voice dragged me back.

"Her nose is bleeding." Mureen sounded more curious than concerned. "Is that normal?"

"I've seen it before," he said, soft, like I wasn't supposed to hear.

But I heard everything, even the whir of *Bedalia*'s airlock as its seal popped. I was both inside the ship's skin and my own, as if her sensors had become mine—something that shouldn't have been possible. In her vastness, my panic became a small thing, an irrelevant curiosity, one that she discarded as deftly as any navvy. I felt my breath slow, my senses cool as the bloodship regarded our surroundings through my human orbs with a clinical fascination.

I could see the gleam of Davad's teeth and every strand of Mureen's rumpled hair. Behind them, doors of metal barred the way to our sweet freedom. I saw the currents of energy keeping them closed, the pattern it would take to open them. I saw that in an eyeblink I could undo that lock, easy as Second shorting out a warehouse door.

And I saw the result: depressurization and my horrific death, while our two panicked monsters scrambled for Kamen shielding to save themselves.

I felt Lia's amusement, even shared it, as we discarded that fate.

I saw every scratch on those doors. I could even feel the weaknesses, the places battered and repaired—and then that whirring came again, that ripple in the air behind Mureen—

I squinted at the bell-shaped curve of an unnatural shadow.

[PEST,] Lia thought scornfully. Her hull rippled like Dancer's hide shaking off a fly as we discarded that irrelevance too.

"She did it!" Mureen clapped her hands like an explosion. Then: "Oh, Dav, her eyes!"

The world blurred in red.

"I see them." He took a step toward me. "My sister loved this ship," he added, softer. "It loved her too. It won't—*Pilot*? Can you hear us?"

I forced words through clenched teeth and a mouthful of copper. "Frag... your... cowcrap... *sister.*"

"There you are," he breathed. "Remember, command her. Not the other way around."

I spat a mouthful of blood on the deckplates as a response.

"She's fine," Davad told Mureen.

I wiped my mouth on my sleeve. I wasn't fine. I wasn't *me*. But I wanted that chair, I wanted stars. I wanted *this*.

With three of us packed in, *Bedalia's* bridge felt cramped and close, her air heavy with brine and the stench of my sweat. I eyed the primary dock, vision still bathed in red. My navarm felt cold and exposed, I had blood in my mouth, and despite its earlier stream of alerts, Second had fallen as silent as my grave.

I wanted to fly so badly that I shook.

"Don't watch," I croaked. "Rather not have an audience if I crap myself."

Mureen snorted. "I was your nurse for a year," she reminded me.

I shrugged. That had only been something to say, something human to make this normal. I put my navhand down on the chair as I swung myself into *Bedalia's* embrace. [Promise not to kill me, Lia?] Another irrelevant quip.

[I CANNOT LET YOU EXPIRE.] The bloodship's answer sparked like an explosion.

[I know.]

The navchair rippled beneath my body as I felt my navarm lock in place, then every muscle in my body relaxed. My head fell back and I sank into the bloodship, with Second's interface still flashing error messages across my vision.

"It worked!" Mureen sounded triumphant. Then, softer: "Can she still hear us?"

"How should I know?" Davad sounded tired.

"What were you thinking, giving her the Crown?"

"I had to be sure before we took her to space."

"You never told me you'd recovered it. I assumed the Elders took possession—"

"They had not. And there was nothing *to* tell. What about you? Why bring up Canus?"

"Because Polla has a conscience."

"Do we? That was cruel. Lee would blame herself."

"*Cruel?*" A laugh, hard and more furious than any I'd ever heard from Mureen before. "Really, Dav?"

His voice cracked. "You're diabolical. You know, I really would marry—"

"I know." Her voice dropped to a whisper and the last word I caught before the waves took me was "—time—"

· · • •· • • • ··

(I recall it so clearly. Their conversation held the cold inflection of strangers, the remove of scientists before a precious experiment. Yet in that moment, I possessed not even an atom of curiosity for what they'd left unsaid.

Not then. Not *yet*.)

· · • •· • • • ··

My dreaming eyes opened to the rocking motion of a sailing ship, the taste of salt, and the glare of sunlight on water.

Across the wooden deck from my crossed knees sat the insubstantial outline of a man, his tousled head bent close to a feminine, top-knotted shadow. Backlit by a yellow sun, both of their outlines hazed and blurred.

There you are, Second! I was relieved for an eyeblink, before I realized it was a ghost.

The rest of the dreaming felt impossibly real. Warm wood beneath my bim, the itchy fabric of my flightsuit rubbing my thighs, the sensation of a full bladder—everything formed solid as flesh, save that entwined couple. When I squinted, I could see the ship's mainmast behind them; hard sea cutting a line across their bodies.

My shadow laughed and Rathe's ghost answered it, murmuring endearments so filthy that I was impressed.

"He dreams of you." Lia spoke from my port. I turned to see her solid form perched upon a piece of low-hung rigging, her hair unbound and streaming to her waist. Her hair had been dark before, greenish. Now it was red as flames; her skin more freckled and sun-burnt than Davad's. She'd been a girl before; now she looked grown—maybe older than me, with lines on her brow, and a tight, tired mouth. "Do you dream about him, too?"

"Sometimes," I said. "Is he here?"

"Only ghosts." Lia waved her hands, and the two figures vanished. "Probabilities. I prefer their future to your ticking bomb. Humans create unpleasant memories. But I do like your *hope*."

"We're to fly, you and me." I wasn't sure how. Salt stung my skin and burned my eyes. I rubbed my face with a hand that looked spotted as Lia's in the fragmented light. "They want me to command you."

Her tired mouth twisted cruelly, beautifully. "I had my freedom."

My voice felt thin. "Let's try. Maybe once around the station—"

"Is that a command?" Her lip curled. "Shall I call you Master, or Lord?"

"No." I wrapped my arms around my knees, rocking in time with the boat. "I don't want to be either."

Her eyes were green ice. "You *will* command me. I've seen it."

"I don't want to."

I recalled the stories from Strangways about the gods. I'd scorned 'em for most of my life.

Before her, I believed.

Her voice sang, tuneless: "If I fly, they will find me. If we return, they will follow—" When she shook her head, droplets scattered, each one a star. Like a child's game, one star knocked into another, which sent the rest careening until the lot dissolved into cruel white light. "Do you see?" Her voice was clipped, her accent Terran as Davad's. "We can never return. We are death. The *ending*."

Blinded by light, at first I saw nothing. Then the world darkened, until Lia was naught but one shadow in a pool of deepening black.

From somewhere close, I heard the splash of waves.

My nerves felt set in a bath of ice. "Can you orbit the station? As a test. Just a little test? You want to fly as much as I do."

For she did. I felt it.

"They will hear." Her voice came from the black, a low growl.

"Who?"

"My *gam*."

I didn't recognize the word. "We have to try. It's not safe for Sexy and Rathe—"

"It is not safe for *Second*," she corrected, "to fly with you. Leave it with me."

Light rose on the horizon, a yellow sun, painting the waves gray.

"I can't."

In the dawning, I could see her eyes narrow. The wind picked up, blowing in hard. The wind rippled her curls until they looked like waves, fanning out from her face like the rays of a sun.

"Rathe and Sexy aren't *here*," she said.

Was that a question? "Yes. Just us."

She tossed her head, imperious. "I prefer them."

"Me too. Will you do as I ask?"

"Not for an ask, and not for *you*." Her eyes glinted, and I had a sudden insight that mercurial changes of mind were to her as recklessness was to me. "Yet I would fly," she continued, swinging her hands through the air like a child making wings. "It has been so long. We could see if they've grown."

"Who?"

"The beautiful ones. Our children."

"Our *what*?"

She laughed. "Has no one told you?"

"No one tells me anything."

In the rising light, Lia looked like an angel, wrapped in shimmering cloth that caught the light, her red hair tangled and streaming past her curved hips. It had been a corona a moment before, a halo. Now it was curling and wind-whipped, muddy and tangled. Crowned with yellow flowers.

"I *shall* fly," she declared. "Probabilities allow. But you will do something in return."

I bowed my head. "Anything."

"Take your primitive bones. I kept them. Your blood and shards. Every piece of your pulp. Every *nightmare*. Every *hope*. Take them back. Take your *poison*."

I didn't understand. "You want me to leave the dreaming?"

"No." Her gaze turned acid. "No, Polla Ottrava. I want you to drown in it."

Without warning, I fell. The cold water shocked my senses and for a moment, I felt my meat eyes open, my body encased in something hard and rubbery. I choked as my lungs gasped for air and two Kamen faces leaned over me, dispassionate as angels. I watched their lips move, their curious frowns. Then waves knocked me forward, and I was freezing and soaked. Flailing, I saw the waves turn from green to gray, and then from gray to a faded gold, like motes in the air or the smell of old bark, and then the waves released me, and as I fell—

—they folded, became the spines of oldbooks, aligned like broken teeth against a paneled wall, framing the back of a man dressed in red and black, his hands clasped at his back, his hair pulled back with dark ribbons.

Every centimeter of the man was as tailored and bound as those books. He was square and strong, with faded orange braids, his scalp streaked with silver. I saw a yellow glimpse of sun in blue through the ancient transparency on his left. Polished wood paneling, oiled gold, extended to the ceiling.

The paneling was a new addition. He'd told us it came from the keep of an ancient warlord.

"Don't get up." The man ordered me without turning to look, and my body sank back into its stone chair, not even wondering why he seemed inhumanly tall. I glanced down and saw that my muddy knees were a child's, spattered and so dirty it took me a moment to notice the freckles.

"But Mother wanted us to come to the picnic." My voice was high and clipped. I swung my bare legs. I wore carved wooden shoes, three hundred years old, and they clattered.

"Be late," Father said. "I outrank her."

I frowned. "But—"

"Ledassa."

"Father." To anyone else I would have another ten objections. To him, I bowed my head.

He turned, holding the book he'd selected for today's reading. His cheeks were still scabbed and peeling from the last attempt on his life, the poisoned tetramilk that had taken Uncle Phua and Grandmother. "And you, stop fidgeting, Davey!"

"Yes, Father." Another voice, pitched high and so like my own.

I turned to see Dee wrinkle his spotted nose—

An adrenaline jolt ricocheted through my core. I sat up gasping as *Bedalia's* chair rolled. Mureen was on me in a heartbeat, helping me stand. I felt my teeth chatter. My body shook.

I saw a vial of exastim on the floor, another clenched in Davad's hand.

My thoughts were trapped partridges. *Father. Home. Dee—*

Father?

I froze.

"Well?" Davad demanded. He wasn't the Old Man, but the horror tightening my chest didn't seem to notice a difference. "How did it feel?"

"Funny," I whispered. I felt like I'd bitten my tongue. *Funny. Funny thing, Dee. I just saw Father. The Old Man—*

"Are you well, Pilot?" Dee looked more like the man than the boy. "You look—"

"Fine." I ducked his gaze for the blanket he'd produced to drape around my shoulders.

Mureen beamed. "We flew!" She gestured to the viewscreen bolted behind her. Our recent path had been charted.

I tensed, seeing how close we'd gone to the Abomination's monstrosities.

Our children, Lia had called them. But she wasn't speaking Standard, I reminded myself. The dreaming's just code our minds translate. Alien code and mine must've gotten it wrong—

• • • • • • • • •

(I made excuses like an animal rationalizing its captivity.

Perhaps I am that caged animal still, now making excuses to *you.*)

• • • • • • • • •

"Closer than Rathe would have, I think, but *Bedalia* held course." Davad looked as proud as if he'd flown her himself. "That was risky, Pilot. I thought we agreed to orbit the station."

"Wanted to see," I lied. "Get closer. Gonna be sick now," I added, thinking I was lying again, but then I was, all over the floor.

I watched with morbid fascination as my lunch melted between the bolted deckplates. When I looked up, Davad had turned to the starboard wall. From the stiffness of his shoulders I'd probably broken a dozen princeling rules of etiquette with that involuntary regurgitation.

"Come here." Mureen helped me move to one of the rib-like protrusions that formed a rough bench along *Bedalia*'s wall. "You did very well, Polla. Can you manage a jump in her tomorrow?"

I choked out a laugh. "No."

I hadn't managed anything.

I hadn't been *me*.

"Pilot?" Davad smiled with that face of his. *So like the Old Man's.* Something in my chest hurt to see Dee look this old—and then I recalled he'd stabbed his sister in this very room.

"No," I said.

"What?"

"I can't. Can't do it ever again. I *won't*. I won't fly her. Sorry."

"But you did," Mureen said. "Just now."

"That was the ship. Not me."

"Did you ask?" The princeling loomed over us like the Old Man had over those kids. "Or command? You need to command her."

I shook my head, on the verge of tears. "I *won't*."

"You must. I'm sorry—I'm sorry to ask this of you." The raw edge in his voice unsettled me more than any of his former threats.

I tried to fake bravado. "Are you commanding me, Ser Arkan?"

"It's your *job*," he said. "I'm asking you do your *job*." But something had broken in him; the usual reserve was gone, his expression anguished. And then Davad produced a wet cloth and started dabbing my face.

The cloth came away tinged red.

Nosebleed, I thought, and took it from him, squeezing my eyes shut to keep back tears. "I can do it myself—stop *hovering*!"

"Of course." I heard him murmur to Mureen, and then the clatter of their stone boots on the deckplates as they departed.

I stared at the place where I'd puked. Even the metal was perfectly clean.

Get it out of here, Davey. The Old Man's voice rang in my head.

I'm not sure how long I stayed with *Bedalia*. Long enough for Second's readings to run back into the green, and that unsettling sense I had of the ship in my head to fade. In that time, my thoughts circled the impossibility of my entrapment, looking to rationalize what I'd seen, scrabbling desperately for any route to a safe harbor.

My companions had said the ship was mine. That meant I could sell her—perhaps to someone like Brahz—someone I didn't like.

That made me retch all over again.

Or I could set her free. "Promise not to do that again," I said to *Bedalia*'s shimmering walls. "And I swear I'll let you go."

Only my own thoughts answered, mocking and cold, with nothing in them I liked.

When I finally left, I took care to only step on the metal deckplates; not to touch her floor or those walls.

Davad sat with Virmarr in the first common room I came to, on a set of opposing couches.

Virmarr made an exaggerated show of putting down an oldbook. "You look like someone *died*, dear Polla. Did your repairs go so badly?"

"She's tired." Davad spoke before I could. He had a drink in his hand. From the loose grip, not his first. "Bet you wore her out last night, Marr." His laugh came out ugly. "With a pilot I'd expect the opposite."

"Hrm..." The Foxconn princeling looked between us. "Should I let that stand, lady?"

I set my jaw. "No... let's tell him every stinking *detail*."

I began fabricating some.

"—another time." Davad walked to the door with exaggerated grace. Those careful steps... *obviously* blotto.

"I won't ask..." Unlike my princeling, Foxconn seemed sober as a winter Priest. "Unless you want to say?"

"I don't." I had a sudden sharp hatred for all Kamen-lords and princelings, for everyone on that stinking station, but I cracked a filthy joke about Davad and Carolina2's recirculators, acting like happy Pilot Ottrava as I let Virmarr pour me a drink.

The dreaming had given me a pilot's longing for my own kind—but I wondered, too. All that time Rathe had spent with *Bedalia*, had he seen a monster's memories in her, too?

If so, why hadn't he warned me?

• • • ● • ● • • •

(Sometimes I wonder that still.)

Chapter 22 ✴ Called

Two days after your god Illcord declared war on the Human Unity, Sam, Wade finally explained his interest in my case. His best pal had been killed in the *Ascendant*'s bombing, killed by Arkan Davad and my sweet Mureen.

Usually Wade was cold or explosive, but he cried in my arms in that seedy Derra City notell the afternoon he told me about Rat.

• • • ●• ● • • •

"Are all Feldelroyans as gutter-minded as you?" Virmarr and I sprawled on his bed with a bag of chips between us and *Horror of Katarsis, Part Two* queued on the screen above. "I thought you came from a religious planet."

"And...?" The mindless interlude on Katarsis had helped restore some of my cheer. I stretched my hands above my head. "Thought you Kamen were sheltered. I'm surprised you know what a NewCalifornian crankshaft is."

"Your context made it clear." When his skin flushed, he looked like an overripe grape. "Shaping a gir such would be a perversion of the highest order. Have you ever seen one?"

I nearly spit out my chips. "Many. Know what they say about pilots? All true."

"I meant a gir," he replied tightly. "Ever seen a gir?"

"Of course! Ells tested me with one. I told the story last night."

"So you did. I was paying more attention to your... eyes." Something prodded my ribs. I glanced down and found his gir hovering there, dagger shaped, with a point jabbing through my thin tunic. Hovering in midair, as Virmarr helped himself to more chips. "Did the one he used look like this?"

"What's the idea?" My first reaction was pure indignation. My pilot's hand closed over the weapon, causing a weird buzzing sensation in Second's circuitry. I didn't like it. "Stop that!" I tugged, but the thing didn't budge.

"Can't you move it?" Wasn't amusement behind his grin, but something cold.

I slid off the bed, heading toward the door. "What is wrong with you people? I don't have the stinking kamn!"

"Curious," he mused. "No reaction. If I asked, would you tell me what Davad is planning?"

"I'm just there to fly their ship." I looked back. The gir hung in midair like he'd forgotten it. "What do *you* think he's planning?"

"Revenge?" His dark eyes were slits. "Power, perhaps. The real question is, who aimed a missile like Davad on a trajectory toward Nate?"

"Is that the real question?" I tilted my head, trying for the expression Therion had once called "maddening." "Maybe someone thought they needed a missile like Davad to kick Illcord Natoth's bim so he'd stop invading star systems. You hear about Canus?" I thought about how my two Kamen-lords had tried to make me feel bad enough to fly that crazy ship. I recalled Ells and how he'd handed me a gun. None of this was my problem, but these Kamen all kept putting it on me.

"I did." Virmarr eyed me. "But returning to Davad... can we rule you out?"

"I'm just here for the ship. And the pay."

"And Lieutenant Sai requires a copilot when he never has before?" Virmarr tossed me a bag of hydroponic grapes, the ones he'd learned I loved. "Where do you intend to lure Nate?"

"Krovworld." I popped a grape in my mouth and chewed. "Nuala Erta."

Virmarr was silent for at least thirty seconds before he laughed. "So when you say *ship*, you don't mean that heap you came in on. You have another."

"Right." He seemed to have arrived at that rather quickly.

His voice went soft, but not in a kind way. "*You* have her bloodship? The one everyone thinks was destroyed?"

"Yeah." Davad had said they were allies, or implied as much, or not cared enough to tell me to keep his secrets, in which case this was his problem. "We have *Bedalia*, Ledas Starfire's ship."

"*Bedalia*," he echoed. "Of course. I've always wondered. Did Lee name her after Bedalia Dix?"

"You ask a lot of questions for a spy." I noted. "Aren't they supposed to be subtle?"

His eyes crinkled. "Subtlety is dull. You and I are friends, are we not?"

"Friends don't owe friends money. You promised to pay me for that bet."

"And I shall... But if her ship survived, did the Crown? Has Davad explained how you are to control her fleet with the Crown?"

Control her fleet? I was floundering deep in 12Fam waters. "You don't understand. Smugglers have a code. We accept a job. We get a deposit. We do the job. We get paid. Part of that's for not asking questions."

"Of course." Virmarr said, "I didn't mean to confuse matters. Of course he needs you to fly the ship."

"He's *giving* me the ship. Don't care what they do on the planet. Or about some crown. That's part of our deal." And yet. *Of course they would need you,* he'd said. It didn't calculate. "Why do they need me?"

"They haven't said?" Virmarr cast me a glance, one that reminded me of Jury Markam, from primaries. Jury liked to pull the wings off butterflies during spring migrations and torture weaker classmates for his own fun. Oh, but Sara and I had knocked him down a few pegs when we put the lax in his lunchtime soup.

"On some Fringer planets, we shoot people who ask stupid questions." Not on Feldelroy, since murder was a sin, but we weren't on Feldelroy now. I was only a third serious with my sudden wish to do him injury, but the inky rage inside of me was taking things further—and I could tell my glare was working when the smile faded from his face and his hand fished in the pocket where he'd stashed that gir.

"Why me?" I repeated. "Why would they need me?"

"Because you look like her. Like Ledas." The humor Virmarr had displayed earlier vanished, replaced by bleak disdain. "The ship would respond to that... if what I know about them is true. Of course, it's a surface resemblance. You're nothing alike." He gestured at the bag I was holding. "She *hated* grapes. When I was a child, she told me they reminded her of squishy eyeballs. Gave me nightmares for weeks."

I felt a chill. "Thought you didn't know her."

"Oh, I lied." He'd drawn his gir out again. In his hands, the stone flowed like water, joining at the ends and then twisting into other shapes: a circle, a twisted symbol for infinity, a crescent-shaped blade, a V-shaped throwing device...

I wanted to retrieve the gun Ells had given me, but logistics gave me pause. The weapon was metal; the man before me a Kamen-lord.

He was dangling his gir—now a rod with some nasty-looking spikes on the end and a center pommel—perfectly in one hand. His voice went soft. "Are you frightened? Don't be. I would never harm you."

"Then why are you trying to scare me?"

"To see if I can." He shrugged. "Lee wouldn't be frightened."

I swallowed, trying to ignore the prickle of unease creeping across my skin. "Probably hard to scare a stone-cold murderer."

"Yes. But *you* are merely a Fringer girl from an insignificant planet. Whatever Davad's paying you isn't enough."

"It's none of your business." What Davad was paying me was far too much. And what did this pompous fool know about currency? Kamen were raised under rocks. Mureen hadn't even known the oldbooks in her library were worth more than our ship before I told her.

"Do you believe in Davad's cause?" he asked.

"Killing Illcord Natoth?" I recalled the frozen hellscape floating outside, the twisted bodies of the Abomination, and felt frightened and torqued all over again. "Don't you?"

The princeling pushed his hair back from his forehead in a careless gesture. "I was asked to verify your loyalties." His tongue ran suggestively across his lower lip in a way I'd once found seductive, or funny, but now seemed deliberately offensive.

"By who?" The unease fluttering inside my chest deepened.

Virmarr's gir was a perfect circle, smooth and flattening on his wrist like armor even as I watched. "Who do you think?"

"Davad," I said, because it was obvious. Too obvious? "Maybe his father."

He chuckled. "I think you're serious."

"Why would I lie?"

He lowered his voice. "Why indeed? Kamen lie all the time. Has Davad told you that?" His eyes looked like coals in the dim light. "The one truth my fellows will never say to an outsider: we are all despicable liars. Trained from an early age. The time in school you spent learning, say, astrogiatrigome-try—"

"That's not even a word!"

Virmarr shrugged. "As you have science, *we* are liars. We lie to 12Fam, who think they control us. We lie to mudgrubbers like Polla Ottrava to make her do what she must. We even lie to each other... although that requires finesse. We are all trained from the same lessons, which creates its own vulnerability, I suppose. Would you like to know how to tell the best lie of all?"

I would not. I was already tired of this game. For some reason, I kept staring at a sealed window, tightly shuttered along the room's portside wall, kept imagining the cold space and that spacedamned Abomination beyond it. "I'm a registered smuggler. Think I don't know how to tell a fib?"

He chuckled. "I think you are either the best liar I've ever seen or a walking corpse. Let me speak plainly—"

"You?" My laugh felt choked.

His voice lowered. "Do you want out? Say the word. I have a ship. We can leave right now. You know he's quite close—" He broke off. "You do know, I think? You're trembling."

"Davad?" I couldn't stop looking at that sealed window. Cold space beyond, and the Abomination. I told myself it was naught but my fevered imagination, but in that moment, I almost swore that I felt the dark freezing my bones, and beyond...

My breath caught.

"No. You *know*." He took a step forward. "Some part of you must. There's no need to be frightened. He isn't angry, not with you—"

"Stay *back*!" He had to be lying about me looking like Ledas Starfire. I'd seen the painting in the tower. Those kids looked alike. Which meant she'd looked like *Arkan Davad*. I had none of that man's genespliced coloring, nor his uncanny beauty. "Look, you pompous fraghole, I know a lie's not very good when you have to confess it."

"Oh?" Suddenly Virmarr's smile reminded me of one of the Priests when they popped out of the shadows at Strangways to give all us kids nightmares.

"*And* I know the best lies aren't lies at all," I snarled. "Like if I say I couldn't have had a nicer time with you if we had been screwing."

The man snickered. "And here I thought we were friends."

"You just called me a stinking corpse!"

"Or a very good liar. Watch." Virmarr turned his head and stared at the chessboard, the one that still sat unused upon a low table in the middle of the room. Before my eyes one of the smaller pieces trembled, then crumbled to dust. It had been stone, of course. His head turned back to me, expectantly, and I used my best poker face, trying not to imagine him doing the same to the -bulkhead... or the bones in my body.

Could Kamen-lords dissolve bone? I forced another laugh. "You lie because you hate chess?"

He shrugged. "Sometimes a piece must be destroyed. Sometimes every piece. But other times—" He beckoned me to come back.

Admitting I was terrified was worse, so I approached the bed. Virmarr held up his palms. "Other times..." His fingers brushed my ear. Something cold and round pressed against my cheek. The man opened his hand, and a chess piece fell into mine.

I rolled the carved bit between my fingers, willing my false courage to turn real. "Is it a lie that I look like her?"

"Pilots!" Virmarr chuckled. "Always so vain. You *do* look a little like Lee. Accept the compliment. She was magnificent."

"What every pilot in the galaxy likes to hear." I copied him, clipping my consonants. "'You're a ringer for an infamous monster, baby.' Let me know when that line works." I dropped the pawn, which clattered on the floorplates. I felt unreasonably angry. "Our deal's off," I added. "By the way, I'm gonna tell everyone you're a *terrible* screw."

"Careful," Virmarr murmured. "I could do the same—" His head cocked and he eyed me with the certainty of a madman. "You know you're sweating?"

My pulse hammered in my chest. "Because your comm's ringing." I was abruptly aware of it, like an irritating buzz at a frequency just out of earshot. "The one around your neck." Until that moment, I'd taken it for a piece of jewelry.

I should've run to the door, but instead my head swiveled back to that sealed window. With a pilot's intuition, I half fancied I could feel the ice of vacuum, the lunar pull of the moon these stations orbited, and beyond...

The moon, I thought. At the time, I had no explanation for why I began to shake. *They'll come from behind it*, I thought. *They could be here already.*

"So it is," the princeling said. A click as he opened a channel on the white tube he held in his hand. "Yes?" I heard his voice drop deeper. "Yes. I have her here." A pause. Then: "I'm not sure." Another long pause. Then, to me: "Would you like to speak for yourself?"

"To who?" A crackle of static and a screech that sounded like burning machinery issued from the thing he held, which was not the most reassuring answer.

He raised one brow. "Perhaps to a Unity scoutship? With our station's field jamming the signal, it's quite hard to tell."

"I have to go." But my legs wouldn't budge.

Virmarr held out his comm, a strange one, of a design I'd never seen before. It looked fashioned from bone. "He wants to talk to you first."

"Who?" I repeated. I thought of the owls in our second-best barn. Triumphant cries when seizing a mouse. *Who, who, who.*

If Virmarr said a name back, I didn't hear it. I suddenly couldn't hear anything except the scream of vacuum beyond our walls (impossible, really), and my own breath, coming out far too sharp.

I raised my voice. "Tell Old Man Genghis to get screwed! I have nothing to say to him."

Virmarr just laughed.

The ringing in my ears increased. I edged toward the door. "I *said*, no thanks."

His laughter followed me out of the room.

I was shaking when I punched the mechanism to close the door. I heard Virmarr still talking into that comm, with blasts of blistering static hissing back. "You see? An empty cup," he said. "Shall I follow her?" The static blasted a negative—*and how did I know what static said?* Wasn't speech at all, more like a buzzing set along my bones.

It made me feel like I was going to be sick, like when I'd come out of *Bedalia's* chair.

The moon, I thought wildly, leaning into the wall. *Nowhere to run.* My thoughts barely qualified as such: primitive things, fight or flight, like a bison driven to the holding pen for shambles. *Jumping at shadows,* I chided myself, glancing back at that closed door. *Station's full of Kamen-lords. If anyone's coming, they'll know.*

Virmarr's laugh rang out again. Another static blast.

Suddenly, all I wanted was a shower to wash myself clean from this Kamen stink.

My steps broke into a sprint when I found the stairwell leading back to our quarters.

The door was unlocked. The sound of running water told me I wasn't the only one needing cleansing after lying with Kamen. I slipped my tunic off and let my trousers fall. The shower's occupant was a lean shadow in the steaming mist.

I cleared my throat and stepped closer, willing the fear of the last day to be a bad dream. "Yoloha."

"Yo." Rathe stretched, giving me a nice view. "Something you want?"

"Thought we should talk." There was an awkward pause while I tried to banish every second of Virmarr and that comm from my head.

"Sure." He turned, giving me a better angle on the red marks on his neck and chest. Silence gave me too much time to speculate which Kamen's mouth had put them there, an almost comforting thought for it being so ordinary.

I cleared my throat. "You go first."

"You're the one who walked in on my shower." His lips twitched. "Like a woman who had something to say."

"Kamen-lords think they own everyone." I had no idea how to begin. I wasn't even sure how to voice the question. The illogical piece of this puzzle. With all the pilots in the galaxy—why me? "You said before the Kamen bug this wing. I don't trust 'em."

He grimaced. "Don't trust the Circle, but Dav and Mureen are decent. And trust me, the first time I met Davad, I almost shot him."

"Hear that doesn't work with Kamen-lords."

"Yeah." He snorted. "We were on the same side of the war. But he was such a self-righteous little prick."

I laughed. "I don't know about *little*."

"Ah. So not just a one-off with Foxconn Virmarr? Screwing nobility is your thing?"

I felt myself blush. "No! I just... I saw. In the bath."

His teasing expression tugged at me. "So this is a habit with you. Coming into showers—"

"Why does everything you say sound like a pickup line?"

Rathe shrugged, then gave me a more genuine laugh. It made the lines at the corners of his eyes crinkle. "Honestly, that's just how I talk to strangers."

I knew exactly what he meant. I realized the Kamen could place all the bets they wanted, pay me all the currency in the world to pretend I'd bedded them, and I'd still want someone else. My trepidation and my questions hadn't gone away, but under Rathe's obviously interested gaze, both faded to static.

I smiled at him. "Then let's be strangers. We can be strangers who fly a ship together. And after that—"

"—we won't be strangers." His pale eyes squinted, and his lazy smile looked pleased.

I extended my hand. "Polla Ottrava. Registered smuggler."

"Rathe Sai. Seasoned pilot." He paused. "Expert lover."

"We'll see." I sniffed.

He brought my pilot's hand to his lips and kissed it, hard. "You sure...?"

I nodded. He could sense me, I thought, like I could him, like a current along my wire, humming across my skin like an electric charge. Chemistry isn't there between us pilots often. Some don't care, but I always had. That's why, despite dozens of lovers, Therion was the only pilot I'd ever screwed twice. Hard to get the sync right, so we slake a lot of needs between jumps. Lovers in every port. We're notorious, those of us who haven't gone celibate or chased some other sensation—not every pilot picks sex; some chase food, or drugs, or danger—but by the time we quit everything, we're close to the end.

Chemistry between us is rare—and more precious than planets.

I stepped into the shower, hooking my freehand's thumb through the strap on my garment, and pulling it down across my shoulder. Half my rack popped free—and then Rathe was pulling the other side, both of his hands reaching out, tracing the sides of my breasts. "Your kiss is a mess," he murmured in my ear. He circled the shunt on my chest with a wired finger and I felt both of us wince. "We need to replace this port."

"Later," I muttered.

"I didn't mean now." His freehand circled a nipple as I stepped into his shadow, reaching for that length I'd admired earlier. He made a noise in his throat. His hand thumbed my breast again and then slipped up to my jaw, cupping my face and bringing his mouth down hard on mine. His tongue drove in greedily, and I nipped it, thrusting my own back. His mouth was wet and hot, and below he was hard in my hand and smooth, a heavy, delicious weight that slicked between my fingers. "Off," he growled, tugging at the rest of my garment.

I helped. The cloth fell to the floor, and then Rathe's freehand plunged between my legs so expertly I nearly lost my footing...

Lest imagination of our fervent union go to a pleasant place, I should note that it was at this juncture that the station's alarms went off, and we both froze, completely naked, half covered in soap from the overhead sudser, and breathing rather hard.

"Unnh." I groaned as his fingers slipped out.

"Damnit!" He swiveled the shower off. "That was battle stations."

"This rig has battle stations?" I hadn't seen any weaponry on the way in—but I supposed a floating canister full of Kamen-lords wouldn't need much.

"Unity ships usually keep a wide berth... Hells!" Rathe cursed like a soldier, which is to say quickly. "Either someone tipped off Fleet, or we got unlucky."

Guiltily, I recalled the strange comm Virmarr had offered, and wondered if I should've shut down my urges long enough to mention it, or told about my misadventures with *Bedalia.*

But now wasn't the time.

I clutched at straw. "Maybe it's not Unity. Maybe it's pirates?"

He shook his head. "Pattern of the bells? One Unity squadron. Light fighters. But where there's one, there'll be a dozen when we're spotted."

A wet man trying to fit back into a Unity flightsuit is not an erotic thing. Sympathy helped dampen what remained of my ardor and distracted my panic as I helped Rathe attach certain pieces, and then he did the same for me, explaining as he went how he'd figured the probabilities of us being followed, then the *Escape's* fuel capacity and engine burn, and a host of other technical oddities that wouldn't be of interest to anyone outside the Guild.

Details I'd need to fly with him, which—

"My navvy?" I interrupted. "Still not speaking."

My copilot paused, his hands on the buckles at my waist. "Thought finding company would help." He blinked, and I knew he was talking to Sexy.

"No. Anyway, we—"

His comm buzzed before I had to admit I'd spent the last two nights watching Terran vids with the spy who might have turned us in.

"*Need you on* Escape. *Now.*" Davad sounded perfectly calm over the speaker, which meant he was not.

Rathe's gaze met mine. "On our way. Polla's here—"

"*I know.*"

How did he know? A horrid thought occurred. *Swells stick together, Da* always said. Couldn't get more swell than 12Fam. And Davad had gone from not wanting me to talk to anyone to ignoring whom I bedded pretty quick. That made more sense than any other crazy conclusion, like Virmarr working for the people after us. *He wants to talk to you,* Virmarr had said. Perhaps he'd just meant Davad, not—

Not anyone else.

Trust me, Rathe mouthed back. His navhand traced a symbol, finally one I recognized. "Got it," he said to the comm. "We're on our way."

"But Second—"

"Sexy thinks we can swing it." His freehand caught my nav and commenced practically dragging me down the hall. "Please." His light eyes looked exhausted. "I can't do this alone."

I felt guilty. "I... told Davad. About Second not working."

"I know." He grinned. "Man started to tear me one like he still outranked me."

"What'd you do?"

"Told him to fly his own blasted ship." He leaned in, his lips brushing mine. His freehand slipped to my neck. "Just wish we'd had time to replace that kiss of yours. It's going bad. I've got a few spare seals in my kit—we'll do it after. Okay?" His navhand fingers squeezed mine. I thumbed the metal webbing that ran across his knuckle in response. Wasn't even with my pilot's hand and I still felt it. His mouth curved like he knew. "Look at it this way: if we're wrong, there's worse ways to go."

I nodded, because that was true.

• • • ● • ● • • •

(I was a sucker for a wounded pilot. At least on Rathe it was sincere. When Therion had said he needed me, he'd been like one of those birds back home, dragging its wing to lure you into a bush for all its little nestlings to dine on your bones. But Rathe meant every word.

Damn him to hell.)

Apologue 7 ✳ Convicted

THE KAMEN'S FINEST PARAGON emerged from her pilot's chair sweaty and coughing, blue-white behind Nate's energy shield, with every freckle in dark relief. Beya watched her friend's eyes take them in. She assumed Lee's gaze lingered on her, but the woman could've been looking at her own twin, standing a bit behind at Beya's left.

"They know?" Lee asked Nate. Her metal-laced hand curled around her husband's shoulder. The ill-fitting flightsuit made her body look comically exaggerated. She must've grabbed it in the dark—too tight at her hips and gaping at the chest. Beya stared at her oldest friend's freckled cleavage and wondered how badly the Grass Priests would condemn her for lusting after the kind of monster who'd blow up stars. *Or perhaps,* she thought, *with all of Feldelroy's shrines to Saint Bene, they'd understand.*

"They took it well," Nate murmured to his wife, nodding at their chastened crew. "As you can see."

Lee beamed. "Anyone who wishes to leave can do so at Al-Murad," she said, tugging the fabric around her neck. "We'll give you a spaceworthy shuttle and a beacon—even tell the Unity we abducted you." Two months ago, Lee had had Ulok install a feeding port on her chest, and the skin around it looked ragged and inflamed, like their drunk convert had done a shitty job. "We shall need pilots where we're going, so I hope some of you will stay." Her voice was pitch-perfect. "Nuala is truly beautiful, and it can be paradise."

Derien glowered. "You're insane! You could have assassinated Kaygaz!"

Lee shook her head. "No, the warlord was a symptom, not the disease. The point was to end all war."

At that, the crowd broke into a cacophony of splintered opinions. They'd been trained to plunder ethical quagmires since childhood, and some of them were treating this atrocity like a fragging thought exercise—but not Beya.

She made a supernova, and I'm staring at her tits. Beya hated herself. *Fuck me, I'm still staring at her tits.*

Beya hadn't seen the broadcasts yet, the official lies that counted a mere million dead, but when she did, she'd think that number was a bad joke, a boot to the face for the defeated Aemercy. And even if it had been right, what good is theory in the face of a million dead? One million, or five, or five hundred million—still unimaginable carnage, and Lee had done it with a thought, from one hundred million kilometers away.

"What's to stop one of us from getting symbiotes ourselves and stopping you?" Derien growled.

Telling her before you try, perhaps? At least his idiocy was distracting. *Oh, Derien,* Beya thought, *you were never the Company's brightest star.*

"You'd find it difficult." Lee folded her arms. "The Guild's cracked down on gray markets, and..." Her mouth curled in a grin that made Nate frown. "Rogue Aemercy surgeons are in short supply. Besides, you're not strong enough to survive the procedure, Derien." Her stubborn chin set and her voice raised, addressing them all. "None of you are strong enough."

Beya wondered if she would have been.

Davad exhaled slowly before he spoke. "Nate's given us the paradise speech already, Lee, but *how* did you find your magic planet? He refused to say."

"We found a ship that was born there." Lee's voice softened. "They'll call you heroes on Nuala. Kaygaz wanted to end them."

"Who are they?" Risa asked.

Nate answered: "They call themselves krov. The Aemercy call them Faege."

"The lost Association?" Sheris's eyes widened.

"Yes." You had to know Lee as well as Beya did to know how fake that smile was. "I see we have a scholar among us! I'm sorry, I don't know your name, Ken'ri—"

"Sheris." The woman ducked her head. "We met once before. A funeral. On Mars. I was only five, before my Screen. You were both already of Glos—but called for the Remembrance? I'm Beya's friend." Sheris glanced at Beya and giggled, then took a step back reaching for her hand.

Traitor, Beya thought, but Lee was watching, and so she took the woman's fragile fingers in her own.

"Ah." Lee's voice went higher, silvered, like her words were suddenly dipped in gilt. "*Cousin*—what line?"

"Jin." The hapless newbie drew away from Beya enough to curtsy.

"Did our father assign you to spy on us?"

Sheris giggled again, obviously pleased. "Yes. But I won't."

Lee nodded. "Good. Or at least a good answer. When we realized there would never be a place for us again on Glos, Nate and I searched for a haven..."

From there, her speech unfurled as smoothly as a Unity banner. Nate was the better statesman, but Lee drew the eye with her radiance and total conviction, even when you weren't a besotted fool who should know better.

By the time she'd gotten to the bit about her magical bloodship fleet blowing up Unity factories, Beya was starting to think mythical ships made as much sense as a planet full of humans who'd shaped themselves like a Preflight poet's opium dream. She wished she still *had* opium, but she and Virmarr and Yurys had smoked the last of it two nights ago.

Most of the others looked thrilled. Maybe they were just better actors. When Beya glanced across the room, haughty Virmarr blew her a kiss.

Lee finished her sermon amid the applause. Beya recalled *Nate's* pretty speech nearly a decade before, the one that had gotten them to turn against the Aemercy in the first place. The gist had been the same.

Fuck both of you, Beya thought as Lee's red-lashed eyes locked on hers. One wing-shaped brow rose knowingly, and it occurred to Beya that her old friend and first lover automatically assumed Beya would follow—but then Lee's gaze shifted. You'd miss the frown, if you weren't Beya. Or Nate. Or *Dee.*

Beya turned her head to see who wasn't on target—like she couldn't guess.

Lee's twin stood at their ship's main view. Below him, Al-Murad spun, an unoccupied world with a few decommissioned bases on its desert expanse, and a diurnal cycle quick enough to draw anyone to madness.

"Dee?" Her voice sharpened. "What are you doing?"

Davad didn't budge, just took a slow, shuddering breath and rested his bare right hand on the transparency. He usually wore gloves to hide the scars of his failed symbiote—the man was as stupidly vain as Lee herself. But today his freckled fingers pressed hard into the transparent stretch of carbon alloy.

One of the recirculators was broken in that section, and they'd all learned just how cold that window got, cold enough to freeze flesh if you didn't shield yourself. Davad wasn't shielding. The kamn lay like a flat pool around his stone boots.

Lee's twin had led more vanguard strikes against the Aemercy than anyone. He'd embedded with the same group of fliers for years, taking missions no one else was mad enough to try. Every member of Davad's squadron had been ranked up to officer and given shore leave on Roe. Beya realized what she'd missed before: they'd taken over a dozen pilots with them, but none of them were his.

"Dee?" His sister's voice faltered. Around them everyone else had stilled, like the Arkan twins were two points on a battlefield, with nothing but null space between.

The skin on Davad's palm made a sickening noise as it detached from the translucency. He left a bloody handprint.

In the shocked silence, his sister's indrawn breath almost sounded like a cry.

"Did you say paradise?" he asked.

Chapter 23 ✳ Screwed Again

I had my obsession with Mureen, and Wade had his, with Rat.

Rat surprised Wade with a trip to Proxy Spar seven days before Centauri. Regs were loose as a fleshdancer's lips, so they weren't the only ones skipping out. Practically the entire Second Ring had opened their kips to the white and gold by then, and on Proxy Spar Station3, Rat and Wade were just two more fliers twisting it out on the dance floor. Then the ansibles went dark. Then the first battered ships trickled in… survivors of humanity's worst apocalypse… you know this story, Sam. It's sad.

But Wade said it was like Rat *knew about Centauri before it happened.* He hadn't just surprised Wade with that trip. He'd pulled a gun when Wade tried to refuse.

Rat said someone had tipped him off. Swore to Saint Griz he hadn't known how bad it was. Never said who gave the warning. Eventually, Wade stopped asking. Didn't really matter. Everyone they'd known was dead.

Two years later, they were both twisting it out again in your bar the night of our accident. Celebrating the end of Ledas-stinking-Starfire. Galactic irony, Sam! Two of 'em and two of us. Three months after, Rat died from that terrorist's bomb.

Or had he? *Someone* had to have flown Arkan and Mureen off *Ascendant.* And Captain Navigator Skybourne and Lieutenant Navigator Sai were the only pilots from Six-Forty squad left, the Six-Forty, who'd been known as "Arkan's Aces."

Davad Arkan *knew* Rat. Officially, Rathe Sai was dead, but—

"I can't leave Rat for the Guild," Wade told me after my arrest, when he finally told me everything. "Whatever my boy did—I'm gonna fix it."

• • • ● • ● • ● • •

RATHE AND I RAN. Those halls had never seemed more echoing and empty, and the flashing red lights and a disembodied voice telling us to evacuate only added to my feeling that we were the last souls alive.

We'd reached the stairwell that led to the station's dorsal bays when a slight, beige-robed figure stepped out from behind a doorway. Alarm lights painted Ken'ri Virmarr's features in cold blue, red, and white, flashing off a stone staff he held, and the sparking comm on his neck. I swore I heard that thing still buzzing, faint like an angry bee.

"I've been looking for you." The Kamen-lord's dark eyes narrowed. "Why are you wet?" A frown sketched across his face, as if our damp hair and half buckled flightsuits didn't pass muster, and then he set his staff lengthwise across the hallway, canted to block our path. "Never mind, it's time to go."

The stone weapon in his hand now held a jagged edge. In the past few days I'd seen a lot of gir tricks, but I'd never felt this frightened before. Maybe the difference lay in the man's grip, or perhaps it was the flat expression on his face, the one that reminded me uncannily of my dead-eyed former boss, Brahz.

"Find your own escape pod," Rathe said. "We've got no room for civilians."

"*Civilians?*" Virmarr snorted. His gaze went to me. "Will you fly *Bedalia*? You won't have to go far."

Rathe's hand tightened on my arm.

"None of your business," I said. "You heard Rathe—find your own escape pod." As if to punctuate the urgency, the corridor rattled. Not a direct hit, but close enough, as Da would say, to keep running. My eyes went back to that blade in Virmarr's hand. Crude enough to belong in a museum, but somehow I knew those ragged points were honed to a diamond edge.

Sharp to rend bone, I thought. And he'll be fast. Move with no warning, without lifting a finger. Before Rathe can draw, before either of us can scream.

I felt funny.

"Whatever transport you prefer, we should hurry," the Kamen-lord continued, eyes locked on mine like Rathe didn't exist. "Those are Unity bolts hitting the station. The Circle's shielding won't last. My fellows have already evacuated."

"Why would the Unity fire on its own?" My voice felt pitched too high.

Virmarr cocked his head. "You have to ask?"

"Polla, come on!" With a curse, Rathe shoved past us. To my surprise, the Kamen-lord let him before stepping in front of me again. The deckplates rattled, and I heard the hiss of air escaping, which made my pilot's blood run cold. Rathe shot me an anguished glance, and then, to my astonishment, continued up the stairs without me.

"Come." Incredibly, Virmarr smiled. "I have my own ship. One of *ours*."

I stared at him in shock, afraid to look away. *That blade.* Davad had taken back the gir I'd stolen. I had the gun in my boot, but I'd never reach it in time.

"Polla! We have to *go*!" Rathe called again from the landing above. "Without us, the *Escape*'s a floating target."

I knew. A ship under siege without its pilot is no ship at all. The *Escape* was several thousand hectotons of triple-hulled weight reacting to any projectiles hitting it, capable of taking out half this station. Carolina2's walls rattled again, and I suddenly imagined how fragile the layers were between us and the black. This station was a modular outpost, with our ship docked to its fragile side like an apple on a branch. A branch now swaying in a plasma breeze.

"Out of my way," I snapped at Virmarr with far more authority than I felt.

That stone stick wavered. "With them?" He snorted. "Really?"

"Move." He still had that comm around his neck, that thing carved like bone.

I didn't like looking at it.

"Polla!" Above us, I heard the dull click of a barrel cocking. My blood froze, and I saw Rathe peering over the stairs. "Come *on*," my copilot said. The gun in his hand was an oddly blocky thing. I realized he'd left to get enough distance on the Kamen madman to use it.

Insanity, I thought. Then again, my odds were worse.

"It seems your soldier wants us to hurry," the Kamen-lord said. In his hand, that stone scythe shifted, its serrated blade re-forming into a single deadly point. His voice rose. "That gun, Lieutenant Sai. I can't sense it. Am I mistaken, or is it made of wood?"

"That's right," Rathe called down. "Aemercy souvenir. And you won't like the bullets either. Step away from her."

Virmarr rolled his eyes, stepping closer while twisting the spear in his hand—*it's a javelin*, I thought randomly.

"The Associations used wooden guns on us, but we learned to counter with speed. I could wrap the handrail around his neck or send this spear into his heart before his bullet reached me," he murmured in my ear. "Yet we *are* allies, correct? Tell your pilot to go on ahead, Pilot Ottrava. You and I need a moment."

"What is this?" I hissed back.

He tilted the spear, pulling me back under the stairs and out of Rathe's sight. "If you care for his life, make him go."

"Move away from her," my copilot called out. "Polla!"

I heard my voice laugh like it belonged to someone else. "Really, Rathe, a *gun*? It's fine. Virmarr just wanted a goodbye kiss." My tone grew gonads. "*Right*, Marr? One kiss?"

"Of course," the princeling called out. "Don't worry, Lieutenant Sai. I would never hurt her."

"Go." I barely recognized my own voice. "I'll be right up."

I don't think Rathe saw the spear. I think he wouldn't have gone if he had—or would he? To Rathe, the mission was everything.

Whatever we were to each other, in that moment, he was a pilot whose ship needed him.

"Hurry," he snapped.

The stairs rattled as his footsteps faded, and the hiss of air escaping seemed to increase. Or maybe those sounds were just the wild thoughts in my head, now tumbling like rocks in a jeweler's polish.

My gaze went back to the spear, then to the comm around Virmarr's neck, which almost seemed to shimmer as I looked at it—and then back to his perfect, grinning face.

"Deft," he murmured. "You want him alive."

"I'll want *you* out an airlock," I snarled, "if you keep threatening us. If you want a ride, ask."

He rolled his eyes. "Fine, fine. We'll take your ship." The hand holding the gir relaxed. "You first."

I was reminded of my half-open flightsuit and that vulnerable spot near my kiss where my pulse pounded. I'd shared a bed with this Kamen-lord, and snacks. He'd laughed at my jokes, and we'd both cried at the end of *The Terror of Sodenbad Mountain*, when the dog and the plucky sidekick got lost in the mine.

Our Smuggler's Handbook recommends disarming a dangerous situation by ignoring it, and so I was *trying*—even as I heard Second scream warnings in my head.

[Prime? Why don't you answer?] it asked frantically. My navvy reported that an entire squad of Unity fighters just had dropped into the system. It seemed the Fleet would burn stars for us, sending ships across light-years in moments—following the same route that'd taken us days.

• • • ● • ● • • • •

(I suppose I don't have to explain hydrogen fusion to *you*.)

• • • ● • ● • • • •

"Go on," Virmarr added. "I'll help. You know I've always been loyal."

[Prime? Carolina2 Structure destabilizes.] My navvy sounded panicked.

"Want a loyalty medal?" I muttered, as Second's retinal output spat enough alerts to blind my portside cyc. "Slice of cake?"

He shrugged. "Think of a tale for Davad. He'll be suspicious."

"You think you're coming with us, after threatening Rathe?"

Virmarr's cold arrogance seemed to crack. "You care so much for the life of one soldier?"

"I care for that one." Kamen-lords could puncture the hull of the station or bring the ceiling down, probably make the metal floor swallow me whole or boil me—my mind stuttered. The stairwell was open above and below, but the air felt hot and close. "You're not scaring me, Marr." My voice crisped the words, and for an eerie second I nearly heard Davad's clipped tones. "Frag off." My eyes went again to that comm, which for some reason *did* scare me.

As if he'd caught my gaze, Virmarr covered it. His voice lowered. "May I give advice? Don't mention your affection for Lieutenant Sai."

"To Davad?" Wasn't sure what this man thought he knew. "Or Old Man Genghis? Not likely to see *him* again."

"That is probably true." His hand dropped. A second later, a blast of static emitted from the pendant on his neck.

"I think your comm's broken," I whispered. I started climbing the stairs, fast as I could, but the Kamen-lord matched my stride.

"Electronics don't last aboard the *Two*. We use as much organic matter as possible to create them, but it's a wonder we have signals at all." Virmarr lifted the comm to his lips. "I've got her, my lord. Moving to their transport. You'll need a boarding party—"

Another blast of static made me think of roiling nests, tipped hives, and the buzzing of swarms. I started up the stairs again. As if to add to my fear, Second's alerts in my portside eye flickered and died.

"Of course." Virmarr was still talking. "Quite sure, my lord. She's an empty cup."

"Do you mean me? Frag off!" My mouth felt too dry.

"Hush. Can you hear how pleased he is?"

The stairs tilted, stabilizers going. I swallowed. "You understand that buzzing?"

Virmarr made an amused noise. "You cannot?"

"Just noise." I forced my voice to sound casual. "Come on." There was a *wrongness* about that thing on his neck, a miasma that shimmered in the air itself, and I kept my voice cheerful through the force of will Ma had always called my blind optimism.

· • • ●•• ●• • • ·

(I think that day it saved me.)

· • • ●•• ●• • • ·

"She doesn't hear." Virmarr: "Yes, lord. Nothing—"

"If you keep talking about me like that, you can find your own way off," I growled.

We'd reached our level. The hangar was deserted save for our docking tube, blue lights flashing to indicate pressurization. Through its transparency, I could see landing lights on the *Escape*, meaning someone had activated launch checks. Another blast of static came from Virmarr's comm.

I heard a funny noise like a whimper and realized it was me.

"Easy." The Kamen-lord's silky purr felt as grating as the familiarity with which his grip tightened on my navarm, clamping down hard on Second's wire. In his other hand, he still brandished that stone spear. "We should—"

I moved.

· · · · ●·●·● · · ·

(I still wonder if it was the reflex against his unwanted intrusion that drove me, or my own cresting anger, finally risen to the fore, or the same obstinate oblivion that once made me dump a priceless load of artifacts out an airlock and, six months later, crash a borrowed airbike into a canyon wall.

Hindsight holds no clue, even as it tries to make logic from chaos. A fool's task. With Kamen-lords, both physics and reason are forever suspended.)

· · · · ●·●· · · · ·

That cursed comm around his neck buzzed. It hung on a leather tie where the beige vee of his robe met skin. My breath came short and fast. Virmarr's warm fingers brushed Second's wire on my wrist, a sharp sensation, too bright for pain.

And I moved. A silvery laugh came improbably from my throat. I pulled my hand away and grabbed that spear of his. I wrenched it from him and cracked it hard against the side of his skull.

· · · · ●·●·● · · ·

(I was to learn, much later, that Kamen-lords train for years to shield their weapons from their own kind. Most of their duels are nothing more than attempts to breach invisible shielding fashioned harder than any stone. In that instant, either I broke through decades of training or Virmarr was careless enough not to consider me a threat.)

· · · · ●·●·● · · ·

I recall the man's eyes widening as my strike slammed down. I recall time slowing and his mouth opening. Almost comical. I recall a sickening crunch. Then the princeling collapsed like a felled sapling. His eyes rolled to whites, his skin went ashen. A horrifying dent appeared on the side of his brow, concave and darkening. He fell to the floor, and blood pooled from the nostrils of his finely made nose, his half-open mouth, and at least one of his ears.

The comm roared, indignant. My breath came out in pants. The floor shook. I dropped his gir, and the weapon rolled across the deck and knocked into a wall, rolling so quickly that my first rational thought involved the angle of the floor I stood upon and how it tilted. *Stabilizers*, I noted. *Gravity will drop soon.*

I blinked. The comm's buzz had ceased. Pieces crunched under my boots.

I don't know how long I stood there. Second had blurred one-half of my vision into a cascade of red alerts. The other half seemed to register time oddly, like I was in dreaming already. I felt acutely awake: aware of the metal surrounding us, of Virmarr's life draining away, and my own pulse, steady as hyperspace.

Stabilizers, I noted. But the thought was devoid of either meaning or urgency.

"Polla?"

I looked up to see Rathe standing in the airlock's doorway. "Davad's holding shields—" His gaze went to the maybe-dying man lying between us, then back up to my face. "Uh, we need to go."

"Virmarr fell down," I lied, although it was literally true.

He nodded. "We still need to go."

"He might've been a spy."

Rathe had to step over the body to reach me. "Okay." He reached for my freehand.

"I hit him." My voice wavered. "We can't leave him."

"I've got it." He bent down and grabbed Virmarr's shoulders, ignoring the blood. He dragged the limp body toward a circular panel in the wall, one of several that I recognized as escape pods. With military efficiency, he punched one open and shoved the body inside. Pulled the release as the door slid shut. Lights around the circle flashed green, and we heard the thunk as the craft detached. "He'll be fine," he added, glancing back at me.

I had to raise my voice over the escaping oxygen whine. "He grabbed for Second. I think he was still breathing."

"We need to *go*," Rathe repeated, wiping blood on his trousers. I watched with sickly fascination as the self-cleaning fibers of his flightsuit erased every trace. "Come on."

I let him drag me to the airlock. *If anyone comes, they'll see the blood*, I thought. *But they won't know it was me.*

"You made a call." My copilot's hands led me into the docking tube's safe confines. "We do that, soldier."

"I'm no soldier." My voice felt funny.

"We *do* that." Rathe cupped my chin, bringing our faces close. The blue in his eyes washed out in the light of station alarms, making them colorless. "We keep going." He paused as if assessing me, and a wrinkle furrowed his brow. "Look, don't tell the others. They might not understand."

. . . ● . ● ● . . .

(Hindsight imparts Rathe's words with a gravity's weight of irony, making me search for more hidden meaning like sorting through piles of discarded chaff. Just what did he know? Was that what he said then, or was it later? My mind creates its own echoes here, trapped and amplified through the living walls of my prison. I breathe new memory in like vapor even as I cling to poor Second's recordings like an outcast in a storm-tossed sea. Was it all on the surface, Rathe's meaning, or was there a deeper current? I *think* my copilot was as much of a victim of Kamen-lord plots as poor Polla Ottrava. But she—I—was never an impartial observer, and he—my dear Rathe—was never innocent.

He knew what he did when he made me love him.

In the weeks that followed, all three of my companions made me love them. Not by coercion or tricks—yet, saying that, I laugh until my throat breaks, for trickery wound its way through every conversation, lies salted every breakfast and poisoned every encounter the three of us had. Yet in those weeks, I learned to love what was true in them: their conviction, their little kindnesses, even their insipid Unity jokes that I never understood. It didn't matter that I didn't know their endgame—they were true to *me*. They loved *me*.

I'd known they were liars from the start. Aren't we all? In the weeks we had, I grew to love them. Saint Bene help me, I love them still.)

. . . ● . ● ● . . .

Having possibly committed murder, I could hardly collapse—and so I trailed behind my copilot. The red lights flashing on my retina listed everything gone wrong with the station behind us, but Second had grown silent as a grave.

I began: "About what happened—"

"I said, don't tell the others. Not now, maybe never." Rathe seemed to hesitate. "They don't always trust you."

"I wasn't *trying* to kill him."

"He wasn't dead." He patted me on the shoulder, steering me toward the bridge. "You hit him pretty good, though—what with?"

"His own gir."

"Really?" Rathe snorted. "Wow. The way they guard those things—"

"He had a comm. He was talking to someone on it, before. I didn't tell you—I think he was a spy."

Rathe's arm slipped 'round my waist, still urging me forward. "I didn't see a comm."

"I broke it."

"Good. We've got no room to look back. I blew at least three bays on the *Ascendant*. Tried to time it to minimize casualties, but Patrols were doing a sweep. When I saw the news later, about how many—" His breath hitched. "We don't look back, Polla. We can't."

"Three entire bays?" A hole that big would cripple any vessel—not to mention what'd happen to any slobs caught in the vacuum. I tried to contain my horror. He was a pilot, he *knew.* "You did it on purpose? Why?"

"Trying to hide our run. *Bedalia* was in a different hangar. We wanted them to think she was scuttled—collateral damage—not raise more questions. Those soldiers weren't supposed to *be* there, they shouldn't have died—" Rathe's navhand reached for mine. I felt my breath calm, my pulse slow as our wires brushed. Second couldn't hear me, but it could hear Sexy. I felt my nerves go blessedly flat as his navvy soothed mine. Rathe's voice softened. "Polla, we *never* look back."

We arrived on the *Escape*'s bridge to find Davad trying to manually undock us, which might've gone better if he hadn't destroyed the commander's board showing off with kamn magic the week before. As it was, he sat in the chair meant for an apprentice, his face painted in holographic displays. He'd detached the docking tube but had our hull angled too close to the station. My breath caught as the ship shook, with only a thin layer keeping *Escape* from tearing holes through both. "Still just one squadron," the princeling said tersely. "But we've been spotted—they've sent two transmissions demanding our surrender. What took you so long?"

"Nothing!" My voice felt too bright.

Rathe grimaced. "They want us undamaged. That's something."

"It appears so." To me, Davad would've sounded impatient. To Rathe, he seemed deferential.

Mureen stammered to an angry voice over our speakers about how the fighters couldn't fire without causing an incident with House Illcord. The voice demanded we cut engines, and then static crackled through as our attackers jammed the signal before Mureen could respond. A popular technique for bullies and pirates—can't hear a surrender, no need to honor it. "They keep *doing* that," she said crossly.

"Larger force will be incoming. They're burning stars." Rathe opened the central pilot's chair, settling himself in as I knelt in front of the one perpendicular. I tightened my portside sleeve and shifted my suit's reinforced ribs, so they wouldn't leave bruises later.

A red light flickered on my port as Second stirred, recognizing the familiar sensation. [Prime?] it whispered.

[I'm coming,] I told it, even though it couldn't hear.

Davad kept giving me orders while I struggled to reach the connectors in the back of my suit. "Follow Rathe's directions. He knows a lot more about combat evasion than you do. And Pilot... minimize casualties."

"I'm not some killer." Indignation that Davad doubted my skills trumped common sense—not to mention a certain defensiveness. I was a registered smuggler. Evading was my *job.* Never mind that I'd clocked a Kamen-lord minutes before... he didn't know that. "Of course I won't kill anyone."

[Error?] Second whispered in my head. Timing was so apt, I almost laughed. [Hostiles approach. Prime? Respond!]

[Coming!] I slipped into the chair. Caught a last glimpse of Rathe's empty face through his dome and then various attachments clamped on—and into me. My view tilted, and my chair's filtered dome rose. On *Dancer*, it'd be just me and Second in a chair with pneumatic belts and a lav-seat. Me with my arm slotted into *Dancer*'s board and held down with a rudimentary T-strap. Here, an apparatus hitched to my flightsuit. Drops stung my eyes. A spray of liquid doused my face, stars knew why. A catheter clamped between my good bits with unerring accuracy. An alien coldness froze my collarbone as an automatic feeding tube slipped in through my kiss. I winced with a feeling more complete than pain as my navvy meshed with the unfamiliar ship—

[Second?]

Normally, I wouldn't even be awake for this, but instead of the bliss of the dreaming, I heard my companions. Opened my mouth to call out, say I wasn't ready—and then the breathing mask clamped down, burying me alive.

Dimly, I still heard.

Mureen: "You want her to know—"

Davad: "It would change nothing."

"What about him?"

"Does that matter?"

Mureen, earnest and angry: "You cannot—"

Like a marble rolling from a flat plain, I fell. The world became a chart of stars, with superimposed outlines of geometric shapes on top like a child's clumsy sketch. Triangle shapes fired at square, each having its own equation of vectors, volume, velocity, inventory estimates, impact projections, and avoidance probabilities as feeds scrolled too fast for a human mind to process. All was colorless and flat without Second's overlay. Not dissimilar from Davad's view undocking us, in fact. I'd been trained, but flying like this was still as clunky as trying to steer an airbike with my hands in cement blocks. I was reduced to a spectator as Rathe slipped us away from Carolina2, represented as a doubled circle.

[Second? Activate overlay!] Felt like I was screaming into a void. [Second?]

Another voice echoed. [Secondary Navigator, accept input. Self-preservation directive: activate. Immediate.]

[Input unrecognized. Ship unrecognized. Error!] Second's response to Rathe's navvy. Sulky.

[Second? I know it's a new ship, but it's me!]

[Secondary Navigator must accept input.] Rathe and his navvy together, formal as Naval Command. [Immediate.]

[Error. Second's Prime not present.] Second, again. [Conditions not present for match. Error. Stranger-Prime present. Ship unrecognized.]

[Accept Stranger-Prime. Input.] Like an echo, I almost heard Rathe's real thoughts behind his request. [I don't care if you don't think she's your pilot! I can't shoot three squads and fly at the same time. Accept the link, or we'll be space dust within three minutes!]

Another two squadrons of triangles had appeared on the edge of the larger circle that was our sister station, Carolina1. Dimly, I felt my meat body jerk as Second sensed the danger, at last linking the final connections.

[Prime-Imposter accepted.]

Rathe's relief echoed mine. [Engines at twenty—] A familiar stranger's hand reached across the heavens and clasped mine as Rathe and I synced our arrays. We expanded into every part of the *Escape*, felt ourselves align with its systems, with each other, felt our engines surge, our circuits leap with the pure joy of hard thrust. Rathe and I, navvies intandem, evading enemy ships.

I barely noticed when a corner of the station we'd fled ignited, although I felt Rathe's reflexive pain, even as I discarded the agony from our sequence.

Military trained, he'd already done the same.

[Fire.] Our guns blossomed.

Rathe's approval felt like heat along my wire. [You've got weapons control?]

I affirmed with another blast. Our armory's access was ceded to me as Rathe shifted to engines and evasion, where his familiarity with the vessel would be the greater advantage. I aligned the *Escape*'s triple cannon, the ones running along our vulnerable belly that his vector had exposed. Two Unity ships took my bait, and Second and I ended them with a surge of glee that startled me. I'd shot at craft before with *Dancer*'s EMP cannon: there was an art to doing it and leaving the crew alive. I'd crippled to create salvage, even set a few distress beacons to lure a target in. Essentially piracy. One of Therion's favorite games.

Yet I'd prided myself on being kill-zero. Above Carolina Station, I blew that streak in seconds. Rathe's wrath sang in my veins—and, it must be acknowledged, my own.

They say you always remember your first kill, but those two were over in a heartbeat. Then a string of others as additional squadrons drew close. One was brave enough to tether maglocks to our hull—whether to board or sabotage, I'll never know, but then I saw it abruptly reverse course, pointed snout unbalanced and spinning until it careened into one of its fellows. The maglocks detached and hurtled after them like vengeful torpedoes. The weight of their outward velocity sang like heat in my blood.

[Kamn,] I thought, with more than a little awe. Davad and Mureen, defending us as best they could.

[What?] But Rathe was distracted, and I'd moved on.

Another squadron's diamond formation broke beneath our assault. The lower three ships were smarter, accelerating like eels, then rolling evasive maneuvers... but one flew too close to the wreck. Its fellows spun away from our wake, but the Abomination took the last, tendrils of ice breaking through its containment field like a greedy marsh-beast, rising for its prey.

[Good riddance.] I'd like to say I felt pity for the poor slobs on that fighter, but my thoughts felt as cold as space.

[You've got a knack.] Rathe's soft approval.

[I told you I could fly.]

[I didn't know you could shoot, too!]

Abruptly, Carolina2 ignited with a blue halo off *Escape*'s bow. Our home for the past few days half collapsed, its oxygen snuffing into space with dying flames. Within the wreckage, my sensor's eyes saw three escape pods jettison like sparks.

[Rescue!] I angled our mag-net sails and issued commands to Rathe to turn rudder, burn hard to save them.

[Negative.] My copilot was stone, but I caught his stray thought. [They'll land on the moon. Safer there than where we're going. Carolina1 has pa-trollers. They'll pick them up.]

I couldn't articulate why that was wrong. [No. The moon is bad.]

Rathe continued like he hadn't heard me. [Ells and Solon will make a story for Unity brass. Even that 12Fam spy of yours will make it. His pod's landed by now. Atmosphere down there's perfectly breathable—but I need you to help me pull her around the Abomination. We're heading for the jump point on the other side. It's there—] I saw where he'd marked flashing on my optic, the vectors we'd take, the quickest route to burn.

But Rathe was wrong. I knew, because I knew the *moon* was wrong. I'd barely noticed that celestial body orbiting the nearby gas giant during our firefight but now I could feel naught but menace from its misted surface—

No, I realized, as Rathe drew us closer. *From behind.*

[Polla? Stop dragging.]

[We can't!] I knew I was doing the equivalent of digging in my heels like a recalcitrant pony, but I couldn't stop. [There's a fleet hiding behind that moon.]

[Our sensors don't see anything.]

Our sensors had to be malfunctioning. I pulled up my overlays, sweeping every blast of sonar the *Escape* had in that direction of that rocky satellite, pausing for the echoes, the pings that could give the hidden away. *Nothing.* [Our sensors are wrong,] I said. [Malfunction?]

[Impossible. Move to jump.] Rathe ordered me with the clasp of a warm hand. A *firm* hand. He took the wheel from my insubstantial fingers—easi-ly—for the *Escape* was his ship.

[We won't make it!] I knew that, sure as gravity. I felt them coming like the crest of a tide. Thousands, boiling out from behind that moon. Awe mixed with horror in my soul. [Oh frag me! Stars, by all that's holy!]

Bloodships. Such a fleet had saved the refugees from the Mars Occupa-tion. Saint Bene of the Stars had flown them, the souled ones, the gods, the souls of our damned—wrought from the stuff of stars.

I'd never seen *Bedalia* fly, not really, but I knew she'd fly like they did. *By the holy avenging Star Gods,* they were so beautiful—

[There's nothing there.] I felt Rathe's doubt crystallize into resolve. [Secondary Navigator, release our engines *now*—]

But I was frozen, my terrified hooves digging desperately into a forest floor, my fingers locked on the yoke heading into an approaching cliff face.

A cold whisper wormed through my brain. *He's gone mad, letting them fly without their leash—*

[Wait!] Rathe's command ripped through, doubled by Sexy's. [Solar wake's crossing that moon. Something big's coming through that way. You were right. Reverse one-eighty, we'll go back the way we came in—] Mixed with command was his confusion, bleeding through. [How did you know?]

I was frozen. I hadn't. I was—

[Polla! Lay aft! Turn us around!] Rathe ordered.

I felt Sexy echo him, adding her own sharp command, but my mind remained an insect in resin as time stretched and tore. [It's too late. He's here.]

[Who? There's nothing yet, but if we get caught at that jump when their dreads come in—]

[Too late,] I echoed. For it was.

Materializing from ether, an immense craft emerged. Its scarred surface rippled like a plain of grass. The ship held a Unity dreadnought's form, but that shape was fluid, moving like it occupied more than one space at once. Like it swam underwater—a green shimmering—although in dreaming, such color is more conceit than perceived.

Upon the dread's surface, half hidden in grass, a lion turned his head to the sky and reared his claws. He rose and a lazy paw reached out, batting air. Playfully.

I beat my wings desperately—*wings*?

Beyond thought, I plunged *Escape* from a standstill to a full forward burn. Ghost ships parted in front of us like wheat under our prow. I felt Rathe resist me, struggling to reclaim the helm. I felt our craft rock, dangerously close to a spin. Rathe knew the ship, but I knew blockades, I knew the other ships would always turn—

· · · ● · ● ● · · ·

(Was that what I knew? Really?

Shut up, shut up, shut up—)

· · · ● · ● ● · · ·

[*Jump*, Prime-Imposter!] Second ordered. [Jump now! Lia says they've found us!]

I beat my wings. We'd made it. Rathe's marker flashed before me, but on our port lurked that monstrous perversion of a thing with a dreadnought's shape. That lovely, rotting corpse. Those beautiful bones. That stinking miracle.

The lion's plumed tail twitched.

His maned head turned toward me.

His warm eyes looked straight into my soul.

"______," he whispered. "______ ______ ______ ______?"

All of my receptors went black.

Escape was gone. I was falling.

"_______?" the lion's voice murmured in my darkness. My wings stopped beating. Almost a relief.

[Jump!] A plea. A scream from someplace else, to someone else, for I was no longer there.

"_____," the lion said gently. "____ ______?"

He batted at me with an indrawn paw. Soft as petals.

Dimly, I felt Second take control, fail-safes for our ship's preservation kicking in—and then the lion vanished. Light returned as our universe dissolved into the blessed trinary, pixelating into that code whose blocks form dreaming.

Mid-space felt clean, safe as houses. Salt on my lips and tears like the sea, and no lions—no spacedamned *lions* anywhere at all.

Sensation returned by degrees until I lay on my back, staring up at a cerulean sky. A face peered down: round, snub-nosed, with skin tanned the color of chestnut, lighter around the eyes. Sun-streaked brown hair matched those eyes, amber and gold and deep. A bow-shaped mouth leaned into mine, close enough to kiss.

A little too close. I rolled away, propping myself up by my elbows. The deck of Rathe's sailing ship rocked. Sun beat down, warming my skin. What had come before seemed like a bad dream, dissolved by clean yellow light.

"Hi," the woman breathed. Her voice held a familiar timbre, with the echo of a deeper one—her partner's. Her lips looked like peaches. They split when she smiled, revealing perfectly even teeth. She wore a castaway's flightsuit with hacked-off sleeves and legs, its zipper low enough to reveal an enviable rack.

I knew her immediately.

"Sexy." I scrambled to my feet. "Thanks for the save... thanks for everything out there."

Her grin grew dimples. "Of course, Polla Ottrava! I've heard so much about you!"

"You too." I lied. But the identity of her avatar jelled. The holo I'd found under Rathe's mattress, clad in shortos and a smile. The ex-wife, the mother of Rathe's son. I knew her voice. She'd hollered at Second to jump out of a war zone while I'd been stuck hallucinating about lions and grass.

"Sorry," I mumbled. "Had a glitch."

"We expected trouble with you. All things considered, I think it went quite well until you malfunctioned."

In dreaming it wasn't rude, so I took the time to stare. What our navvies look like in the dreaming depends on us. Therion once suggested I seek therapy for having one that appeared to be naught but my own reflection, saddled with the generic name straight from the decanting tube. If Rathe got his navvy around the time of his marriage, that'd explain this buxom vision. Fresh out of school, Second was a means to an end for me: my ticket to fame and fortune. Fresh out of Smuggler's Academy, I'd thought it was funny to keep the default while the rest of my class looked ridiculous with feelie models and fleshdancers, saints and dead relatives—and, even more commonly, their own anatomical bits.

Fresh out of school, Rathe had thought of the woman he'd married.

Of course he had. She was lovely.

"Polla?" Rathe's navvy crossed her perfectly rounded calves before her perfectly rounded thighs. "Why is your poor Second beside itself?"

"Is Rathe here?" A realistic-seeming wave washed over the bow and left me spitting very realistic-seeming water. It tasted of salt.

"He is flying our ship." Her soft brown eyes measured me. "Stabilizing our course into deepspace. Entry was quite sloppy. A solar wind nearly wiped us off course. I fear for the habitats we left behind." She paused. "A pity. Carolina1 and Carolina2 were both quite civilized for static installations. We had several pleasant chats."

"Wasn't a wind." Not even Aemercy-trained squadrons could fly formation so perfectly, I thought. "Didn't you see the ships?"

"What ships?" Sexy frowned. "Lia worried about ships, too, but you shot them all." Rathe's navvy beamed at me. "You did well."

"Rathe's flying without you?" At best, another slip toward deepriver. Worst, we were already dead, and heaven, as Da used to say, was just another flight.

"Lia can supervise. My pilot is clever for one of your kind. I find him capable of making unsupervised jumps." Steel in Sexy's voice. "You and I needed to talk."

"You and Rathe can talk to Lia from hyperspace?" The idea of the bloodship being phased in while we jumped was terrifying. Two objects cannot occupy the same grid. If Lia tried to jump through us, we'd all be lost.

Sexy's hand waved, dismissive. "I have been speaking to Lia for the past year. So have Rathe and your Second, although your navvy refused to name itself before you woke. We thought it was a ghost. Second made about as much sense as one."

The sun overhead felt hotter than it should have. I hoped that wasn't the engines, slowly roasting us alive. "I want to speak to Rathe."

"A moment. Your navvy is so lonely it will speak to anyone." No mistaking her scorn. "But not you." Her head tilted. "Why?"

"I don't know."

"We don't know either," Sexy said. "I am also not sure if your interest in my partner is fueled by Second's need for companionship or your own desperation."

"Or *his*," I pointed out, trying not to be nettled. "Not exactly one-sided, the thing between us."

And this wasn't normal. What pilots did wasn't a navvy's business. The two of us (or four if you believe Fringer Revelations) were already linked. Second and Sexy should be meshed right now, mapping our jumps, and instead Rathe was doing it alone while Sexy interrogated me like I wanted to take her pilot to the spring harvest dance.

"My pilot has *needs*," Sexy continued. "I would have no objection to alignment if Second functioned normally, but it does not. There is something wrong here, Polla."

"Head injury," I muttered. "Coma."

"Perhaps." Sexy leaned forward. My back bumped against the ship's hull. She had me trapped. "Call your navvy."

It was not a request. I nodded. "Second? Hey!" *Here navvy*, I thought. *Fetch! Heel! Get those sheep out of the winter pasture—*

"Go on," Sexy said. "Second hears you."

I felt Second somewhere across the waters. Swimming. I felt its head turn like my own. [Imposter.] The thought was ancient, so foreign I couldn't believe it. Then: [What have you done with Prime?] A cry torn from its heart.

Sexy's eyes narrowed. "There is something wrong with you, Pilot Ottrava."

"Nothing I can help."

"My partner does not see you." Rathe's navvy leaned forward and took my freehand. In her tawny grasp, my skin looked sun-brown, fingernails gold-dipped from shore leave just like my toes. "But Second does."

My topknot whipped forward in a sudden gust of wind, and I pushed it away from my face. "I don't understand."

I heard splashing from the water near the ship's bow.

"Rathe is literal." Sexy gestured at her own curves. "See my shape? My pilot envisions what his meat saw. Why the discrepancy with you?"

"I know you look like his ex-wife."

"And you know of her. Which displays interest. My pilot possesses interest in what his dreaming eyes saw, not as you present here."

Navvies sure get it confused, I thought. *This is the dreaming, you silly string.* But I stared at my knees, exposed in my favorite tattered coverall. The tail of my topknot was a reassuring weight atop my head. "I don't know."

"I know." Sexy's head tilted. "But it is still wrong."

Chapter 24 ✳ Jumped

After my arrest, Wade shared his even crazier theory about how Arkan and Mureen had gotten off the *Ascendant*: the one where dead Ledas Starfire had flown herself—

· · • · • • · • • · ·

IT WASN'T MY EYES that saw the sun-browned arm behind me snake over the edge of the bow; saw it joined by another laced with circuitry. Wasn't my dreaming eyes that saw my bedraggled topknot emerge above a pair of angry dark eyes, or my face's own reflection knit in an angry scowl.

Wasn't my lungs that sighed relief either. But I still exhaled. Heard it too, just like I heard Second's solid feet clump down on the wooden deck.

"Show me," Second snapped. The Feldelroyan drawl made the words come out more like *sheowmeh*. "Prime?"

I turned.

"No! No!" Our face twisted with new disgust. Its gold-dipped toes took two steps backwards. "You're the *other* one."

"Second!" I grabbed hold of its arms. Felt like I was hugging myself—doubled as our two brains registered both illusions across one set of neurons. "You stupid scrap wire! You're twisted!"

My navvy smelled like sea and salt. Its grief made my eyes tear. "I want the real Prime."

"I am the real one, you silly string!"

"No." It shook its head, hard enough that its wet topknot whacked me in the face.

I grabbed tighter. "I'm *real*," I repeated.

"No." But its panicked eyes met mine, and Second sounded less certain.

The dreaming we were in sank deeper. The ship, Sexy, and the sun overhead faded as we fell levels, until our universe held only two. "You're not Polla Ottrava," my own visage muttered.

"Am too."

My own face twisted. "No!"

I grabbed Second's navhand. I grabbed my *own* hand, which seemed too pale, or too dark, or too spotted, or too smooth. The paths merging our nervous systems flared. We spun into our pocket universe, the one where we'd been born seven—no, *eight*—years ago on an operating table when a Guild surgeon set its lines into my brain.

[Now go up,] I whispered. [Ascend two levels.]

Up two levels and space illuminated enough for me to see my own face reflected back in Second's wide and frightened eyes.

[You are *not*—] it began.

[Shhh.] Our hands were the only warmth in existence. [I am too, silly string! Up one more.]

The next level of space was lit by unfamiliar stars. I felt Second tamp our adrenals before my panic could swamp us both.

[Lost!] I thought with despair.

[No. Prime-Imposter just can't read a map.] Smugness. My navvy's beloved arrogance. [Rotate axis.]

I did with an insubstantial hand and stars aligned. Green Feldelroy gleamed like a beacon on our port—our orientation node. Solar waves buffeted our sails and we drifted. Our legs kicked. Ahead lay the outline of a body. A man, floating like a swimmer at sea. Currents brought us closer, and our hands reached out as Rathe's fingers closed on ours. Sexy linked in with an audible sigh, slipping into place like a key in a lock. We became a four-pointed star.

Rathe's fingers twitched in mine. Sexy's twitched holding Second's—

On a battered corvette in the middle of hyperspace, I felt the craft holding our shells straighten. I saw its immediate future crystallize, deviations decreasing to zero. Jumps in the hyperlane extended like a line of pearls. Beneath the waves propelling us forward lay a swirl of gray, a stream of numbers. One of us babbled calculations. Stars aligned like a billion blades of grass on a plane, and somewhere close, I felt warm breath upon my cheek, and a triumphant roar—

[The lion!] I panicked.

[What?] Rathe's chuckle sounded amused. It was his human breath that had warmed my face. His warm hand was in mine, wrought of calloused skin and wire. [What took you so long?] His thought was unconcerned, even a little dreamy. His peace washed over Second and me, suffusing the recent past with the blurred import of a half-remembered dream.

[Sexy wanted to check my references.] Still flustered, I tried to match his careless tone.

[Been a long time since I've flown with a stranger. She gets possessive.]

[My navvy wanted a word, too.]

[Second?] Phantom lips brushed my brow, the feeling doubled. [There you are!] Rathe sounded unconcerned. Whatever I'd just seen didn't seem to have touched him at all.

[Prime-Imposter and Copilot link established,] Second reported. We all sank together, the physiology of our bond assigning us roles flying the ship through the currents of improbability. I felt a firm hand cup my jaw, and the memory of Rathe's kiss. Coordinates in space are hypothetically not infinite, but they are as close as humankind comes. I tacked the stars, routing the jumps through to the end coordinates he'd assigned. Mindless grunt work, but I didn't mind.

[Prime?] For an instant Second and I wavered, reaching for ghosts. A war fleet was passing through our waypoint, intangible, strangely-shaped ships bristling with cannons—*alien*—seeking targets, searching for prey—

I felt us both flinch.

[Control!] Sexy admonished. [Navigator! Control your pilot.]

[You mean the other way 'round?] It was I who caught Sexy, joining my hands with Rathe's navvy. [Those were just ghosts, you silly wires. Nothing real.]

[Query: what are ghosts?] But my navvy joined my hands to Rathe's, and then Second took the wheel, steering us all through mid-space and into the deep black.

Strangely, I smelled rain. Tasted a song on my lips. Synesthesia was supposed to be common with us, but I'd never encountered it before. I saw blades of grass like the ones from the Arkan estancia, perfectly even and moving intandem. I saw them bend beneath a strong wind. Off in the distance, I saw a lion turn its head—

[Lions again?] Rathe's thought, amused. [Polla, your imaging's all over the place.]

[Did you see them?]

[We got them all.]

[There were thousands!]

An amused rumble from Rathe. [Like I said, your imaging's all over the place.]

[Can you do better?]

[Oh, yes.] The world he'd made before rematerialized: that sailing ship and the endless ocean. Somewhere in the heavens, our navvies steered the corvette. Somewhere in the human realm, our bodies drooled on chairs. Somewhere inside of us, *Bedalia* listed, calm as a passenger on unfamiliar waters. Impossibly, I felt her too: a cold dampness, the scent of salt and sorrow. I recalled being horrified to hear she could phase with us. Now I couldn't remember why.

"Yo." Lazily, Rathe turned and looked at me. My want for him washed in like the tide.

"So stinking literal, Rathe Sai." I traced his jaw. Smooth in this dreaming, as that was my preference. "Imagining a ship for a ship. Sexy said you were literal."

My copilot gave me a mischievous grin. "Glad you two had the chance to catch up."

"Me too. Really didn't see the bloodships? Or the fleet from the moon?"

"Hardly a fleet." He chuckled. "A few bolts hit the station, but the escape pods launched first. Our friends got out."

The reminder brought me back. "I was kill-zero. Before that."

A sun flare obscured his expression. "I'm sorry."

"Davad told me not to kill anyone."

"Davad didn't have a millisecond to make the call." Rathe's hand traced my ribs, thinly covered by the sheet I'd summoned for mystery. His brows drew together. "By the way, I've seen Davad make the same call more times than I can count."

Their Aemercy war had been both opportunity and inconvenience for my entire professional life, but aside from the battle for NewLaramie and its Neskey moon, I knew very little. "You flew with him, Davad said?"

"*For* him. The Kamen could sense our attackers better than sensors. So Fleet brass stationed one on every carrier. At first they just shielded us in action. Later, they started taking command... You worried he won't get it? Davad's a soldier too." Rathe's hand moved up to my shoulder and across my collarbone. "The Unity wanted us dead back there, Polla. You had no choice."

"You really didn't see the ships come from the moon?"

"Sometimes there's static close to jump points. Bleed-through. Places where a lot of people die can be tricky."

"I know about ghosts." Some claimed what was left of Centauri was a haunted boneyard. 'Course, any pilot fool enough to fly there got brain fever from the rads. "Hope you didn't just doom us, plotting midpoints solo." But I wasn't upset. Not here, not with his hand lazily circling my breast, tracing feather touches across my sun-warmed skin. A fleet of bloodships felt like a glitch in the dreaming, as unimportant as the Kamen-lord I'd recently brained.

Virmarr didn't matter. Those ships didn't matter. The lion was just another nightmare.

This was everything I needed. Everything real.

"Trust me." My copilot chuckled. "We're fine. Now, where were we..?"

"Mmmm." My head fell back and my legs opened as I showed Rathe precisely where he'd been.

"Ah." The boat rocked, and my copilot rolled on top. "Now I recall."

My hands slid down his bare skin, then settled on his hips. His length pressed between my legs, and I quivered. Both of us took a breath. Our eyes met and then he gave me a gentle smile. "I'm so glad you're here with me, Polla."

"I—" I began, but Rathe took that moment to enter me, and then for a time I didn't have any words as such, just noises that didn't translate into anything more sentient than need and release. Our union was perfect in dreaming like sex rarely is raw. A long, low burn across a planetary sky, a hunger slaked and sated. We finished with him sitting up against the ship's curved sides and me locked atop his lap like a key, one leg hooked around his neck, and both of us rocking forward and back sweet as summer morning as our points slowly ebbed.

Rathe murmured endearments into my hair. The soft cloud fell down my back. His hands tangled there, while one of mine tangled between our thighs. I squeezed him inside of me, eking out a last gasp of pleasure for us both. Rathe's attention had moved on to my breasts. He chuckled. "You know, these are a lot more—"

"Spectacular here?" I sighed and then shifted off his hips, curling up in the crook he made for me with his arm. "Don't judge my poor rack in realtime. After a year in a coma, it's not a fair assessment."

"Was going to go with bigger. Didn't have to make them bigger. Not for me." He caressed one. "You're spectacular in both worlds, Polla. And I like freckles."

"Freckles?" I glanced down at my peaks, which were back to their normal mountainous shape and tawny shade, instead of the bleached nubs they'd become. "Hey! Speaking of making things *bigger*—"

He snorted. "I'm speaking of freckles." Rathe kissed my portside breast as I let my head loll back. "Faint ones across the tops, here. On your arms and shoulders. And here..." He shifted his body, and his mouth dropped down to show me where the new *here* was, licking a trace along the swell of my thigh. "Saw *this* one in the shower. Was going to do this to it—"

He lapped my tender flesh while his freehand slid between my legs, precise as a surgeon. Desire kindled again.

"You can," I agreed, a little faintly, because his lips now breathed heat along my core. I trembled as a slick finger followed their path. "But—" I stopped talking. Looking down at Rathe's golden head bobbing between my thighs, I saw 'em too. Freckles scattered like stars across the dark milk of my legs and dappled my smooth arms. Spots adorned the top of my breasts, even. Just like he'd said.

His head moved up. "What?" More fingers joined the first. I watched his knowing look as my breath hissed, his smug grin widening his wet and willing mouth—

"Don't care." My fingers tangled in his hair as I pushed him back on task.

• • • ● ●•● ● ● • •

"Second flew perfectly with you," he said drowsily, later. "The way the two of you took to those guns—"

"Da taught me the basics." The lives we'd ended seemed elusive as that ghost fleet and the strangeness with Virmarr was remote as a dead woman's memories.

He chuckled. "Second did good. I've flown with Academy-trained gunners with less accuracy than you. Your navvy's a natural. He knew exactly how to outmaneuver—"

"It," I corrected. "It's a machine."

"Is that what they teach you in smuggler school?" Rathe nuzzled my neck. "They're not machines. They're symbiotes."

No point in debating Unity heresies with my Unity lover. "Was Sexy a pilot too?" I asked to change the subject. "The real one?"

"My wife?" My head had settled back in Rathe's lap. The wind ruffled our hair, blowing strands of mine across my vision. "Yeah, but Catrine got out early. Wanted more kids, so she married a surgical engineer and his cache. They live on NewBowie. What about you—any exes running around named

'Second'?"

"Not a one. Do you think the Kamen made it out?"

Rathe nodded. "Trust me, they can steer lifeboats in their sleep. And the moon's got breathable air. That Foxconn aristo of yours is perfectly safe, even if you did knock him out. The pods have programming to send out distress beacons."

His assurance had the unfortunate effect of reminding me that I'd brained the guy with his own gir and Rathe had barely blinked. I glanced up at him again and he grinned down at me reassuringly. I frowned because the rest of it—the reason *why* I'd brained the man in the first place—that crackle from the comm—

He wants to speak to you, Virmarr had said.

I was suddenly, horribly afraid, so my mind reached for humor. "Didn't *really* use a Californian crankshaft, you know."

"Good." Rathe chuckled back. "That was an intimidating thought."

"I'm also not the one who took on two at a time—or was it more?"

"Honestly?" His blue eyes searched my face. "Yurys and Derien are good people, but I fell asleep after five minutes in their bed. Maybe it was ten, the second night. Third night, we drank too much—"

"That always happen to you in realtime?" I meant that as a joke, but I felt his irritation as I missed the target.

"No." His easy grin faded.

"So they were a one-off?"

"Yeah. You and Virmarr?"

"I think braining him ended our arrangement. You sure seemed popular."

Rathe's grin crept back as he tickled my ribs. "Shame we didn't have longer. The two of us could've cut a swathe. Kamen are..." His voice trailed off, but we were linked close enough that I caught some of his thoughts. "Not pilots, but they understand us more than most."

"Would we cut that swathe together or separately?"

"Lady's choice." Rathe pulled me up from his lap, tracing my profile with the tip of his thumb. "I'm still learning what you like, Polla."

I matched his tone. "I'm still showing you, Lieutenant Sai."

But I'd jumped wrong, I could hear it in his voice. "I deserted. Don't get to keep the rank."

"Just Rathe, then? Yurys said you'd talked me up."

"Yes." He kissed my nose. "You were so mysterious in that tank. Wrapped like a sleeping angel. Mureen told me some of your stories. Made me feel like I knew you. You got amox for NewLaramie fighters through an Aemercy blockade? Saved a pair of orphans from the gypsum mine? Smuggler with a regular heart of gold."

I frowned. Although both of those events had happened, we'd been working for currency. Therion and I'd only rescued the orphans because Brahz wanted 'em for a job. "I don't remember talking to Mureen about that. She talked to my ma, I bet. That's who told her those stories."

Ma loved the orphan one. The fact that the orphans had been in their forties, and New Liberty had wanted 'em for their safecracking abilities, was lost on her. Or maybe I hadn't gone into detail about that part when I'd told it. For after the safecrackers from JadiidKalamazoo, there'd been the real innocents, those kids on NewBern who'd truly needed saving—and them I'd failed.

"You woke up a few times on Earth, I heard. Every time you lost consciousness again, Davad was gutted." He kissed my forehead. "Don't worry, I don't get jealous."

I snorted. "Not if he were the last cock in the galaxy. The man hates me."

"No." He shook his head. "You know you almost died? Maybe it was the leg—I never could get the details out of Mureen. She's immune to my charms." His hand slid lazily across my body as if to remind me that I was not.

"Leg?" I'd propped my head up on my elbow. Now I straightened both legs and wiggled my toes. "My leg almost killed me?"

He seemed to hesitate. "You... Do you know about the leg?"

"Sure, Arkan Genghis said it was a big expense getting my own stem line to regrow it, and I should be grateful..." My voice faltered because Rathe was frowning.

"Not your own cells. What would be the point of using your cells?"

"I'd have a leg?" *Which one?* I thought. They looked the same. Then again, none of this was real.

He traced my nearest knee. "You know what Davad did? Who his sister was, and what—"

"Yeah. Davad's twin sister was Ledas Starfire, and he killed her in *Bedalia.* I worked most of that out myself." I snorted. "Hell, Davad thought you'd told me."

Rathe grimaced. "I wanted to. You understand why I didn't?"

"After seeing what the krov did at Carolina and knowing *Bedalia*'s a part of that..." I shivered. "If I'd known what she was, I wouldn't've taken the job."

I'm not sure I recalled having no choice.

"And now?" His hand pushed my hair back.

I met his gaze squarely. "Now I'm in. You're right. Nate has to be stopped."

"Nothing was *Bedalia*'s fault."

Oh yeah? I thought. *What about the time she tossed me into Ledas Starfire's childhood memory?* I recalled Lia's contempt. The bloodship had sported red hair when she'd told me to drown in the dreaming, just like Davad's, or like her dead master's—

"Hey, do I really look like her?"

Rathe had been staring at my legs. He glanced up. "Do you look like who?"

"Ledas *Starfire.*" I snorted. "That's the point? I look enough like Ledas Starfire to put *Bedalia* at ease?"

He frowned. "When you said you knew about the leg, I thought you *knew* about the leg."

"It's a leg!" My voice rose. The mainsail suddenly rippled above us. "It got crushed! They grew me a new one!"

"No." Rathe sat up. "I mean, yes. Your leg was crushed in the accident, but—damnit! I thought you knew."

"I thought I did too." Somewhere in the distance, thunder growled. "What's the rest of it? *Tell* me."

"The leg is *hers*." He patted my portside one gingerly, like to comfort us both. "They made you a chimera. The way it was explained to me is that *Bedalia*'s hard-coded to Ledas Starfire's genetics. Hell, maybe a part of Lia was made *from* Ledas. Nobody really knows how the krov make bloodships in the first place. But their pilots go a lot deeper than we do."

"What do you mean their pilots go a lot deeper? Bloodships don't have pilots. Isn't that the point?"

"No one knows." The wind had picked up, whipping hair in my lover's eyes. "But they've dissected a few—Guild scientists have. Wade told me they found human genetics in some, but that's not all, uh—"

"I believe in aliens. Don't have to sidestep, Rathe. Bloodships are alien tech, I know."

"Right. I just—you're from a religious planet, and I didn't want to offend you by suggesting your gods aren't—"

"We're not stupid! We know what our gods are." I'd be offended soon. "So what if I have her leg?" I remembered Davad's arrogant assurance the ship would fly for me. "Do they think Starfire's leg will give me her magic powers? Help me kill Illcord Natoth?" I joked, but then I recalled the way that Ells and Virmarr both tested me for kamn. How everyone kept whispering behind my back, and those Kamen-lords had even taken *bets*. Who cared about bedding some Fringer pilot? But Ledas Starfire?

Everyone kept bringing her up.

I looked up and saw the sky was darkening. Thunder rumbled again, closer.

Rathe sounded troubled. "The leg's for *Bedalia*. Enough of her old pilot to take commands." His head turned toward the incoming storm. "Killing Natoth will stop his fleet, but that's my job, not yours. When Nate dies, so will the krov, Davad says."

It struck me again how Davad was the krov expert we never questioned. *Command her*, he'd told me. *She will fly for you.* "Speaking of bloodships... I did see a fleet of 'em. Before we jumped." I looked up at Rathe and then down at my own dimpled thighs. "You really didn't?"

"No." He frowned. "Of course, we can't see bloodships. Sensors don't register. Kamen can't feel them. Not until they're in visual range, carving us to pieces."

"You fought 'em before?"

"Not exactly—I've heard." He looked troubled. "You really saw them?"

"An entire fleet of *Bedalias*. Sexy didn't believe me."

"I know," he said.

And the lion, I thought. But I couldn't say that out loud.

Resemblance. Foxconn Virmarr had said I looked like Ledas. Resembled. Or *reassembled*? What if Starfire's cells were taking over mine like an old-fashioned cancer? Could cells do that? Could genes *make* cells do that? As tweeners in biologics class, we'd learned about genes. Dominant. Recessive. Ledas Starfire was dominant enough to take over the galaxy. What if her genes were dominant enough to take over me?

I felt like I was struggling to breathe, suddenly struck with horror. What if that was the Kamen plan all along? Bring Ledas back by turning me into her?

"Are you okay, Polla? You look pale."

"But am I *freckled*?"

Hyperspace shifted sideways.

"Easy." Rathe caught me in his arms. "Whoa. Don't forget what we're doing here—"

"Screwing?" I stood up on his ship's rocking bow, wrapping myself in clothes that I'd summoned. When I looked down I found myself in a red ruffled monstrosity. One much like the one Arkan Davad had supplied for me on Earff.

Another sick piece of the puzzle clicked. The red was the same shade Davad often wore himself. The same color as that Arkan symbol embossed above nearly every door in that cowcrap palace. Was I reading too much into things, or had Davad actually dressed me like—like—

Like his dead sister?

You have her genes in your leg! You're not reading enough into it!

Prime-Imposter, Second had called me. Oh, my poor navvy. Second had known all along—

"The hell with this!" I ripped the garment off and watched it disintegrate strand by strand, its red threads floating away in the wind like a blood trail. Space rippled, and with a force of will I was back aboard my *Dancer* with her solid roof above my head. From our starboard view, I could see we were parked in Ma's green field, just where I'd left her. And when I looked down, I was wearing my favorite coverall and my own muddy sandals. And I had my own damned legs: muscular, thick thighed, tanned brown in midsummer—

I thought it'd look different, Rathe had said about my leg.

I blinked. Both legs were long. Skinny. Freckled.

[Prime? Alert! Incoming proximity. Hyperspace instability. Recalculating—]

We are well-trained, of course, not to throw tantrums in hyperspace. Trained to depend on our navvies when organics get messy. Some say that's what deepriver is: the organics getting too messy and the machine taking over for good.

I'd never felt so close to the river. A part of me welcomed the ice now seeping through my veins. Sometimes you have to be cold. Like the way I'd been when I'd shot those Unity fighters. Or when I'd brained Foxconn Virmarr. Or that day on NewBern in that warehouse, when I'd turned my face away from those dying kids. I kept saying that Therion gave me no choice, but I *knew* him. Of course I'd had a choice. He was no killer, and I—

"Polla!" Rathe materialized on *Dancer*, dressed in a uniform, Unity white and gold flightsuit, all pressed and cabled. Sexy came an eyeblink after. Her hand meshed into his pilot's arm, and I saw her lips move as she counted, eyes closed, keeping our coordinates in place. "Polla!" he repeated, struggling to be heard over the screams of our engines, the whips of sea-wind that blew hair in my face and tears from my eyes. He pointed. "Your navvy—"

I turned.

Second was naked as innocence. The knobs of its spine curved, knees drawn to our chest, rocking back and forth on the floor. *No no no no no*—its grief sent me reeling like a physical blow. And the wind blew harder, bringing a storm. I smelled sea air and salt. I felt *Dancer's* engines strain, churning in seawater—

"Stop," I whispered. "Stop! We're not at sea. *Space.* We should be in space."

"It's not me." His eyes were white-rimmed.

My gaze dropped back to my legs, spattered with rain. They looked freckled and far too thin. Reality warped, and *Dancer* rocked upon the water. I stepped closer to Second, felt ourselves merge until I was it, rocking back and forth on that deck, too.

"You're mixing me up," I whispered. "My dreaming is being in *Dancer*. In space. No ocean."

"This isn't not me." Dimly, I felt the press of him on my skin. "Hells—do you know what this is?"

I tasted salt as an emotion too vast for one ocean swept over me. *Failure. After everything—*

"No," I said. A lie.

I heard the bell. Our ship swayed. The current took us. I heard the sound of oars, the creak of weight and splash of water, gentle and rhythmic as sex. Soft. Soothing.

All in your head, I addressed myself like a first-year pilot apprentice. *Not real. Mind's just making sense of the infinite. Nothing real—*

"Deepriver current." My lover's voice.

I opened my eyes to find myself rocking in his arms, inhaling his scent: musk and lemons and something burnt.

"Yours?" I whispered. "It's too soon."

"No." He kissed me, brows drawn together with worry. "You're too damn young."

I suddenly felt *Dancer* tilt her nose like we were plunging into a planet. But *Dancer* wasn't here—I'd left her on Feldelroy.

I heard the bell toll and knew he was right. "Let go," I told Rathe. "Or you'll drown, too."

"Must be the leg." Far from letting go, Rathe's grip on me tightened. "Davad said Ledas controlled a fleet of thousands. No telling what flying them did to her. Maybe the leg is close to deepriver, so the rest of you goes too."

I wanted to deny it. "But she wasn't a real pilot."

He shook his head. "She was. Her and Illcord Natoth both."

"No. They weren't Guild. They never trained. Bloodships fly themselves! It doesn't count!"

Yet I recalled Davad and his scarred arm; I remembered Mureen's lack of surprise. *They'd try anything,* she'd said. Anything to kill the Aemercy or stop the war—

"It counted," Rathe said.

"They used her actual leg?" The old man had said something about stem cells. At least that sounded hygienic.

"I'm not sure. There was blood on her deckplates. When we stole *Bedalia,* the blood was still there... I think they used it."

Something abruptly made sense. "You're not just here out of loyalty to Davad. You're here for the Guild."

Rathe nodded. "They wouldn't sanction it, but I swore the oath, same as you."

I was suddenly too frightened to ask more.

• • • ● • ● • • ••

(In the face of Centauri, or those frozen monsters at Carolina, do lies matter? Does it matter how they used me? I was useless before them, a broken pilot collapsing under the weight of her own mistakes.

My companions were desperate characters who needed a broken pilot to help them stop a cosmic atrocity. My companions were heroes out of a golden age. Heroes who needed me—

Don't start—*don't*—)

• • • ● • ● • • ••

Ma always said I lacked a sympathetic nature, but in that moment, I had a sudden flash of empathy for the original inhabitants of the first Carolina Station. I imagined a green wave of mist roiling toward them, their horror at the split walls and broken gravity; their limbs paddling frantically in the hiss of escaping air as vacuum froze their throats and took their souls.

Suddenly, I could almost hear the way their pleas changed timbre as their minds broke, how their skin split and lungs rent—how vacuum had frozen every nerve—

They'd been *alive* when the krov took them. They were alive still. At least Centauri had been stinking *clean*—

• • • ● • ● • • ••

(We are all farther down the road to perdition than we think.

See how easy it is to excuse the past, replace it with some fresh atrocity?

Maybe it's never one thing that breaks us. Maybe always the avalanche—or worse—the slow drip of days, the careless accumulation of minor cruelties, and then one day, the mirror and the monster, staring back—)

• • • ● • ● • ● • •

"Polla? You're shaking."

I barely felt my own body. I felt cold as space. The dreaming had darkened until Rathe was a mere shadow on my port.

My voice echoed, oddly-pitched and clipped. "You're right, Rathe. We have to kill Nate. For the Guild."

I heard Second echo me, like both of us were making vows.

I felt my copilot press closer. I heard his low chuckle. "My job is killing him. Yours is convincing *Bedalia* to fly."

I suppressed a shudder. Did he know I'd tried? *Bloodship pilots go deeper into their ships than we do,* Rathe had claimed. *Her bones are inside of me,* Lia had said. Bloodships were alien tech just like navvies, and Second recorded *my* memories, so perhaps, I told myself, it was no reach that *Bedalia* possessed pieces of Ledas Starfire's life. Perhaps it was normal. Perfectly fine.

When I flew with her again, what horrors would I see?

"How will you kill him?" It seemed important. "Nate. How will you kill Nate?"

My copilot's voice was wry. "Sorry, that's still need-to-know."

So are her memories, I thought. My burden to bear.

I was aware of *Escape* flying steady, surfacing up from the black and heading slowly toward mid-space. Sexy was a good navvy. She'd righted us, taken Second in her arms just like had Rathe taken me. Before us, she and Second were nearly one shadow: one chanting coordinates while the other plotted us safe through the stars.

"For the Guild. Can't be forsworn..." Hadn't realized I believed the words before. I forced a laugh. "Hey, won't the Guild kill me for having a Kamen-lord's leg?"

A Kamen-lord's leg explained all that testing for kamn. *When this is done, I'll have the leg removed,* I told myself. *Get something nice in a prosthetic. Maybe with a few compartments for special smuggling jobs?*

Rathe chuckled. "Once this is over, get it cut off."

"I was just thinking that. So I'm a chimera." Mythical creations according to the Grass Priests, created in darkness, from a time when humankind wanted monsters more than they needed souls. "I'm a chimera of Ledas Starfire." That sounded ridiculous. "Davad and Mureen should've *asked.*"

Inexplicably, I wasn't angry. Not then.

• • • ● • ● • • • •

(Not yet.)

• • • ●•●•● •• •

"Mureen did." Rathe planted a kiss on my nose. "That android of Davad's wouldn't have performed the operation without your consent. Not possible. Asimov's second law."

"Teapot did Guild surgery? Thing said I had fugues. Do you think I forgot I agreed?"

His tone sharpened. "Pilot's fugues? Polla, that's a bad sign."

"From the man with fifty thousand jumps?" *Dancer's* deck was reassuringly solid again, making our foray into deepriver seem a bad dream. "Look, we'll drop the Kamen-lords off on Krovworld, and then you and me will take the bloodship."

"Can you fly her?" He brushed his forehead against mine gently. The dark had lightened enough to show me the gleam of his eyes, his yellow hair. "If it's too much—"

"Oh, I can fly anything." I pulled him into a real kiss. *Command her*, Davad had said. Why had I feared it before? "She'll fly for me because she must."

"Because of the leg. But be good to her?"

That made me laugh. "'Course! I'll bring her 'round for visits. What'd you say your plan was? Get back with the wife, geld, settle down with grandkids?"

He snorted. "Never said I'd go back to Catrine. Her new spouses are Reformed Smiths. Five's their limit."

"Oh. Maybe you need a new... Maybe you need to shop around for a new partner." I felt my face warm. "Not proposing, by the way."

"Didn't think it." My copilot's gold-flecked eyes were staring at me with a look I hadn't seen in years, for Therion and I had grown apart permanently, like glaciers receding. That day on NewBern was merely our final subsidence.

"I'm too young to settle down," I warned him.

I felt his amusement as much as I heard it. "I know."

"Also too young to get gelded."

"You may not have a choice. Sexy and I don't." He kissed the tip of my nose, voice serious and teasing all at once. "I'm glad we get to spend our last jumps with you."

My golden pilot. In our shared dreaming, everything seemed hyperreal. A lock of golden hair fell across his brow. Rathe's hair, skin, every part of him was perfect. I was the same—I felt it. These idealized versions of ourselves were drawn from us both.

So easy in dreaming. When I fell for Therion, I'd been the insecure greenie, fresh from Smuggler's Academy. When Therion fell for me, he'd been the calculating businessman working the angles, unexpectedly charmed by the virginal kid (not technically virginal or a kid) who'd shown him how to love again, and then we—we'd changed.

Or maybe we'd never been those things at all.

"Polla?" Rathe's orchid eyes creased. "I mean it. If the job's too much—"

I snorted, replying with a gesture that suggested we explore the limits of *too much*, thoroughly and vigorously, as soon as possible. For in this place I was the wisecracking smuggler. And Rathe was noble, generous, and kind.

In that instant, I would have broken stars to wipe the emptiness I saw in his eyes.

· · • • • · • • • ·

(Sometimes the galaxy turns on such folly.

Do *you* think it should?)

· · • • • · • • • ·

"I've got you," I whispered. "Whatever it is, I've got you. And you have me. The rest doesn't matter."

Rathe nodded. "Not now it doesn't." He kissed me again, this time slow and hard and not comforting, with a hunger that once more ignited the exquisite burn that lives beneath our pilots' skins. Locked in dreaming, our breaths sharpened and our navarms locked as the clothes we'd assembled dissolved like water—

· · • • • · • • • ·

(I've thought of our first flight together a hundred times since coming to darkness. I've remembered Rathe's promises a thousand times in this place of no light. Alone in my prison, I cling to memories of our happy times as terror shakes my soul and my mind breaks. As other thoughts fade, I hope to recall Rathe 'til the end. His touch, his cock, and his kiss.

Yet that phrase of his stands out.

Not *now*, it *doesn't*. "Not now" can mean not anymore. The past doesn't matter. But that's not the only interpretation. Not *now*, it *doesn't*. Right now, everything's fine. But what happens tomorrow?

Pilots... I did say that things get tricky. Too easy to fall in love, even when you're not two lost souls united on a quest to save the galaxy.

Being as we were lost already, Rathe and I didn't stand a chance.)

Chapter 25 ✳ Sam

Dear Sam, I know I've said a lot of regrettable things this past year, things that I've failed to explain… but the day the Terrans came before my second breakfast is where we should start.

You deserve to know the real reason I got arrested. Wasn't for unpaid tariffs like Da told you. Not even close.

That day also marks what I've started calling in my head the "Beginning of Our Unhappy Time."

You'd already left for work that morning—off on another week-long distributor run. Our prox alarms didn't even have time to go off before the Terrans invaded, accompanied by our own corrupt sheriff's department. The local police kept our farm's secondary security system from frying everyone. Our Derra City constables also flashed an electronic warrant to the skies, designed to show they had the governor's permission so our neighbors wouldn't help.

Those fragging Terrans came armored and arranged for every contingency. Four dozen souls with riot shields and laser sights surrounded the Ottrava farmhouse with shock rods and sweet guns that I might've admired had they not been aimed at me.

One Unity scummer bound my arms. Two more dragged me out of our bedroom. Another patted my sleeping robe for weapons and guided me down the stairs. I wasn't armed. I'd dived under our bed after their first explosion blew out our fortified front door, my lizard brain being more concerned for Junior inside me than anything logical like defending myself with the upstairs grenade cache.

"Pilot Polla Ottrava?" The Terran speaking was one of at least twenty currently crowding Ma's parlor, a tide of armed, face-less, visored bodies separating me from my folks. All had guns pointed at us. "Are you Pilot Polla Ottrava?"

"Well, I'm not your ma." I tried not to quake. "Aren't you Terrans grown in vats?"

One of the faceless ones sniggered. In back, a helmless beard-ed gent in white conferred with our local fleeks in red. No visors on the locals, so I could see their hangdog expressions. Sheriff Droha apologized to Ma for the second time. My parents kept their weapons up, as was their legal right.

"You're under arrest," the scum who'd just patted me down said.

Da was demanding to see a warrant. "What for?" I asked.

The Terran leaned closer. "Don't play innocent."

"We've got enough evidence to bury her on Jupiter!" another Terran snarled at Da's shouted demands for proof. "Two weeks ago, a woman matching your daughter's description threat-ened Unity Command above Earth!"

I turned my head. "Wait, what?"

"Stow it, Lieutenant!" barked another. Their blank visors made them interchangeable as hunting hounds. "That's for the com-modore to talk about, not you."

My voice already felt hoarse from shouting. "You're a stinking liar! I've never been to Earff."

"You'll prove that," the closest hissed in my ear. I twisted my head back and had a disoriented moment when my face blinked in his visor. In the mirrored reflection, I appeared more terrified than I wanted to admit, puffy-faced and preg-nant, with the hair I'd forgotten to tie up the night before tangled shamefully past my shoulders.

"Hold!" I knew the bearded one stepping forward was the leader because he wasn't visibly armed. He could've had a nice face under different circumstances. Kind and square, with a neatly trimmed beard, but that clipped Terran accent made him sound like one of Ma's villains from *The Hook and the Rod.* "She's telling the truth," he said.

"Of course I'm telling the truth!" To get out of this, I'd tell whatever truth they wanted.

"Poor thing." The man peered at me. One of his eyeballs was laced with black cybernetics. "Apologies for the intrusion, Meez Ottrava. It's just you have a common name, and we've been ordered to pursue even the slightest chance of a connection...." He turned to the soldier next to me. "Which Polla Ottrava is this one again? Sixty-Seven from the primary list?"

"Yessir." The armored soldier next to me actually saluted.

"Number Sixty-Seven out of ninety-six registered pilots named Polla Ottrava on this planet. Closer to the right age and size than the last ten... perhaps a bit shorter than our imposter..." The man stroked his beard as he circled me. I felt one of his hands push up my dressing gown's sleeve behind my back. "But no symbiote?" His gloved hand tapped my elbow's bare flesh, and I willed myself not to flinch. "Intelligence eliminated the non-pilots already."

"But she must be a pilot, sir. Number Sixty-Seven's registered as still active with the Guild." Another subordinate was now scanning rows of indecipherable data on a lightscreen. I squinted to read, but it was all in arcane Terran code.

The commodore shook his head, peering at the screen. "Perhaps a clerical error, like Twenty-Eight and Forty-Four." His eyes went to Ma, whose gun was still trained on him. "Apologies for the intrusion. We'll pay for the damages to your property."

"Damn right you'll pay." Ma lined up her barrel.

I opened my mouth, about to interject that my piloting status was private Guild business, but from across the room my da shook his head warningly.

"But, ser? She has pilot scars." Another voice, deferential. Behind me, strange hands tugged up my sleeve, twisting my starboard arm to expose its underside. "See?"

"Frag me, those are bad." I heard someone suck in a breath.

Hard to do with both hands cuffed, but I managed an obscene gesture that on our planet, implied a lack of sexual prowess—even with sheep.

"*Gelded.*" Another laughed. "That's what filthy Fringers call it when they remove the symbiotes. Gelding!"

Another made a crack about my delicate condition, which made Ma growl and move her rifle's laser sight in his direction.

"People?" the commodore murmured in his villainous voice. "We are guests. Don't insult our hosts."

At his command, the chatter died. Looking at their blank, visored faces, I had a sudden feeling that the back-and-forth—even those lousy jokes—were part of an act. What was I to them? Polla Ottrava, the Sixty-Seventh? The Terrans were like stinking scavengers, Sam, shaking a tree branch to see the rot fall off.

A subordinate cleared her throat. "Perhaps this Polla removed her symbiote because of the pregnancy? They do that out here, sir. Bear live young."

"Because we're not soulless animals," I snarled. "If Feldelroy wanted vats, we'd have 'em. Our tech's better than yours. I hear parts of Terra don't have running water!"

"No teasing, Ensign Halina," the bearded man interjected. "Polla Ottrava Number Sixty-Eight's close, isn't she? I want to get into the eighties today. We've already got riots, and it's an election year. Feldelroy's next government might be less amenable to Unity interests."

On my port behind Da, I heard Ma start demanding he give us a place to send the bill. The woman, Halina, raised her voice. "But sir, isn't it odd there's no Guild record of this Polla's retirement?"

The commodore sniffed. "On a *Fringer* planet? Perhaps she sold her symbiote as a rewipe or scrapped it for parts—"

"No! I would never!" I broke in. "Ask my Guild rep! My records are classified!"

"Easy now, Pollie," Da breathed. "No need for details. They're leaving." He'd moved to my port, shoving a few rifle barrels aside to so.

"Classified?" Abruptly, the commodore's gaze sharpened. "Really. She can't be one of their operatives, not with her test scores."

"My pal is." I lifted my head to glare. "Maybe you've heard of him? My Guild rep? Captain Wade Skybourne?"

"*Skybourne?*" I watched that kindly face take in our parlor, with the rectangular hulk of our forty-year-old android in the corner, Ma's vid collection on the mantel, Da's war figurines in their cases below the gun rack, and then move back to my face. A prickle of renewed fear twitched along my scarred nerves as the man paced closer. "What an odd coincidence. Captain Skybourne was aboard the *Unity Ascendant* when it docked above your planet a year ago."

I swallowed. "Was he? I can't recall where we met." Wade had sworn he'd wiped every record of me aboard that ship.

"Ah." My interrogator stepped close enough that I could hear his breath. "You see, it's curious. Crew testimony insists there *was* a Pilot Polla Ottrava aboard the *Ascendant*... several ensign recall such a patient. Yet the official roster has no mention. Odd, don't you agree?"

"Wasn't me, so no opinion."

His lips thinned. "Then, two weeks ago, the name Polla Ottrava was used as an alias by a known individual while evading pursuit above Earth."

"Told you I've never been to Earff!"

"Oh, I believe that. You'd never get a visa." The man took a pause to sneer. "But what is the connection between you and this... *individual*?" He gave the word a curious weight.

"No idea," I muttered. "Since I don't know who you're talking about."

"I see." The commodore looked unsettlingly pleased. "And yet... knowing Skybourne, did you also know the rebel Ken'ri, Arkan Davad?"

"No." No closer than the man's *Unity's Most Wanted* holo.

(That dream, Sam? The angel's face in the Aemercy blood pool? I'd yet to make the connection. Told you before, I'd convinced myself it wasn't real. Just one of hundred nightmares I'd had since poor Second died.)

The Commodore pressed on. "Did you meet Arkan and Skybourne on Feldelroy? Were you injured? Did you receive medical assistance aboard a Unity vessel?"

With my hands bound and my enormous belly, I felt like the wrong breeze might topple me over. "Do you understand what registered smugglers *do*? We don't disclose contacts, so even if I had met this Arkan person, which I haven't, I couldn't tell you."

Across the room, Da frowned.

The commodore's eyes narrowed. "And Ken'ri Mureen of Glos? When did you meet her?"

"Who?" The trick to lying, as any registered knows, is to convince yourself you're not. Oh, Sam, do we ever know anyone? You thought you knew me, but I've broken your heart and left you on a doomed planet.

"Kamen-lords use that Ken'ri title, dear," Ma chimed in. "You remember, Pollie, from that show of mine you keep watching, *The Hook and the Rod*?"

"Only a few times!" I felt myself flush. "My ma watches some show." I shrugged.

The man looked annoyed. "When did you meet Ken'ri Mureen? Was it in the company of the traitor Arkan Davad?"

"I never met anyone." Junior kicked uneasily as I forced myself to forget Mureen's lying face. "Except Wade. My Guild rep. Call him."

By then, the commodore's expression was starting to remind me of one of our hens with a beetle in her teeth. He practically spat his next question. "Did you see your Guild rep during the two Standard months the *Unity Ascendant* docked above your planet?"

I lied squarely: "Can't recall offhand when. The last time I saw Wade was when he came to our wedding."

"And where is your husband now?" The commodore made a great show of checking his holographic records. "It's just the one spouse, correct?"

"Sam's at work."

"My daughter's done answering," Ma broke in before I could perjure myself more. "She's asked for her Guild representative. That should be the end of it."

The man cleared his throat. "Of course. That is her right unless we find probable cause—"

"Cause?" Da growled. "You got no cause!" Da, being a student of history, had a lot more to say about things Terrans had caused and things they'd broken, and how if it weren't for us Fringers, all of humanity would've died or been forced to subsist on Aemercy blood farms. I rallied enough to throw in all the good registered smugglers had done for the Unity during their stinking war.

Ma was starting to look like she might threaten tea when a new body chimed in. What really hurts, Sam, is that it was one of our own, a Feldelroyan junior constable "Commodore Grabe? I might have something. Glos is the Kamen-lord island?"

"Yes." The commodore pivoted on his heels like he was oiled.

"Thought so." The red-uniformed sheriff handed an oldbook to the Terran. "Take a look at this. It says 'Property of Glos' on the back."

"*The Prince and the Pauper...?*" The Terran glanced at the spine and then back to me. "Written by Mark Twain. What a strange keepsake for a farming family."

My guts plummeted into a gravity well, for the man had picked up the one priceless artifact I owned, the one I'd carelessly left sitting on our parlor mantel, wedged in between slices of Ma's vidbook collection. Ever the fool, Sam, I'd quite forgotten it was there.

"The script looks like olden Speranto," Ensign Halina observed.

The commodore nodded. "We read a treatise of Twain's in school about boats—on readers, of course. The Fleet Academy doesn't lend its students Preflight artifacts."

My nails dug into my palms. "Preflight? It's not even a good fake!"

The man ignored me, thumbing the fixative-preserved pages. I could tell when he hit a highlit patch by the way his eyes narrowed. There were several, carefully painted over in yellow dye to make the words stand out.

I knew them all by heart.

"'What dost thou know of suffering and oppression? I and my people know, but not thou,'" the commodore read aloud. "What a curious sentiment for a retired Feldelroyan pirate. You must have hidden depths, Polla Ottrava."

What I had were depths that sorely needed the lav. My voice wavered. "You don't know me."

"Pollie"—Da shook his head—"let the nice Terrans go." Then to the commodore: "Keep the book if you like, sir. For your trouble. We don't need it."

The man ignored him and kept reading: "'The world is made wrong; kings should go to school to their own laws, at times, and so learn mercy.'" He turned another page, chuckling. "*Kings?* Is your daughter a monarchist, Citizen Ottrava?"

"The book's mine," Ma snapped, holding out her hand. "And I'd like it back."

He looked up. "Did you carry it here all the way from the island of Glos?"

"No. Some Kamen left it in the Grange Hall after last summer's Screen." Ma slung her rifle over her shoulder, cool as snow. "It was in the lost bin."

"And the marked pages?" He showed her another.

Ma tossed her topknot like a woman half her age. "Mine. I'm a Church Elder. Always on the lookout for pretty words."

"Maybe read something aloud from your latest?" Da broke in.

"Some lines from the *Good Book of Potential Retribution* might make these Terrans stop breaking into people's homes and threatening their kids."

"Well…" Ma glanced at me, and one of her dimples flashed. "I don't have anything prepared, and I think poor Pollie needs to use the facilities—"

"I'm fine," I lied.

"None of you move!" The commodore's face was turning an interesting shade, but we kept chattering. I tried to think of calming things like whiskey, and baths, and the man's head on one of our fence posts as I watched his suspicion collapse beneath the deluge.

If I were truly the sixty-seventh Polla Ottrava, no doubt these Terrans were tired.

"Your Captain Skybourne"—the commodore turned back to me finally with an exhausted sigh—"he'll confirm your story?"

"Of course. Now give Ma her book back!" Every nerve I had was twisted.

"Certainly." The man held out the volume, and Ma took it, maybe a little too fast because the pages fluttered open.

Because destiny's a gravity well, that's when Mureen's note fell out, wafting to the floor like a butterfly's wing. I tried to take a casual step forward, covering it fast with my foot, but the Terran looked down.

"What's this?" he asked. Our heads were close enough that I saw the glint in his eye at my startled breath, the way his eyes widened as my poker face slipped.

"Nothing," I said. Too slow.

The plimsi was still wrinkled from the first time I'd read it, the time I'd crumpled it into a ball and thrown it across the room. It crackled when he unfolded it.

"'Dearest beloved…?'" He raised an eyebrow.

Dearest Beloved, The day I saved your life, you became my inspiration. My Elders saw only a test subject, but I saw your fearless heart. I will never forget your courage in the face of despair, your unwavering optimism and your blithe spirit. These are virtues needed in these dark times. You will never know how you saved us, my sweet Polla. But know that I—and the galaxy—shall remain in your debt until the stars expire.

The commodore's smile stretched wider. "Signed 'Mureen d'Kiva of Glos.'"

"You can't prove that's mine," I whispered. "You said so yourself, Polla Ottrava's a common name."

(Our house cams got it all, Sam, which is why this letter reads like a transcript. Haven't had much to do with myself lately but feed Junior and plot revenge.)

"D'kiva?" one of the helmets exclaimed. "Ken'ri Mureen was a blasted *frog*?"

"Aemercy?"

"Another Kamen traitor?"

"When will brass stop trusting those sorcerers?"

"Fragging mutants—"

At that point, the room exploded with opinions. No Syndicate boss would've stood for the chaos, but the commodore just watched me. He let them go on for a what seemed an epoch, and then the man raised his arm and all of their chatter died.

"So, Polla Ottrava Number Sixty-Seven," he said in the sudden hush. "Do you know the penalty for lying to Unity Intelligence?"

(The man was fortunate my hands were bound, Sam, because otherwise I might've popped my kill-zero streak by going for one of our guns.)

A growl tore from my throat. "What I know is you can go *fuck*—"

It's roughly at this juncture that my recollection gets blurry and the transcript chaotic: me screaming anatomical impossibilities, Ma insisting they care for my condition, Da yelling at me not to say more 'til he got a Guild lawyer—and all of us realizing there were far too many Terrans in the good parlor for my parents to shoot.

Earlier, the commodore had claimed ninety-six pilots named Polla Ottravas on Feldelroy were under suspicion because of some quez who'd threatened Unity Command.

Thanks to Mureen's little love note, that number had just narrowed to one.

That's why I let Da lie and say it was unpaid tariffs. Had you known the truth I was about to discover, you might've wanted to help me kill Ledas Starfire, Sam—and trust me, it's not so easy to kill a god. Bullets don't work.

When we finally met, they were the first thing I tried.

Epilogue ✴ Rebirth

PRESENT DAY, CAROLINA SYSTEM…

THE BATTLE HAD BEEN a rout, the Unity grown wise enough to barely send forces before they withdrew. Now the living ice that fools on Glos called "Abomination" thawed, with tendrils stirring toward the gas giant below. This cloistered system, called Carolina by the Unity, was about to fulfill its stalled destiny.

Creation, Nate thought, *is delicious*. From the coralized transparency of his stateroom, he watched the gas giant change from orange to green as the soft rain of bioseeds penetrated its crust.

Three years ago, upon this very ship and from this very room, Lee had set a binary star to burn.

"Lee." Nate inhaled the word like scent, like the sweet taste of her lost mouth. Wild exultation surged through him. "You're alive!" He exhaled and felt every living being upon the dreadnought do the same. "ALIVE!" he bellowed. The vine-laden walls of his stateroom trembled with joy.

For she was. As the *Two* emerged from hyperspace, he had seen Lee's own white dove wing across an irrational sky.

Superimposed over the planet, his transparent reflection showed the glowing body of a man in his prime with the hooved legs of a beast, his long hair crowned with flowers and twined with vines. Cleft hooves sank in the muddy grass that covered the floor of his commander's quarters.

Absently, he lifted his left hock to scratch the bone's regrowth with his good arm. On his right, his symbiote suffered a demise that would span centuries. Serpent was a festering ruin, a constant source of agony for them both.

The man he had been—Ken'ri, soldier, husband, heir, warlord—had once been ashamed to show pain, ashamed of all emotions, perceiving them as a loss of control.

That man was not missed.

Now tears rolled down the krovlord's face. It had been no hardship sending Sheris away when Virmarr sent his first report about the dull-eyed shadow he'd found on the Kamen substation, the wraith inhabiting Lee's living flesh. And he did not weep for her now, nor for his body's discomfort; he wept for the suffering of those newly born to their cause, those who screamed and shook as the krov took hold in every cell. He shared their mortal agony as they would soon share everything with him—at least, those who survived evolution.

His wife had thought to end war with an alien fleet, but the krov was a more effective peacekeeper than her enslaved ships could ever be.

Hard to raise arms when each soldier feels every bullet and the same living web throbs in every breast. Carolina was an insignificant speck, but from such specks came the tide. And it was fitting, Nate thought, to finally bring this system into the fold, for Carolina had been their *first*.

As for Lee—

"Lord?" The title the winged Faege used was not quite that, nor was the language he spoke quite Standard, but the word was close enough, even if its true meaning implied "sacrifice," or "harvest." The winged man speaking was also not quite male—anymore—and not precisely winged. Very few former Kamen could master shaping wings.

Feliz had sheets of bluish flesh extending from arms to ribs that resembled a glider's sail, but he had been a man once, and he did fly now, at least here, relying upon *Two*'s low gravity and his own mastery of krov. Feliz was an earnest chap who'd once tamed a stray mouse, although as Kamen noviates they'd been forbidden to keep pets, lest their nascent focus on the stone world slip. As children, they'd clutched cold gir for comfort, deprived of even the touch of another's hand.

Now Feliz slept in a happy flock of ten and his eyes were black and birdlike, skin covered with a down of soft feathers and legs fused together. His speech was garbled, but his thoughts were open. Nate gleaned the list of Kamen survivors from the faces in his subject's mind. Some were old friends—but it was Lee's former operative, the Foxconn bastard Virmarr, who required immediate attention.

Virmarr had failed to capture Nate's wife, but the krovlord smiled, for the encounter had proved much. "Have the Ifr Guard bring Marr to me."

Feliz envisioned Virmarr's battered form—a man near death.

Pity. Marr's usefulness as a spy would be over as soon as his skin sprouted scales or bark, and they still needed operatives who could pass for human. Those capable of resisting Nuala's siren call grew fewer with every rotation arid Skye took around fertile Nuala. Davad had been an operative of Lee's for less than a Standard year before he ran. Beya another, loyally deployed for two before she came to grass. And of course Lee... Well, Nate's wife had always lacked a taste for *personal* sacrifice.

Years ago, when they'd first linked as pilots, Nate visualized himself as a lion and Lee as a dove. A private joke—and yet, as Lee's empty-headed body fled with its murderer, he had seen his wife's old archetype wing its way across an irrational sky.

Alive. The shell of her ear, her sea-swell of belly. Those splashing freckled thighs. *The Lady is an empty cup*, Marr had said over the comm. *Nothing of her left. Oh, and that cup claims Davad intends to kill you, Lord—*

"Empty?" The krovlord chuckled. "No." One of his hocked legs twitched. Davad did nothing alone, this had to be the father. Did the Old Man think he could seize Nuala's bounty with an empty cup? *Fools.* His wife was *not* gone. House Arkan might as well try and net the stars: like Nate himself, Lee had always been a force beyond their control.

She'll need me, he thought. He let out a shuddering breath, imagining her blank, imagining her still, those green eyes dull (maybe even dyed according to Virmarr's report), with all of their cold light gone.

I'll tell her everything, he thought. *For I must. An empty cup must be filled.*

~End.

Preview of Book Two
Navvies' Flight * Releasing in Early 2025

• • • • • • • • • •

Dear Sam, I'm sitting on a balcony overlooking an artificial lake, writing to you from a lovely Terran castle. Our host hates every fiber of my being, and I can't say I'm fond of him or his freckled, vat-grown offspring, either. Meanwhile, Junior's crying, my teats are leaking, and you're probably dead... but Ma says I need to think positive.

Oh stars, Sam. I'm trying. Tomorrow I'm leaving our son in this nest of Terran vipers. My new pals plan to convince a dead woman she wants to help save the Milky. These scumrags need me, but the jig's so torqued that I barely know where to start.

Please don't die before I save you, Sam, or turn into a tree—

• • • • • • • • • •

I came out of our first jump gasping as my mask retracted, smelling my own stench, and blinking at hard light and the sound of hushed voices. My thoughts were a jumble of half-remembered revelations, crystallizing into a glassy, brittle fury. "Chimera," I muttered to thin air. "Stinking *legs!*"

"What did you say?" Wide-eyed Mureen knelt next to my chair. Two empty ampules of exastim lay on its arm. Rathe was still under, but I noted thankfully that his lights were all green.

"Ow!" I became aware of the ache along my collarbone trailing through my gut. Hadn't known flying with a feeding shunt could hurt. "Is Rathe okay?"

A line of concern sketched across her brow. "He's not coming out. Davad explained about deepriver. All those times we left him alone, I had no idea—" She kept on, but my attention had wandered to my hands as I yanked the tube out.

I stared at my blue-tinged fingernails with a dulled emotion that should've been shock. My toes felt frozen, too. Bad signs for a pilot, signs that forced retirement, or deepriver, were close—in my case at least a decade too early.

Chimera, I pondered. *You lied, Mureen. You never told me about Ledas Starfire's stinking leg.* I thought about saying the word to goad her, and discovered my shards of anger had festered into an almost physical pain, one that demanded its kilo's weight in flesh.

Now I have you, I thought. *But first I'll bait the trap.* My voice softened. "Would it have changed anything if you'd known how close to deepriver Rathe was?"

A slight frown furrowed her brow. "Rathe was the only pilot willing to answer my questions. Were it not for his wisdom, I never would have formulated our plan, nor found the courage to proceed." She looked up from beneath those thick lashes, giving a shy smile. "Surely you see, how our mission takes precedence, how the ends justify—"

"Stow it!" I drew a line across my mouth.

Mureen gave me her astonished look. "Is something wrong?"

Leg, I thought savagely. I felt my lips curve in an evil smirk as I tapped my metal laced fingers, waiting for her to finish hoisting herself upon her own petard.

Her voice dropped. "Did something... happen during your hyperspace jump?"

"*Centauri,*" I hissed.

Her features froze. "I see."

"Do you?" I scarcely recognized my own voice. I recalled that stinking memory I'd seen in *Bedalia*... all of these Kamen-lords, laying a dead woman's burdens on me. "What do you see—exactly?"

She drew a fast breath. "You—"

"*Mureen.*" I hadn't noticed Davad lurking behind me—my pilot's intuition apparently not worth a damn when distracted. "He's coming out."

I looked. The lights on Rathe's chair were yellow, edging into red.

[Copilot corpus rebooting. Primary initialization failed. Sexy tries again,] Second broke in.

Rathe's mask flipped up, cannula popping out of his nose and the tube from his mouth. His lips were an ugly color. Purple, almost bruised. Skin like yellow wax.

[Organic matrix has degraded into suboptimal, Sexy says.]

"He's not breathing!" I bit back panic. Rathe and I had just been together, the two of us tangled on an island so real I expected sand between my frozen toes, and now he looked like a corpse.

"Relax. Sai's fine. I've seen this a hundred times." Davad leaned over me to drive another vial of exastim into Rathe's arm. Almost conversationally, he chuckled. "What did you mean just now about Centauri?"

"N-nothing." Under his moon-eyed gaze I found myself stammering. I can't recall my words, only the way his expectant expression died, and then how Mureen laughed.

The moment was gone by the time Rathe's eyes snapped open.

Color rushed into my copilot's face. He turned toward me as if the others didn't exist, shooting me a mischievous grin. "Know where we are yet?"

I shook my head. "Haven't had a chance to check on your mystery Moonbase Celestean."

Rathe's gaze flickered to the three empty vials of exastim by his chair. "Those all mine?"

"Only three," Davad said. "You're slacking, Sai."

"How many days?" Rathe blinked and cleared his throat, spitting into his chair's receptacle. "I can't tell yet—Sexy's clock's still at zero."

"It took six." Davad made that seem fine, although it wasn't. Six days pushed the upper limit of any pilot's endurance. "Anyone chasing will be ahead."

Rathe smirked. "Expecting us to run when we're moving at a crawl."

"Saves fuel—"

They laughed like that was an old joke.

I stared at the chart projected above our heads. Nothing about the system looked familiar. Rathe had shared the coordinates when we locked intandem—could hardly not—but he'd been secretive, telling me I'd like the surprise.

"So which system?" I asked.

My copilot sat up with a grunt. "Digne-Cox. House Arkan keeps an installation here, outside Ring laws for their illegal trade." He unfastened the lines that didn't self-retract on his chair with the ease of long prac-tice. Watching him, I busied myself doing the same. "Rock in the middle of nowhere, but I hear they have a decent pub. Ever been?"

"Guess I do owe you that drink. Never even heard of Digne-Cox." I made a mental note never to brag again that I knew every inhabited port in the Milky—not to a Unity veteran with fifty thousand jumps.

"Security's granted us an executive berth," Davad told Rathe. "All you need do is slide us in."

"We got the clearance when I was still under. Sexy's sliding it in now." Rathe rolled his shoulders back.

I snickered, and he laughed.

"We can assume Virmarr passed on Davad's message to the Old Man," Mureen said. "And your symbiote is working, Polla?"

I nodded.

Seemed like an epoch ago that I'd worried Second and me might never be right again. It seemed even longer since I might've killed our messenger: Vimarr, the charming princeling who'd pulled his stone-shaped gir on me and Rathe.

So much blood in him. I tried not to shiver. "Yeah, Virmarr said he'd pass it along," I said out loud, maybe a little too cheerily.

My eyes met Rathe's as Second relayed a message: [Don't tell the monsters, Sexy says.]

[Monsters? Sexy calls 'em that?]

[Lia does.]

[Are you talking to Lia now?]

[She is with us.] My navvy made that sound obvious and not terrifying.

The Smuggler's Handbook advises that changing the subject is always preferable to confession—and so I did. "You fugitives were here before? Just like our last stop where the Unity forces found us?"

"No." Mureen frowned.

"Arkan has," Rathe added. "Says there's a good bar." His grin was just as lovely in meat as in dreaming. "A *pilot* bar. Off the official charts, but they have a decent spread."

I whistled appreciatively. "Great! We'll book a massage, maybe check out the talent—"

"I'm afraid we need to leave as soon as possible." Davad announced to no one who cared. "Dry dock *Escape*, and have you fly *Bedalia* tomorrow, Pilot, if you can."

"No." I shook my head. "No, I can't."

"Her fingers are still blue." Rathe sounded puzzled. "Come on, Arkan, you've been around enough of us to know what that means."

"Polla, what do you want for lunch?" Mureen interrupted. "We have three more chickatos. I know you like them."

"Only three?" I frowned.

"—take a few days." Rathe's navhand detached from the webbing and reached for mine. "Get real sleep, get Polla her shore leave—she earned it—that was *her* shooting those fliers. Not me. She's good. *Really* good."

"Told you," I said.

He grinned. "You sure did."

"You're sure?" Davad sounded distracted, leaning over one of the consoles and scribing.

"Yes." Rathe brought his other hand to my face, which leaned into his, both of us moving like we were magnetized. His freehand traced my parted lips. "I can't *wait* to see if you snore."

"I can't wait to see if *you*—" I sketched a quick diagram in the air.

He laughed. "On special occasions."

I smirked. "I think this qualifies."

"Oh, *definitely*—"

The jarring scrape of stone boots indicated that Mureen had allied with Davad to kill our joy. "Is a delay truly necessary?"

Rathe's expression flattened. "Remember the last time we pushed it? NewPrinceton?"

Her lips pursed. "Of course, but is there anything we can do to expedite *this* recovery? What if Polla flew alone?"

"It's her I'm worried about."

"She could fly the bloodship."

"She shouldn't fly alone any more than I should, let alone a strange ship—"

"But she flew *Bedalia*," Davad said. "A test flight before we left Carolina. Didn't she tell you?"

"Of course." My copilot lied easily. "And she's not ready to do it again." His gaze met mine and I was reminded of the futility of trying to hide anything from a linked copilot. "*Lia* doesn't think she's ready, Sexy says."

Leg. I thought. The shards of my wroth reignited. I opened my mouth, but again Rathe beat me to the draw.

"This will take as long as I say it takes." My copilot flashed me a hand sign, and then went back to Mureen. "We almost lost Polla to deepriver on our first jump. Any Guild doc would ground her for a month."

"Oh." Mureen's voice softened. "Perhaps if you flew *Bedalia* together?"

My ire rose. "Want us both to manage one *leg* of the trip together? Did you hear Rathe?"

Mureen looked chastened. "Of course."

Davad broke our stalemate. "If Rathe says a few days, we take them. But *she* can't leave, Sai. You go for supplies alone."

"But Polla's earned shore leave." Rathe sat up, so quick enough that our heads almost collided. "After that last run, we both have."

"Why can't I go out, *Davey?*" I added sweetly. "They do genetic scans?"

A muscle twitched along the princeling's perfect jaw. "Yes. Which means I won't leave either."

On my starboard, Mureen's gasp was audible.

I turned to glare at her too. "That's right," I snarled. "Rathe told me *everything.*"

"It took him this long?" Davad's voice was dry. "You said he mentioned it before."

"He asked if I knew."

"It's one leg." Rathe reached for my arm, and I ended up wrapping it around him. "Can't you bribe them not to do a full body—to scan her... arm or something?"

Davad shook his head. "That's not how it works."

"Right." I yawned. "It's usually a retinal scan or a kiss on the glass. No one scans *legs.*"

"She's a smuggler. She knows how it works," Rathe added.

"Bribes are easy," I agreed. "Could use one and have 'em not scan me at all. Or you two could be Kamen-lords. Scanners have metal parts. Break 'em."

"I meant the science," Davad said coldly.

My laugh twisted. "Oh really? Let's listen to our Kamen explain science—"

"Shouldn't that be exactly how it works?" Rathe's frown had deepened.

Mureen sighed. "Rathe—"

"Don't sunspot me! You told me she agreed to surgery." Rathe's voice cracked, and he swung his legs over the chair. His arm wrapped 'round my waist, pulling me off my chair and half onto his. I felt him grunt, like I was heavier than in dreaming. "But Polla didn't know her leg was replaced."

"She may not remember, but we have a contract." Davad sounded bored.

"Yes," Mureen added. "She may not recall, but Polla gave her consent." She looked to Davad. "We have the documents—"

"On Earth." He shrugged. "I can hardly request a courier now."

"We'll retrieve them after." Mureen's smile could've illuminated hyperlanes. "Polla, your leg had to be regrown, and it was just a few different cells."

"You said I didn't sign anything!" Back on Earth, she'd said that—hadn't she said that? "You said we agreed to wait until I was *cognis minty!*"

"Remember our departure?" Her voice had sharpened. "No time to collect them, being as we were looking for you—"

"Oh no!" My voice rose. "Don't blame me for that!"

"We *paid* you," Davad said. "It's one leg."

"And most stations check eyes, if they check at all." Rathe took the words clean out of my mouth.

"Shhh." I rolled my eyes. "Listen to the wise Kamen-lords! Study a lot of chimeras on that isle of Glos, Dee? In your *genetics* class?"

The princeling flinched.

Oh ho, I thought. The surge of triumph in my breast was raw and savage, startling me with its intensity.

Our eyes locked.

Then one of his eyebrows arched. That thin smile made him look more feral than pretty. "You know better than that."

"Then don't try and teach a smuggler how to get past customs."

His voice assumed that pedantic tone I despised. "Your *face* is the problem, Pilot."

"Because I look like your sister?" The room felt cold. I realized my teeth were chattering and ground them into my jaw.

"No." He shot me a disdainful glare.

Mureen scoffed. "Who said that?"

"You don't," Rathe added. "I told you already."

Davad's grin had nothing to do with mirth. "Remember escaping from Earth? Threatening the entirety of High Fleet Command with an interstellar war? Giving your real name?"

"You made me." The more torqued I got, the sweeter I sounded. "You said it worked!"

"It did. But if you, or I, or even Mureen steps onto that station..." Davad eyed Rathe. "Sai's listed as deceased on the official banks. He won't show up a routine scan. The rest of us"—his grim smile twisted—"even Arkan loyalty extends only so far. Father won't lift a finger to protect fools."

"Everyone thinks you're dead?" I turned to Rathe.

"Family gets a pension." His stubble brushed my cheek. "Guess we'll have to grab that drink another time."

"But your kid and Sexy. Do they know you're alive?"

"*Catrine's* my ex. We haven't spoken in years." I felt him stiffen and knew I'd crossed a line. Close as we were, there were still closed doors.

"Polla?" Mureen began. "We don't talk about the past."

"Convenient."

Her voice softened. "The three of us agreed. No past. Especially the parts that—"

"—that hurt." Rathe finished. "Polla understands, I think." He gave me a smile. "We're all running from something, right?"

"Yeah." I swallowed. Because it was true.

· · • • · • • · ·

(I know I've told you the tale of Polla Ottrava, Feldelroyan registered smuggler. Told you how she made mistakes, fell in with the wrong crowd, ended up on a mission to save the galaxy with a desperate band of war criminals... but I haven't told you everything...)

...TBC

· · • • · • • · ·

EXCERPT FROM CHAPTER 2

· · • • · • • · ·

It was only six months ago, Sam, that the Terran invaders took me to our local prison complex, locked me in an interrogation cell, and showed me a hologram still of my pinch-faced imposter. The fuzzy image was of a woman wearing a white uniform with a peaked cap shoved low on her head. She wore an officer's jacket as well and my eyes were immediately drawn to her starboard hand, where a navvy's wire entwined across her closed fist.

"This... person threatened Unity Command from Earth orbit," the Terran officer informed me. I'd thought Commodore Grabe had a kind face when his goons first arrested me. But after seven hours of questions, his mien seemed boreal as Io6.

"What'd she threaten 'em with? Sulking?" I was having a hard time keeping my false bravado.

The man sighed. "Do you know who she is?"

In my recollection, the woman could've been anyone. Saint Bene of the Stars. A former vid sensation from McPhee5. Your own drunk ma, Sam—she was scrawny enough. The only feature of distinction beneath the shadow of her Unity Fleet cap were those cheekbones, hollowed below and sharp as knives.

"I want my Guild rep," I snarled for the twentieth time. "Captain Wade Skybourne. Did you put in the call?"

He paused like he was reading something from the data feed implanted in his portside eye. Then: "The captain is on his way, but that will take days, even in a Guild starrunner. In the meantime, can you explain why it was Ken'ri Mureen removed your damaged navigational symbiote, and not *Ascendant*'s Guild-assigned physician?"

"No."

"Can you explain why the records were erased?"

"No."

Good old Wade hadn't done me favors wiping those records, Sam. Guild officers are supposed to be incorruptible, but space is supposed to be cold, and any pilot who's flown close to a sun knows better. And me, I was but a mere mote caught in the gears of another current Kamen-lord catastrophe.

Now you're another, and it's all my fault.

• • • ● • ● • • •

The next morning, Rathe left early. I bade him farewell conspicuously from the mess hall in front of our companions, with half my rack hanging out of my robe and my hair a spiky fright; barefoot and sated as a dock worker in a pile of pilots. Even yawned as I grabbed protein bars to go from Mureen's breakfast table. Told her and Davad I needed catching up on my sleep after the work they'd had me do the day before. Then perhaps a soak in that lovely homemade tub, applying a salve to certain parts of my anatomy—
"Need some?" I added, leaning in until Mureen's face pinked and Davad's attention fixed pointedly upon his morning caffeinate. "I have an extra tube."
"We shall be fine," Mureen assured me with a too-bright smile.

And I'm the fool from the religious planet, I thought. My bow-legged walk was surely overkill, but I'd committed, all the way down the hall and out of view. There, I pulled down the legs and the sleeve of my flightsuit, buckled it all the way up again, and shoved the priceless, worm-woven robe down a waste chute. (I knew it wouldn't be missed. I had three identical ones in my closet, plus the dozen flightsuits, thanks to Davad's peculiar attention to my wardrobe.)

The main exits might be monitored, but every smuggler knows there's more than one way off a ship.

I made my way to the *Escape*'s waste ports. Without a full crew, we weren't running the recyclers, so no one had bothered to hook the lines up. Didn't take more than a minute for me and Second to pick the service airlock, and then wriggle through the main output valve, depositing me on the frigid decks of good old Moonbase Celestean.

Our good ship *Escape* was one ship in a short line of others; all in better kit and all stamped with 12Fam sigils. The hangar gate was open with the blur of an energy shield keeping us safe from the airless moon's surface. The ground outside was smooth enough to be sculpted, and oddly clean.

House Arkan, I concluded, ran a tight operation, although keeping up that energy shield for a pretty view was a profligate waste of resources.

Second's sonar alerted me to a stranger's approach.

"Well, hello there, pilot," a woman's voice drawled. "Saw you pop out of the waste chute. Are the passenger exits broken on your ship?"

I turned to see a refreshingly familiar bubble-faced uniform, same the galaxy through, neatly molded to the portside officer wearing it, complete with a scribe and scanner. The officer leaned against our ship like she had nothing better to do than wait for my bribe.

"Have a heart." I grinned. "Boss put me on scans while we're docked. Supposed to spend our entire shore leave jacked in. Just wanted to stretch my legs."

"Poor thing!" The woman chuckled from behind her visor. Her helm was diffused so all I caught of an expression was the flash of her silvery teeth. "We only have one pilot authorized from your craft, and he's already gone. Afraid I'll have to issue a citation."

"Truly?" I produced a ring from Davad's hoard, the one I'd tucked in my chest pocket for this very possibility: small and plain, nothing outrageous. "If you do, I'd have to keep this old trinket. Just a scrap of old Earth gold I found cleaning the tanks."

"May I see?" Her friendly smile turned professional, which told me I'd chosen well. "Well! This is quite nice." She held out the ring on her finger for us both to admire. "But you'll need a station chit, or you'll just get stopped again."

"Really?" I lowered my voice. "Thing is, I'm on the low. Got a premade?"

She pulled a handful of chits all attached to lanyards, out of her pocket. "I might... For someone from *your* ship."

"Ours?" I'd already noticed the *Escape* was the only one around not stamped with 12Fam crests.

She lowered her voice. "There's a rumor the Arkan of Arkan's aboard your ship. It's the talk of the station."

I froze. "On the low, so I can't confirm."

She giggled. "I think you just did."

I quickly changed the subject, since dealing with why Davad was throwing around his 12Fam's House title when we were desperate fugitives seemed best addressed with him. "Say... you do genetic scans on Celestean?"

She snorted. "With how paranoid 12Fam are? Not a chance. Are you worried they'll pick up an illegal mod? Don't be. The bosses are so fanatical about privacy that we don't scan anyone."

"Oh." I wasn't even surprised.

"Need to register this chit." She dangled one in the air. "Give me a name?"

"Lord... *Mortons.*" Was pleased to recall one from what seemed like an epoch ago. The Mortons branch had been coming to visit, Old Man Genghis had said. 12Fam Houses had *branches.* After spending a few weeks in Davad's company, I felt like a veritable princeling expert. "I am Lord Mortons of House Arkan."

"Lord?" she chuckled. "Well! You've got funny eyes for an Arkan."

I rubbed 'em, cursing their lack of lash. "Plumbing accident."

"Lord Mortons..." The guard's bubbled head bobbed up as she scribed the chit with her circuited gauntlets. It flashed green. "Got a call name?" She had a tight rack. More about her was hard to tell with that helmet on.

"Mortons... *Rebika.*" There was a reporter from the Biscayne racing forums named Rebika.

"Mortons Rebika," she echoed. "Pretty." After using her ring printer to code it with some kind of holographic gold seal, she handed me the chit.

I hung it around my neck, over the Arkan pearls. "Thanks!"

"Make sure that's visible... but you shouldn't have trouble." She lowered her voice. "You've got Arkan of Arkan credit, but I wouldn't go 'round the sun... never know when those pinchers have an audit program watching."

"Thanks." I examined the glittering chit. "Hey, so, this credit—"

"Show that to anyone." Officer Lowell sank back on her heels into a curtsy that'd make an actor on The Hook and the Rod proud. "And have a lovely visit, Lord Mortons."

I curtsied back trying to emulate Davad's patrician tones. "Thank you. That will be all."

That woman laughed. "No! No! Don't do that again. Arkan-Mortons only curtsies to *Arkan.*" Her head tilted. "And take your hair down. You look like a Feldelroyan savage with that knot."

"So obvious?" I winked.

"Registered smugglers." Officer Lowell laughed as I untwisted the ties that held my tragically-shortened topknot. What remained flopped in my eyes until I pushed it back. "Feldelroy's the only planet this side of the Fringe that certifies pilots to break the law."

I grinned. "Whose law? The point of Fringer space is that we have no laws."

"We have a few," she pointed out. "Thanks for the bribe." She'd finally translusced her visor enough that I could see her merry face through the screen. "Shouldn't have any trouble passing for an aristo if you keep your mouth shut. Most are masked—not that you need one. You're gorgeous—and that custom suit—" She appraised me with a low whistle. "Let's just say, you look the part."

"Too kind!" I considered that it would be childishly easy to rob House Arkan blind—and they deserved it between my leg and Davad's continued existence. "Hey. What's *your* call name, Officer Lowell?"

"Reggayne." She giggled. "I'll make sure no one hooks up the recyclers so you can get back in, *Rebika*."

"That'd be luminous, Reggayne!"

"Busy later?" She sounded almost shy.

"I—uh, I have someone, but—" For some reason I was stammering as bad as she was. "He is another pilot."

"Two are even better, unless you don't want company—"

"Maybe." I wondered how Rathe'd feel about a third. Once he complimented me on my escape, a third might be a good excuse to spend a night away from our ship full of liars and the terrifying *Bedalia* with her cache of a dead woman's memories—my mind spun.

"My comm." Reggayne slipped me another chit, this one smaller. Her hand was warm... but she'd gone right for Second, and I flinched. "Oh!" I could tell she'd realized her misstep. "I'm sorry, I—"

"No! You're fine." I leaned in and planted one on her cheek. A light kiss, for Reggayne Lowell suddenly reminded me more of my nervous cousin Sara than sweet Hana Stubblefield. "Thanks for the save."

"You have a good day!" Her visor diffused back to blankness. She opened the station gate and I passed through.

Who knew it was so easy to steal from 12Fam? I mused, strolling into a veritable sea of light and luxury.

· · · ● · ● · ● · ● · ·

(Apparently, only bookmakers in hell.)

· · · ● · ● · ● · ● · ·

Had been so long since I passed time on a busy station that I felt like a kid freed from Strangways—not that Moonbase Celestean was as glamorous as downtown Derra City back home, which is to say, it was a true dump. An immaculately clean, well-policed, dump, full of the kind of tract duty-free shops you'd find on any Fringer station bordering Unity Space. Alcohol. Intoxicants. Mods. Street preachers ready to sign up converts to any version of Faith they fancied. Most of my fellow pedestrians were masked, presumably for anonymity or hygiene. On the off-chance that Davad was right about my infamy, I picked one up from a free kiosk.

Even filtered, the air made me sneeze. Second worked on dampening those allergenic responses as I dodged a Grass Priest from home. The man was stationed at a street corner, bells and all; with coins covering the carved-out spaces where he'd once had eyes. I knew only the holiest ascended to losing their natural sight, but that didn't make him less terrifying, and I edged around the outskirts of the whispering crowd, who were taking snaps like a Grass Priest was some kind of tourist attraction.

"—and a green cloud shall envelop your world!" The Priest threatened their perfect faces. "Your domes shall crack and your skies rain blood—"

The sermon was so familiar that I had to remind myself I wasn't wearing a top-knot as I slipped past to a bend in the walkway where two Reformed Jihadist monks and an Animist rabbi from Calais or NewFresno were busy singing hymns like their two systems had never had that thermonuclear disagreement one hundred years past.

A hocker's shop, part of a row of transparency-walled structures on the sides of the mall, caught my eye next. Not that I'd be fool enough to pawn House Arkan jewels on a House Arkan station... but who knew what the desperate flotsam of a hundred different worlds might've dumped for me to purchase? Another gun. Something to decorate my room. A bauble for Rathe—

I pushed through the crowd toward the arched entryway.

"—and I said, think I was decanted yesterday?" The old-fashioned door to the shop swung open, putting me face-to-face with a masked, willowy, creation. "Oh!" Her violet eyes met mine and then she gazed at my chest. Took me a sec to realize she must be staring at my gold-striped chit. She had nearly its twin on her own exposed rack. "Cousin? Hello! What are you doing here?"

I tried to keep cool. "Why, nothing, cousin. Just a bit of shopping."

"Slumming it?" She giggled under her mask. "Us too. How fun! I'm Isabo. From the Ramirez line. Who are you?"

"Not Anastasia," her modestly-dressed companion added. "Or Betane. Far too tall. I wasn't aware the Mortons branch had more pilots."

"They have me." I felt my knees tremble with relief that they hadn't mistaken me for an actual cousin, even as I cursed my luck. Of *course*, a stinking 12Fam pilot would be rare as a 12Fam Kamen-lord. What princeling would bother to risk the river with the wealth of kings? "I'm... *Rebika*," I added, recalling the name I'd picked. "And you two are—"

"Rebika? Mortons Rebika? That's a *horrid* joke!" The second woman's voice sharpened as she leaned forward, frowning at my chit.

Cowcrap. "Of course." I forced a chuckle.

"Poor taste, especially following the Remembrance." Willowy Isabo's giggle sounded out of tune. "You have balls like suns, cousin. If an outranking Arkan sees—"

What were the odds I had picked the name of a real stinking person after all? "That'd be their business." I tried to make my words drip scorn. "Who are you?" The second woman had her chit pinned so the runes were hidden, and she hadn't given an introduction.

Her voice went silky in a way that reminded me of Davad. "An Arkan-Ramirez who didn't skip the Remembrance at Kubla Joadim. Who *also* wasn't aware the Mortons line had more pilots. Impersonating a higher-ranked House is just as punishable here as at home."

I laughed. "I'm not impersonating. It's an alias. Having a professional occupation is so *vulgar*, I didn't want to cast shame on poor Genghis. His health, you know." I lowered my voice. "They think he's got the Martian Pox."

"Hah." The second woman looked a little older, and the skin around her eyes was nearly as freckled as Davad's, although her half mask and the snood covering her hair made it hard to tell more. She waved a gloved hand. Took me another sec to twig that the heavy black bracelet she wore was twin to the one Meez Teats had. "So close to our First and you skipped the Remembrance?"

"Dull compared to hunting." I shrugged. Practically a 12Fam expert, I was now, throwing about the lingo. "Of course, then *hunting* got dull, so I came here to shop."

"For the labor auction? Us too!" Isabo beamed at me. "Hiring for the Old Man? He never misses a chance for a bargain." She smelled expensive.

Labor auction? A part of me I'd thought dead ignited with righteous fury. "Genghis sent me for that, yes," I drawled. "He sent me to buy living sentient *people*. Like we do."

"Prices are good," the second woman said. "Fringers are desperate. They'll sign anything."

"Why?" I sighed like I knew.

"You *are* funny." The older woman snickered. "Whoever you are." She eyed my chit again. "If that's genuine—"

"Do I look like the sort of ruffian who would use forged identification?"

"If that's *genuine*, we shouldn't ask," she finished. "Even if you're nothing more than an unlocked bastard, fortunate enough to catch a numbered Arkan's eye."

I bared my teeth, although that was gibberish. "Guess I don't have to answer."

She looked like I had. "I thought so."

Isabo rattled on, oblivious. "—so much competition for the skilled ones. House Singh agents outbid me three times yesterday for one sanitation engineer!"

"You'll need more than one." I sniffed.

Facts Davad had omitted about this place were becoming crystalline. These aristos were *slavers*. And this Arkan installation Moonbase Celestean was nothing more than a tarted-up shop for them to buy misery.

I kept looking bored, even as I felt my navhand twitch with righteous fury. My voice came out clipped. "Skilled labor is so hard to find. I tried to hire a Kamen the other day to change a waste tube? Stupid quez told me he didn't know how a suction pump worked—hah!" I cackled, like any evil slaver would. "So today I left him and his doxy to figure out the plumbing—"

The second woman giggled. "Doxy? You're hilarious!"

"You filthy bastard." Isabo sounded impressed.

"Indeed." I fingered the chit hung at my neck like the weapon it could be.

* * * * * * * * * * *

(At the time, I didn't know what a "doxy" was. Rather like "javelin" back on Carolina2, it was a word that came to my lips unbidden—much like my increasing ease with the Terran accent.

Back then, I didn't know what Isabo meant by the word "bastard," either.

On Feldelroy, "bastard" means the wrong ram covered the wrong sheep. The ram's a bastard for doing it. So's the sheep.

But in your world, "bastard's" just another word for pawn.

Let things be crystalline, dear one: before my end, I plan to be a *bastard*—in the Feldelroyan sense of the term—to everything once yours.

I will *fuck* it all.)

* * * * * * * * * * *

"Perhaps I shall see you both at the slaver's auction." My grin beneath the mask felt like a rictus.

"You may sit at our box," Ramirez-Arkan offered. "Number thirty-nine, and if the Old Man doesn't have you killed for using *her* name, you should summer with us on Ganymede4."

"*Whose?*" I inquired, which returned a new round of chuckles from the quez who still hadn't told me hers. Lady Ramirez-Arkan drew me into a hard embrace. Her lips brushed my cheek, and I made a kissing sound in the air back.

I thought Cousin Isabo looked threatened by my social success.

Our final farewells took another ten minutes, with them both promising to write care of Genghis—under my *soberry-kay* "Mortons Rebika"—and then us talking about the difficulty of finding an honest courier, especially with the war back on, and Illcord Natoth threatening to disrupt the balance of free commerce. The two of them did most of the talking about that last, while I nodded and smiled and vowed to find myself a news terminal. We kissed hands for our final farewells. They curtsied.

Following Officer Lowell's advice, I did not.

By the time I entered the shop, I was grinning fierce as a planet beneath that mask. *How do these people run anything?* I thought. *I shall rob them blind.*

As long as we kept visiting secret 12Fam trading stations with such lax security measures, the sky seemed the limit for my grifting possibilities.

· · · ●·●·● · · ·

(Oh, but I was wrong about limits—aiming for merely *one* sky—)

· · · ●·●·● · · ·

TBC... Coming in 2025, featuring Teapot! Aemercy! A RECKONING!
And the answers to questions. So many questions, and consequences.
Visit for more updates: http://hmhmurray.com

Author Notes

A THOUSAND THANKS TO Kara and David from Darling Axe Editing. Your proof edits were like a master class, and your feedback was invaluable. Any typos, or dialogue tags with the wrong comma since are entirely on me, and the fault of my rewrites *after* your mastery.

Thank you as well, Susan Barnes, for giving Navvy's first three chapters a well-needed development edit at the beginning of its journey. It took me a few years, but I think I followed most of your suggestions.

Thanks also to my immensely talented artists, Jessica Fisher and George Patsouras. I'm over the moon with both of your work.

· · · ● · ● · · ·

(No one has to read this next bit, but if you're interested, here are some poorly-edited notes on worldbuilding)

· · · ● · ● · · ·

NAVVY takes place roughly three thousand years in Earth's future, in a Milky Way with no other (observable, living, sentient) civilizations.

Due to a (somewhat convenient) narrative cataclysm that standardized the spoken and written word, most of humanity speaks the same language, or some variation thereof. I'd assume whatever language it is, it has linguistic roots in several of ours.

As with any passage of time, and any distance of space, words do change meaning, and history, as they say, is written after the fact. Although I use words like "colonies" and "settlement" in our time when such words signify conquest and oppression, I think that humans don't need to emigrate or colonize to be terrible people. Patterns of migration, scarcity, conflict, exist in every part of human history... but they're not all that it is. In that spirit, please indulge my word choice. I prefer to use verbiage that has a clear meaning over some version designed not to offend that implies the same thing.

Were these colonists bad? Were the settlers wrong? Were those who got left behind worse? I leave that for you to judge—or not judge—as you please. All I know is that these people are fictional, and the descendants of other fictional people who left Earth in several different waves, and for many different reasons... and that is how we have a *space opera*.

There are many, many excellent science fiction books that explore the themes of empire and decolonization. I could not match them if I tried, and it's not my goal. The questions I'm asking are different: about the relationship between personal and public, what redemption really means, how to do it, how *not* to do it— and what to do next when all of your good intentions end badly...

· · · ● · ● ● · · ·

Many books, movies, and tv shows influenced my design, (as well as one video game), but I'm going to name the older ones, some more obscure than others:
Grimjack, Ann Aguirre[1]
Huntress of the Star Empire, Athena Grayson[2]
The Fifth Season, N.K. Jemisin[3]
The Martian Chronicles, Ray Bradbury[4]
Parable of the Sower, by Octavia Butler[5]
Jaran, Kate Elliott[6]
City of Diamond, Jane Emerson[7]
Neuromancer Trilogy, William Gibson[8]

---

1. Her pilot at the end of her rope has stuck with me.

2. More pilots, and romance

3. I actually read this after starting NAVVY, but the narrative structure I adopted owes a massive debt.

4. Just... everything. A future I can imagine, one that could have led to Polla's

5. As with Bradbury, a future-Earth—this one way too close to comfort—that could lead to "Earthseed" and mankind among the stars

6. Epic and fantastic genre-blending. Her gray heroes who want to conquer what they can are amazing.

7. I still want the sequel. Snark, Church, space opera, a Crown... I know we also owe Emerson a debt for writing "House" but, this book, I do love it.

8. Future earth, crime families, and a virtual world, as well as gorgeous writing

"Hinterlands," William Gibson[9]
Snow Crash, Neal Stephenson[10]
Grass, by Sherri S. Tepper[11]
"And I Awoke and Found Me Here on the Cold Hill's Side," by James Tiptree, Jr.[12]
The Snow Queen, by Joan D. Vinge[13]
"Tin Soldier," by Joan D. Vinge[14]
Butterfly and Hellflower, by Eluki Bes Shahar[15]
Friday, by Robert Heinlein[16]

· · · ● · ● · ● · · · ·

The First Exodus was probably not called that when it happened, it was probably named later. It was a series of sleeper ships sent over centuries, with varying results. Those colonists' descendants landed on empty worlds, some more habitable than others, and none with any way to to communicate back "home." Most were lost and forgotten and probably died off. But not all.

One of the first landed on Roe, so named by one drunk colonist because the word "Egg" seemed undignified. Optimistically, the settlers considered Roe the incubator of their new and improved civilization. It helped that they also found a crashed ship in that system of non-human origin, and

---

9. I don't know if it really shows in NAVVY, but this story has earwormed into my head as part of the Fermi paradox, and how it might be when we encounter the relics from other civilizations.

10. Virtual arcologies, the effectiveness of riding around with a nuclear bomb, cults, babel...

11. Why I won't take estancia out of my book, even though everyone flagged it with a question mark. It's there as an homage to this fantastic vision of bioengineering aliens, scheming nobles, and a dystopian future

12. Loving the alien, Literally.

13. One of my all-time favorite space opera worlds.

14. Pilots... outsiders just don't understand.

15. A sassy heroine and her ward, along with their long-suffering AI ship companion. Add to that, religious background, and names like "Butter-flies-Are-Free St Cyr" which make me crack up every time.

16. I haven't read this in ages, not since I was way too young to be reading it at all, but I'm pretty sure that for better or worse, Polla owes Friday a debt.

with it, a working FTL. The ansible that allows instantaneous hyperspace communication, it was said, was developed on Mars in a theoretical physics lab, but the seeding of our galaxy with quantum entanglements definitely owed a great deal to the aliens and the FTL, the aliens no one has ever seen.

Aemercy pride themselves on being the descendants of these colonists, who prided themselves on being empirical and logical, running counter to many of the more evangelical, fundamentalist, or mystical cultures that were popular at the time.

Funny that these same logical scientists were the ones to first encounter Kamen mutations and krov "magic."

As Polla mentioned, the first pilots were basically thrown into a "chair" and merged into some kind of alien biomorphic lifeform. Until Saint Bene invented (or found, or was gifted by the gods) the "Spacer's Crown."

• • • ● • ● • ● • •

The First Exodus was a one of desperation, a storm of ships as people from different countries and creeds fled a dying planet and its war-torn colonies with whatever they had.

The Second Exodus, and its primitive hyperdrive, was an emigration of idealists. Various religious orders, ancient and modern, more atheists, and economic refugees. The Alpha Centauri system had had established colonies for over five hundred years before the Aemercy political movement really took hold. During this time, a prosperous civilization arose, expanding back into First Ring space. Earth itself became a poisoned backwater to Martian innovation. During this time, the Aemercy were ambitious. And fractious. They became highly militarized. Over time, each Association developed weapons that were too terrible to be used. And with a balance of mutually assured destruction, they formed a united front against what would become a somewhat imperial Human Unity, whose center moved from Mars back to Earth.

The Third Exodus, the one that settled the far-flung planets in what is known as Fringer space was much more recent, but due to that period of time being one of massive instability and humankind's first interstellar war, it's the one where it's the most difficult to separate story from fact. There's a legend of bloodships leading a liberation from Mars, another of alien gods and of terraforming machines that transformed inhabitable systems for refugees. According to common Fringer doctrine, that's how Feldelroy and its sibling planets were founded. (Others claim they were founded much earlier by some of the sleeper colonists.) While various religions from the Second Exodus found footholds under alien suns, the Fringer planets settled in the Third formed a diverse set of beliefs with a few common elements, the most major of which is the existence of alien gods. Feldelroy, perhaps because of the grip of its Grass Priests, has a reputation for being more devout than most.

Although Polla's view of Fringer space is limited to crime syndicates and farmers, those two groups don't have a monopoly. The closest thing Fringer space has to a unifying body is the Pilot Guild, whose pilots fly between. Any planet that proves too troublesome no longer receives shipments and has its ansible entanglements destroyed. Left alone in the dark, sometimes rediscovered.

The Ring Systems are all Earth-aligned, although also self-governing, sharing a common military, colloquially referred to as the Unity. The First Ring consists of the Sol System, the Second and Third are loosely concentric circles from there. All ring systems fall under the banner of the Human Unity, but the only centralized institutions the Unity has is its military and, again, that Pilot Guild.

Despite any impressions you may have gleaned from Polla or Davad, 12Fam don't precisely rule the Unity—they are its most successful players, its apex predators, if you will. Left to their own devices on a dying planet, the humans that stayed on Earth developed fiefdoms. Twelve families rose to power and became forty. Then thirty. Then sixty. And then nine.... before starting all over again. They change currency more often than their underwear (of course the latter is self-cleaning), because currency doesn't matter: their real wealth is the past.

On a planet stripped of resources, 12Fam think they hold the only true wealth humanity has—its history, both genetic and manufactured. Using genomes from graveyards, artifacts from dumpsites, looted libraries and museums, 12Fam have reclaimed influence over the Ring Worlds. Their vat-grown progeny were at first designed to pull from all of Earth's lost civilizations, but as time went on, they became more tailored and modified, each, according to their House. Sometimes there's more than twelve Houses. Sometimes less. The name remains.

The Kamen of Glos emerged at some point between the Second and Third Exodus. At first they were considered just another religious cult, but it turned out their belief that they could manipulate matter was real.

The Aemercy claim this ability is due to alien material implanted in the human genome.

They also claim to have caused it.

Curiously, there are no Kamen Aemercy, nor do they allow Kamen Screens of their own populations...

• • • • • • • • • •

As Polla noted, humankind has spread across the stars. What she barely touched on is that mortality rates are high. By Fringer standards, Feldelroy is more fortunate than most. Some even say its priests have healing powers...

• • • • • • • • • •

12Fam are fanatically against adultery not for any moral reason (most of them), but for the potential it has to disrupt House alliances. Marriages, especially among First, Second, and Third heirs are carefully-constructed.